Royal Affair

T0345458

Royal Affair

A Royal Scandal Novel
Book 1

PARKER SWIFT

FOREVER
YOURS

New York Boston

This book is a work of fiction. Names, characters, places, and incidents are the product of the author's imagination or are used fictitiously. Any resemblance to actual events, locales, or persons, living or dead, is coincidental.

Copyright © 2017 by Parker Swift

Cover design by Elizabeth Turner. Cover copyright © 2017 by Hachette Book Group, Inc.

Hachette Book Group supports the right to free expression and the value of copyright. The purpose of copyright is to encourage writers and artists to produce the creative works that enrich our culture.

The scanning, uploading, and distribution of this book without permission is a theft of the author's intellectual property. If you would like permission to use material from the book (other than for review purposes), please contact permissions@hbgusa.com. Thank you for your support of the author's rights.

Forever Yours
Hachette Book Group
1290 Avenue of the Americas, New York, NY 10104
forever-romance.com
twitter.com/foreverromance

First published as an ebook and as a print on demand: February 2017

Forever Yours is an imprint of Grand Central Publishing. The Forever Yours name and logo are trademarks of Hachette Book Group, Inc.

The publisher is not responsible for websites (or their content) that are not owned by the publisher.

The Hachette Speakers Bureau provides a wide range of authors for speaking events. To find out more, go to www.hachettespeakersbureau.com or call (866) 376-6591.

ISBNs: 978-1-4555-9803-8 (ebook), 978-1-4555-9804-5 (POD edition)

To ER, because fiction doesn't hold a candle to the real thing.

Acknowledgments

Tremendous thanks to the early readers of this book. In particular, thank you to Marci Gleason, for your wise feedback, generous encouragement, and endless enthusiasm. And to Susanna Fogel, for the *multiple* readings of this book, for the hours spent Gchatting about plot lines and characters, and for saying this book was good—whether you knew it at the time or not, I needed to hear it, and it energized me through each turn and chapter. I'm so grateful we refound each other when we did.

Additional deep gratitude to Taryn Aronson, Kara Carroccia, Amie Rapaport, Grainne Fitzsimons, and my family for their support, and to the Johnstons for providing the ultimate writing retreat for two overworked parents/writers.

Thank you to Caroline Acebo and everyone at Forever Yours, in particular Megha Parekh, for bringing Dylan, Lydia, and their world to life.

An enormous thank-you to Kimberly Brower, who made this book better. A lot better. Thank you, Kimberly, for staying up to read Dylan and Lydia's story that night in Canada. Thank you for taking me on. And thank you for getting on board this train and helping me believe it can get there. Let's keep going!

Finally, every word in this book reflects the love, generosity, and support of my extremely talented husband, Ethan, the first writer of the family. From the moment you said "Go for it," through teaching me how to write just a little bit better, you cheered on every inch of progress, and I am so grateful for how enthusiastically you went on this journey with me. This book reflects lunches you packed, dinners you made, and probably some words you didn't get to write because you were busy explaining dialogue to me. Thank you for that, because there's no bigger gift. I promise I appreciate every minute.

Royal Affair

Chapter 1

Lydia? Can you hear me?"

Barely, was the answer.

The voice of my best friend, Daphne, was coming in and out no matter where I seemed to stand in the palatial suite. The beautiful if not a little *too*-perfect bedroom was straight out of a Pottery Barn catalogue, or more accurately what Pottery Barn was trying to imitate, and had been mine for the three weeks we'd been in northern Québec. It was lined in a delicate blue toile wallpaper and wainscoting, filled with floral accents, and located in the guesthouse on a large estate overlooking the Saint Laurence River. "The Cottage," and the enormous country property it sat on, belonged to old college friends of the Franklins, the family I was travelling with and nannying for over the summer.

I tried resting on a large white linen tufted couch, just so I could relax for a minute, but I couldn't hear a word Daphne was saying. I stood up and walked to the window, which had worked earlier. As I pressed my hand to the warm glass, the phone crackled back to life, and I squinted into the hot August sun.

"Well this is a first," she said, speaking up, hoping to overcome our reception difficulties. "Lydia Bell has finally lost patience with Maddy and Cole Franklin. It's no wonder you're exhausted. I mean, I know you love those kids, but you've been travelling with them for nearly three months!"

"Feels like three *years*," I said. "Remind me never to have six-year-old twins of my own."

I hadn't thought that there was a limit to the amount of energy I could put into Maddy and Cole, but now I could see that limit on the horizon, fast approaching. The money was good, and I really did love them, but I hadn't had a day off in two weeks, and that included a ten-hour car ride from Martha's Vineyard to northern Canada, during which we'd watched *The Sound of Music* on repeat on the in-car video system. I still had "Edelweiss" stuck in my head and thought I might scream if asked to reenact the puppet show scene one more time.

It was one thing when I was babysitting for the Franklins back in New York City, but now, three months in, I was getting edgy for the summer to end. I'd seen amazing places with them, we'd stayed in beautiful homes in exclusive summer enclaves, and I'd gotten a taste of the way the fabulously hip and well funded spent their summers. But the truth was that I couldn't wait to get back to gritty New York for a few days and start getting ready for my big move to London.

"Well," Daphne said, "you're not missing anything here. It's so hot the whole neighborhood smells like a sewer."

"I doubt that I'm not missing anything," I said. "That's ridiculous. You live in New York. *I* live in New York. Or, I used to, at least." I sighed and looked out the window. "I love these kids. And I appreciate that the Franklins hired me for the whole summer. I'm just tired."

"Yeah, I know you needed to get away for a while," replied Daphne. "How are you doing, by the way?" she asked hesitantly, the way people do when they're referring to someone having died. Not wanting to say or do the wrong thing. People had been talking to me like that a lot recently.

As of April, I was officially an orphan, and Daphne had been keeping an eye on me, almost waiting for the moment I would fall apart. My father had finally lost his battle with cancer, a battle he'd been slowly losing for almost eight years. I could hardly remember a time when taking care of him hadn't been my priority, when my days hadn't been marked by trips to the doctor or helping him with his medications.

When things had been particularly bad—during a new clinical trial or another round of chemo—I would stay home to be with him. It was especially hard for him during these times, knowing that he was pulling me out of the college life I was supposed to be living. So we'd joke about it, the only way to really cope with what was happening. He'd ask, at least once a day, with an effortful smile across his face, "Now, sweetheart, are you living life?" and I'd reply, with a cheerful cheerleader's pump of the fist, "To the fullest!" and we'd both crack up. Now I owed it to him, to myself, to actually go out and do that: live my life to the fullest. I'd promised him I would.

"I'm ok, Daphne, really," I replied, and I meant it. "I mean, being out of New York is good. I'm really ready for London, ready for a fresh chapter, and honestly, ready to get to work. I mean, non-babysitting work."

"Have you thought any more about looking for her?" she asked.

I knew she was referring to my mom, and I could almost hear her cowering behind the couch as she asked, not sure how I would react. I'd never known my mom. My parents had divorced when I was only a year old, and she'd set off for some European adventure. My father never told me about their marriage, anything about them as a couple, why she left, or even her name, and so now, more than ever, the love that brought me into this world was a total mystery. I had been floating for a long time, but now I was completely anchorless.

"Daphne, I adore you, but please stop with that—"

"Ok, ok, ok," she said defensively. "Sorry."

"I've gotta go, Daph," I said as I walked out onto the balcony. "I promised the twins I'd take them swimming before this cocktail party we're going to tonight. I also have to think about packing before we leave here in a couple of days, and the movie they've been watching is about to end."

"A cocktail party? Does that mean you'll finally be able to wear that adorable dress? And maybe flirt? Just a little?" she nudged in her classic Daphne way.

Daphne was constantly trying orchestrate blind dates. She was determined to get me into what she would call "a proper relationship," by which she meant one that lasted more than three dates and included physical contact beyond an awkward kiss at my front door. She respected that I had my reasons for not really dating, but she hadn't exactly tried to hide the fact that she thought I'd be happier if I did. She was the only one who knew how that night had unfolded when I was sixteen and found out my dad was sick, how I'd gone on my only real teenage bender. I emerged after a month of drinking, skipping school, and sneaking out, no longer a virgin by a long shot.

One night, at the end of that month, I'd come home in the

early hours of the morning to see my father asleep in his recliner, facing the door. His skin was sallow, the worry etched into his eyebrows, even in his sleep. There was a thin trail of dried blood below his nose—a stark and harrowing reminder that he, my father, my only family in the world, was sick. Really sick. In that moment I realized that there would be no room in our small life for my teenage antics. No room for not facing what was happening. No room for the normal giddiness of proms or hours spent contemplating when or if a boy would call. My dad needed me, and I was going to be there.

The saving grace, and probably the only reason I didn't emerge from that month diseased or pregnant, was that I'd had a careful and sweet boyfriend. But while he may have been happy with his suddenly-eager girlfriend, he didn't exactly know what he was doing in bed, or with me. It wasn't his fault. What seventeen-year-old boy knows how to handle his girlfriend finding out her dad is sick? What seventeen-year-old boy wants to have the I'm-terrified-my-father-is-dying-and-my-world-is-falling-apart existential kind of sex?

I didn't give up on sex or guys right away. I tried six months later with a new, yet short-lived, relationship, and again in the form of a one-night stand with a friend's older brother on my nineteenth birthday. But never once did I feel that urgency that people describe. Never once did I feel safer in someone else's arms than I did in my own. Not once was it good enough to leave my dad at home alone or allow myself to be distracted from the life in front of me.

But Daphne was doggedly optimistic. And I did try. I would go on a date, sometimes even a few dates. I'd think, *Maybe with this guy, I'll feel the "butterflies."* But inevitably my pessimism was justified, and I'd gently extricate myself from the situation.

With taking care of my dad, putting my all into school, and then work, I simply couldn't afford to devote the time it took to date anyway. Isn't that what they meant when they said you couldn't have it all?

The only problem was that twenty-five was right around the corner in September, and if I wasn't careful, I'd be looking at a full six years since the last time I'd had sex.

"Oh, lay off," I said, teasing. "Plus, this party is geared towards the forty-plus crowd—not exactly fertile ground for flirting." I started to hunt for my bathing suit and sunscreen as we wrapped up our phone call, and sighed heavily into the receiver. "I am so ready for a cocktail. But *first*," I said, trying to sound like the world's most earnest camp director, "to the pool with the most rambunctious, precocious twins on the planet."

"Oh, please, a pool sounds amazing. I am going to the movies just to bask in the free air conditioning."

"I can honestly say I wish I were with you. I would do anything to be having a drink with you on your roof." Daphne huffed back incredulously. "Same time tomorrow?" I asked.

"You know it," Daphne said, but then the call was dropped before I could even tell if there was a goodbye.

I missed my best friend, and on afternoons like this one I wondered if I should have spent the summer with her. But I'd had to get out of New York. I'd had to get out of the city where my dad had just died, and nannying gave me the perfect excuse to get away. I'd timed it perfectly so I'd only have to be back there for a day before leaving New York for good. In just two weeks, I'd be boarding a plan to London, to my fresh start. An internship at the Fashion Institute of Technology, four years working at two different couture boutiques, and a fashion merchandising minor had paid off—I'd landed a job as the second assistant to Hannah Rogan, an on-the-rise British fashion designer. And I had a one-way ticket to London to go with it.

I closed my eyes and let the idea calm me down. Just two more weeks.

* * *

The pool at La Belle Reve—the massive country estate had an actual name—was dark blue instead of the standard turquoise and separated from the large main house by an expansive lawn that smelled of chamomile and thyme. We'd spent nearly every afternoon out there splashing around, and I had deep tan lines that betrayed a summer chasing kids in my swimsuit.

Maddy and Cole were jumping off the high stone ledge bordering the pool, and I stood by the side judging their jumps like an Olympic coach. The well-honed routine included holding a fake clipboard, blowing a whistle, and shouting out scores as they giggled and swam for the edge.

My shoulder-length blondish brown hair, highlighted from the sun, had settled into a permanently wavy just-out-of-the-pool mess. I'd completely given up putting any effort into grooming, and I was constantly sweeping my overly long bangs out of my eyes. The estate had been empty the three weeks we'd been there, except for the occasional delivery person or the many gardeners, so I was startled when I saw four adults approaching from the main house, where staff were busily preparing for the cocktail party.

As they got closer I could see an older couple leading the way, followed by a younger man and woman strolling behind them. All dressed and styled to a T, they looked the perfect wealthy vacationing family. The trim older woman wore a knee-length floral-print pleated skirt with a navy button-up blouse, pearls, and delicate leather sandals, her sandy hair blown dry to perfection. The gentleman, her husband judging by the way he gripped her hand, was her perfect preppy match right down to the loafers with no socks. The young woman, who appeared to be about my age, looked far more urban, with a grey V-neck maxi dress, a long dark braid over one shoulder, and Grecian sandals. I couldn't quite see the younger guy, his back now turned, head down, and tucked in behind the others.

"Your grandfather laid this pool in the forties, Emily—no one over here had swimming pools in those days," said the older gentleman, directing his comments to the young woman in an unmistakable posh English accent. "Isn't it marvelous?"

They were just far enough away that I didn't feel I had to say anything yet, but close enough for me to hear their conversation. I toned down my embarrassing Olympic-judge routine while I tried to eavesdrop. He sounded quite impressed by this grandfather's pool foresight. I surreptitiously squinted into the sun, trying to get a glimpse of the younger guy, who'd just stepped up with his parents. He wore slim dark-brown pants and a denim shirt tucked in around a trim waist, attached to what appeared to be an unbelievable body. He was looking down, eyes hidden behind aviator shades, buried in his smartphone.

Hah! I thought to myself. *Good luck with the reception.*

As if on cue he said, "I have to go back to the house. I need to sort this project out, and there's no goddamn mobile reception anywhere out here." He was curt, and he radiated annoyance. He turned stiffly and lifted his head, clearly getting ready to voice further disapproval of the whole no-reception fiasco, but he halted when he saw his family's pool inhabited by small splashing children and a raggedy babysitter. My jaw dropped a little. If I'd been in a Saturday morning cartoon, someone would have pushed it back up to meet my face.

Holy shit.

This guy was off-the-charts gorgeous.

Chapter 2

There was no other word for him but stunning. He was definitely older than I was. Late twenties, maybe? Early thirties? He was built but not bulky and exuded lean, guarded strength and power, like he could use it when he wanted but didn't have to show it off. I was getting that lightheaded feeling that happened when I glimpsed a celebrity on the subway, like I wasn't sure if I was still in my own life. Only this time it was way more intense, and definitely more unexpected.

"Darling, it's unseemly to be rushing off as though the office can't survive without you," replied the older woman.

"Quite right," chimed in the older gentleman.

"Yes, well, it can't be helped," Mr. Aviators replied under his breath, a world of irritation in each word.

His mother sighed heavily and waved a hand at him, clearly resigned. "Well, do be down by half six. Amelia will be there, remember," she added. But he was now looking my way and didn't budge.

They'd gotten closer, so I could finally appreciate him in his entirety, and I could feel my jaw sinking even lower. His dark brown hair was cut short on the sides—short enough that his barber probably knew more about him than his mother—but it was slightly longer and messy on top. It looked hip, but still refined, suggesting something roguish beneath all the restraint. Before I knew what was happening I was imagining running my hands through it, clamping it between my fingers. The sleeves of his shirt were rolled up, snugly hugging his biceps in a way that left no doubt to the hours he must have spent at the gym.

But it was his face that somehow upended me. He had a strong jaw peppered with a visible layer of stubble. I couldn't see his eyes behind his dark sunglasses, but he had the bone structure of a model—just the right combination of chin, cheekbones, and brow. He looked intellectual and sophisticated, but also a seemingly impossible combination of ruthlessly sexy and tender.

I was definitely staring. I noticed his hand gripping his phone, and my mind immediately shifted to imagining those strong hands on me, grabbing my own hair, holding me. I was mindlessly enjoying taking in every detail of this guy until I realized he was watching me back, and, *Oh god.* I slowly realized that I was still holding my pretend clipboard and had a whistle hanging off my suddenly dry lip.

I straightened, let the whistle fall from my mouth, and licked my lips just as Maddy splashed me from the pool. "Lydia! What was my score on that one?" she shouted.

I jumped up and shrieked in surprise like some kind of startled animal—this was just getting better and better. My skin, hot from the sun, was now dotted in cold water, bringing goose bumps to the surface and making me shiver wildly.

"Maddy! For antagonizing the coach you get a penalty! A

six at best! Three extra cannon balls!" I sternly instructed her. I
heard a subtle chuckle coming from my right. Maddy pretended
to be affronted but quickly giggled, hoisted herself out of the
pool, and ran back to the stone ledge.

I took a deep breath, trying to calm my heart, which was currently drumming violently in my chest, and turned to the older
couple. I dried off my hand with a towel and reached out. "Hi,
I'm Lydia Bell," I introduced myself. "I'm travelling with the
Franklins this summer. Are we in your way?"

Mr. Aviators was hanging back. He was still smiling
wolfishly—surely amused at my situation. Suddenly I wished my
cover-up wasn't on the other side of the pool. I felt completely
inappropriate and weirdly shy in my bikini, like I'd shown up in
underwear to a swank dinner party.

"We're quite pleased to have you use the pool, my dear, delighted," the woman said. The word *delighted* dripped from her
lips as though it was an often-repeated part of her how-to-be-
cordial script. "Charlotte Hale, and this is my husband, Geoffrey." The older gentleman reached out his hand, which I shook
as firmly as I could: two strong arm pumps while maintaining
eye-contact, just like my father had taught me.

"How do you do?" Mr. Hale asked, clearly not really expecting an answer.

Mrs. Hale continued, "La Belle Reve belongs to Geoffrey and
his sister, Eloise, and their parents before them, of course."

"Of course," I replied. "I've heard lovely things about your
family." It must be Eloise that the Franklins were friends with, I
thought. I certainly hadn't heard about any children, especially
not any aviator-wearing gorgeous-but-most-definitely-trouble
sons.

"Living in London, we don't get to Murray Bay often." Mrs.

Hale gestured to the expansive property, talking more to herself than to me. She looked at her son, who still hadn't departed, despite his previous urgency.

His stance had shifted. He lifted his sunglasses from his eyes, and, sliding them onto his head, stepped forward. He reached out to shake my hand. "Dylan Hale," he stated, nothing more.

His eyes were an implausible shade of blue—warmer and brighter than the ocean, almost lapis—and framed by endless eyelashes. My breath, suddenly shallow, felt as though it was barely escaping my lungs. As I reached forward to shake his hand, I tripped on a foam pool toy and only barely regained my footing as he grabbed my hand in both of his.

My first thought was: At least I was wearing a sporty, secure bikini.

And my second thought was: *I am touching the most gorgeous man I've ever seen.*

In that moment, skin touching skin, all the energy that had gone to breathing was now focused, like laser beams, on our meeting palms. "Hi" was all I managed to squeak out, coughing on my words. "Nice to meet you." Since when was I unable to greet someone like a normal human being?

He grasped my hand firmly with both of his in response to my shakiness, essentially holding me up. "All set?" he said, looking directly into my eyes. I caught a hint of a smile, which just made the embarrassment worse. I withdrew my hand as soon as I could manage and brought my arms back to my waist. Then I went to smooth my skirt, remembering too late that I wasn't wearing a skirt. I turned it into a little thigh tap, which probably looked bizarre, like: *Yup, I've got legs.* At this point, I kind of wanted to disappear.

"You're quite the taskmaster," he said.

I looked at him, puzzled, and then I realized he was looking at the children. "Oh! Well, you know, kids these days. They just aren't willing to put in the hard work it takes to be an Olympian." I glared at Maddy lovingly. When I looked back at Dylan he was smiling. God, those eyes were captivating. The eyes alone could have seduced me.

"Did I hear that you'll be coming to London in the fall?" Mrs. Hale asked with a polite-at-all-costs energy that struck me as exhausting.

Dylan's eyebrows rose, and I swore I saw his jaw tighten.

"I am. I'll be working for Hannah Rogan, the fashion designer."

"Lovely," replied Charlotte, but she clearly wasn't paying attention. As soon as I had started talking her gaze had shifted behind me to the view and then to her son, who once again seemed determined to head back to the house.

He turned to me and made steady eye contact. "Pleasure to meet you, Lydia."

"You too," I replied, replaying the way the word "pleasure" sounded with his upper-crust English accent, melting away at the end almost as if he'd never meant to say it all. He started to turn to the house. "And try the east side of the house for cell reception," I added, smiling. He looked back and nodded quickly, eyes wide, clearly surprised that I'd caught his tirade earlier. And then, just like that he was gone, ascending the lawn up towards the house.

"Enjoy your swim, dear," Geoffrey said to me while looking at his watch and already turning away, his daughter and wife in tow.

Enjoy my swim? I'd just had the wind knocked out of me by the most gorgeous guy I'd ever laid eyes on, somehow managed to politely converse with his parents, and by some miracle not allowed two children to drown in the process. I didn't think I'd be able to walk, let alone swim, until I got Dylan Hale out of my mind. Part of me wanted to will him back down to the pool, to somehow prolong our interaction. But the other part of me was so grateful he was gone. I had no doubt that he was the precious boarding school type, aware of his carefully curated charms, the power contained in those eyes, and all the more deadly for it. I needed time to recover—the intensity of the encounter was going to have me reeling for a while. Maybe a swim was exactly what I needed.

* * *

A few hours later, refreshed, I descended the steps of the guest cottage with a child holding each hand. I had dressed both in their summer finest—garden party outfits that probably cost more than my ticket to London. And I finally had the chance to wear the little black V-neck dress I'd brought. It had capped sleeves and was short enough to make my legs look longer—I needed all the help I could get at five foot three—but not so short as to be inappropriate. With the Hannah Rogan silver heeled sandals I'd scored at a sample sale and some cobalt dangly earrings, I felt like I could hold my own at an upscale cocktail party.

"Oh, Lydia, you look lovely," Kate said as she saw me come down the stairs. She was standing by the waiting chauffeured SUV, and looked slightly chagrined. "I was hoping to catch you before you all dressed, but, well, I am just off the phone with Eloise, and the party is adults only." She had a look of apology on her face.

My disappointment must have showed, because Kate quickly added, "But we'd love for everyone to meet the children, so I suppose it's good that they're not in play clothes. You can spend the first part of the evening exploring the grounds around the main house, and then duck in for a quick drink before we leave?"

I nodded in reply, hoping my defeat didn't show. After so many days working, I'd been really looking forward to mingling with adults. And now, instead, I'd be playing tag in my only nice pair of heels and getting eaten alive by mosquitos as the sun went down.

On the upside I still felt slightly unhinged by my run-in with Dylan Hale, and perhaps it was better if I had a chance to come down from whatever that was before interacting with anyone. I'd been feeling the reverberations of our handshake all after-noon, and it was just a handshake! Meanwhile this guy was probably having actual sex in his actual life with his actual gor-geous girlfriend at that very moment and not fantasizing about an aunt's friend's gawky babysitter. Enough—I wasn't going to let being *attracted* to a guy completely derail me.

Must not think of Dylan. Must not think of Dylan. Must not think of Dylan. I continued to repeat the mantra to myself as we climbed into the SUV and headed across the estate.

* * *

The main house was a large stone manor—symmetrical, sandy brown with white trim, and simply mammoth. It looked like the kind of place people might rent for weddings. It was hard to believe a relatively small family owned the entire thing and didn't even live in it full-time. When we pulled into the wide circular drive, there were lines of cars already there, all black and silver, and many with drivers leaning against their hoods. I enviously watched Kate and Charles make their way to the front door and accept flutes of champagne from a server waiting by the entrance, and then I sighed and ushered the kids around the side of the house, and into the gardens below.

Finally, after an hour and a half of scampering with Maddy and Cole in the late afternoon sun, and dousing myself in bug repellant, I saw Kate come out onto the patio and motion for me to bring the children inside. I must have looked positively feral.

As soon as we entered the elegant living room, Maddy and Cole scampered to their parents' sides, and Kate and Charles began the process of proudly showing off their children. I stood in an empty corner letting the cool air-conditioned air settle over me and took in the vast light-filled room. One side was lined with tall French doors facing the river valley below, and the pink of the late afternoon sun was pouring in. Enormous rugs and several elegant couches made this a living room officially, but without the seventy-five or so elegantly dressed partygoers currently orbiting its fine antique furnishings, I could only imagine it would feel far too enormous for actual living.

I spotted a tuxedo-clad waiter carrying champagne and made a beeline towards him, narrowly dodging an older gentleman wearing pink pants. Only, when the waiter was finally at arm's distance, the hand of a tall sophisticated blonde in a killer cream-colored shift dress snagged the last one. Figured. As I took her in, along with the other guests' smooth elegance, I decided it would probably be wise to find the bathroom before drowning myself in cocktails. I needed to assess the damage from playing hide-and-seek in the hedges in the late summer heat.

The bathroom, which I found through the cavernous main hall and down a short hallway, was the size of a studio apartment. After retaming the soft waves I had carefully blown dry and reapplying lip gloss, I ventured back into the hall. I was nearly at the door to the party when I felt a cool hand on my back bringing all my blood to the surface. I turned around to find myself face-to-face with Dylan Hale offering me a drink.

Chapter 3

Here," he said as he moved to my side, putting the drink in front of me. "It's a gin and tonic."

So much for my mantra, I thought. I was completely tongue-tied, registering his presence in my body before my brain. He wore a slim navy suit that hugged him exquisitely and a trim light-blue shirt open at the collar. Now that we were inside I could appreciate his refined but also salty earthy smell—he had the scent of elegance with something primal lingering just beneath the surface, like sweat and fresh laundry in the perfect ratio. If I looked like I could just barely fit in at a stylish cocktail party, he looked like he was born into one. And he probably was. Too long a moment went by, and I was still silent.

"It's for drinking," he said, eyebrow raised, cracking a wry smile, still holding out the drink for me.

"So that's what it's for," I said, and our fingers touched around the sweating glass. I brought the rim to my mouth, and took a tentative sip. "Thank you. That's amazing. You're like my alcohol-delivering knight in shining armor, riding in on a white

horse, gin in hand." He smirked slightly, almost if he was allowing me to poke my fun.

"Hardly. I simply couldn't imagine being trapped out there,"
he gestured to the windows flanking the large main entrance
to the house, "when air conditioning and cocktails were to be
had in here." His English accent added charm to everything he
said. He could have been describing the toilet, and it would have
sounded elegant. I also couldn't help but cringe at the possibility
that he had seen me scampering with the kids outside. I must've
looked like some overheated Muppet out there. Mortifying.

He swung in front of me to grab the door handle, and at the
same time his other hand returned to the small of my back, ushering me into the room buzzing with chatter. My mind went
fuzzy at the contact. It sent shivers of the best kind running
straight to the apex of my thighs. This was the third time he'd
touched me (apparently I was counting), and each time the
world around me seemed to zoom out of focus, and he zoomed
in. It didn't seem possible to be this attracted to someone with
whom I'd exchanged only a handful of sentences.

Just as I was managing to convince myself to break away and
regain some focus, his mother stepped over and grabbed Dylan
by the elbow. "Darling, we've been looking for you," she said.
She looked directly at me, and then through me, as if I were a
potted plant. She returned her gaze to Dylan, and, radiating impatience, said, "Amelia has arrived with Piers and Louise—did
you know she just returned from doing humanitarian work in
Tanzania? It's quite marvelous."

As his mother tried to urge him away, he paused and held
back, giving her the universal one-minute sign with his finger.
He leaned over me, forcing me to look up into his eyes. His
height was more apparent now that he was so close, and his in-

toxicating smell filled the air around me. I gulped, feeling my face heat up under his determined stare. I felt intimidated by this gorgeous, confident man in front of me, but in that moment I also felt stripped bare, like any façade I might manage to construct would crumble under his gaze. It was captivating, and also infuriating. He tucked a stray lock of hair behind my ear, grazing his fingers against my cheek. I could feel my pulse everywhere.

He leaned farther in and whispered firmly, "I'll be back."

I gulped again, and watched him walk away from me.

What the hell was *that*? For that one moment we'd been the only two people in that room. Only now that he was gone were the voices of the party slowly creeping back into my consciousness. His instruction to stay put was implied, and for some unknown reason I felt compelled to obey. I sank against the wall where we'd stood, hidden between a large antique highboy and an even bigger indoor tree, and thanked all that was holy that I had an alcoholic beverage in my hand. The cool wall was like a balm for where Dylan's hand had been—I could still feel him there when I closed my eyes. When I opened them, I saw that Dylan had found his way into the heart of the party, and was now engaged in deep conversation with Miss Cream Sheath Dress.

She was laughing at his every utterance. He said something to the group, and I saw her lean into him and place a kiss on his cheek. His back was to me, and I couldn't see his reaction, but an unexpected stab of jealousy spread through my chest. I took a long gulp from my drink, hoping to restore my sanity. Surely *this* woman, who fit right into this cocktail party world, was whom he should be making feel the way I was feeling a moment ago. In fact she probably was feeling that way, and that seemed far more appropriate.

My ruminating was interrupted by Charles's singsongy voice, made even more singsongy by a few rum punches. "Ah, there you are, Lydia," he said. He looked over his shoulder, glancing back into the party where a slightly irritated-looking Kate stood with the children. "You'd better be off. Maddy is beginning to sing that chimney song from *Mary Poppins*, and well, as adorable as we both know she is, it'd probably be better to spare these folks. The car is outside waiting." He gestured towards the driveway. "We'll see you back at The Cottage in a bit." I followed him back to his family, abandoning my woefully unfinished drink on a coaster along the way.

After herding the kids out of the room, I paused for a moment before leaving the house, wondering if I should interrupt Dylan to say that in fact he wouldn't be right back, because duty was calling me away. But the whole thing just felt too absurd. You don't say goodbye to someone you've just met. Or, at least, you don't make a production out of it.

"Come on, Maddy," I said, grabbing her hand. "Let's go."

"I don't want to," she whined. "It's more fun here. Everyone's listening to me. Did you hear my song?"

"I did. It was wonderful," I told her. "You're a wonderful singer. Who needs to go to bed. You too, Cole." And I took both of them, protesting, up the driveway.

As I was about to hoist Maddy into the car, I heard someone approaching on the gravel driveway behind me, and then suddenly there was a hand on my shoulder, stopping me. Turning around, I found Dylan looking at me expectantly and letting his hand slowly slide down my bare arm to rest by his side. And sure enough, there was the world zooming out of focus.

"You ran off," he said dryly. Maybe even disappointed?

"Sorry, but it was time for these kids to get home, and you

seemed to be busy. I didn't want to interrupt." A conflicting mess of emotions rose in me, telling me both to run away—to escape the intense physical reaction simmering in me—and also to stay right there, looking into those preposterous eyes. "Thank you for getting me the drink. I really didn't mean to be rude."

He moved his hand to my forearm, holding it gently, and despite my best mental efforts to remain unaffected, the electricity of his touch coursed through my body, settling between my thighs. At twenty-four perhaps I should have been able to be around someone I was attracted to with more grace, but this was new to me, and apparently, my body would not be handing control over to my brain anytime soon.

"Are you available tomorrow night?" he asked. "I'd like to take you for a drink." The way he said this wasn't an invitation, but more like a reminder. As though he and I having a drink together was a fact I'd forgotten, an inevitability. I was paused in shock when I heard a screech of delight erupt from Maddy, who I'd forgotten was standing between us.

"Are you asking Lydia out on a date?" Maddy looked up at Dylan with a huge grin on her face. Oh god. I felt all heat leaving my lower half and going straight to my face. *Stop stop stop*, I wanted to tell my blush, but it wasn't listening. I'd always wondered if you could actually faint from embarrassment, and I was about to find out.

Dylan looked down and replied directly to Maddy, without missing a beat. "I am," he said. "Is that alright with you?"

Surprised and pleased with the authority just granted to her, Maddy replied, "I guess it's ok, but Lydia *never* goes on dates. She's too busy." She recited the line I'd told her parents so many times before when they'd asked me about my love life.

"Is that right?" he asked, either to Maddy or me. I wasn't even sure anymore.

"Do you love her?" she said. She had a huge grin on her face and practically sang the word *love* as she twirled in her flouncy dress. *Oh god.* I was pretty sure actual death from embarrassment was now on the horizon.

I tried to usher her into the car with Cole, hoping that maybe just maybe we could all pretend she hadn't just asked him that. But she was glued to Dylan, hanging on him, waiting for an answer.

"Madly," he said to her, completely straight-faced. He was *really* good. Turning to me with a hint of a smile, he asked, "Well?"

I nodded shyly—no one in my life would ever have described me as shy, but against my better judgment I found myself agreeing quietly. He moved his hand briefly to my face, brushing my bangs away from my forehead. His look was almost curious, like he was trying to figure me out.

"I'll pick you up at The Cottage at eight thirty."

"Right," I said, finally finding my ability to speak. "On your white horse."

He smiled back, giving me a knowing smirk. I had a feeling my snarky humor wasn't fooling him. Surely he could perceive my violent blushing and flustered response. My body was completely at attention, betraying me with each shallow breath. I had to focus. I lifted Maddy into the car and quickly followed. I looked out of the window as I shut the door, and I waved as the driver pulled away. Dylan stood there looking back, hands in his pockets, appearing completely unflustered. So unfair.

* * *

The next morning I managed to get Daphne on the phone, who was all ears about the guy who had totally mystified me and thrown my body into a tailspin.

"This sounds so steamy and romantic, Lydia! What do you think he wants? I mean, you're only there for another couple of days. Do you think he wants to have a one-night stand?"

"What else would he want?" I said. "Seriously. He was so good. He must do this all the time."

"Do what?"

"Pick up the babysitter," I scoffed.

Daphne was the perfect person to pick this apart with. We'd begun our inseparability sophomore year when we discovered we took the same train from Brooklyn to NYU together every day and had the same monstrous Intro to Conversational French professor. Now she was entering her second year in law school. Her career was actually under way, while mine was still in the planning stages.

"Maybe you should let him," she said, and laughed. "I mean, from the sound of things, I might drive up there and let him."

We'd hashed out every romantic encounter over long dinners. Or I mean, let's be honest—her romantic encounters. My romantic encounters wouldn't get us through the appetizers. And she was the only one who knew the extent of my recent celibacy.

"While you think about that," she said, interrupting my brief wonder at the idea that I might actually want to have *sex* with Dylan, and it might actually *happen*, "I'm going to Google him. What's his name again?"

"Dylan Hale," I said. "I have no idea what he wants! And also, it doesn't matter, right? I'm not going to sleep with a man I hardly know, no matter *how* attracted to him I am…I mean, am I? Gah!" Feeling this attracted to someone for the first time, well, ever had me spinning, and I was *not* used to spinning. "I leave here in two days. Then we're back in the Catskills for over a week, I'm with you for a day, and then I'm off to London. It's easier to leave this whole riotous out-of-control feeling behind me. Daphne, I was talking about knights in shining armor and white horses. I mean, what is *wrong* with me?"

Daphne laughed. "Ok, ok, first, stop reminding me about this whole London thing—I'm still in full-on denial mode about you leaving New York. But also, isn't this guy British? Why couldn't you see him again over there?" This was a fact I had been purposely ignoring. For some reason visualizing a future beyond this date with Dylan felt strangely dangerous.

"And, Lydia, look—I know that with everything you've had to do for your dad you've never been able to really... Well, it's been easier to keep things simple. But, you don't have to do that anymore. Your dad's—" She paused, and I could tell she was worried she'd gone too far, that I wasn't ready to hear what she had to say. But of course I knew she was right. There were times when the fact that Daphne knew me so well was more of a curse than a blessing. And she knew that I hadn't let it sink in that my dad was really gone. Or what that meant for all of the ways in which I'd been holding it together for years. My dad *was* gone. I knew that, but she also knew that I might not be ready for my world to become one that didn't include him. Living life to the fullest is harder than it sounds.

"It's ok, Daphne. I know. I just... Anyway, London is enormous! It's a city of eight million people, and I have a feeling we don't exactly run in the same circles. Not that I even have a circle. But damn, Daph, I'll admit that I don't think I've ever found a guy this... this... intoxicating before. It was like I was a magnet, and all of my little magnetic cells were pointed in his direction or something. There was just something there. I had goose bumps! Plus, I get the feeling he's trouble. He's just too good-looking, ya know?"

"I can't believe Lydia Bell goes to Nowhere, Canada, finally finds someone who she wants to do it with, and he's a sexy, mysterious Brit." There was a moment of silence while I could hear her typing. Then the typing stopped and she gasped. "Oh my god. Make that a sexy celebrity Brit! He is all. Over. The Internet, Lydia."

"What do you mean?" I asked impatiently. I could feel my blood pumping. "You have to tell me. This place doesn't have Wi-Fi, and my cell data doesn't work up here. So charming until you need to Google the hot guy who asks you out, and then suddenly it isn't."

"Ok, ok, calm down there, lady. So apparently he is an architect and has designed a bunch of buildings in London...and in every other major city. Um...He is a prodigy of some sort—he won some big award for architecture when he was really young. God, Lydia, these buildings are pretty incredible." I could practically hear her going into fantasyland over what she was seeing on her screen.

"Don't get distracted!" I scolded her.

"Sheesh, ok...So there are all of these links for events he speaks at and attends, like red carpet stuff. He looks *great* in a tux." I could practically hear her scanning her computer screen. "English gossip blogs and tabloid sites love this guy."

"What else? This is all because he's an architect? And gorgeous?" I asked, looking into the hallway to make sure neither of the kids were eavesdropping.

"I don't think so...It's mostly like crazy *Downton Abbey* shit, society page stuff," she said. I could hear the keyboard clicking.

"Dude. You should see this family crest, and this house. I think he is like old-school aristocracy...Holy shit."

"What?"

"His grandfather is a fucking Duke!" Daphne's voice had reached an octave I was pretty sure only dogs could hear.

"Wait, seriously?" I asked. I knew he was rich, but that seemed beyond the pale. Although, somehow it also didn't come as a surprise. Power, independence, and status oozed from him, like he didn't have to brook disappointment. Ever. I suddenly remembered talking to him and wondered if I'd committed some kind of antiquated royal faux pas. Should I have curtsied or something?

"You heard me. The Duke of Abingdon, which apparently makes Dylan the Earl. Leave it to you, Lydia, to get asked out by an Earl."

"He didn't exactly ask," I said. "It was more like he just told me it was happening." I was all of a sudden embarrassed by my knight-on-a-white-horse comment. "An Earl. Oh yeah, that's just my style."

"Says the girl who's spent her summer riding around in a chauffeured SUV." Sometimes Daphne could simply be annoying.

"As the help! Come on, Daphne, focus. What else?"

"Um, let's see...I don't have time to click on all the links, but he has his own architecture firm in London, and he's thirty. He's clearly very philanthropic—there's a lot about large donations to x, y, and z. Um, everything else is about his family and, like, family history stuff. There's clearly more to read here, but I have to run."

"Great, so I'm going on a date with Lord Grantham, and you're back in our normal life. I feel like we're crossing space and time barriers here."

"Not Lord Grantham. Or maybe like, Lord Grantham from his young wild days? Lydia." She sighed in frustration with me. "Go have a drink with him, and just relax. Have *fun* with him!" I could practically hear her ordering me to let my guard down. "Just let loose a little. And if nothing happens, come home, fantasize about him, get yourself off, and get it out of your system."

I laughed at this. But of course, that had been my idea too. "What will I do without you this year?"

"We'll do this—gab our faces off on the phone. Every day. I gotta run, Lydia—Matt's here." Matt was Daphne's long-term boyfriend, a super-sweet hipster she met in law school. "See you next week! We'll have to make the most of our one day together."

"Great, you can assist in my reeducation—I feel like every ounce of Brooklyn grit has been sucked out of me by the chauffeured car and dates with Earls. I need to go to a dive bar and mainline cheap beer."

Daphne laughed. "Gross," she said. "How about a slice at Grimaldi's, followed by cocktails on our roof—Matt's been bartending, and the man can make a mean Dark 'n Stormy."

"Perfect! Tell Matt I say hi!"

* * *

When I came downstairs after my phone call with Daphne, the Franklins told me I had the morning off. I think they felt bad about my having to leave the party so early the night before, because they told me to borrow the family car and head into town if I wanted. I resolved to use the time to distract myself from the Dylan issue. After a long run around the estate to clear my head, and a desperately needed shower, I put on my best skinny jeans, ballet flats, a fitted tank, and a cropped jacket. I needed to feel like a real person, not just a professional kid chaser.

The town of La Malbaie was twenty minutes away down twisting hilly roads dotted with French road signs, tiny B & Bs, and little shops filled with local crafts. But in the heart of town was an upscale coffee shop with reliably good coffee and croissants. When I got there, I found an isolated table in the window, got myself a latte, and settled in with a stack of fashion magazines. I needed to get my brain back in gear in anticipation of entering the fashion world in two weeks.

In some ways it was ridiculous for me to be pursuing a career in fashion—I'd never been drawn to the glitz of it, and no one would accuse me of being ahead of the fashion curve—but there was just something about it. It was an arena where art met the real world. Clothes could undo things, change people, create clean slates. Even though my own artistic prowess began and ended with the drawing of spirals on the margins of my notebooks, fashion was an art I really wanted to be a part of.

But as much as I tried to focus on the magazines in front of me, my mind kept drifting back to Dylan. I was completely hopeless—trying not to think about him was like being at war with my physical body. My blood had been humming and my skin buzzing ever since I'd met him. I half expected to see him on the pages of the magazines in front of me, lounging in some fashion spread, torturing me in a Tom Ford suit or a Banana Republic field jacket.

It was no mystery why *I* found *him* attractive—you'd have to be blind not to see the appeal—but I was startled by his attention to me. It's not that I thought I was unattractive—I knew I could work it in a pair of heels and a dress when I tried—but I was the cute, sweet, overly long-bang girl who talked with her hands. I just didn't have that sophisticated, mysterious thing going on that guys like Dylan seemed to go for.

But, also, why him? I had dated a few guys, some of whom had been distinctly not ugly, but Dylan was the first one whose clothes I wanted to tear off his body, and quickly. Or more accurately, I wanted him to tear *my* clothes off.

If I closed my eyes, as I was doing at that moment, I could easily imagine his strong hands on my body, starting in my hair, sliding down over my collarbones and smoothing over my breasts. I could imagine him pinning my hips down with those muscular arms. This fantasy wasn't one of the vague scenarios that I normally conjured in order to have a pathetic but much-needed orgasm. This fantasy was specific. I actually wanted to imagine a guy, *this* guy, entering me, taking me. And as I imagined just that, I squirmed in my seat, starting to feel the delicious tension pool low in my belly. The scene was getting torrid, more aggressive, and more inappropriate to be thinking about in public when I heard a coffee being placed on my table, and a familiar voice say, "Lydia."

Chapter 4

Gah!" My eyes shot open, and I nearly fell off my chair. I found myself looking directly at the star of my fantasy. "You scared the crap out of me!"

Flustered, I crossed and uncrossed my legs and tried to regain composure. "Um, hi." I coughed. My hands were white-knuckled, gripping the edges of my seat for support.

"Hi." He leaned forward, smirking and pressing his palms onto the table with locked arms. "I didn't mean to startle you. Am I interrupting something?" He smiled as he said it, making me feel like he could see right through me again.

"No. Um, I mean, yes. God, are you like, everywhere?" I replied, talking mostly to myself. He smiled again, knowingly, while I resettled myself at the table. "I was just thinking about my new job, trying to brush up on what I've missed in the fashion world this summer." I pointed at the towering stack of magazines in front of me, as though it was completely normal to read magazines with your eyes shut and head leaning back. Not to mention the magazines were all closed.

"Dylan!" A shrill, determined voice echoed through the small shop. We both turned towards the entrance and saw his mother and the tall blonde from the night before through the screened door, their noses nearly pressed up against it. "Did you get my cappuccino, darling? And one for Amelia?" Mrs. Hale looked at me with disappointment and then at him with impatience.

"I'll see you tonight, Lydia. Be ready at eight thirty." He said it so matter-of-factly, and that commanding tone did something to me.

"Wait," I said, and he turned back to me with a raised eyebrow. "I'd prefer to meet you there, er, wherever we're going." For some reason I felt like I had to explain. "It's just easier—the doorbell wakes the kids, and I'd prefer not to interfere with the Franklins' night." It was a lame excuse, but the idea of Dylan ringing their doorbell and picking me up for a date in front of Charles and Kate was more than I could bear. I was sure that if they saw us together, they'd know immediately what kind of thoughts I was having about him. Not to mention the risk that Maddy would mortify me again.

He leaned back down, getting close enough to make my heart rate go up another notch, smiled, and asked quietly, "Are you always this much trouble?" My breathing hitched—god, there was something so goddamn masculine about the way he said things like that. "Meet me at the Lucky Fox pub at eight forty-five." And he was gone once again, in and out of my life like a specter.

* * *

At eight thirty, using a map Charles had drawn for me, I found myself walking through the gardens and navigating down a narrow wooded path through the property. With the moon shining through the canopy of trees and the smells of the flowers sifting through the warm air across the narrow footpath, I felt like I was in a production of *A Midsummer Night's Dream*. The path let out at the edge of the road, and the pub was just across from it—it looked like a perfect version of a small English local with its wooden painted sign hanging over the door: a fox with a bow and arrow.

As I reached the door, Dylan was suddenly there behind me, appearing out of nowhere. We both reached for the door handle at the same time.

"I got it," I said, pulling on the door handle, but he stopped my progress.

He looked shockingly handsome and alarmingly seductive in a soft black leather jacket over a perfectly cut linen shirt and the most amazingly well-fitting, worn-in jeans I'd ever seen. Since we were so far north, the sun was still setting and his aviator shades were back in place. He had this refined *Top Gun* thing going on and it was totally working on me.

He looked down at me, eyebrow raised. "Can't I open a door for you?" Somehow he packed both a sweet gesture and a scolding into his tone.

I smiled and gave him a grin, gesturing towards the door as if to say, with more than a little snark, *By all means.* I don't think one guy I'd dated had ever thought to hold a door for me. But, as I walked through the open door, I was surprised that my snarky defensiveness gave way to something else, something slightly foreign but also pleasant. I felt taken care of.

The pub was a classic dark low-ceilinged affair, smelling of polished wood and warm fried food. It was making me hungry with anticipation for England. "Only two more weeks," I hummed under my breath.

Dylan gently put his hand at my back and led us to the back of the pub with purpose. "It's quieter back here," he said by way of explanation. The way he said *quieter* made me smile and remember my Lord Grantham comment earlier. I had the feeling that as posh as this guy sounded, he was *not* the staid, reserved lord of the manor.

I slid onto a bench lining the back wall, and Dylan addressed a passing waiter as he slid in next to me. "We'll both have the Laphroaig fifteen, on the rocks."

"I'd prefer wine, I think," I said before the waiter could leave, and the waiter had the gall to look at *Dylan* for confirmation.

Dylan smiled. "Fine," he said. He looked at me briefly before turning this attention back to the waiter. "I'll have the Scotch, and she'll have a glass of the 2012 Bourgogne Blanc." The waiter didn't even bother looking to me for approval—Dylan's authoritative tone didn't leave any room for questions. I had a feeling this was how most interactions went in his life—Dylan ordered and others followed. I gave him a raised eyebrow.

"They stock that wine when I'm in town," he said in response to my skepticism. "You'll like it." I tried to summon another snarky retort—it should have been reflexive given the circumstance—but oddly his whole gentleman-in-charge demeanor was wearing me down. Maybe it was a whole summer of being in charge of two scampering cavorting uncontrollable children, but there was something about having him take control that took the edge off. It settled me.

He removed his jacket and leaned back, looking at me. "You look lovely," he said with appreciation. I was pretty sure the lump in my throat made my *thank-you* come out as six syllables.

It wasn't that I was nervous, although I was a little; it was that I didn't recognize this feeling, this pull, like a long-shut door was being pried open.

I made a point of looking around the bar, away from him, attempting to regain some control, but I could feel Dylan's eyes on me, pulling me back. Every inch of my body was responding to him, tingling as though champagne were bubbling just underneath my skin. He reached over and tucked my hair behind my ear and swept my bangs aside, which was becoming his signature move, and my nipples instantly hardened beneath the thin lace of my bra and even thinner cotton of my tank top. I shifted back in my seat, hoping to hide the evidence of my arousal.

There was a part of me that screamed to run back into my safe hole and wondered what the hell I was doing out with a man who had me this on edge, but it didn't stand a chance against the part of me—the majority of me—that was intensely drawn to him, to the way it felt to *be* drawn to him. But I was so tense, my whole body engaged in this battle between opening up and protecting myself. The air was letting off sparks around me, as though this tension was living on my skin and interacting with the atmosphere.

"Relax, Lydia." He leaned forward as he spoke. "This is the part where we get to know one another."

Our drinks arrived, and I took a swig. *Just enjoy this*, I told myself. I lifted my chin and smiled. "So, what do you want to know?"

He smiled with approval. "When are you coming to London?"

"I arrive at Heathrow the morning of the sixth." I loved saying *Heathrow*. That small detail reminded me that it was really happening.

"And you'll be working with Hannah Rogan when you get there?" I nodded while taking a long sip of my wine. "Is that what you want to do for work? Be a fashion designer?"

I looked down at my clothes and gave him a skeptical look. "I think we can both agree I wouldn't get that far as a fashion designer. I want to work *in fashion*, but not design. I've had plenty of experience in retail and some internships, but I'm really interested in the business aspect, which I will be learning more about in this job. I'll be able to see the design-to-market process, from beginning to end." I began to breathe more easily, adjusting to being the sole focus of this incredible-looking man in front of me.

He looked puzzled. "But why fashion?"

His question surprised me. No one had really asked me that question before. Daphne and my dad had just trusted it was what I wanted to do. "I'm in awe of fashion designers, what they do. Creating something that represents *them*, as artists, but also works on a moving body and has to become something so personal for someone else. It's not like a painting, simply there to be admired. It's functional. I've seen people feel transformed by clothes, and it must be pretty incredible to feel that way."

"What way?"

"So beautiful, to be so transformed, especially by someone else." The words tumbled out of me, and, as I spoke, I realized that what I had just said about fashion could just as easily be said about architecture. Buildings gave people literal shelter, for crying out loud.

He took my response in and looked surprised. "You've never felt that way? Transformed? Beautiful?"

I looked down into my glass, feeling too exposed. I'd never asked myself that question, and I wasn't sure I even knew the answer. For some reason *transformed* and *beautiful* felt like some-day words—they applied to a woman I wasn't, at least not yet.

Dylan gave me a reprieve and continued, "Where are you from?"

"I lived in Connecticut when I was little, but I feel like New York is really home. It's where I've grown up." Although I was seriously beginning to doubt that I had grown up. Looking at the man in front of me looking back at me, I felt like I was being seen as a woman for the first time, which oddly made me feel more like a girl than ever before.

"Oh?" He was intrigued. "And why is that?"

"Oh…Um, well, we moved there when I was a kid, and then I stayed—"

"To go to NYU." He finished my sentence. It wasn't a question. I looked at him suspiciously. "Celebrities aren't the only ones on Google, Lydia," he explained. *He'd Googled me?* There'd been an article in the student newspaper about me around graduation, which must be what he had seen. "You're quite accomplished," he said admiringly.

Two could play at this game. "So are you," I said, challenging him. He smiled, bigger this time, but it quickly shifted into a stern, even worried, look.

"Don't believe everything you read." *What?* Oh great, now he was mad.

"I just saw an article about the architecture award you received and your buildings." I felt compelled to reassure him, although why he would need reassurance was beyond me. "If it makes you feel any better, I didn't read anything, really. I only had time for a quick search on my phone." I figured he didn't need to know I'd been blabbing about him to my best friend. "And all I saw, as I said, was something about the award. I think the word 'prodigy' was even thrown in there?" I smiled, hoping he could see my teasing was meant to be gentle.

He still looked suspicious, almost resigned, like he was waiting for something else, but I didn't continue. "So, no questions about being a Marquess then?" he finally asked, with a hint of disgust under what he was trying to make a normal question. He was almost wincing, as if he were thinking, *Here we go.*

"The Internet said you were an Earl," I said as generously as possible. Maybe I should be more intrigued by this part of him than I was, but it just didn't seem real. The architecture stuff made sense in my world, but I didn't even know where to start when it came to the aristocracy.

"Right, well, I was, until my grandfather died. Just last month, actually," he replied, looking down at his drink for a moment.

"Oh god, Dylan, I didn't know," I said, having enough familiarity with this to know when not to continue. He nodded and looked back to me. "And no, no Earl or Marquess questions...Unless you want to tell me about it, or unless I'm supposed to call you 'My Grace' or walk two steps behind you or something." I hoped this was the kind of thing one could joke about. Or was I supposed to be reverent about it?

He gave a weak smile, apparently relieved. I had him back from whatever dark place he had just receded to. I felt like I'd just pulled our evening back from the ledge. "Definitely not."

"Were you close with your grandfather?" I asked. I was determined to get *some* piece of information from him that I wouldn't be able to glean from the Internet.

He nodded. "We got on well. He's the reason I'm here actually," he replied, his last word hanging in the air with a sadness he seemed to be guarding. I looked at him, urging him to con tinue. "La Malbaie was his favorite place on earth, and I promised him we'd get back here together, but he died before we could. I came to spread some of his ashes."

"That's so sad, but I can see why he loved it. It's beautiful."

Dylan looked thoughtful for a moment, as though he were remembering something. "Yes, well, just don't tell the cemetery at St. Helen's—they don't need to know that we only buried half of him there," he said, smiling devilishly. "And don't tell my parents either—they wouldn't approve." I smiled back, imagining him with this secret and all of a sudden I felt a small chink in his steely armor. "Back to you, Lydia. Why London? There are plenty of fashion designers in New York."

I hesitated, debating only for a moment about how much to open up to him. To tell him my feelings about London, about that particular part of me, was more than I could give. "I've never been."

He could tell there was more to it than that and looked at me disapprovingly. "That's all I'm getting?" He waited, commanding me to open up with his eyes, but in this case I had no trouble resisting. Yes, that was all he was going to get.

"Why'd you Google me, Dylan?"

"The same reason you Googled me, Lydia."

His acknowledgment of this strange attraction emboldened me. "Well, I'm sure Googling 'Lydia Bell' blew up your Internet," I joked, and he smiled.

"You might be surprised. I learned that someone holds a darts record at a certain Brooklyn bar."

"Oh god. Really?" I hid my face in my hands to conceal heat rising to my cheeks. Great Lakes had been my father's favorite bar, and I'd practically grown up there. I was beating the other patrons at darts well before I was legally allowed to drink.

He chuckled and pried my hands from my face. "But I want to know more. Keep talking." He looked like he was actually enjoying himself, and to my surprise I was too.

I told him the story about the darts record, about my life in Brooklyn, about Daphne, about how much I loved New York. He listened about school, my jobs and internships, and nannying, and he seemed interested in all of it, asking questions, probing. He let very little slip about himself, but I was beginning to the get the sense that taking a woman for drinks was somehow as unfamiliar to him as it was to me. He seemed insatiable, like we had to make the most of this time while we could.

After I told him about my stint volunteering at New York Fashion Week, there was a pause in conversation. He was looking directly into my eyes in a way that was beginning to feel familiar, pulling all the blood to my cheeks. For a moment, I felt like we were on the same page. I felt myself opening up, my eyes getting bigger, waiting for him to acknowledge this tension in some palpable way.

I was silently begging him to touch me, kiss me, something. The bubble he'd created had me feeling safe, so I summoned the confidence to make my own move. I turned towards him, and in that moment I was his completely. One of his hands was on the back of my chair and the other on the table in front of him, as though I was being embraced in an oversized hug without us even touching. But I *wanted* to touch. I began to lean forward, hoping, praying he'd meet me halfway. The pit in my stomach told me I was taking a huge risk, and it screamed at me to pull back, but I wanted this. I wanted him. I looked at him, straight into his deep blue eyes and thought, *Please, please show me what we're doing here.*

Chapter 5

Suddenly he pulled his hands back and leaned away from me, his lips tight. "Lydia, don't—"

I pulled back just as quickly, instantly regretting opening myself up. Instantly feeling like an utter fool. All of the relaxed warmth and delicious excitement drained from my body in a flash. What did I really think was going to happen here? Did I think this guy, this feverishly hot and apparently famous, accomplished *Marquess*, was interested in me? I felt completely confused around him and now, humiliated. I had to get out of there.

"I need to be going, Dylan. Thank you for the drinks," I said, more bitterly than I intended.

"Lydia, sit down," he ordered, exasperated.

But I ignored him and headed out of the pub with my don't-fuck-with-me walk, the stride I reserved for walking back from the subway late at night. I could feel tears dangerously close but held them back. I summoned all my strength, all my bullshit-detecting badass-ness, and firmly began to convince myself that the last thing I should waste my tears on was a confusing, arrogant, although undeniably sexy, asshole.

I could feel him right behind me, pushing chairs aside as he followed me out of the pub. "How are you getting back to the cottage?" he demanded.

"You know, would it kill you to speak to me with a little less annoyance when it was *you* who just rejected me?" I let out in a frustrated grumble. "I'm walking."

"Lydia." He sighed impatiently. "You're not walking alone at nearly eleven in the evening."

"Don't be ridiculous—I'm not a damsel in distress. We're in the most pristine, beautiful, idyllic page from a children's book," I huffed back at him. I was walking, and he was following right next to me, and it was driving me crazy. "My dangerous walk home will be paved with hydrangeas and rose petals, and I'll be greeted by a butler. I don't think I have anything to worry about. Plus, I'm a Brooklyn girl—I can take care of myself." I could feel the anger rising.

"Can you now?" he said, clearly doubting me. He pulled ahead, grabbing me by the hand gently but with no question as to who was leading the way, and we marched down the path towards the cottage.

"Really, this is completely unnecessary," I muttered, my hand still firmly ensconced in his as we continued at a brisk pace. "Do you do this often? Rescue helpless young lasses from the wilds of manicured gardens and quaint country pubs?" He still didn't bite, and we were fast approaching the end of the path. "Do all women fall for this I-won't-talk-to-you-but-I'll-somehow-still-get-under-your-skin routine?" Nothing. "Do they teach you this delightful technique at boarding school or something?"

He stopped. We were on a narrow bit of path, harbored by

a canopy of trees. Apart from the moonlight filtering through, it was nearly pitch-black. He looked down at me with a combination of fury, restraint, and what I hoped to god was lust. He let me go, and he placed one hand over his eyes, his thumb and forefinger pressing into his temples in irritation.

"Goddammit," he hissed through clenched teeth.

Before I knew it, he'd pulled me into him, my whole front pressing, molding into his, our faces nearly touching. He grabbed my wrists with his hands and firmly swept them behind my back, pinning them there in one of his large hands and using them to push us closer together. He backed us against a tree behind me, and I stepped up onto its roots, bringing my face level to his. His forcefulness should have scared me, but it didn't. It felt *necessary*. All I could focus on were all the places our bodies were suddenly touching, a manifestation of the energy between us. He slowly slid his free hand beneath the side of my tank top, skin on skin. His cool, broad palm nearly covered the expanse of my warm side, his fingers wrapped around to my back, his thumb stroking the tender skin just under the band of my bra, rhythmic, gentle. He pulled me closer.

Our foreheads were touching, and I'd already stopped breathing in anticipation when he gently touched his lips to my own. He held this simple kiss for a beat longer than I ever would have expected given the determined expression in his eyes. I felt his tongue slide across my lips, urging them to open. He gently tugged on my lower lip with his teeth before slipping his tongue into my mouth and kissing me in earnest. In the next moment, he leaned into me, feverishly stroking my tongue with his own, pressing my back firmly into the tree behind me. He was in total control. In no way were we kissing. He was kissing me, and it was the fiercest, deepest kiss I'd ever experienced. Every gesture seemed to resonate in my whole body, bringing fresh life to my skin, alerting all of my senses, and making me instantly wet. I had no idea kissing could be like this.

There was no way I was going to let him have all the fun. I twisted my hands free and brought them into his hair, pulling him even closer. He let me kiss him back, which I did just as ferociously as he had kissed me. Both of his hands at my waist, on my skin, and pulling, almost lifting me into him. This kiss had its own beat, its own rhythm, and I was totally lost to it.

Finally, he began to trail gentle kisses away from my mouth towards my ear, ending our mutual assault. Our cheeks barely together, his mouth hovering by my ear, he whispered, "Fuck." He said it with curiosity, almost wonder.

I looked at him, stunned, still feeling like I was on some kind of Tilt-A-Whirl, trying to regain my balance. How had we gone from him rejecting me to him taking me over completely?

"Are you ok?" he said, looking imploringly into my eyes, and holding my face in his hands. He asked it like he'd never had to ask it before, like maybe he was just as surprised at his behavior as I had been. I nodded, touching my swollen lips and still trying to get a grip on what had happened.

"I can't keep my hands off of you. But, Lydia—" He looked around us, as though making sure no one had seen or heard us. "I shouldn't. I can't—"

Suddenly he looked more resolved. He backed away from me and turned to head back towards the pub. He turned around after a few feet, looked at me with piercing, resolute eyes, and quietly said, "I'm sorry."

And then he was gone. Again.

* * *

The next morning we had the car packed by 7:30, and I was just double-checking I hadn't left anything in my room when Charles found me.

"Lydia," he said, startling me out of my reverie. "Sam just swung by to say goodbye and gave me this for you." He handed me a small white envelope. As I took it from him, I could feel its heftiness—it was thick expensive-looking cream-colored stationary.

"Thank you, Charles. I'll be down in a moment." Charles left me alone, and I sat once again on the beautiful tufted linen couch and fought off a yawn. I hadn't slept a wink the previous night, going over every minute of my interactions with Dylan, trying to figure him out. Trying to figure *me* out.

I opened the envelope. Inside was a single ivory notecard with the initials DWLH engraved in navy ink at the top. A foreign phone number was written in large print, and in bold, masculine handwriting below:

RING ME WHEN YOU ARRIVE. —DYLAN

Chapter 6

The flight attendant woke me from my half sleep to let me know we were landing at Heathrow. I'm not sure I'd had a full or decent night's sleep in the two weeks since the crazy kiss-on-the-path business, but I'd been doing my best to chalk the whole thing up to a weird end-of-summer fling, the kind of story I'd tell my daughters one day when they were old enough.

My last day in New York was split between trying to hone my pathetic wardrobe into something that could be packed into luggage but also wouldn't leave me feeling embarrassed to be working for a fashion designer, saying goodbye to my friends, and spending as much time with Daphne as possible.

I'd been waiting for this day, the day I'd arrive in London, for what felt like my whole life. I retrieved the photo from my bag to look at it for the zillionth time—the only photo I had of my parents together, the only photo of my mother at all. There wasn't even a photo of their wedding day, which, according to my dad, had been a spur-of-the-moment Tuesday afternoon at the local register's office. In this picture they were leisurely picnicking atop Primrose Hill, young teachers living abroad, clearly in love, sitting on a tartan blanket. My mother was heavily pregnant, and her head rested on my dad's lap while he played with her hair. They looked like pure, relaxed bliss, like they'd just been laughing at some inside joke.

London was the city where they'd been happy together, where I'd been born, and I'd been dreaming about breathing its air since I was a child. Even though had no memories of being there, I had always imagined that park, Primrose Hill, would feel like home, that if I were there, where they'd been, sitting in the same green grass, I'd feel the family I'd never really had. More than anything, that was why I was going to London. As the pilot came over the speakers announcing our final descent, I safely tucked the photo into my oversized caramel-colored leather tote bag and let the contentment of finally being there settle under my skin.

Getting off the plane took ages, and my whole body ached from sleeping in an awkwardly coiled hump in my tiny cramped seat. After collecting my luggage, clearing customs, and finding myself a latte "for takeaway," I made my way towards an exit promising a taxi stand. If I hadn't turned my face to wipe the latte foam off my lips, I would have missed the formally clad chauffeur holding a sign that clearly read LYDIA BELL. I stopped in my tracks and met man's gaze. "Excuse me," I said. "Um, I'm Lydia Bell. Are you sure there isn't some mistake? I'm arriving from JFK."

"No mistake, Miss Bell. My instructions are to drive you where you wish to go."

Wow—they certainly treated second assistants better in London than they did back in New York. This was fabulous. The chauffeur introduced himself as Lloyd, took over my baggage cart, and led me to a large silver Mercedes sedan at the curb. It looked longer than the typical car, and after he opened the door and helped me in, I could see why. The black leather seating was spacious, with more than ample legroom, and there was a partition between the cab and the seating in the rear, which looked to have a window that could rise and fall.

"Would you like me to close the partition, Miss Bell?" Lloyd asked from the driver's seat.

"No, thank you, Lloyd," I replied. It would have felt so formal and odd to be separated from the driver. Even in New York, I was one of those people who ended up chatting with the cab drivers.

Once we were off, I gave Lloyd the address of my new home. By some winning-the-lottery variety of luck I'd managed to arrange to housesit for a couple in Notting Hill. They were both academics and friends of my favorite journalism professor at NYU, and they happened to be on sabbatical in Turkey. It was mine and mine alone for a year, which seemed like plenty of time to figure out where I would want to—and could afford to—live for the long haul. I obviously hadn't seen it yet, but in pictures it looked to be the tiniest, cutest English house straight out of my anglophilic fantasies. All I had to do in exchange for staying there was water their plants and send them a package once a month with their mail. I was assured it was walking distance to the tube and to the famous Portobello Road Market. I couldn't wait to be part of a neighborhood, especially one as picturesque as Notting Hill.

As the car smoothly flew down the highway, or the "motorway" as Lloyd had called it, I was glued to the window, trying to soak up my new city. In most ways, the houses we passed weren't that different from those back in New York and Connecticut, but there were subtle differences, leaving no doubt that I was in a foreign country. Something about the tone of the brick, the lack of wood clapboard houses, the clothes on the laundry lines all told me I was somewhere new. I'd get glimpses of drivers on the right sides of their cars and was startled into remembering my own foreignness. All of this was strange and exciting to me, not them.

As we entered London proper, the homes got bigger, more regal and elegant, and I began to see the familiar London of postcards and movies. Lloyd darted around other vehicles expertly and navigated the complicated roundabouts with ease.

"Excuse me, Lloyd?"

"Yes, miss."

"Could you tell me if we pass Primrose Hill?"

"I'm afraid we won't be passing that spot on this trip, Miss Bell. Would you like me to take you there instead?"

"No, no. Thank you, though."

"Anytime, miss. Holland Park is down that way to your right, and if we continued up this way you'd see Hyde Park and Kensington Palace. You'll find a map in the console there, if you like." A long shiny wooden-paneled console lined my side of the partition, and I found the map in a drawer, along with bottles of sparkling water, wine, refreshments, and a package of breath mints. It was an entire hotel minibar. Man, this was the way to travel.

Outside my window, stylish Londoners were going about their business, and I couldn't wait to be one of them. An old man in a tweed blazer and cap sat on a park bench with a newspaper. A young woman in killer heels and a perfectly tied trench coat walked by him with purpose, a long umbrella firmly tucked under her arm. I peeked into a taxi stopped at a traffic light and saw a father straightening his son's tiny tie before the car sped away. I saw a gaggle of high school students in their uniform blazers whispering and circling each other as they stood outside a newsstand. A tired-looking chef ducked out the back door of his restaurant for a cigarette. So many of these little pieces of a city I'd seen before—New York was just as lively—but somehow they had a different quality here. A look in one direction, and I could be in Virginia Woolf's London, and in another direction I'd see British punk rounding the corner. Surely it was just the rose-colored glasses of a new arrival, but I was hooked on this place, and it wasn't even ten a.m. on my first day.

* * *

After a shower—well, after figuring how to work the shower and then soaking in it for twenty minutes—I began to unpack some of my belongings and take stock of the surroundings. I dressed in the first thing I could find—my favorite jeans, oxfords, and a loose cotton sweater—ran a brush through my hair, grabbed my tote minus all of the magazines I'd been lugging around, and headed out to explore. I felt far livelier than I deserved given my lack of sleep, but it was like fresh blood was pumping through my veins. A British transfusion. I couldn't have stayed inside if I'd tried.

The first thing I'd need was a cell phone. The house phone had been disconnected, and I needed to let Daphne know I'd arrived safely. My old phone was beyond the point of software upgrades and apparently didn't have any international capacity, so I'd tossed it in a trashcan at the airport. Doing that had been surprisingly liberating. I was truly leaving my old self behind.

In the back of my mind I was still debating adhering to Dylan's invitation, his order, to call him. For the past two weeks, I'd been fraying at the edges from our kiss on the path. When I thought about it—and I had, in explicit detail, repeatedly—I felt part of myself coming alive. I could feel my cheeks flush and belly clench every time I remembered his lips and hands on me. And beyond that, I felt almost new, like I was meeting a different part of myself. In essence, I was simply insanely, outrageously attracted to him.

But I couldn't pin him or his bizarre behavior down—kissing me and then apologizing before disappearing. Hell, I couldn't pin *myself* down when I was around him, and I was afraid of throwing myself in his path unless I had a better handle on where we'd be headed. No matter how well I avoided it when talking with my friends or pushed my thoughts of my father into the recesses of my mind, I knew my grief was still right there, lurking, waiting to make me feel lost. And something about Dylan made me feel like I might lose my tenuous grip on myself, like somehow he had the power to bring me out of the fog I'd been in, and the truth was, well, I wasn't sure I was ready for that.

I walked up to Bayswater Road, the main thoroughfare, and started to head towards Marble Arch and Oxford Circus. According to Google maps, which I'd consulted before leaving New York, I'd eventually land in a sea of shops and restaurants. Plus, this allowed me to take in Hyde Park, Speakers' Corner, and all the people enjoying the last of the summer sun. As I entered the fray and began to duck down the winding side streets, I couldn't help but peek into all of the beautifully curated boutiques, catering to singular and refined tastes. I knew I'd have months to explore them all, but I couldn't get enough. I passed tiny mahogany-lined shops catering to gentlemen, offering bespoke suits and ties, and others selling artisanal high-end toiletries *since 1790*. But there were also fish 'n' chip stands, large chains, and stores selling soccer gear. It was a total mélange of high-end and low-end, a commercial concoction for every need. I absorbed every smell and took pleasure out of every cobblestone, letting my nose and eyes guide me down narrow passageways and across major roads.

One store tucked in a narrow walkway between a noodle shop and a tiny French cafe caught my eye. Fancy hats and fascinators were perched in the window, something I'd never see in New York. I still hadn't found the cell phone store, but I couldn't resist. I was the only one in the spare and elegant shop, and I luxuriated in the serenity of the space, hidden from the bustle outside. A lit candle made the store smell of jasmine, and I inhaled the relaxing scent and took my time fingering each dress and accessory. I could imagine the months of becoming a Londoner falling into place, like I was absorbing the fabrics of this new place. My hand paused on a small cobalt-blue tailored dress, and I pulled it from the rack to get a better look.

"I still haven't seen that on anyone." The salesgirl's voice seemed to come from nowhere—she'd been so quiet. "I'm sure it would look fabulous on you." I knew what she meant in that my small-breasted figure worked with low necklines, and this dress had a deep v in the front. It was sleeveless, and looked to hang to mid-thigh. When I pulled it from the rack I saw its killer feature—a cutout diamond at the lower back, sexy but not risqué. I had to at least try it on.

The look on the salesgirl's face when I came out of the dressing room told me that I was pulling it off, and I figured I could always throw on a jean jacket and wear it to work if an actual dress-appropriate occasion never popped up. The price tag—nearly three hundred pounds—was a chunk of my savings I shouldn't have been parting with, but I vowed to myself to be more frugal going forward. I wasn't paying rent, and I'd get my first paycheck before too long. Maybe it was careless, but it felt like a small celebration at having arrived in this place I loved, of all the newness.

After finally purchasing a cell phone and finding the grocery store and picking up some essentials, I was ready to drop. Whatever adrenaline had seen me this far was now failing me. I hailed the nearest cab, and nearly passed out on the short ride to my new home. In order to avoid falling asleep at six p.m., I called Daphne.

"There you are! How was your flight?" Daphne's enthusiastic voice was exactly the jolt of caffeine I needed.

"Oh, you know, lap of luxury. I'm pretty sure the guy I slept next to had clinical-level BO problems, and my ass is still numb, so you know, typical day for me."

Daphne laughed. "Well at least your sense of humor made it over intact. So what's it like? What have you been doing?"

"Oh, it's effing adorable. I saw this old man today dressed completely in tweed, a pipe hanging out between this teeth, and he was swinging his umbrella with every step, like a cane, in this way that was just, well, perfectly British."

"And you brought him back to your apartment and shagged him rotten?" Daphne interrupted, saying the last bit with her best English accent, which was unfortunately indistinguishable from her Austin Powers impression.

"Obviously," I said, nearly choking on my laughter. "Anyway, yeah, I spent the afternoon wandering around and getting acclimated. My feet are sore—I walked forever." I rubbed my toes as I held the phone between my ear and shoulder. "Ooh, and I got

the most amazing dress!" I proceeded to tell Daphne every detail about the house, the neighborhood, and my shopping trip. I
loved that I could tell how happy she was for me.

Daphne finally stopped my rambling and interrupted me.
"So. Are you going to call him or what, Lydia? Don't think I
don't see what you're doing here, talking about shopping and
old tweedy men, avoiding the whole thing completely." She saw
right through me. It was almost like I was hoping I'd fall asleep
while on the phone with her so I wouldn't have to make the de-
cision.

"Call who?"

"Oh yeah, right."

"Daphne, I'm sure he's not as hot as I remember. I mean
that old guy on the street probably *was* Dylan. The fact that I
hadn't seen an actual man in three months when I met him was
probably clouding my vision. The magical Canadian summer air
was probably hiding his weird English teeth and wonky eye." I
looked in the mirror and realized I was actually making a wonky
eye face as I was saying this.

"Lydia!"

"What?!"

"Stop deflecting. You're not going to joke your way out of this
one." Daphne was using her no-nonsense, there's-a-lecture-just-
over-the-horizon tone with me. "Call him. You were obviously
into his whole high-handed I'm-an-Earl-and-the-world-turns-
the-way-I-tell-it-to thing, which—"

"I was not," I tried to interrupt. "Plus apparently he's a Marquess, whatever that is."

"Whatever! You were. You are. I get it. It's kinda hot. I know
it freaks you out to let go, but you need to branch out. We
have already talked about this. Get off the phone with me, and

call him! I love you. We'll talk tomorrow. Ok, bye!" She sped through the last few sentences and hung up.

Argh! Sometimes she drove me crazy! But I also knew she was right. She knew how preoccupied I'd been by him, and she knew I hadn't been able to get that kiss out of my mind. It's just that, well, on top of me feeling so upended by him, he had a freaking *title*.

It was after seven. Surely he'd be at some formal dinner or something and wouldn't pick up. A safe time to call if there ever was one. I dug out his card, crumpled, folded and softened from two weeks of me thumbing it in my pocket, and dialed. My whole body relaxed when voicemail picked up. "Hi, um, hi, Dylan. It's Lydia Bell. I hope you remember me—we met in Canada." I mean, of course he'd *remember* me, right? He wasn't senile. I was embarrassing myself already. "I arrived in London this morning, and thought I'd give you a call. Hope you're well. Talk soon."

Well that was only half-mortifying, and at least now it was over. I put down the phone half hoping never to hear from him again. The ball was officially out of my court. I was halfway to the kitchen to make some tea when the phone vibrated. I looked at the screen and saw the number I'd just dialed; the pit of anticipation quickly took up residence in my stomach.

Chapter 7

Hello?" I said, as if I didn't know exactly who would be on the other end.

"Lydia." His voice was just as delicious as I remembered. He sounded firm, authoritative, and so sexy, and incidentally like there was no need to remind him who I was.

"Hi, Dylan. How are you?"

"You arrived safely."

"So it would seem," I replied. Was it possible I was hearing him smile?

"You thought I might not remember you?"

"Well, who knows? Two weeks might be a long time in the life of Dylan Hale."

"That kiss isn't one I'd forget."

I inhaled loudly, and I'm sure he could hear it. Was it possible he'd been thinking about it as much as I had?

"So, when can I see you?" he continued, and his voice spoke straight to the nerves pulsing through my body.

I felt like I should play hard to get a little, but the reality was I didn't know a soul here or have any plans. "Well, let me look at my calendar. Hmm, all it says here is 'get over jetlag' and 'learn how to pronounce Mara-la-ban.' Marlee-bonee? Maree-lee-bone? Your language is chaos." I had walked down Marylebone High Street that day and had been trying to figure out its pronunciation ever since.

"English, you mean?" he said, teasing.

"Is that what you call it?"

"It's Mar-le-bone, and tomorrow night then. We'll have dinner. I'll pick you up at eight."

"Sounds lovely." Thank god he was making this easy on me. "Where will we go? I don't want to dress inappropriately."

"My place. Wear whatever you'd like." I heard him shift into business mode and say something to someone on the other end. "I'll see you tomorrow. And, Lydia, I'm glad you're here." He hung up without another word. *Wow.* It was definitely still there—all of that sensual tension that arose in my body in response to him. Even over the phone he was able to turn me on. I didn't stand a chance.

That night I drifted into a long, calm, and dreamy sleep, thinking about dresses, blue eyes, country paths, and absolutely perfect kisses.

* * *

It was a Tuesday morning, my first day at work, and I left the house with plenty of time given that I didn't really know where I was going. I walked up to Bayswater to get the tube, very happy I'd decided to stow my heels in my bag and wear ballet flats for the walk. For my first day I went with slim black cigarette pants, a loose blouse with sailboats on it, and a well-fitted black blazer. Blue suede heels Daphne had given me would make the whole thing less corporate, once I had a chance to put them on. With my umbrella tucked under my arm, and a coffee in hand, I hoped I looked as at home with all the other people on their way to work as I felt. One transfer later, I stepped off at Green Park, and made my way to the Hannah Rogan offices in the top floor of a beautiful old building deep in Mayfair. I was practically skipping, I was so energized and excited to be there.

I rode the tiny antique elevator, swapping my shoes on the ride, and was greeted by a young, thin, gorgeous guy in a drapey grey t-shirt, just putting down the phone. "And you must be Lydia." He smiled, and I couldn't help but giggle back. If I didn't get used to the English accents soon, it would start to get awkward. "I'm Josh—we spoke on the phone when you interviewed?" Also, clearly gay.

"Of course! It's so nice to meet you in person! You were so helpful during all of that, and I was so nervous. Thank you."

"Oh, I've been there. Not to worry," he replied, smiling broadly at my enthusiasm. "Hannah may have a bark, but really she's a great boss. And I have it on good authority she was impressed with your interview."

"Oh, that's a relief to hear. Thank you. I don't look too nervous now do I?" I looked down at my outfit and then back to him. Hannah was known for having high standards, and the truth was that I *was* apprehensive about meeting her and her staff.

"Not even a smidgen," he replied kindly.

"Whew," I said with a dramatic brush of my forehead. "And thank you for sending a car to the airport—that was so welcome after a long flight."

He looked puzzled by my appreciation. "Huh. Wasn't me. Perhaps Fiona? I didn't even know we had a car to send. Anyway, do you know where you're headed?"

"Not a clue."

He pointed down a long hallway behind him, and said, "Last door on your right, and you'll find Fiona, Hannah's other assistant." I nodded. "The loo is that way," he added, pointing down another hall. "Oh, and we're going out for lunch at one—you should definitely come."

"Oh, that'd be great. See you in a bit then." I was so relieved that the first face I'd see every day at work would be a friendly one.

I knocked on the frosted glass door as I entered, noticing there were two shiny white desks, one of which was likely mine. The office was large, light-filled, and very modern, with windows looking down at the bustling street below. "Hi, Fiona? I'm Lydia." Fiona, tall, buxom, and with killer style, rose and reached out to shake my hand.

"Welcome! Here, have a seat, and I'll fill you in."

Over the next three hours I learned that Hannah was only in the office a couple of days a week, preferring to work from a private studio, especially with London Fashion Week fast approaching in three weeks. But the office was where we handled everything related to the business. We'd be noses to the grindstone until Fashion Week passed, and I realized that if I was looking to see all sides of this business, I'd arrived at the perfect time.

It was just after noon when we were walking at a clip to the Caffè Nero around the corner. "So, Lydia, you just arrived yesterday morning? Aren't you completely knackered? Was the flight just *awful*? Do you miss New York terribly? You don't *look* like you missed a night of sleep!" I could tell Josh's speed-talking exuberance was going to bring me great joy. It was simply infectious, and I laughed out loud.

"Oh, well, it's probably all of the cocaine I've been doing," I replied, deadpan, and he acted playfully shocked.

"Oh, I'm going to like her," Josh said, pointing at me and looking at Fiona.

"But, seriously, I think I've bought this fair city out of coffee already," I continued. "So, unless you're horrified by my asking, what's the office gossip? Can you fill me in? Catch me up so I don't feel like such a newbie?"

"Well, first, and I'm not supposed to tell anyone, because officially I don't know," Fiona glared at Josh with an I'd-better-be-able-to-trust-you vibe, "but Hannah's going to be opening a private client studio in a few months. There's been enough interest that she feels like it's time to move the fittings out of her regular studio and into a more posh setting. Lady Amelia Reynolds alone has already tapped Hannah to dress her for six events before the end of the year. And now her friends are following. It's great for us." Josh's eyes got wide. "No, don't worry, Josh. This isn't one of those things that will result in you losing your job. Lydia, Josh is always panicked that we'll get purchased by one of the big conglomerates and there'll be redundancies. This isn't *that*. I'm sure she'll tell us all soon, but I have a feeling not much will change, except maybe now we can order in from the good Vietnamese restaurant instead of the dodgy one."

One of the reasons I'd wanted to work for Hannah Rogan was because she was a smaller house, established enough that a couple of celebrities had worn her dresses on red carpets and business was hopping, but not so big that there were knockoffs of her handbags on Canal Street. And certainly not big enough that she was being peddled by one of the few major luxury goods operators out there. She was still an artist, and still in charge, which I loved. I hoped to learn a lot from being around her, both about the business and about art and design.

"Well that was better gossip than I'd expected," I replied. "Although, still pretty tame. I mean, what? No office romances? No one making out under the desks or anything?"

Josh jumped in, "Ooh, I've got one! I overheard Stephanie, our media booker," he clarified for me, "talking to her boyfriend in the loo. It sounds like she thought he was going to propose, but he didn't, and she was in a snit and bloody impossible about it."

"Josh! What were you doing in the ladies toilet?" shrieked Fiona.

"Oh don't be such a prude, Fee!" He hit her playfully. I knew I was going to have fun with these two. "Oh, and Fiona has a fabulously fit boyfriend, Lydia, so don't think of falling in love with her."

"Good to know, Josh," I replied, giggling. "And how about you?"

"He wishes!" Fiona laughed, "He's too busy breaking hearts in every club in Soho. What about you, Lydia, leave any suitors behind you in the States?" My mind drifted immediately to the night ahead of me, and I paused, completely distracted and taken out of the moment. "Hellooo?"

"Oh, sorry, no. No boyfriend for me. I'll just have to work my American charms over here."

The remainder of lunch flew by in a sea of boisterous chatter. I felt instantly comfortable with Josh and Fiona, and had a sense I wouldn't be friendless in this new city for long.

On the way back to the office my new phone buzzed in my

pocket. I looked, and my skin came alive the second I saw Dylan's name on the screen.

TUESDAY, 1:45 pm
What's your address?

TUESDAY, 1:46 pm
You don't have to pick me up. It's the 21st century. Women can use the tube, have the right to vote, etc.

TUESDAY, 1:46 pm
And the right to be impossible. Address, please.

TUESDAY, 1:47 pm
Ah, but will we both fit on that white horse of yours?

TUESDAY, 1:47 pm
I'm sure we'll manage. Polishing the saddle as we speak. Address.

I smiled and texted him the address. I couldn't help it—the grin was spread ear to ear. I was just grateful that he couldn't see just how happy his texts were making me.

TUESDAY, 1:48 pm
Now was that hard? See you at 8.

The afternoon back at the office moved just as quickly as the morning, and before I knew it I was slipping my flats back on and heading out the door.

When I climbed the stairs from the tube onto the street, dark clouds were moving in, and I immediately picked up my pace. I just made it to the door of my house before the heavens opened and big, thick raindrops began to fall. Fumbling with my keys, I nearly tripped over a huge bouquet of flowers on my stoop. I leaned over to grab them, rushing them and myself inside before we both got soaked. After settling in, tying my wet hair in a ponytail, and pouring myself a glass of wine, I returned to the flowers. Two dozen white roses, which I now noticed were absolutely perfect, stood in a beautiful porcelain vase, not the typical crappy type sold by florists. I opened the card.

For your first day. Delivered via horseback, *naturally*.
See you at 8. Be ready. —DYLAN

I could actually hear Dylan saying these words, imagine the way his accent would make the words bleed together, and it brought a big stupid smile to my face. No one had ever sent me flowers except for my father, on my birthday, and for a moment I dipped into that ever-present well of sadness. He would have been so happy to know a man had sent his daughter flowers. And these were stunning. After a moment, I took a picture and quickly texted it to Daphne.

TUESDAY, 6:43 pm
He sent these! Having dinner tonight. Wish me luck.

I looked at the clock, and it was already 6:45. If I was going to shower, I was going to have to hustle. For some reason, I didn't think his *be ready* comment was to be taken lightly.

I shaved my legs, plucked my eyebrows, and spent about twice as long as usual in front of the mirror attempting an elegant messy ponytail I'd seen in a magazine. After holding up every article of clothing I owned and deeming each one subpar,

I decided if there were ever a night for the blue dress, this was it. The reality was I didn't really own anything that felt appropriate for hanging out with a man like Dylan Hale. I had a feeling this was the make-it-or-break-it night for us, and I was going to need all the confidence I could muster. I quietly willed myself to shed my nerves and vowed to just have fun with him.

At 7:52, I was throwing on black heels and applying a second coat of lipstick.

At 7:56, I was grabbing my jacket off its hanger.

At 7:58, I was sitting on the bottom step of the staircase willing the next two minutes to go faster.

At eight p.m. sharp, the doorbell rang.

Chapter 8

I hesitated a moment. I couldn't believe I was actually going to see him again. The uncertainty and the waiting had elevated our moonlit kiss to an operatic level in my mind. It had been replayed over and over, and now he was just outside, a few feet away.

I finally opened the door, and it was like seeing him for the first time all over again. Jaw drop and all. I would have thought my memories were exaggerated, but they hadn't been doing him justice. He looked back at me, a different Dylan: architect Dylan, urban Dylan, London Dylan, Lord Dylan. He was clean-shaven and wore a crisp white shirt unbuttoned at the top and a sleek grey suit, which he wore perfectly. It looked like it had been sewn right onto him, and it probably had. His blue eyes smiled at the corners, and I swear I sensed joy mirroring back at me.

"Hi, Lydia," he said, smiling his rakish smile. He was standing in my doorway, and he rested one hand on the doorframe, half leaning into it. He looked so calm and relaxed, the exact opposite of the riot that was taking over in my body. His hair, freshly cut, begged for me to run my fingers through it. And his eyes, the fathoms-deep blue eyes, held my face and made me blush. I gave him a huge smile back, unable to hide my appreciation. I wished just for once that I was able to play it cool. My fingers felt long and tingly at my sides, and my skin seemed to light up under his gaze.

"Hi," I said back, still smiling.

He stepped through the doorway and reached out, using one of his hands to grab mine and placing the other firmly on my hip. Part of me was surprised by his brazenness, by his touching me the way he was, but of course he'd already kissed me. We'd already crossed into a world where it was ok for Dylan Hale to wrap his fingers around my hip. And when he did, it sent sparks flying straight between my legs. He pulled me closer and said, "You look unbelievable, not an ounce of jetlag."

I looked up at him, resenting the few inches of space that remained between us. "Thank you," I replied. "You're not so bad yourself."

"Better than you remember? Or worse?" A smile and boyish eyes lit up his words.

"Wouldn't you like to know." If there was a time to channel my sassiest, most confident self, it was now. "Now, feed me, Hale. I had a busy day at work, and I'm hungry."

He laughed out loud, a smile spread across his face, and he pulled me through the front door of my own home, shutting it firmly behind me and testing its lock. As we approached the street I saw the same long silver Mercedes that had picked me up at the airport, with Lloyd at the wheel. I stopped short and shot him a look. "It was you? *You* sent the car to the airport?" I said it with more force than I'd intended. I was more confused than angry. It had, after all, been lovely.

"You're angry?" He was puzzled.

"No, just...How'd you...I mean, it's kind of a kidnapper-y move."

He shrugged, looked at me in a way that was somehow both disapproving and charming, and said, "You need to learn how to accept chivalry, Lydia. I wanted to know you'd get in from the airport safely. I didn't like thinking about you lugging your suitcases into a cab on your own, or worse, the tube." Lloyd was holding the car door open, and Dylan gave me a slight nudge, encouraging me to get in.

"It's not chivalrous when you don't know who's doing it." I stood my ground. "The creepy kind of outweighs the sweet in this situation. I mean, how did you even know what flight I was coming in on?"

"You told me."

"No I didn't," I stated firmly, crossing my arms over my chest and racking my brain for when I might have told him. "When?"

"At the pub. You said you were coming into Heathrow the morning of the sixth. I sent Lloyd there before the first morning flight arrived."

"Oh." I guess I had. "Good thing for Lloyd I arrived at eight in the morning. What if I'd been on a flight that arrived at eleven?"

Dylan just shrugged as if to say it wouldn't have mattered.

"So, wait, you already had my address when you asked me for it today?"

"I had *access* to your address. You'd given it to Lloyd, not me. I felt like you should give it to me on your own. If I'd just shown up out of nowhere that *would* have been creepy."

"You're kind of splitting hairs, but..." I sighed in defeat. "Ok.

Thank you for the airport pickup. It really was lovely."

He smiled slightly. "Not so kidnapper-y then?"

"A little less, but you still should have warned me." I felt slightly chagrined, but I also saw Dylan rolling his eyes and caught Lloyd smiling. I smiled back. "Hi, Lloyd."

"Hello, Miss Bell."

Lloyd held open the door, and Dylan helped me into the car, his hand somehow never leaving my body as he climbed in after me. We darted through Tuesday night London traffic in silence. I was looking out the window, taking in my first real night out in my new city. Finally, I looked to him. "So, what have you been up to?" If there was any way I was going to see through all the attraction and actually talk to him tonight, I'd have to start somewhere.

"Oh, the usual," he deflected.

"But you love the usual?" He seemed in his element here in London, far more at home than he had been walking across that lawn with his family.

"It's what I do," he shrugged. I got the sense he was being modest.

"And what exactly is that? What did you do today?"

"You know I'm an architect," he said, and I nodded. "Well, today, I began work on a personal project. I also checked in on a library in Athens and a residence in Jordan, both under construction."

"You were in Athens and in Jordan today?" I replied curiously.

"No. These were remote check-ins. Virtual tours of the building sites," he clarified.

"Oh. Of course." I blushed. Presumably what I suggested had been impossible.

"I'd be there in person if I could be. I'm very…particular." He grabbed my hand and held it across his lap. "How was your first day at work?" he asked, clearly wanting to change the topic.

"Oh!" I remembered, turning to him in my seat. "Thank you for the flowers—they are gorgeous!" He smiled and tightened his grip on my hand. "No one's ever sent me flowers before."

He turned slightly to face me and frowned. "That won't do. I don't believe for a minute that you haven't left behind a line of chaps, pining, all wishing they'd thought to send you more flowers about now." Forget sending flowers. No man had even *looked* at me the way he was at that moment. I wanted to hold on to it. Keep it.

"Hardly! But thank you for the undeserved credit. I'm quite sure it's never once occurred to any guy I've gone out with to buy me flowers."

"You don't see yourself very clearly, do you?" He wasn't asking, he was stating in wonder, and it made me melt a little. He lightly brushed my palm with his thumb as we rounded a tight corner onto Sloane Street.

"You're clearly blind, old man." I scoffed and huffed at him, turning to look at the stately neighborhood outside my window.

But then I felt his finger tap the edge of my chin, prompting me to turn my gaze to his. He looked dead serious, no trace of humor on his face. He said, with pure authority in his voice, "Don't do that. You're lovely."

I gulped and nodded in reply. I felt instantly shy, vulnerable, and surprisingly, riotously turned on. The words, that attitude, cut through any date-like awkwardness that could have been there. I got the sense that he would never let me be falsely modest or play games with him, never let me just act the part of being a girl on a date, never let me be dishonest. That clarity, that authority, brought the sexual tension between us into high relief and every cell of my body to attention. There would be no skirting around this thing between us. He was going to throw us into the fire. I could feel it.

"I'll ask again. How was your first day?" he continued, still bossy but softening, as though he were exercising patience with me.

"It was actually…great." I started slowly. "I think I'm really going to love the people I work with—they're hilarious and welcoming. Spring Fashion Week is coming up, so things will be getting busy, insanely busy, soon. In fact they already are—I think they're just easing me into the fray." He nodded, stroking my hand as we talked.

The car made a couple of tight turns through the elegant Regency-style neighborhood and pulled up in front of a large white home, standing tall on a corner. The house was in Belgravia, which I knew from a *60 Minutes* special on some Middle Eastern oil tycoon was one of the most expensive residential areas in the world. Lloyd opened the door, and Dylan ducked through and held out his hand for me.

"This is me." And he gestured to the manse in front of us.

He had his hand to my back from the moment we left the car, removing it only to unlock the huge glossy black door, and he ushered me into an expansive high-ceilinged foyer painted a warm hunter green. Dylan placed his keys on a large dark wood circular table in front of me, and the scent of the enormous arrangement of flowers perched there mingled with the cool rush of air that came when he closed the door behind me. A beautiful parlor was off to the left, and there were signs of a kitchen down a long hall ahead. A huge regal staircase wound up to the floors above.

The house was all polished wood and carefully chosen paint

and finishes. Each accent seemed perfect for the space, a combination of sleek modern male taste and distinguished English elegance. I caught glimpses of large oil paintings and photographic prints, a careful juxtaposition of contemporary and traditional art. It wasn't the home of a soulless mega-mogul bachelor. It obviously wasn't the home of a family man either, but it had a warmth and lived-in feel that suggested a distinguished sophisticated gentleman rather than a bachelor playboy.

Dylan stood behind me and lifted my jacket from my shoulders, halting as he brought it down my arms and encountered the cutout at the back of my dress. I heard him inhale deeply.

"God you're gorgeous," he said quietly, placing my jacket on the bannister of the stairs and eyeing me up and down. He placed his hand on my bare back, and I felt cooler and warmer in the same instant. He stroked his thumb against my skin, and I found myself trying to steady my breathing. If I never wore this dress again, it would still be worth every cent.

As he turned me towards the hallway leading towards the kitchen, I was caught by an enormous glossy photographic print of an ocean horizon on one wall of the foyer.

"This is stunning." My eyes were glued to it, taking in the surprising red hues on the crests of the waves in the picture.

"Isn't it?"

"It's otherworldly."

"You've got an eye." He tugged my hand and led me back to the warm light of the kitchen. The room was lined with large white subway tiles and accented all over with butcher block and stainless steel. It was a cook's dream.

"This place is incredible, Dylan." I took it all in as he reached into the fridge for some white wine. "Is it a family home?" I asked as I found a place on a high stool at the marble kitchen island. I had thought he'd live in some glass tower, and I was frankly surprised to see him in this traditional English building.

"It was," he started, looking at me like I'd touched on something he hadn't expected me to. "It belonged to my grandfather. Wine?" I nodded, and he began to pour. I was going to need all the liquid courage I could get. "He inherited it from his father, who had the misfortune of being a drunk and a total wanker by all accounts. He lost much of the fortune he had inherited. Not high times for the Hale family. So when he died at the ripe age of fifty, this house and the one where my parents live now were the main assets, apart from his title, that he could leave his son. My grandfather sold this place when he was young and used the money to start his own business—"

"Hale Shipping?"

"That's right." He looked faintly surprised that I had done my research. He pulled two plated meals from a warming drawer behind him and placed one in front of me. The food—steak, polenta, and some kind of leafy green vegetable—was perfectly arranged and steam rose from its surface. He sat next to me, and we both began eating. "The money from selling this house helped him build a business of his own, on his own merit, and he was able to hand down the business to his son, my father."

"You admire that." I could see the pride and reverence in his eyes.

He nodded. "Not that my father cared. He's far more concerned with being the sixteenth Duke of Abingdon than running the business, although he certainly reaps the rewards." He said this with clear disapproval.

"What does a Duke do, exactly?" I asked sheepishly.

"Nothing," he replied curtly. "Not these days anyway. My grandfather represented the Queen on State visits a few times and organized the State Opening of Parliament, and there are some other command performances. Apart from managing the estate, it's all pomp and circumstance. Presumably my father will be doing some of that soon, though if I were the Queen I wouldn't let my father near anything of import." There was obviously a story there, and not a good one, but it didn't seem like the time to explore it. I certainly wasn't ready to talk about *my* family, or lack thereof.

"And what exactly is a Marquess? I'm sorry for not knowing."

"Don't be," he replied firmly. "I'm the son of a Duke, that's all. It's a title and excuse for people to be interested in my personal life." This was obviously not his favorite topic.

"Anyhow," he continued, "the house had been bought and sold and broken up into flats, but a few years ago I made the owners an offer, and here we are." There was a subtle pride in his voice.

"Buying it back on your own merit."

He gave a subtle nod in acknowledgment. "Many of the furnishings once belonged to my grandfather, though I've added quite a bit of technology and sustainability features, and you'll see that the upstairs has been modernized quite a bit." He paused. "More wine, Lydia?"

I gulped and nodded. "You think I'll see the upstairs? Confident, aren't you?" I had no idea where my occasional bursts of self-assurance were coming from. Dylan exuded total competence, and I was pretty sure I was completely out of my depth.

"Always," he said and smiled knowingly.

We ate in silence for a few minutes, and I could feel the tension rising. "You're not eating much," he observed.

"It's delicious. I'm just…distracted." I crossed and uncrossed my legs, attempting to curb the growing need between them. My skin was beginning to heat up. The way he looked leaning on the island in front of him, his shirt unbuttoned and exposing a hint of chest hair, left me breathless. He was so goddamn *masculine*. He checked my body over, clearly taking in my flushed state.

He shoved his empty plate aside and turned to me. "Tell me about your previous relationships, Lydia. You don't have a boyfriend back in the States, do you?"

I shook my head. "There's not much to tell." I shrugged. "You know, town harlot and all that," I said, willing a joke to somehow make me feel like I had a better grip on what I was doing. It seemed we were about to get somewhere, and my body was on high alert.

He barely smiled at my feeble attempt at humor, and continued his interrogation, sweeping away my plate. "I don't believe you. Has there ever been anyone serious?"

I shook my head. "No one lasting more than a couple of months."

"Why?" He was genuinely puzzled. He leaned on the far side of the kitchen island, his forearms resting on its shiny surface.

"I've never been that interested. I mean. Before—" I stopped myself, and he smiled.

He leaned in further, reaching over the island, and whispered conspiratorially, "I want you too."

I gulped and felt the tension thicken between us. "Have you had many girlfriends?" I asked. I was talking, but I was only half processing anything other than the sensations beating through my body.

"I don't have girlfriends."

"Ever?" He shook his head in confirmation.

"Not in a long time. I don't do relationships, Lydia. You should know that before we go any further."

"What do you want then, Dylan? I feel like I'm being courted here—effectively, I might add." He smiled knowingly at the compliment while I crossed my arms in front of my chest, trying to protect myself a little, as futile as it might be. "Or I *was* being courted…" Dylan got up and came to stand before me, making me pause.

"Lydia," he said, looking straight into my eyes. He grazed my arms with the backs of his hands, and my skin hummed with his touch. He was looking right into me. He cupped my chin with his hand, and drew my gaze up to his. He placed a gentle kiss on my lips, instantly calling all of my blood to my cheeks. Then he said, in a playful but firm whisper, "I want to fuck you."

Chapter 9

I could barely breathe with him standing this close; my chest was rising and falling in an exaggerated beat, hunting for more oxygen, and for another kiss. I gulped. "So, just sex, then?"

He smiled with a hint of mischief in his eyes. "*Just* sex? What I have in mind will be far better than 'just sex.'

"I hope you're not offended," he continued, in a near whisper. "I'm afraid it's all I'm good for, but I promise I'm very. Very. Good at it." He moved in even closer, parting my legs with his, and wedged himself between them.

"You know, it's a real shame about your self-esteem," I said, feeling the room around me fade into the background.

He held my face in his hands with surprising softness, and he leaned over and kissed me again, laying gentle pecks across my cheeks and neck. "The fact is, cheeky girl." Kiss. "I want you." Kiss. He grazed one hand up my leg and brought his fingers tantalizingly close to my center, barely grazing me over my panties. "And I want *this*." Kiss. My body sang with desire. He brought both hands to my face and pulled me into a deeper, more demanding, possessive kiss, skirting my lips with his tongue.

"Dylan—" He brushed my bangs from my forehead and stroked my cheek with his thumb. "Do you ever have relationships?" I asked.

He shook his head slowly. "No. Only casual. We do this my way, or not at all." He smiled knowingly. "Trust me," he continued, "I'm complete rubbish at relationships anyway." There was a long pause as I took this in. No matter how attracted to him I was, no matter what direction my own feelings took for him, Dylan would be uncompromising on this last point—he said it with an utter finality.

"What about other women?"

"What about them?"

"Are you seeing any?" I asked, almost not wanting to know the answer.

"Not at the moment. For as long as we're sleeping together, it will just be you." Well there was that, at least. "Also, there's something you need to know and understand. It's important." He looked more resolved all of a sudden, and he moved his hands to my waist. He searched my eyes for a moment, to be sure I was listening.

"*No one* can know."

It's not like I thought we'd be spending holidays together after he'd so firmly established that we'd be casual, but he couldn't mean *no one.* "I think that goes without saying. I don't actually want to be the town harlot, so I think this would be private to say the least."

"Completely private. Like I said, I don't date, Lydia. I'm a very private person, but I'm also a public figure. I attend a lot of functions, give many speeches, and I get photographed and written about. Frequently. I won't want you anywhere near that circus. Do you understand?" I nodded. "This is nonnegotiable, so think about it, Lydia. No family. No friends. No double dates. Just you and me, in private. You need to agree to that before this goes any further."

What the hell? My first instinct was to be pissed off. What right did he have to unilaterally call the shots? But after a moment, I realized what he was saying. If he was really the man-about-town he claimed to be, I could see how it could get messy if every time he started to have a relationship, or whatever this was going to be, it got splashed all over the *Daily Mirror*. And hell, the longer I thought about it, I wasn't sure I would want it to be anything *but* completely secret. If he was such a player, and I actually agreed to have this *thing* with him, did I really want other people looking at me and thinking I was being played?

He looked at me intently, impatiently. "Lydia, it will be good, I assure you." He began running his fingers down my arm softly, and he whispered, "I'm going to fuck you a thousand different ways."

Another moment passed, and he was clearly waiting for me to say something, to reassure him that I understood what he was asking, to agree to this version of what we would be—casual, secret sex, for I guess however long it lasted. But I couldn't. Not only because I was practically having an out-of-body experience—every move he made and every look he gave me connected me more firmly to the insane chemistry we had—but also because I was completely off-kilter. None of this was going how I thought it would. Was I really ok with meaningless sex? With Dylan?

His hand had drifted back down between my parted legs and rhythmically stroked my inner leg right above my knee, and I was pretty sure that if he kept it up I might come right there, from goddamn *knee touching*.

He stood before me, waiting, wanting, and I'd never felt more desired. "Talk to me," he said quietly. "I'm dying here, looking at you in that dress, with your hair off your neck, your lips hanging open like that. I'm about to lose it. Are you in?" All of this was said while he stroked my leg, ready to pounce when I gave him permission.

I wanted to. I wanted to fling my arms up around his neck, feel that scruff against my skin. Him wanting this, wanting me—it was an aphrodisiac. God, he was so deliciously alluring, and maybe that was all he had to be. I didn't even know him; maybe a casual fling is all *I'd* want.

I could do this. Hell, I was only twenty-four, I *should* do this. Suddenly, I wasn't remotely concerned about any of the things I should have been: Why did we need to keep this a secret? Would this only be a one-time thing? How many other women had there been?

The one thing paralyzing me was my ninety-nine percent certainty that I would somehow embarrass myself, that the fact that I hadn't had sex in so long would be immediately clear to him.

"I understand," I began. His eyes widened with excitement, and he started to move in, clearly taking my words as a green light. But I held up my hand, placing it against his firm chest. "But..." He stopped, looking wary. "You should know that it's...it's just that it's been a while since I've..." I stared down at my hand, afraid to look him in the eye. He didn't need to know that a while was actually nearly six years.

But he just stood there, quiet, thoughtful. I couldn't tell what he was thinking at all. Was my inexperience a turnoff? Was he now afraid that I couldn't handle our casual fling? I was beginning to get that embarrassed pit in my stomach, which had the unfortunate side effect of pushing all the delectable turned-on feelings aside. The air between us suddenly felt cold and empty, where just a moment before it had been hot and thick with potential. I was getting ready to get up and admit this wasn't going to happen when he leaned into me. He put his hands behind my back, skin on skin, and pulled me off the stool and into his arms.

"Well, baby," he said, "don't you think we should remedy that?"

The term of endearment put me over the edge into total comfort, and all the warmth seeped back into the moment. I completely relaxed into his arms. He had one hand wrapped firmly around my waist, holding me to him, and he moved the other to my hair, holding me in place completely. He pulled back so he could see my face. "God, I have to have you. I've wanted to get you under me from the moment I saw you in that bloody bikini." He searched my eyes, looking for my answer. "Say you'll stay."

I could feel his possession already—it was bleeding into the air between us. I could feel myself bowing to his will, and there was nothing I wanted more. I didn't care what he wanted from me ultimately, and I still had no idea how this whole secrecy thing would play out, but *this* I knew I wanted. I couldn't take my eyes off of his, and for a moment it was almost too intense. I needed to regain at least a semblance of control.

"Meh." I shrugged. "I was thinking I might actually go home now." I faked a yawn and gently turned to walk away in jest, but he quickly and fiercely pulled me back to him.

"Not on your life."

I smiled broadly at him, tight in his hold. His hands, which had been soft and tentative all night, became steady, fierce. I had officially given him the green light. His grip around my waist tightened, and he let his hands firmly roam over my dress. Any hesitancy about where they might tread was gone.

He reached down my sides, his hands taking in the shape of my hips, and he grabbed the hem of my dress, pulling it up to my waist. With one hand on my back holding my dress, he slid the other between my legs, starting at the top of my inner thigh, but quickly moving right to the dampness in the center.

"My god, Lydia, you're soaked. I can even feel it over this thong. You're so ready for me."

He pushed the thin strip of underwear aside and sank his finger deep inside me. I gasped. I had my hands on his shoulders and was shivering with anticipation. I was in a pleasurable fog, not believing what was happening. I tried to bow backwards to absorb some of the raw pleasure, but he effectively held me in place. I started to quiver.

"Not yet," he said. "Let's get you upstairs and out of this dress." He withdrew his finger and wiped my wetness on the inside of my thigh—the move was dirty and deliberate and crazy sexy. He reached down and grabbed me by my bare ass, lifting me. I swung my arms around his neck, so our faces were centimeters apart, and I wrapped my legs around him, kicking my shoes off and letting them drop to the floor.

He kissed me hard—not in a wild messy way, but with deep, strong, slow movements, his tongue sweeping into my mouth in a patient rhythm. He carried me upstairs and into his vast white bedroom. The lights were off, but the streetlights below flooded the room and cast the perfect glow onto his low bed. He sat down in an overstuffed sunken chair in the darkened corner, continuing to hold me to him, so I was straddling him. He grabbed the zipper of my dress, and began to slide it down.

The blue fabric pooled between us, still wrapped around my waist, and he buried his face between my breasts, stroking my nipple through the fabric of my thin bra with his nose. "You smell incredible." His words shook me—this was really happening. He reached behind me and unclasped my bra, slowly pulling it forward down my arms and dropping it to the floor by the chair. His finger traced the fading tan lines at my shoulders, and down to my pale breasts. He leaned in, laying soft kisses to where my bikini top had left its marks, and palmed my breasts, letting them fill his hands. He thumbed my erect nipples, kneading them, lengthening them.

"Lydia, you're beautiful," he whispered, and he fell forward and licked both of my nipples, watching them pucker under his attention.

His hands gripped my ribcage, and he lifted me to standing. No one had ever moved me around so effortlessly—it was intoxicating. He hadn't exerted himself at all, and I could feel the hard tight muscle beneath his shirt. The dress fell to my feet, and I was left standing in the moonlight before him in just my panties. He reached through the space between us and drifted the back of his hand from my neck, down between my breasts, and settled at the top of my low-slung thong. He dragged his palm across my lower belly, his fingers just inside my underwear. I felt his other hand's fingers wrapping around my hips, and he pulled me against him, letting me feel the expanse of his warm chest against my breasts.

I arched my eyebrow up at him. "Surely, you're going to have to take some clothes off too. I mean, I know it's been a while, but I'm pretty sure we're both supposed to be naked," I said, trying to keep any lingering fears of embarrassing myself at bay. He unbuttoned his shirt, and I reached forward to pull it away from his chest. He was perfect. His pecs were exquisitely outlined above his six-pack. "It's too bad you're so out of shape, though, Dylan. I can only imagine—"

He put a finger over my lips and gently shook his head before I could crack a joke, as if somehow he knew I was trying to create distance. He wasn't going to let me deflect—he was going to make sure I experienced every second of this. I sighed, trying to fully relax, and I let myself slide back into the moment.

His chest had a smattering of dark hair, and unable to help myself, I ran my fingers through it. He sucked in his breath in response. I realized that no other guy I'd ever been with could correctly be described as a man. *This* godlike creature in front of me was a man. He bypassed my slow moves and made quick work of his belt, pants, shoes, and socks, leaving us both in our underwear.

I hooked my thumbs into my panties, but he reached out and grabbed my wrists. "Let me. I've been thinking about this for two weeks, and I want to do it my way."

I smiled, and I dropped my arms to my sides. He slowly dropped to his knees before me and spread kisses along my hip, moving his face to the gap between my thighs. My breathing hitched. This felt so much more intimate than any sexual encounter I'd ever had before.

"I'm going to savor every minute of this, and I'm going to drive you wild before I let you come."

"I'm practically there," I whispered. I could barely get the words out. My breathing had bottomed out, and I was arching my back, pushing my hips towards him, absorbing every ounce of him I could. My hands went to his hair, and I wrapped my fingers around his nape and dragged my fingernails through the short hair.

"Can't wait to be inside you," he hissed. His crude words fueled the fire he was building. He brought his hand between my legs, first palming my ass, then dragging his fingers forward to my dripping entrance. He snapped the lace of my panties at my hip, and I jumped at the slight sting of the elastic against my skin. His fingers hooked into each edge of my underwear and slowly dragged them down my legs.

He picked me up as he stood and laid me down on the bed, my back suddenly cool against the sheets, and he hovered above me, looking down at me, into me. Putting his weight on one arm, he began caressing his other hand back and forth up my side, leaving an echo of feathery touches in his wake. His fingertips alerted every cell in my body, setting each one on fire, and I shivered, ripe with anticipation. When he leaned down to kiss me, I hooked my arms over his shoulders, pulling his face to mine. I needed to kiss him, taste him. As I tentatively bit his lip, he let out an exhale, and his hands drifted south. I instinctively spread my legs a little wider and lifted my hips into his touch. I wanted him to start, to get there, but he pushed my hips back to the mattress.

"Don't rush me, Lydia."

I gave him an exasperated grunt, and he smirked back at me as he reached between my legs. His fingers found the hair between my thighs and gave it a gentle tug, causing me to buck into his hand. "Hmmm. We'll see about this."

I gave him an "oh will we?" look, and he tugged harder, inciting a shriek from me, followed by a groan. How could he do this? It was like he knew what my body wanted before I did.

He rolled to my side, keeping his fingers on me while propping himself up and sliding his knee beneath my thighs, spreading me. He looked down at me in appreciation, sighing as he sank into me with his deft fingers. He alternated between teasing my clit with his thumb and applying perfect pressure inside me. As soon as one move would have me trembling, about to come, he'd slow and shift his attentions. I gripped the sides of the pillow beneath my head and attempted to close my legs, trying to counter him and maintain control over the mounting pleasure, but he shook his head.

"Open, Lydia. I want to see you spread out for me," he ordered, and my knees fell back down in compliance. I began to moan with pleasure and with frustration.

"Please. Oh god, please, Dylan," I cried his name. He was making this all about me, and it was clear he could read my body like a book.

"Your body is incredible, Lydia. Look what I can do to you." My moans reached a fever pitch in confirmation, and he took me all the way, my body crumbling under his touch. Sensation and pleasure convulsed and converged, radiating outward. His breathing was harsh and quick—making me come was turning him on. "Has anyone ever made you come like this, this hard, with their fingers, Lydia?" he whispered, almost grunting.

"Never. Not like this." I groaned. The orgasm was still reverberating through my limbs, by far the most intense of my life, when I heard a drawer open and saw Dylan holding a condom. I closed my legs to gain some sense of relief and ran my sweaty palms down my still-shaking body, trying to both quell and savor the tingling sensitivity humming on my skin.

He quickly shed his briefs and sheathed himself out of my field of vision. He tented himself over me, perching himself on his forearms, and he used his knees to swiftly separate my legs again. I felt him position himself, parting me gently. He slowly fed his huge cock into me and easily slid through my wet folds. The fullness radiated through my every limb, and I bucked my hips, wanting to feel all of him.

"Slow, baby. I don't want to hurt you," he said. He was holding himself back, going at a glacial pace, and it was agonizing. "You ok?" he asked, pausing.

"Yes. God, yes. Please. More." I could barely breathe. He remained still while I accepted him into me and adjusted to the intrusion.

"Fuck, Lydia. You're so tight." Once he was fully acclimated, he began to move slowly, thrusting carefully but purposefully. When he'd established his rhythm, he reached down and grabbed one of my legs behind the knee and pulled it up, deepening his place inside me. I winced—there was no way my body could accommodate another inch. I tucked my foot behind his back, and he nodded. "That's right, baby."

And slowly, I began to feel the build begin, my body tensing and releasing in quick succession. I couldn't believe I was about to come again so soon. No orgasm had ever been like the one I'd just had, and my whole world was opening up.

My back was sliding against the sheets, catching as his thrusts pushed me back and into the mattress. These sensations I'd been imagining with him for the past two weeks were so much more potent, so much more complicated and rhythmic, than I ever could have conjured. He was both using me and attending to me with every move, and both were vital, both were making this so outrageously erotic.

"I want you to come again," Dylan said, looking into my eyes with feverish determination but also with great care. "I can feel you. You're close."

"Please, Dylan." I moaned and relaxed even more, allowing him in completely. He leaned down and kissed me hard as he shifted, angling himself perfectly. I felt entirely possessed. It felt in that moment that there was nothing of myself I wouldn't give to this man. It was a flash of unguarded willingness that I'd allowed, for this moment.

"I'm letting go, baby, come with me." He grunted through his movements. My body closed in around him, spiraling through the orgasm, closing out the world around us completely. He pumped into me, each thrust deeper and longer, each one penetrating me more wholly, energizing the continuing riot in my body.

He cried my name as he came, and as he stilled inside me, he raised his head. My eyes were closed, but I could feel the weight of his stare, his hands on my hips as he withdrew. He quickly rolled over to shed the condom, and returned to my side. My body was still tingling and alert, my breathing still deep and heavy, shaking. He leaned up on his side, one hand in my hair, the other resting low on my abdomen.

"So, is that what you had in mind when you said 'just sex'?"

Chapter 10

I smiled, but I couldn't bring myself to speak yet.

"Open your eyes, Lydia. Look at me." I obeyed, turning my face to him. "Well? As good as you remembered?"

I wasn't ready to talk. I was still feeling the reverberations of whatever he had done to me. I'd never had an orgasm—or orgasms—like that. My limbs were limp in utter relaxation. I turned to look at him, and replied, "Wouldn't you like to know?" and brought my arm up to cover my eyes.

He chuckled. "I think I do know." And he pulled my arm away to find the grin that I couldn't sweep off my face.

"My fantasies may need some updating," I conceded, and he gave a hearty approving laugh.

"You fantasize, do you? Get yourself off now and again?" he pried, teasing. I blushed. "Tell me, Lydia." He was doing his best bossy tone, but he couldn't hide his playfulness.

"Doesn't everyone?"

"I don't care about everyone at the moment. I care about you." I knew those words were true and tried to ignore the *at the moment* part of that statement. "Have you fantasized about me?" His smile was wide, because he knew the answer.

"You know I have," I said, pulling my arms back over my face. But he quickly removed them and pinned them on my belly. "Or maybe I'd just forgotten how good it could be."

"Or maybe you've never had it that good," he replied, seeing right through me. He paused for a moment. "How long had it been, exactly?"

I hesitated, not wanting to tell him. "A while."

"Lydia."

I shrugged and turned away from him, resting my head on the pillow. "Six years."

He pulled me back around, turning me towards him. "You were eighteen years old the last time you had sex?" he asked, incredulous.

"I'd just turned nineteen," I replied and silently pleaded with him not to dig any deeper.

"Well then," he continued, and he pulled my body flush against his. "We'll have to catch you up."

"Pretty confident that there'll be a repeat performance, aren't you?"

"If you enjoyed what just happened half as much as I did, there would be no doubts about doing this again, and often." He paused, drinking me in, looking at me as though he were searching for signs of injury. "I probably should have warned you: I'm terribly bossy in bed."

I playfully guffawed. "Who? You?"

He laughed, clearly not feeling like he had to explain. Plus, I had been grateful that he had taken charge, not to mention completely turned on. "You know I'll look after you, right?"

I smiled up at him, and he began strumming his fingers in the hair between my legs. I found my hips bucking up to urge his fingers down.

"I know," I replied, hoping it was true. In spite of all of my doubts and his insistence on secrecy, I did believe that at least he *wanted* to be good to me. I closed my eyes and took in his movements, letting him play with me.

"So, really? None of your non-flower-sending American boyfriends enticed you into bed?"

"They weren't the enticing types." He looked at me, waiting for more. "They were mostly sweet, but also..." I was searching for the right word and also trying to handle the returning ache between my legs. "Boys."

"And I'm not? A boy?" He began skirting the edges of my entrance and I groaned in frustration.

"You...ah...oh god...You are most definitely not a boy." I closed my eyes and took in his movements, letting him play with me. I moaned, suddenly ravenous for more of him. "Oh, Dylan. Touch me, please."

"Again?" He smiled a huge grin, and I nodded. He rolled over on top of me, our faces nearly touching, and he dragged his knee up between my legs, spreading me. "God, Lydia..." He looked at me with a kind of reverence I almost found unnerving. "Hmm. What to do with you." I could see his imagination running away with him, and he was scanning my face with his eyes.

"Shower." He bounced up, energized, then leaned down to lift me.

I let out a laughing howl in revolt and rolled onto my stomach, burrowing my face into the covers. "What? But I'm so comfortable! A shower isn't exactly what I had in mind."

"Out. Up. Come on, damsel." He grabbed my ankles and dragged me towards the edge of the bed. I squealed in fake protest, dragging the pillow behind me. He flipped me over and hovered, looking so sweetly at my face, and brushed my hair away from my eyes. "I'll carry you, if you don't behave."

"Voting, working, walking, getting to and from the airport. All things women can do."

"Incorrigible." He swept down and picked me up, throwing me over his shoulder so my ass was in the air. I kicked in protest, and laughed into his back, as he carried me across the room to the master bath and stood me in front of the vanity.

As he went to get the shower running, I took in my reflection. I felt warm, replete. I couldn't help but smile.

When he returned, he came up behind me, his eyes travelling over my reflection. "Look at you. You're glowing." He was right. He stroked my back, and then he gently pushed me forward, causing me to bend at my hips, and ran his palms down my arms. He leaned over me, into me, and laid a kiss between my shoulder blades. He firmly planted my hands on the vanity, under his own. "Keep your hands there. Understand?" I nodded at him in the mirror. "No moving." Then, he grabbed my hips and pulled them back, so I was bent over fully. "Spread your legs." I complied, moving them a couple of feet apart. "Wider," he instructed, and I moved them again. I suddenly felt so exposed and available. He whispered in my ear, sweetly, firmly, "Bossy, remember?"

"I know. I think I like it," I replied in a matching whisper.

He ran his long fingers down my spine and slid them through my wetness. "I can tell."

He reached over to my side, opened a drawer in the vanity, and grabbed another condom. Did he have them stashed in every room in the house? I wasn't sure I liked what that implied, but I pushed the unpleasant thought aside, determined to enjoy this, enjoy him. The room was beginning to fill with steam as he positioned himself at my entrance, holding his tip right there, grazing me.

"This time," he said, breathing into my back and kissing my neck. I started to quiver, desperate for him to enter me again. "I'm not going to be quite so gentle."

"Oh *god.*" I grunted as he entered me.

He was right. This time was fierce and uncompromising, and my knees were going to buckle under the intensity of the orgasm headed my way. He reached around and began strumming my clit in sync with his thrusts, and my back arched to try to absorb the pleasure. His feet were firmly planted between my own, preventing me from closing my thighs and curbing the oncoming tidal wave.

Finally, he leaned over, and whispered harshly in my ear, "Come now, Lydia. I want you to come *now.*"

And his words kicked me over the edge. My orgasm was a ship and Dylan was its captain. He'd willed it with sheer determination. He reached his climax and held himself firmly buried in me for moment. I collapsed, leaning backwards into him, my own reverberations still pulsing through me. He withdrew, turning me and letting me sink into his chest, my cheek buried against him, and he brushed my hair from my face.

"I can't get enough of you, Lydia. I've never known someone so…" He paused, breathing into my hair.

"So what?" I asked, catching my breath against his skin.

"So alive."

* * *

We showered, soaking up the heat together. He washed me carefully, tenderly. He glided his soapy palms between my legs, and I winced as I became aware of the growing soreness.

"How do you feel?" he asked, rising and pulling me into a slippery soapy embrace, my back to his front.

"A little sore." I leaned back into him.

"Good."

I turned to look at him with a "what are you, a sadist?" look.

He smirked back. "You'll be feeling me all day tomorrow." He was gently stroking me between my soapy legs.

God, that sounded sexy.

I had no idea how late it was, but I was completely wrecked. I also suddenly realized that I had no idea what his expectations were. "So, I'm hoping that sleeping over is part of this deal; otherwise you'll have to carry me home."

I felt him flinch and tense next to me. He paused, but then gave me a slight smile. "A bit knackered, are we?"

"A wee bit." I gave him my best English accent. "Turns out you're an absolute beast in the sack." I stepped out of the shower, and he followed, handing me an enormous white fluffy towel.

"And that was only our first go."

"And second," I said.

He smiled. "Sure, spend the night."

Why did that feel like a concession? It was clearly going to take some stumbling to figure out the boundaries of this secret sex fling I was embarking on.

I sat on the edge of the bed and combed through my hair with my fingers, waiting for Dylan to join me. He came and swooped in behind me, wrapping his arm around my waist and pulling me into bed with him, whisking away my insecurities about whether it was ok for me to stay. He pulled up the covers around me.

"So, um," I began, "the bossiness thing…"

"Just tell me if it's too much." He must have sensed that I wanted more information, because he continued unprompted, "There is enough that is unpredictable and fast-paced about my life, Lydia. I may not have freedom and control in certain things, but when it comes to sex…" He paused for a moment, looking as though "sex" wasn't quite the right term for what was happening. "When it comes to this, I need total control, no surprises. None."

He was lost, thinking of something else, and a quick coldness flashed between us, but then he came back to me. He curled around me, and with his hand spread across my stomach, he pulled me against him.

"I'll make it good for you, baby. Always. Now sleep, Lydia," he instructed.

And I did. I fell into a deep, sated sleep, dreamily aware of the big, strong hand that lay over my hip the whole night, and silently trying to convince myself that I was fine with just being Dylan's well-attended-to secret friend with benefits.

Chapter 11

Lydia, wake up. It's nearly seven."

Where was I? I opened my eyes and took in the expansive white bedroom. I had only seen it in the dark, but I now appreciated the unfinished wood accents and subtly masculine features of the space. The enormous bed took up only a fraction of the room. Past the end of the bed was the wide entrance to a sitting room with another fireplace and lined with built-in bookshelves, filled perfectly with enormous art and design books and rows and rows of old-looking leather-bound volumes. Off to the left were two enormous elegant windows bordered with long natural-colored linen drapes that pooled at the floor. I saw the low chair in front of the windows and blushed remembering the way he'd unzipped my dress there the night before. Off to the right were doors leading to the bathroom and, presumably, a closet. This guy had mastered the combination of cool modern and old English—there wasn't anything snooty about this place, but it was undeniably luxe.

I propped myself up and took him in as well. He was showered, dressed in another perfectly fitting suit and crisp blue shirt. A thin striped tie grazed my breasts as he leaned in for a kiss.

"Up," he commanded. "I'm going to head off now. Lloyd will be back at half seven to take you to your place. I just ask that you leave through the rear door."

He had every right to ask—that was our deal, after all. A secret. I was going to have to retrain my brain not to interpret requests like that as hurtful. But oddly, the way he avoided my eyes when he asked made me think that, just maybe, he didn't feel great about asking either.

"Ok," I agreed and pushed my hair away from my face.

"There's coffee," he said, pointing to a steaming mug on my bedside table. "Make yourself at home." Why did this feel so awkward in the light of day?

He looked at me, surely sensing my hesitation. "Lydia, last night was lovely for me. Not my usual situation, but lovely all the same." He was inserting cufflinks and straightening his shirt beneath his jacket, all while making his way to the door.

Not his usual situation?

I thought what we were doing was *exactly* his usual situation—casual sex. "What do you mean?" I asked, holding the duvet against my chest.

"You spent the night," he clarified matter of factly.

Oh.

"Dylan." I stopped him before he had a chance to leave. "Thank you for dinner. I really enjoyed it."

"Oh, I know," he said, with a wry smile. "I'll call you," he added, turning back towards the door.

And he was off. I got up to use the bathroom, and then returned to his bed, living it up in his million-thread-count sheets with my steaming cup of coffee. I thought I could seriously get used to that, but then I remembered it probably wouldn't happen again. This retraining my brain thing was going to take some time.

When I next looked at the clock, it was already 7:25. I scampered into my dress and jacket, but I couldn't find my panties anywhere. After looking for a few minutes in the bedroom and bathroom, it dawned on me that I probably wasn't going to find them. I probably should have found it gross that Dylan had obviously stolen them, but I couldn't deny that the idea of him taking them, thumbing them in his pocket, and maybe getting off while holding them was making me wet. If I'd had more time I would have gone right back to his bed and taken the opportunity to get *myself* off. Fuck, what had gotten into me? One night of hot sex, and I was a crazed fiend? I downed my coffee, headed downstairs, and was just putting my cup in the sink when I saw Lloyd pull up to the side door.

* * *

On my walk to the tube from my house, where I'd gotten ready for work in record time, I checked my phone to find three texts from Daphne.

TUESDAY, 9:43 pm
Those are gorgeous!

WEDNESDAY, 1:13 am
How was dinner? I want to hear everything

WEDNESDAY, 6:09 am
These texts are expensive and you're leaving me hanging here. Call me!

Shit. This was going to be a conversation. She'd be thrilled that I was finally actually sleeping with someone, but I could hear her worry already. After weeks of talking about Dylan, convincing her that I could roll with the casual non-commitment secrecy aspects of thing would be a hard sell. She was going to be worried for me, and maybe she had a right to be. I was going to put off talking to her until I'd sufficiently convinced myself. I replied hastily before descending the steps underground:

WEDNESDAY, 8:23 am
Dinner was good. Details later. Xo

She would not be satisfied with that.

I walked into the office at 8:45, and everything was already abuzz. Josh quickly caught me up that Hannah had just been notified that a dress from her upcoming collection would be on display at a museum gala on Friday, and everyone was frantically putting together media materials, tracking down a model, and anxiously checking things off lists. I could see Hannah behind the glass wall of her office, talking on the phone. Just as I was about to duck into my own office, she looked up, caught my eye, and gestured for me to come into her office.

I was nervous to be meeting her on this busy day, but at least this way I could jump right in and be helpful. I dropped my jacket and bag quickly, picked up a notebook and pen, and quietly ducked into her office. She gestured to a chair, where I sat down, back straight, waiting to make a good impression while she wrapped up her phone conversation. "I'm honored, Tom, really. Thank you for thinking of me.... We're busy making the selection right now.... Terrific. Thanks again... Sure. Cheers." I looked around as she chatted and took in the perfectly hip and modern office. She was surrounded by fabric swatches and sketches. She put the receiver down and looked at me. "And you must be Lydia."

"Yes. It's such an honor to meet you in person, Ms. Rogan—"

"Hannah. Please," she said while looking at something on her desk in front of her. I straightened my back and refocused. She obviously wasn't the buddy-buddy maternal type.

"Hannah. Yesterday was a great day, and I'm thrilled to be here. I know it's a very busy time of year, so I hope I can hit the ground running. Fiona has been extremely helpful in getting me settled."

"Terrific. You're ready for this? You don't need any additional time to acclimate to the time change?" she asked, without looking up at me. I had the feeling this was a test.

"Absolutely, Hannah. No acclimating required."

"Good. I'll need you here until at least six tonight, and later going forward," she said, still looking down at the paperwork on her desk.

"Of course," I replied with as much confidence as I could muster.

"Good. Let Fiona know if you have any questions. I think we'll get along fine." She glanced up and towards the door to let me know that the introductory gabfest was over. I rose from my seat and turned to leave.

"And, Lydia," she said. I turned around, slightly anxious. "Great skirt," she said, looking back down at the work on her desk.

My shoulders sank in relief. I'd taken a risk on an extremely bright, practically neon pencil skirt with a white blouse and nude pumps. I figured it might distract from my unshowered ponytail hair and hasty makeup job.

I had a feeling that while Hannah might not be the person I went crying to when I missed home or broke a nail that I was going to learn *a lot* from working with her.

The rest of the morning went by in a blur. My soreness was a constant reminder of the night before, just as Dylan had promised, and the fact was I loved being sore from him. But given that it was day two at my new job, I did my best to distract myself. Fiona was out scouting the space for this museum gala that would be featuring the works of contemporary designers and artists, including one of Hannah's gowns. I was fielding calls and scheduling appointments with a few important clients whom Hannah would dress for this party. It was apparently one of the big social events of the year, and even some of the royals would attend.

I was grateful that Josh and Fiona were both unavailable at lunch. I needed to catch a few moments on my own. I'd barely had a second to even register the night before since it had happened. I grabbed my tote, and carted myself to a nearby park with a coffee and sandwich.

I couldn't believe it—I was sitting here, light, *happy*, and the previous night I'd had incredible, mind-blowing sex with Dylan Hale. For the past few years I'd become increasingly afraid that I was never going to want someone, that I'd never know the crazy, giddy, glowy attraction I'd seen on Daphne and my other friends, that sex was always going to be for someone else. Until this moment, I hadn't realized how terrified I'd been that it would never change, what a sad weight that had been.

The one therapist I'd seen when I was nineteen thought I'd formed some kind of association between my dad's illness and sex, but that time would heal it. And maybe it had. Or maybe it had been Dylan. I honestly didn't care. I wanted to do it again and again. With him. It killed me that I didn't know when I would see him again, but I knew my role was to play this cool. And that—having to play it cool, having to be a secret—was something I just couldn't question at that moment.

I wouldn't.

Because if I let myself go there, let myself reflect on the fact that I was walking headfirst into a one-hundred-percent casual non-relationship with Dylan, that I was probably going to end up shattered by this thing between us, there was a chance that everything that had been perfect about the night before would disintegrate. So for now, I was going to embrace playing it cool.

I felt my phone vibrate in my bag. Surely it'd be Daphne. But I looked down, and it was Dylan:

WEDNESDAY, 1:12 pm
What are you doing?

Shit. My grin was face splitting—playing it cool was going to be harder than I wanted it to be.

WEDNESDAY, 1:13 pm
Reminiscing

WEDNESDAY, 1:14 pm
About?

WEDNESDAY, 1:14 pm
Well, I'm having trouble remembering the details. Something about showers and being sore?

WEDNESDAY, 1:15 pm
I'll jog your memory. Come see me tomorrow. My office. 6pm. Lloyd will pick you up from work.

How the hell was it possible for a text to make me wet? Just knowing I'd be seeing him again made me shiver with anticipation. He was still thinking about me.

WEDNESDAY, 1:15 pm
I'll be there.

WEDNESDAY, 1:16 pm
Also, for the record, stealing panties is kind of pervy.

WEDNESDAY, 1:16 pm
But worth it to be able to imagine you in that dress with nothing on underneath. Plus, I'm willing to bet you were turned on.

WEDNESDAY, 1:17 pm
See you tomorrow.

WEDNESDAY, 1:17 pm
Busted, damsel.

Chapter 12

By the time I got home at the end of the day, I felt like I'd lost hours. We'd been up and moving and on the phone the whole afternoon, trying to get things ready for the museum event on top of preparing for London Fashion Week. When I left, the office had still been buzzing.

As soon as I walked in the door of my little house, I changed into jeans, poured myself a glass of wine, and decided to sit on the patio in the back and soak up what was left of the day's warmth while I watched the sky darken.

I was letting the day's busyness slide off of me when I heard a very loud, very boisterous "Well, hello there!" I nearly fell off my chair and lost half my wine in the process. I looked up to see my neighbor in his backyard looking over the low wall with a chummy how-do-you-do smile on his face.

I wiped the wine off my jeans, and pulled myself together. "Um, hi."

"Sorry, didn't mean to startle you. I'm Michael, the neighbor. Obviously." He said it in that classic English self-deprecating way. And he was handsome. No one would have argued that point, although my definition of handsome had recently been shifted by Dylan. No one stacked up anymore. Michael was wearing the remains of a workday suit, with his purple-checked sleeves rolled up and collar unbuttoned. His floppy dirty-blond hair gave him the air of a jovial tennis-playing collegiate type.

I stood up and approached the wall. "I'm Lydia Bell," I replied with as much cheer as I could muster after having my solitude interrupted. "I'm housesitting—"

"Yup yup. I heard. How's it going over there? Any problems?" He was leaning on the wall now in an inviting way, as if to offer his services should I have any needs. He was flirting, and the truth was that while he seemed harmless and it was always nice to be flirted with, it was starting to make me feel guilty, like I was being disloyal to Dylan, which was of course ridiculous. In fact I *should* probably flirt back. I needed some anchor out in the world to stop me from falling into Dylan-land any faster than I already was.

"Not one. It's a great place," I said, trying to keep the conversation polite. I couldn't bring myself to fully engage, but I needed to make *some* effort. "Have you lived here long?"

"A couple of years. It's a fabulous neighborhood. Have you been to the Market yet?" I shook my head. "It runs most days, but Saturday is the most frantic, of course. Bloody insane, really. It's quite a giggle if you can stand the crowds."

"Of course I've heard of it. I'll check it out soon," I replied before he had the chance to invite me to go with him. "So, what do you do, Michael?"

"Ah, just a boring old finance schlub I'm afraid. Nothing sexy. But you know, it pays the bills."

"Finance will do that if you're not careful," I said, leaning on the wall. "Have you always lived in London?" We made small talk for a bit, and then I was grateful to hear my phone ringing inside. "I should get that." I took the opportunity and excused myself.

I'd have to remember Michael. Maybe I couldn't muster the excitement about him now, but I had a feeling I might need a rebound in the near future, and he could be just the ticket.

* * *

The phone call had been the Franklins, but I was too tired to talk to them. I had a feeling they were going to want a rundown on everything, and really I just wanted to bask in the evening by myself. I broke out the laptop and decided to do a little Internet research on Dylan.

I did an image search and scrolled through recent pictures. He looked to be honest about not having relationships. Most of the pictures were of him alone or occasionally with his sister, exiting a restaurant, a hotel, or his car or attending some kind of event. Jesus, this guy must own thirty different tuxedos. The related articles seemed to speculate about his relationship status or flag him for being an eligible bachelor attending society events. I scrolled past the articles about the Hale family lore, bypassing family photos and logos for Hale Shipping.

The cover of a big coffee table book of Dylan's work showed up repeatedly. There were also a zillion pictures of his buildings, all of which were modern and beautiful, revealing actually. Whatever emotions Dylan kept at bay in his personal life he clearly poured into his work. I studied the detailed shots of the museums, hospitals, office buildings, and astounding private residences he'd designed. I read about his fearsome reputation—apparently he was known for being completely uncompromising in his designs, which came as no surprise. There were stories of him walking off half-finished projects without a second thought. It appeared from these design blogs that people either worshipped him or considered him arrogant and impossible.

I continued clicking on various links and began to form a picture of this young but shockingly accomplished man. He was a member of all sorts of arts and design organizations, on the board of the Green Building Initiative and several charities and hospitals. There were as many pages outlining his illustrious and aristocratic heritage, complete with family crests and pictures of enormous country estates. Dylan was clearly a tabloid favorite, and I was beginning to feel like an idiot for not knowing about him before I'd met him, but his efforts to retain his privacy seemed to have paid off. I had yet to stumble across anything that would really enlighten me about him.

But as I scrolled down the fifth page I found some younger photos of Dylan. While he was apparently no stranger to the press, there had clearly been a time when he was making the British news on a daily basis. These weren't red carpet photos—these were paparazzi shots.

I was seeing shot after candid shot of a younger, longer-haired Dylan, followed by picture after picture of whom I swore was Princess Caroline, the eldest granddaughter of the queen and a total knockout. And plenty of them together. I clicked on one of the corresponding links and found myself face-to-face with evidence very contrary to Dylan's no-normal-relationship rule:

PRINCESS CAROLINE ENGAGED TO WILD GUY DYLAN HALE.

I stood up immediately, dropping my laptop on the table. He'd been *engaged*? To a fucking *princess*? Why was this so upsetting to me? I guess I hadn't realized just how public a figure he was. I read through the headlines and corresponding news articles.

"*Princess Caroline Going through a Bad Boy Phase*," paired with a picture of the Princess in a floaty flirty dress with Dylan next to her in that amazing leather jacket.

"*Queen Furious About Nudies With Dylan*" above a photo of Caroline and Dylan on a sailboat somewhere sunny and with black bars covering their nether regions.

"*Palace Confirms Royal Engagement*" with a professional posed photo of the two of them, looking weirdly stiff and uncomfortable.

The articles described Dylan as an aristocratic, out-of-control bad boy. A loaded and irresponsible architecture student lucky to still be enrolled. In short, the opposite of the Dylan I'd been getting to know. I read about antics in clubs, run-ins with the police that seemed to bear no consequences other than being written about by the press. And tons and tons of pictures of him cavorting around town with Princess Caroline, often looking drunk or hungover. It was a totally different man. This was not a guy who started his own business and took the architecture world by storm. There was nothing in charge or in control about the man in these pictures. The dates on the articles were from about seven years earlier. What had happened?

I kept scrolling, and then came across "*Engagement Off, Caroline Mourns*" accompanied by a picture of Caroline in enormous sunglasses, head down, walking through Knightsbridge. *Is this why he wants so much control over his relationships?* Had they been in love? Had she broken his heart? Had he broken hers?

A few more articles displayed images of Dylan or Caroline alone, photographed by paparazzi in various situations, all speculating at the cause of their demise. I couldn't help it, and I had no right, but jealous bile rose in my throat. He wasn't mine to mourn, and she didn't seem to have any hold on him, but this all felt like too much. I mean, a *princess*? What had I gotten myself into? How could I possibly compare?

I poured myself another glass of wine, ran myself a bath, and sank into the hot water. In the span of twenty-four hours I'd gone from feeling euphoric, optimistic, and on top of the world in this new city, to feeling strangely alone and exhausted. Maybe it was Dylan, maybe it was my new fast-paced job, or maybe it was jetlag, but I just needed to cry it out.

* * *

By morning I had recovered my resolve. I wasn't going to let Dylan's past haunt me. I wasn't sure if I was going to ask him about it or not, but I was going to do my best to push the feelings aside. The past was the past. If I thought about it for too long, a zillion questions came into my mind about how and why he'd gone from being someone who would be engaged to being someone who didn't even date, and from being someone who had apparently been barely staying in school to being someone who was internationally renowned at his job. My mind would run wild with stories if I let it.

Maybe the Queen paved his way when she thought he was going to marry her granddaughter, maybe everyone all of a sudden wanted the husband of the future Queen to be their architect even if he was a party boy, or maybe this was just how life as an aristocrat worked: You could completely and irresponsibly blow off your youth and still land on top.

But none of this seemed like Dylan, and the truth was I couldn't know. And the real question I was trying not to ask myself was: *If he actually is capable of a committed relationship, why is that such an impossibility with me?*

So, right.

Back to trying not to think about it.

By my trip to the office that morning, my third official trek to work in London, I was starting to feel like one of the pack, cramming onto the tube, making sure the belt of my trench coat and my bag were tucked in before the doors closed, and offering my seat to pregnant women. Today was cool and blustery and giving a hint of the English fall to come, which suited my more subdued mood.

When I got into the office at eight thirty, there was a note on my desk to call Hannah on her cell.

Hannah answered on the first ring. "Lydia."

"Yes, Hannah. How can I help?"

"There are two important client appointments today at the same time—people I'm dressing for the event tomorrow night. The first is someone you may not have heard of, being an American and all, but she is a big deal over here, so brace yourself. It's Princess Caroline."

Chapter 13

Shit. Seriously? I hiccupped slightly, but recovered quickly. It was a huge deal for Hannah, no matter my own quickly shifting feelings about the royal family.

"Oh, wow. Is that the first time she'll be wearing you?" I tried to disguise the slight panic in my voice.

"It is," she said. "The second is also a wealthy and very important client and the daughter of a Baron and all that, but, well, not royalty. An 'it' girl, so to speak. I'll need you and Fiona to meet her at my studio. Her stylist will be with her, so you'll just have to show her the gowns, which I've left on a rack with her information on it. Then Fiona can help you process the sale."

"Of course."

"Great. It's at ten a.m., and Fiona knows how to get there."

* * *

At 9:50, Fiona let us into Hannah's sprawling studio on the third floor of a building nearby. There were several covered racks des-

ignated for Fashion Week, but there was another rack near the
door holding only four dresses. As I approached I saw a sign
hanging off the rack: *Amelia Reynolds*, in bold print atop an
empty sales slip.

Why was that name familiar?

Moments later, in walked Miss Cream Sheath Dress from the
party in Canada. Amelia. *Oh god. Seriously?* I immediately hid
behind the rack of gowns, pretending to look them over. Surely,
she wouldn't recognize me, but I just needed a moment to recover. I don't think I'd ever realized I had a jealous streak before,
but it was certainly getting a workout now, and my self-doubt
was blossoming right along with it.

Behind her entered a muscular—and very gay—man, who
introduced himself as Rocco, Amelia's stylist. Rocco? Did becoming someone's stylist require you come up with a bullshit
name to go along with it? Ugh, my bitchiness was rising right to
the surface, and I needed to quell it fast. I decided to hang back
and watch Fiona work. I rehung dresses and brought new ones
from the rack. Amelia examined herself in the mirror wearing a
pale blue gown, very low-cut in the front. On her figure it actually managed to look slightly gauche, which I hadn't thought
possible for one of Hannah's gowns. She was too buxom, and she
was overwhelming the dress.

She turned to Rocco. "What do you think? Is it too much?"

He scoffed. "Do you want him drooling?"

"Obviously, but I don't want to appear desperate," she replied
while pouting at him in a false coquettish way.

"Mmm. Yes, well, it's a difficult balance to strike. Hale doesn't
strike me as someone who would fall for the whole boobs-
spilling-out thing, darling—it's just not a very Dylan thing to
do. I think you should go more subtle."

I froze and my eyes went wide. Fuck, *Dylan* was going to be at this party? With Caroline *and* Amelia?

My anxiety shifted into high gear. And even as it did, the ticker tape across my brain was reminding me that I had no right to be jealous, that he hadn't promised me anything. Dylan had ushered a level of internal drama into my life that I'd never known before but with which I was becoming all too familiar. Sure, my life with my father had been challenging, and it certainly had included its own share of drama, but I'd never felt so raw, stripped of any armor. Fiona interrupted my rumination and sent me a side glare, as if to say, *What the hell? Are you going to help me, or what?*

I took a deep breath and brought over the next dress.

Amelia continued, "I could, and I mean, I know you're right, but I just… Well, I have to feel and look fabulous. I just have to." She shimmied out of the blue gown and barked over her shoulder, "This is wretched! I need something else." Her attention never left Rocco. "He's been looking even better lately. I heard he's been training with some ex-military something or other. Have you noticed?"

I brought her the next gown, which she swiped out of my hands without ever looking at me. This woman was literally the worst, but she was also, even I had to admit, rather stunning. Seeing her in her underwear made me cringe. She had a flawless body, was about five inches taller than I was, and exuded a finishing school polish that I'd never be able to pull off. Her arms were perfectly defined, suggesting long mornings with a private trainer, and her strawberry-blond hair was shiny and long and perfect. I could just imagine that someone named Franco had probably signed her head somewhere, marking his accomplishment. Her designer underwear fit her perfectly. I felt like a troll all of a sudden. She slid into the raspberry-hued dress, far more elegant, with off-the-shoulder draping.

"Meems, you'd have to be blind not to notice him," Rocco said. *Meems? Blech.* "Ahh, this is better I think. Less is more, and all that. And you still have a fabulous tan from your safari."

Hah! Humanitarian work in Tanzania, my ass.

"Did I tell you his mother called me again? She is obviously trying to bring us together," Amelia said with pride, as though having Dylan's mother on her side made her a shoo-in for the next Duchess of Abingdon. Although, having Charlotte on her side was certainly more than I had.

I was supposed to be invisible. I was supposed to use the back entrance, and was driven home early in the morning before anyone else was awake. All I had was fuck-buddy status with a clear indication that nothing more would ever come of it.

Rocco leaned over, resting his chin on his palm, and replied to her, "Well, *that*, darling, will only work if he cares what his mother thinks. Does he strike you as a mummy's boy?"

Amelia looked dubious. "I didn't think so."

"Do you think chandelier earrings? Or a necklace instead?"

Her stylist eyed her critically while she continued, "Well, regardless, he can't remain a bachelor forever, and his parents aren't the only ones getting impatient. He's always been stubborn, even when we were kids, but he'll come around. It's well and good to have his youthful fun, but if there's ever going to be an eighteenth Duke of Abingdon, he's going to have to start taking his position more seriously, and I'm going to be there when he does." She interrupted herself to consult with Rocco again. I had become literally frozen in place as I took all this in. She sighed and finally stilled in front of the mirror. "Well, what do you think?"

Her stylist gave a final appraisal and then confirmed, "Yes, this is the one. It makes your skin look divine, Meems."

Amelia shrugged out of the dress and practically tossed it at Fiona. "This one. Have it delivered to Brown's Hotel. By noon tomorrow—not a minute later—or don't bother." She dressed, gathered her things, and finally approached where I was standing by the exit. She met my gaze and paused, looking puzzled for a moment, but continued walking out, never directing another word to either Fiona or me. I wanted to throttle her. First for being able to openly desire the man I couldn't get off my mind and second for treating Fiona and me like scullery maids.

I excused myself to use the toilet as Fiona finished up the details. Leaning against the sink, I took deep breaths and tried to figure out what the emotions swirling inside me were. Jealousy? Unfortunately, yes. Possessiveness? Again, yes. I definitely felt possessive. But also, sad. She was obviously trying to orchestrate Dylan's life, and she wasn't alone in it. I wasn't actually worried that Dylan Hale, the man who seemed to negotiate with no one and brooked no disappointment, would allow that, was I? And she'd known him as a kid. Suddenly I felt like such an interloper, like such a foreigner. This wasn't my world.

Worst of all, if Amelia knew what she was talking about, Dylan would be at this museum party with both of these women. I hated this feeling. What had been Dylan's excuse for keeping us a secret again? Something about protecting me? I was beginning to understand Dylan's desire for control. This sucked. It was seeming more and more likely that I was a fun thing on the side, and he didn't want me to get in the way, especially when women like *Princess* Caroline and *Lady* Amelia Reynolds were floating in the mix. And you know what? I felt my resolve building from deep within me—that was fine. He could be my something on the side too, right? I wasn't going to let any of this take away from the other night with him. I'd just have to keep all these feelings buried. Not let deeper feelings—the ones that I knew lingered terrifyingly close beneath the surface—take hold. Just have my fun. I could do this.

* * *

The rest of the day flew by in a haze of preparations. At five thirty, Josh, Fiona, and I were all in the reception area chatting, coming down off the day. Fiona all of a sudden remembered our morning. "Hey," she said, looking directly at me, "what happened this morning with that client? You looked like you'd seen a ghost."

"Oh, you know," I started, figuring out how I'd bend the truth. "I realized halfway through her appointment that I'd actually met her, or not met, but seen her this past summer on vacation in Canada. Isn't that weird? It just took me by surprise is all."

"Where were you that you were hobnobbing with the important and beautiful?" asked Josh, all of a sudden very interested. "Do you have a secret exciting life we don't know about?"

Oh, if only he knew.

"Hah! Hardly. No, I was babysitting this whole summer for a family from New York, and *they* are the well-connected ones. I was one hundred percent the help. I promise."

Hannah walked in, looking slightly frazzled, and we all straightened up. "Fiona, Lydia, don't forget that I'll need you two at the museum Friday night."

Fiona looked totally unsurprised. "Of course, Hannah."

Well, this changed things. At least I'd be around to witness Amelia's pursuit, even if it just meant having a front-row seat to Dylan choosing her over me. The idea of being with him, or, more accurately, not being with him in public was somewhat nerve-wracking.

"Lydia, Fiona will fill you in, but for the most part I'll need you two there early to make sure the dress is in order, and then for a little bit after it begins to make sure the model is taken care of. After that you're free to stay and enjoy or jet off. Just check in with me first. And, Fiona, show Lydia the closet." She waved an exhausted wave and headed to the elevator.

" 'The closet'?" I looked at Fiona and Josh, who were jumping little jumps and clapping their hands in unison. They grabbed my hands and practically dragged me down the hall to a set of double doors. Fiona pulled them open to reveal a huge walk-in closet, lined with racks and racks of Hannah Rogan clothes, mostly gowns.

Fiona was beaming, and explained, "These are samples, previous year's runway looks, dresses sent out to magazines, all of the extras, so to speak. Hannah rarely lets us take advantage of this. I was here *a year* before I was allowed in here. You're here, what, *a week*, and you're in? So unfair. Anyhow, since you and I will be orchestrating the whole thing tomorrow night, we have to look good, and *this*—" she spread out her arms, gesturing to the racks of gowns "—is where we'll find dresses."

Josh jumped in. "And the shoes, and the bags. Ugh, you two are so lucky! When will she start doing menswear?" he grumbled jealously. "Lydia, we are totally going to make you over—we will Hannah you into submission before you head out the door to that party."

"Well, thank god for this. Seriously. Left to my own devices, well, you'd probably get a glimpse of my high school prom dress." I looked at my watch, and saw that it was 5:40. Lloyd was probably outside already. "Sorry, guys I have to run. Can't wait to dive in tomorrow!"

I tried to contribute to the enthusiasm, but my brain had already fast-forwarded to when I would be in Dylan's office. I darted into the bathroom, straightened my top and skirt, reapplied lipstick, and pinched my cheeks. And I literally ran out the door.

* * *

Outside, Lloyd was waiting in a navy blue Jaguar, and for the first time he wasn't standing outside the car, ready to open my door. As soon as I stepped in, he greeted me and said, "Forgive me, Miss Bell, for not opening your door. Mr. Hale thought this might be less conspicuous." Ahh, well that explained it.

"I've been his chauffeur for nearly a decade, and I'm known by many of his associates, you see, and, well." Poor Lloyd was clearly struggling. He probably had never *not* opened a car door in his life.

"Please," I said, rescuing him, "it's fine, Lloyd. Thank you so much for the ride." I could see Lloyd's expression relax as he pulled out into traffic. "I am guessing that explains the change in cars, as well?"

"Yes, Miss Bell. The other vehicle you've ridden in is the only one like it in the city, custom-made, you see, quite recognizable. He keeps this car for more private matters." I nodded. I guess Dylan really was taking this whole keep-Lydia-a-secret thing seriously. The thought tugged at me, but I pushed it aside.

We pulled up outside a glass and brick building right on the south bank of the Thames in Butler's Wharf. It looked like an old warehouse or factory that had been retrofitted. "Thank you for the ride, Lloyd."

"Of course, Miss," Lloyd said from the front seat. He glanced at me in the rearview, and smiled. "I know Mr. Hale would prefer you not take the tube."

As I rolled my eyes, I heard my phone buzz, and looked at the incoming text. It was from Dylan.

THURSDAY, 6:00 pm
I'm waiting. Top floor.

Lloyd remained in the driver's seat while I sprang from the car, and I had to stop myself from running to the elevator as I had out of my office. Although I was still irked from being unwillingly thrust into a catty jealous frenzy about Caroline and Amelia, my skin was already tingling in anticipation, the familiar goose bumps rising to the surface. I wanted him.

The elevator doors opened, and there he was, standing right outside my car, hands in his pockets, looking urbane, completely relaxed, and in control. Images from the Internet flashed into my mind, and I couldn't reconcile the man before me with the shaggy bad boy in those photos.

"Hello there," he said, his lips curling into that unbelievably sexy smile. He spoke so seductively I lost track of myself and forgot to move. He leaned in and blocked the closing elevator door. "Are you coming, Lydia?" He smiled, clearly amused by my sudden paralysis.

"I'd imagine that's on the docket," I told him. I couldn't believe I'd actually just said that. Operation Remain Cool was in effect. His jaw dropped in mock shock.

He grabbed my hand and pulled me out of the elevator. "You cheeky girl. Come here." He pulled me right to his chest, holding my hand and keeping one at my back, almost like we were slow dancing. I inhaled that salty-sweet smell of his, and let it feed my memories of our evening together. I was just beginning to warm inside his embrace, when suddenly he released me and stepped back, hands back in his pockets. I was confused until I saw a smartly dressed middle-aged woman walk into the elevator bank.

His whole posture had shifted, and the woman wished him a good evening. He nodded at her and wasn't even looking at me when he said, "Right this way, Miss Bell." The tone of his voice was casual and businesslike, like he'd never met me before in his life. It was an impressive shift, so expertly executed that I suspected this wasn't the first time he'd had to do it.

"Thank you, Mr. Hale," I said, playing along. I followed him past the woman waiting for the elevator and into the vast space. Apparently most of the offices were on lower floors, because this space seemed mostly taken up by scale models and large tables. The design was stark, clean, light, and modern. It was open with insanely high ceilings and exposed brick.

"How many people work for you?"

"I'm the only principal. I have six other architects that work for me, and we have an internship program for students. And then several administrators." I didn't see a paper or pen out of place anywhere, and I wouldn't have been surprised if the boss's preferences for control extended down to rules about clean workspaces. We passed a large central space that was wide open with enormous drafting tables and computers hooked up to multiple monitors. A few diligent types were leaning over the tables, working hard.

We were about to enter through a set of tall grey double

doors, when we were stopped by a nervous-looking younger guy, an assistant presumably, who said, without looking Dylan in the eye, "Sir. Excuse me, but—"

"What is it, Thomas?" Dylan demanded curtly. "I said no interruptions."

"I know, sir, and I apologize, but I've just had a call from the Sheik's secretary informing me that he doesn't like the balcony structure. He's worried about access, and—"

"Thomas."

"Yes, sir." Poor Thomas seemed like he might be sweating even from his ears.

"Have you ever known me to alter my designs? For anyone?"

"No, sir. But I thought, because he is who he is—"

"I understand, but no. Please pass on that if the Sheik isn't pleased with my design there are several other architects he could work with."

"Yes, sir." Thomas looked terrified and turned to sheepishly head towards his desk. Dylan looked at me, and I was pretty sure he could sense my intimidation or maybe my sympathy for Thomas, because he heaved a sigh and then looked back towards his assistant. "Thomas, email me the contact details. I'll make the call myself."

"Yes, Mr. Hale," replied Thomas, visibly relaxing.

Dylan looked at me, shaking his head as though he couldn't believe that he'd just given in, and he ushered me into his office. The evening light flooded in from the large industrial windows on two sides of the room, but I barely registered the cavernous stylish space. Now that we were alone and away from the gaze of strangers, all of my attention was zeroed in on the strong beautiful man before me. He immediately closed the door behind us, locked it, and grabbed my hand firmly in his own.

Chapter 14

Worried we'll get caught?" I said, following him across the gleaming dark floors to his desk. He took off his jacket and tossed it onto his chair, then pushed me against the smooth pale wooden surface, the edge digging into my ass, and leaned into me, over me. I had to brace myself with my arms pillared at my sides. I looked up at him, breathing him in, our faces so close. Every inch of my skin tingled.

"We won't," he said with total certainty. He was caging me in, his arms firmly pressed against my sides, and his stare was bearing down into me. "How was your day, damsel?"

He reached down and put his hand between my legs, slowly bringing it up and my skirt with it. He moved slowly enough that I was desperate for him to get to his destination, but fast enough that I didn't have a chance to think. I had no choice but to listen to my gut, which was telling me to throw myself at him with abandon. He leaned down and kissed my neck.

"Informative," I replied breathlessly, his touch already detonating sparks in my body. He lightly brushed my entrance with the side of his finger through my panties, and then moved his hand around, smoothing it over my ass. Grabbing the edge of my underwear from the top, he pulled them down, edging them past where the desk met my legs, and let them drop to the ground. He picked them up and quickly deposited them in the garbage can next to his desk.

"What? You're not going to add those to your stash?" I protested. "You know I might need them later. You're awfully—"

He cut me off. "No underwear," he said. "Not with me. Ever."

I started to open my mouth, but he laid a finger over my lips and kissed me, effectively silencing me. I should have been fighting against this more, but *Christ*, it was so possessive, so *hot*.

"You—" he brought his hand back up my skirt "—are drenched."

I gripped his upper arms with my hands, closed my eyes, and leaned my head back as he stroked me. I could feel my insides start to pull and tighten just from his feathery touches. He leaned farther into me, and I felt his straining erection against my leg. In that moment, all I wanted was for him to be feeling the pleasure I was feeling, to have my lips wrapped around him. Images of Amelia and Caroline were flashing through my mind, and I wanted to possess him, claim him, even if it was only for this moment. I moved my hands to his belt and started to unbuckle it, but he grabbed my wrist, shaking his head.

"I'm not finished with you yet."

"Fine," I conceded, because I was already so close, "but I'm going to get my turn."

"I'm counting on it," he said while taking both of my hands in one of his and locking them behind my back, using his other to taunt me. He leaned into me, kissing me hard, making me feel like I was going to fall back onto his desk. His free hand continued to graze me, tease the crease between my sex and my thighs, laying whispers around the edges, almost touching me where I needed it the most but not quite. I could feel the sweat surfacing, and my legs starting to grow weak with need.

"Dylan," I groaned. "God, holy mother of... Please."

"Please what?" He was getting closer. He quickly swept over my clit, making me gasp, but was once again at the edges.

"Touch me."

"Look down, Lydia," he said. "Watch me make you come."

I looked at his eyes, fiercely searching mine, and then I looked down. I saw my skirt hiked high above my waist. I saw my flesh exposed to him, spread for him, and I saw his hand rhythmically stroking me, toying with me. He sank his fingers deeper into me, stroking the front wall inside, hitting that perfect spot. I came fast and hard into his hand, and my chest shot forward as the peak of my orgasm tore through me. He met me, his mouth on my neck. He bit me, hard, and I let out a yelp. The slight pain was the perfect accent to my pleasure, and I felt ravished. This was no teenage finger fucking in your parents' basement.

My breathing came down, and my eyelids were heavy. I fell forward as he released my wrists, and my head met his chest. He pulled me in and stroked my bare ass before lowering my skirt.

"I've been thinking about getting you off all day," he said, holding my face. "Open your eyes."

I looked at him with a sleepy smile and replied, "Lucky me."

He lifted me completely onto his desk before backing up, and I dangled my feet. He moved around the office, collecting things, wrapping up his day.

"I saw Amelia Reynolds today," I said, with as little emotion as possible. He paused at her name.

"Oh?" he asked with a cool clipped tone.

Ugh. I felt like he was a million miles away all of a sudden. I didn't want to get into a fight, but I also wanted him to know that I wasn't ok with being lied to or being made to feel like I had to compete for him. I also just wished I didn't *care*. But I did, and I hated myself for not being able to hide it. This is why I had always known that letting myself go would be dangerous. I wasn't built for playing it cool.

He looked at me, waiting. I could feel his eyes on me. "Look at me, Lydia. What is this about?" He was stern all of a sudden, demanding.

"She's one of Hannah's biggest clients. She was picking a dress for this museum event with her stylist, and all she was talking about was *the* Dylan Hale." Yes, I could do this. I would just tease him about it, relentlessly. Keep my anxiety at bay with humor. "And about how she and your mother see wedding bells. It looks like someone's going to get lucky tomorrow night. I mean, I've seen her nearly naked, and you could do a lot worse. If you—"

"Stop," he commanded. He said it so firmly, so decisively, that I didn't hesitate. And his tone cut through all my bullshit. He wrapped one arm around my waist, pulling me tightly towards him. "I don't do relationships, Lydia. With anyone—that's not about you. And you're the only woman I'm getting 'lucky' with—I told you that." He had told me, but this whole situation was new to me, and knowing that there were women like Amelia out there required a level of trust, a gamble, that I wasn't entirely sure I could embrace. "Plus," he continued, "Amelia Reynolds is a spoiled twat."

I smiled, hating to admit that I felt reassured, and put my forehead against his chest. "She is, isn't she?"

After laughing, he held my face in his hands and tried to read my eyes. "Was there anything else?"

I didn't really want to go into the Caroline thing, and I probably should have just kept my mouth shut and ridden the reassuring wave. But I must have been silent for too long, because as if on cue, he asked, "Lydia, what is it?" He could see right through me.

"I may have Googled you again, and," as I said it, he look resigned and sighed. He knew exactly what was coming. "Just tell me one thing," I started, without any real sense of what I'd say next. *Fun*, I reminded myself. *No strings*. It's what I'd agreed to. I hated how raw I felt, how stuck I was between embracing the hot casualness of this arrangement and letting myself want more from him. I needed to get back to the place where we were giving each other outrageous state-altering, forget-your-own-name orgasms. I needed to take back control, if not over our sex then over the emotions. I smirked mischievously. "Did you tell Princess Caroline she couldn't wear underwear, too?"

He smiled and eyed me, suspicious of my ability to roll with this whole royal-ex-fiancée business. "No," he started quietly. "Just you." He leaned in and said directly into my ear, "Yours is the only pussy I can't bear to be separated from by fabric, no matter how thin." Then he kissed me with a sweetness in direct contrast to his crude words.

He brushed my cheek and looked at me with concern, somehow letting me know that I was fooling no one with my cool act. "Lydia, Caroline and I know each other from grammar school. We were only twenty-three when we got engaged. And it was—well, it was a disaster, actually. But it's been over for a long time, and we're just friends. It's all we ever were, really."

I shook my head. "You don't need to explain." Although I

wanted nothing more than an explanation at that moment. Well, almost nothing more.

He moved his thumb back and forth across my cheek and kissed me so gently. He licked my lips and grabbed my lower lip between his teeth, sweetly tugging. And as he toyed at my tongue with his, I felt the anxiety drop away, too easily, probably, and it was replaced with the lust lingering just below the surface. His hands glided over the silk of my blouse, and he unbuttoned the top several buttons and slid his hand in. He freed my breast from my bra and began stroking his thumb over my tight nipple.

"Trust me, Caroline and Amelia are the farthest things from my mind."

I couldn't tell if that was the truth or if he just wanted me to feel reassured, but I didn't care. It was what I needed in that moment. My head fell back, and I arched my spine, pushing my breast into his hand, begging for more. He could bring my arousal to the surface in an instant.

"Alright, damsel…" His fingers slowed and shifted to a gentle coaxing, and he tucked my breast back into place, leaving me feeling bereft. "Your turn." He looked at me expectantly.

He had just been fondling me, working me up, and now he was going to *stop*? I gave him a look that I hope communicated the depth of my sexual frustration.

"Getting greedy? Don't worry, I'm not done with you yet, but I want to know what you were going to do if I'd let you unfasten my belt." He looked down at his growing erection, and I licked my lips. I'd been thinking about getting my mouth around him for three weeks. It wouldn't be my first blow job, but it would be the first one I'd ever actually *wanted* to give.

He lifted me off the table and stood before me, waiting. I slid down to my knees before him. He freed himself and stroked his cock a few times as if offering himself up to me. I looked up at him through my lashes and gave him a you-have-no-idea-what's-coming smile. I put my lips to the tip of him and began to work myself down, licking, lapping my way. I swallowed him, creating suction that made him fist my hair and slide back on his heels. I could hear his breathing getting deeper, feel his arousal growing between my lips.

"Fuck, Lydia!" he uttered between gasping breaths.

I used my hand to cup his balls, stroking the underside gently. I glided him into my mouth, taking him as far back as I could, and then I willed myself to take him just a little farther. Opening wider for him than I ever had for anyone else, I found my rhythm, and he found it with me, gently bucking into my mouth as I took him whole. I tried to soften and relax my throat more with each thrust, allowing him greater purchase.

"Lydia, I'm going to come soon. Ahh...Christ, baby...If you don't want to swallow...Fuuuck, please swallow," he said, groaning.

It fueled me. I couldn't wait to have him spill into me. I increased my pace and flicked the end of him with my tongue, sucking as I took him back in. His hands gripped my hair, and I could feel the tension in his hands. Then he came, wet and hot, and I swallowed fiercely to keep up. When I felt him finally still, I pulled away, licking him clean. I sat back on my feet, and smiled up at him. He backed up and fell onto the couch behind him, leaning his head back as he let the end of his orgasm pulse through him. I rose and climbed on top of him, straddling him so his still hard cock rested against my slick entrance. I could feel the warmth of my own mouth against my flesh, and it felt so raw, so shamelessly wanton.

He looked at me, his arms wrapped around my back, stroking

up and down with his fingertips. "That was unbelievable," he said, twirling my hair in his fingers. We stayed like that for a few moments—his eyes closed, his face appearing so sated. I leaned down and lay against his chest, and he steadied me, held me in place, by wrapping his hands behind my ass.

"You know what I can't get out of my mind?" he asked.

"Mmm?" I muttered, my own eyes closed, my chin resting on his shoulder.

"You. Outside that party in La Malbaie."

"When I was babysitting?" I asked incredulously, and I felt him nod in affirmation.

"You had taken off those high heels, and you had those children running, playing, literally hanging off of you. That pink sun was framing you. I never get to see anyone—the women I'm around, especially—be so...unrestrained. Open. Real...You looked absolutely stunning."

"You've lost your mind. I looked like a wild animal," I said, rising and rolling my eyes.

He stilled my face with his palms, and looking steadily into my eyes, said, "Not to me."

I smiled, but I had no idea what to say. I held his gaze, and the playfulness crept back into his eyes. He stroked my cheek with the back of his hand.

"Now." He smiled.

He stood, bringing me with him, my legs wrapped around his trim waist, and placed me on the conference table in the corner of the room.

"Lean back, Lydia. Ass to the edge." I did as I was told, and my feet dangled off the edge. "Feet on the table. Show me that beautiful cunt of yours," he demanded as he put himself away.

I complied, surprised that exposing myself to him so fully in the broad daylight of his office didn't feel awkward or embarrassing. He made me feel coveted, beautiful.

"Good girl. Now grab the top of the table, above your head, with your hands, and keep them there. Understand?" I nodded and reached my hands up. There was no way I could get a word out now. I was glorious with anticipation, and my limbs were already deliciously unsteady.

I heard the sound of a desk chair wheeling towards me and felt his warm hands settle atop my knees, gliding up my inner thighs, pushing them apart as he moved in closer. My legs shamelessly bent outward, falling even farther. I was spread wide open for him. Using his thumbs, he parted me and laid one kiss where all of my energy was focused.

And with that one kiss, I was falling.

With slow, agonizing touches and gentle feather-light flicks to my clit, he barely touched me. Gasps and pleas for more filled the air, and I knew they must be mine, but didn't recognize my own voice. I was already lost in him, greedy. I could feel him smile and chuckle against my skin. My pleading moans were louder than I intended, and the reminder that it was *Dylan* between my legs made me convulse, my hips arching upward.

"Still, baby." His voice was heavy, breathy, a gruff whisper, and he pinned me back down.

He brought me to the brink over and over, sensing my body tighten against his mouth and retreating just enough to drive me insane, escalating my desperation. I wanted him in me, on me, with me. I want him to stop. To never stop.

Fuck.

My shoulders arched away from the table, and I gripped the table edge for dear life and writhed as the tidal wave arrived. The orgasm worked violently through my body, undulating, pulling me under. I just had to pray that my cries and throaty calls of his name didn't make it out into the hallway, because I was completely incapable of reining them in.

As my wrecked body finally settled, he gently kissed my raw throbbing pussy before backing away. "You taste so good." I lay on the table, spread open, my skirt bunched around my waist, and I slowly regained consciousness, becoming aware of the dampness of my skin and how my arms still gripped the table edge. Dylan slid back in his chair, taking in the view. "And you look fucking gorgeous."

I managed to prop myself up and give him a disapproving look, eyebrow raised. "So, you really only want me for my body, don't you?"

He leaned over me to help me up. "Your delectable body, your cheekiness, your humor. All of it, damsel." He stood me up in front of him, and pulled my skirt taut, tucking my blouse back in, and straightening me up. "It'll have to do, I'm afraid. Put your hair up."

I leisurely searched my bag for a hair tie as life returned to my limbs. He was right that the last thing we needed was for me to leave his office looking like I'd just had brain-frying orgasms.

"I have a business dinner to go to, so Lloyd will drop you home. You'll be alright?" he asked as he stroked my cheek and tucked a stray hair behind my ear.

I was being dismissed, and it was a stark reminder of what this was. A glorified, extremely high-quality booty call, but a booty call all the same. I could fight it or I could embrace it. It stung a little, but this was how things were. I nodded.

I would be ok, but I would also be thinking about him nonstop until I saw him again, which reminded me. "I'll see you tomorrow night," I added.

"Tomorrow?" he asked, surprised.

"Hannah has a gown in the show, and I need to be there," I explained.

"Oh? It'll be lovely having you there." He was straightening his tie, slightly distracted.

"Should I act like I don't know you or something?"

"Just follow my lead. And don't make plans for after."

I looked up at him with curiosity. "You have big plans for me?" I asked, smiling.

He walked in my direction and leaned over me, looking seductive and serious. "After the week I've had, and after what you just did to me, I'm going to want to sink into you and stay there. You think your pussy is sore now…"

I feigned shock, dropping my jaw and widening my eyes. "Tell me," I said, "do all the nobility have such a way with words? Or is it reserved only for Marquesses?"

He shook his head and gave a wicked predatory smile. "For that comment, I'm taking Saturday too."

I shook my head in disapproval and rolled my eyes. "Daphne isn't going to believe me when I tell her about you."

He looked instantly panicked. "Lydia," he said with a thick tone of warning, but I shrugged him off.

"Calm down. I won't tell anyone else. I promise. She's my best friend. She knows about the kiss in Canada and that we were having dinner the other night. I've been dodging her calls. I can't lie to her—she sees right through me. You two could probably start a club, in fact—people Lydia can't seem to keep a secret from."

"I—" He started warily.

"I'll tell her it's top secret. Look, I hate to break it to you, but people in the States aren't that interested in the love lives

of aristocratic British architecture prodigies." I was smiling, rib-
bing him. "And I don't think Daphne is going to be calling the
Daily Mirror when we get off the phone." I looked at him imploringly.

He was smiling now. "Fine. But no details. And only
Daphne." He'd caved, and it looked like it killed him to do it.
Years of not having to cave for anyone, I suppose. "You are impossible." He came over and kissed me again, quickly, but firmly,
and swatted me on the ass. "Now go. I'll see you tomorrow."

Chapter 15

It was two thirty in the afternoon New York time, and Daphne should be free. I had my knees curled up under me, was full of my favorite pasta dish, had a glass of wine, and was ready for a gabfest with my best friend.

She picked up on the second ring. "Finally! Lydia, where have you been? Does London not have cell towers or something?"

"I know, I know. I'm sorry! It's been crazy busy, and then I get home and flop into bed."

"Who cares? I've got you now, and I want to hear everything," she said, and I could practically hear her digging in, getting ready for a good long chat.

"Well...I have some news." She knew exactly to what and to whom I was referring. Daphne shrieked an endless piercing shriek on the other end of the phone.

"You did *not*! You *slept* with him? That didn't take long. Good for you, Lydia. Tell me everything."

"Well, he's very...commanding. And he definitely knows

what he's doing. But, seriously, Daphne, I mean. It was so…God, it was just…I can't even."

"That good, huh?"

"Yes." I was grinning goofily, images running through my mind of our night together.

"God, listen to you. Finally! Jesus. I was wondering if you were going to turn out to like being celibate or just give up and sign up to be a nun or something. But this is so much better. You sound totally smitten."

"I think I am."

"So you really enjoyed it?" I could hear the concern. She knew that I had had a complicated relationship to sex. She knew I liked Dylan, and she knew the heartbreak potential. I had finally let someone in. Or I was starting to.

"Daphne, it was better than I'd ever imagined. Honestly, I had no idea it could be like that. I mean, good *god.*"

"Good," she said through her laughter.

"I wish I could tell my father about him. I mean not *all* about him, but you know what I mean."

"Oh, Lydia, I know. You know he'd be happy that you're having fun, right?" As Daphne spoke, I could picture my father, always cheerful, always curious about my life until the end of his. I knew he regretted that I'd spent my high school and college years looking after him, but I was his daughter. Where else would I have been?

"Yeah, I do, and it helps to think about that. I mean, to be clear, I don't think it's going anywhere, but—" I continued, suddenly remembering the most important detail. "Oh! Before I forget, you can't tell anyone."

"What? What do you mean? I mean, it's not like I am going to buy a billboard or something, but why is it a secret? I don't like that, Lydia."

"He's bizarrely skittish about his privacy. You saw. He's all over the Internet, especially over here. He's like this man-about-town—he was *engaged* to Princess Caroline when he was younger!"

"*What?!*"

"I know—he hasn't really filled me in on that one, but it sounds like it was some kind of rebellious early-twenties thing, which is funny, because that's what he probably is to me, but anyway. His picture is in the paper all the time. You know all this. He said that when he has dated in the past the press has gotten in the way, and he doesn't want this to be public. So we're just keeping it private and casual. Also, I mean, we've only seen each other a couple of times. Who knows how long it will last, right? He's pretty clear that he's not in the market for a girl-friend."

"Hmm. I don't know, Lydia. This doesn't sound good. Are you sure you're cool with this? You deserve someone who will shout it from the rooftops: 'I banged Lydia Bell, and she blew me, then blew me away, and I want to love her for eternity!'"

I laughed out loud, both because I loved Daphne's ability to perfectly articulate her love for me, but also because the idea of Dylan shouting anything of the sort was ridiculous to me.

"I know. I would be lying if I said it didn't bother me at all, but I'm going to give him the benefit of the doubt. I know in my gut that he doesn't want to hurt me. When I'm with him, there's nowhere else I want to be. I feel really safe with him—is that weird? But also like I'm actually living my life. This is the first time since my dad died that I've felt anything other than numb, ya know? And I'm just so goddamn attracted to him." Images from his office were flying through my mind, and I could feel my skin tighten instantly.

"That sounds amazing—"

"Right." I cut her off, trying to get my mind out of the gutter. I was fully in my stream-of-consciousness mode. "But then when I'm not with him, I wonder if I'm crazy. I know I am thinking about him in ways you're not supposed to think about the man you're just casually sleeping with. Is this the dumbest thing I've ever gotten myself into? This is going to end, and I'm going to be completely, utterly screwed, aren't I?"

"Um," Daphne started, clearly overwhelmed by my rant. "I don't know what to tell you, Lydia."

I grunted. "Why? You know me better than anyone. You're always right about these things. Tell me what to do!"

"Listen, for years I've been hoping you'd dive into something, have someone sweep you off your feet, open yourself up to actually being with someone. But this sounds so intense. And I'm not going to lie—I don't like the sound of this whole 'casual only' thing. I swear to god, if he hurts you, I'll kill him."

"He probably has bodyguards. Daphne, you should see his house—it's like an *Architectural Digest* mansion in a neighborhood where a studio apartment costs two million pounds."

"Lydia, look. You can't get your mind off of him, right?"

"Unfortunately."

"Well there's your answer. You'll just have to see what happens. It sounds like the sex is incredible, and if anyone deserves that it's you. So enjoy. You have my blessing. What's the worst that could happen?"

"I could be utterly destroyed and ruined for any future love with anyone else," I stated.

"Exactly."

"You're infuriating," I protested, and she laughed.

"I agree that you need to be careful and protect yourself. This is your first time out of the gate, and I don't want you getting crushed by this, either. But, Lydia, you need to remember: You can never cross the ocean until you have the courage to lose sight of the shore."

"Did you just quote a fortune cookie?"

"A refrigerator magnet. I'm at my mom's." Only Daphne could have me laughing this hard while in a relationship crisis.

"But, Lydia," she continued, fighting off a fit of laughter herself, "in all seriousness. You sound good. I mean, frantic and a little crazy, but also better than I've heard you in a long time."

Apparently I needed Daphne even more than I realized. I proceeded to tell her all about the job, and the friends at work. She caught me up on school and our Brooklyn friends. I missed her terribly, and now that I'd told Daphne about Dylan, it was like it had really happened. It felt real.

"Before we go, I have to tell you something." Daphne sounded serious all of a sudden.

"Ok. Everything alright?"

"Yes, yes, of course. It's just that Matt and I broke up." I could tell she was nervous about telling me.

"Oh god, Daphne, I'm sorry. What happened? And why didn't you text me? I would have called earlier—I'm so sorry." I felt like a complete asshole for having taken up the entirety of our conversation with my dumb sex talk.

"You know, it was just done. He asked me to move in with him, and—"

"That doesn't exactly sound like a precursor to a breakup," I interrupted.

"Yeah, but I didn't even need to think about it," she continued. "My answer was no right off the bat. Matt's great, and in so many ways we're good together, but even after two years I still felt like we were two separate people just meeting up for dinner. Good dinner and good sex, actually, but I don't know how to explain it—we just weren't intertwined or interconnected the way I always expected to be with someone I moved in with. It's like, I *could* imagine life without him, and that seemed like a bad sign. Does this all make sense?"

"I think so," I replied, but really, what did I know? "How did he take it?"

"Surprisingly well, which was a kind of confirmation itself. He admitted that he thought that living together might get us there, but I just don't believe that. Anyway, it was very civil and friendly. Nothing dramatic."

"Right, ok then. Well, you sound very adult about all this. And I suppose this will free you up to come visit?"

"Obviously! I have to meet your fancy sexy famous architect."

"We'll see. Who knows where that's headed?" I said it like I meant it, but the truth was I was beginning to have a hard time imagining *my* future without *him*. "But you're really ok?"

"I really am."

"I believe you," I said. "And, I love you, Daph. I really miss you!"

"I miss you too, nutcase. Talk soon, ok? Love you!" I heard her sigh, quickly, before the call was cut.

My best friend had just admitted that she never felt interconnected with her boyfriend of two years. Was it weird that I already felt interconnected with Dylan? Like we were embedded in a back-and-forth, even when we weren't together, like he was making me feel like I was part of something bigger? I tried to put the thought out of my head. It had only been a couple of days, I knew that. But something had been moved—jarred loose. I was out of my element, but for the first time I didn't mind. In fact, I loved it. It was like the moment when you are in the water and suddenly you can't feel the sand beneath your feet. You're free.

* * *

The next day at work flew by in a haze until around three thirty, when all the work that could be done for the party that night was done. That left us about two hours to primp before we had to leave for the museum. Fiona and Josh dragged me back into the closet to begin their assault.

"You're lucky, you teensy-weensy Yank," Fiona said, emerging from the racks. "You'll fit into all of these. I need to find something among the very few in my size and that will accommodate these bristols." Fiona cupped her boobs and sighed.

"Well, I may have a small waist, but we're going to have to hem the hell out of anything I try on with mountains of tape!" I was holding a gown by the hanger, my arms stretched far above my head, and the fabric was still grazing the floor.

"We all have our limitations." Josh sighed.

After about thirty minutes and twelve dresses, we all agreed I should wear a black off-the-shoulder dress with a long gauzy skirt made from overlapping panels of chiffon. There were yards of fabric, but because it was so light, it was subtle and hung weightless to the floor. I would have felt self-conscious in anything too flashy or big. Apparently it had been hemmed for a shorter celebrity who had borrowed it for a movie premiere. Josh helped me tame my flyaway locks into something resembling a messy braided bun,

Fiona and I stood before the vanity, covered with our various cosmetics, and looked into the mirror to admire our handiwork.

"We clean up rather nicely, don't we?" she said and smiled at me. I smiled in agreement, but I was starting to feel a combination of nerves and excitement about the evening. I just wasn't sure how to act when I saw Dylan, or whether or not I'd be able to restrain myself if I saw Amelia making a move. I knew I'd want to go to his side, and I wished I could go to this as Dylan's date, but that wasn't the situation, and it never would be.

Chapter 16

By 6:45 Fiona and I were done with our tasks and had snagged a couple of glasses of champagne from the first waiters to enter the room. The party was held in a huge gallery of the museum, lined with portraits of famous British people: everyone from poets to royalty and actors. It was a mesmerizing place for a party, with endless fodder for conversation. And at the moment, the space was relatively empty. Only a couple of guests had arrived, so we just took in the art and exchanged stories.

Fiona had grown up in Yorkshire and gone to university in Manchester. She had five brothers, which seemed insane to me given that I was an only child, and they'd had a bucolic postcard-perfect English country life from what I could tell, gallivanting on the moors and celebrating Boxing Day, basically living my English fantasy. Her boyfriend was a Londoner, a graffiti artist, and lived in Hackney. Fiona described late-night tagging adventures, which she confessed scared the crap out of her, but she was completely falling in love with him. She looked positively glowing as she talked about him.

We were still gabbing when I saw Dylan enter the room, his eyes scanning, searching. I felt all the color rise to my cheeks, and I shivered, the goose bumps coming to the surface. The actual quality of the air had changed now that he was here. He looked like a modern James Bond in a perfectly fitting tuxedo with a black straight tie—custom-made, I'm sure. There was something about a man in a tux, especially *this* man in *this* tux, that made me swoon. I could see hints of his impressive muscles beneath the tailoring of the jacket and his shirt. He had a restrained power—even strangers moving about the room seemed to sense that he exerted a gravitational force.

I couldn't believe that twenty-four hours earlier this debonair man walking towards the bar had had his face firmly buried between my legs. I tingled just thinking about it. Finally, drink in hand, his gaze met mine briefly, but he pivoted and walked across the room to someone I couldn't see, ignoring me completely. And there was the sting—fast, sharp, and inevitable. I didn't blame him for wanting his relationships secret. The problem was that it was getting harder to deny that I wanted more.

Fiona was chatting in my ear about her new flat in Hoxton that she was sharing with two other girls, when I noticed Dylan drifting closer with a group of people. They were all admiring a sculpture, some kind of conceptual piece made of Bible pages, and a photographer stood behind him, waiting for a good shot. Dylan was clearly on the to-be-reported-on list.

"Ooh, Lydia. *That* is Dylan Hale. Have you heard of him?" Fiona was nearly shouting at me in a hissed whisper. "He is basically London's most mysterious and eligible bachelor. Not to mention one of the kings of the art and design world. Oh god, isn't he just gorgeous? People say he is a total arse to work with, though, like completely insane about his work. But, ugh, can you even imagine what he's like in bed? He just oozes sex, doesn't he? He's probably got an outrageously huge nob." The champagne was clearly working on Fiona—her Northern accent was getting thicker, and she was channeling Josh pretty effectively at this point with her rapid-fire assessment.

I nearly choked on my champagne. "He really is attractive, isn't he?" I replied, taking down a large sip. We were both following him with our gazes, and I got the sense he knew it. He easily navigated this scene, mingling with his highbrow social circle.

"He is all over the society pages," she continued, "and look at him—he knows everyone in this room!" I glanced over and saw a continuous stream of people approaching him. "Can you imagine the women who throw themselves at him? Didn't you hear Amelia Reynolds, that client, talking about him? I mean, he's a *Marquess*. I think every socialite in London would die to land him."

This was not helping me. In fact, as Fiona went on about how eligible and desired Dylan was, the sting of being Dylan's "piece on the side" was becoming more apparent. I tried to remember his words from the previous night, that he wasn't interested in Amelia. But right now, watching him make other women—and there were other women; a gaggle of them had settled around him—laugh and swoon, I was keenly aware that that didn't mean he wasn't interested in others. And I couldn't get Amelia's words out of my mind, that he was going to have to settle down eventually. Was I just going to be last in a long string of flings before he made England's nobility proud and produced heirs or whatever he was supposed to do?

Fiona and I continued to chat and wander, and as we were inhaling our fourth mini quiche, there was a commotion at the main entrance. It became immediately clear why: Princess Caroline had just arrived, and holy hell she looked incredible in person. I'd seen plenty of photos of her, of course, but she was taller and leaner than I expected as she drifted into the room with a group of friends. I gulped. I couldn't help it. I felt like the ugly stepsister in some kind of twisted fairy tale—I mean, she was a goddamn princess.

Fiona gave a little shriek. "Ohmygod, Lydia. I can't help it, but I need to get a closer look. Shall we go stalk the royals?"

"Oh, you know, my feet are kind of aching from these heels. I'll ogle from afar."

Fiona was already off, pretending to be looking at art mere feet from where the Princess and her entourage had convened.

I looked to where Dylan had been standing, and he was also walking towards Caroline. Her friends parted to let him enter the group. He kissed her on both cheeks, and she smiled back. Their welcome was warm—it was clear that they felt incredibly comfortable around each other. They chatted amiably, laughing and looking around. Then he leaned over and said something quietly to her, and I saw her eyes dart up to him and then scan the room in my direction. He continued to speak, whispering directly into her ear, and her eyes seemed to fix on me. What was he saying? Fuck—I would do anything to know what the hell was going on. She looked at him and smiled, squeezing his arm. Was he telling her I was his latest conquest? Was he talking about me at all or was her looking my way a coincidence? They chatted for a few more minutes, and then he fell away and migrated to a group of suits nursing their tumblers of Scotch.

I was still reeling and trying to make sense of what happened when Fiona returned bubbling. "Oh god. Did you see Amelia Reynolds? She actually looks pretty incredible in Hannah's dress. I hate to admit it since she's such an awful bitch, but the woman is bloody stunning, isn't she?" God, out with one threatening woman and on to the next. Would it never end?

I followed Fiona's eyes and saw exactly what she meant. Amelia looked amazing and was out for blood. And Dylan was a red-blooded man. I watched Amelia search the room until her eyes settled on him. His back was turned to her, and he was still engrossed with the businessmen. She approached him from behind and tapped him on the shoulder. He turned and gave a polite smile, introducing her to the group. She lingered and leaned into him, but he remained tall and shifted to keep their stance less intimate. After a few minutes, I saw him excuse himself and head for the bar. My shoulders sank with relief. Looking back, I saw a befuddled Amelia, posture slumped as she presumably tried to figure out how to extricate herself from the conversation.

Suddenly I felt Fiona's posture stiffen, and I registered Hannah approaching us with a satisfied expression on her face. For Hannah this was beaming. "Have you seen the way people are responding to the gown? This is perfect." She looked at the model on the pedestal with approval. She glanced around the room and filled us in on who was who, pointing out the important people from the British Fashion Council as well as other designers and artists. Apparently being included in tonight's showcase was a real coup, an honor reserved for the most prestigious of London's working artists. A friend of Hannah's who was a painter joined us with her husband, and Hannah introduced us. It turned out that they'd taught at NYU for a year, and we quickly fell into reminiscing about favorite coffee shops and the school's latest bureaucratic scandal.

At a lull in conversation, Hannah glanced down at the dress

I was wearing, giving me a pleased once-over. "That gown looks marvelous on you, Lydia." Hannah held my arms out and took me in thoughtfully. "You know, I don't think I realized that this neckline would fall this way on someone who was so petite. It works perfectly."

"I couldn't agree more," said a familiar voice from my side. My head snapped up to see Dylan, looking appreciatively, not at me, but at the gown I was wearing. He was so practiced at feigning indifference—it was a little disconcerting. He reached his hand out to Hannah. "Dylan Hale. I love your work, Hannah." Hannah blushed at the compliment—it was clear that Dylan was the more renowned of the two in these circles. He knew the other couple as well, and the conversation quickly resumed, but everyone somehow silently deferred to him. He had this way of being in charge even here.

He had positioned himself so he was standing slightly behind and next to me, our backs hugged to the wall, and he guided the group to appreciate the pieces of art on display, speaking eloquently about their origins and bantering about their merits with the others. He was clearly incredibly knowledgeable. He still hadn't acknowledged me in any way, and now that he was right there, next to me, my position in his world, notably one of inconsequence, was just that much more obvious.

But I couldn't dwell on that nagging unpleasantness for long. His art-world banter turned out to be a very effective strategy for keeping the attention faced away from us as he began his seduction. His hand holding the glass of champagne gestured to the pieces in the middle of the room, and the others' eyes followed, but his other hand was firmly spread across my lower back, and was drifting decidedly south.

My breathing hitched, and I began feeling the familiar spread of heat and anticipation. Every hair on my body stood up, and I wanted to melt into him, have that delicious anticipation soothed by him. His hand spread broadly across my ass, cupping the cheeks, almost lifting them. I couldn't believe he was doing this here, in front of all these people, including my boss! He seemed adept at executing these moves without notice; his stance barely shifted, and I thought—hoped—the others were naïve as to what was going on. But god, this was insane!

I squirmed and shifted slightly when one of his fingers began pushing the fabric of my gown between my legs. He pinched me, hard, on my ass, and I did my best not to squeal. I got the message: I was to remain still. I was now dripping in anticipation, in longing. There was no way he'd be able to alleviate this need, to make me *come* while standing here—it was going to be pure torture. He found a separation in the panels of my skirt, and slid his hand in. Skin on skin. His thumb found the border of my panties, right where my pussy met my thigh, and suddenly he paused.

Oh, shit. He'd said that thing about underwear. Had he been serious? He couldn't have meant no underwear *now*? When I was essentially at *work*? Suddenly he withdrew his hand, leaving me hotter and hornier than hell. He excused himself and walked towards the entrance.

What the—?

I smiled at Hannah and ducked away, letting her continue her conversation with the couple. I passed Fiona, waved, and headed for the restrooms. If I didn't find Dylan, then at least I could find a bathroom and discreetly relieve the tension myself.

Chapter 17

As I rounded the corner into the dark hallway, Dylan reached out and pulled me to him. Our entire bodies were flush up against one another, and we were only just blocked from view by a column. "You. Are a very. Very. Bad girl, Lydia," he whispered and smiled, and I could feel the bulge between his legs pressing into my side. He looked so turned on, like he was struggling to maintain control.

"What did I say about underwear?" I knew it wasn't a real question, and he knew the answer, so I responded with a kiss instead, fiercely molding my mouth to his own, following the lines of his lips with my tongue. He reached his palm around the base of my head, into my hair, and pushed me further into my kiss. Just as suddenly, he pulled my face from his own and leaned into my ear. "Say your goodbyes, and go around the corner. I'll pick you up on St. Martin's Street. Five minutes." And he was gone in that way only Dylan seemed to be able to disappear.

I hurriedly told Fiona that I needed to be off, making up an excuse about delayed jetlag that didn't make sense and no one should have believed, but she kindly did. Just as I rounded the corner, I saw the tail of the Mercedes peeking out from a delivery alley, the passenger door slightly ajar. As soon as I slipped into the car, Dylan hauled me onto his lap. "Your place or a hotel?" His tie was loosened and the top button of his shirt unbuttoned. His eyes were glowing, and he was ready to pounce.

"Why not yours?" I asked, and I began kissing his neck.

"There was a photographer there when I left tonight, and we shouldn't go there anyway. Too risky," he replied as he kissed me back. I paused, but willed myself to ignore the sting, kissing him again.

"Then mine," I answered.

"Lydia Bell's house, Lloyd." His huge hands were covering my back, as though he were trying to touch all of me at once.

"Yes, sir," replied Lloyd from the front. I turned to look in the direction of the front seat, and then looked at Dylan warily.

"Don't worry," he whispered. "Lloyd is nothing if not discreet. But we'll wait till we're there. We're close." I tried to slide off his lap, but he held me firmly in place.

"I can't believe the way you were touching me in front of those people," I whispered.

"No one saw. I would never let anyone see." Of course he wouldn't. He didn't want anyone to know.

I tried to push away the nagging, uncomfortable feeling about the secrecy issue and focus on enjoying the insane and delicious sexual tension blossoming between us. I rested my head in the crook of his neck, trying to maximize the areas of our bodies that were touching. Suddenly, I remembered, popping my head up to look at him "What did you say to Caroline?"

He shrugged, and gently urged me to put my head back where it had been. "You told your friend. I told mine." He reached down to fondle my ankle and began gliding his hand up my leg and under my skirt. "On second thought," he said, as he pressed a button. The tinted partition rose between where we were sitting and where Lloyd was driving. "I can wait to fuck you until we get home—barely—but let's get these off, shall we?" He tugged at my panties. The fact of his impatience made me feel coveted, so attended to, and so turned on.

"Wait." I tried to close my legs to stop him so I could get the rest of the story. "What did you tell her?"

"I don't want to wait, Lydia." He pushed my legs apart. I rolled my eyes and consented. I braced myself on his shoulders and raised my hips. He went about expertly separating me from my lacey thong, and he tucked it into his jacket pocket. "Are you going to tell me everything you told Daphne?" The panels of my gown were pushed to the sides over my hips, so I was completely exposed on his lap. He placed his hand against the inside of my bare thigh, and strummed his thumb against my hypersensitive skin, barely missing the edge of my pussy. It had the effect of coiling me even tighter.

"Um, definitely no."

"Well then." He was staring into my lap and driving me crazy. Not only did I want to know what he'd said to Caroline, but he was teasing the edge of my slit in a way that had me close to coming. I needed him in me. I attempted to shift towards him, forcing his fingers into me, but he removed his hand completely for a moment. "Ah ah, Lydia," he chastised, before resuming his assault. "I want me inside you as much as you do, but I say when…Do you think I could make you come like this? Without even touching you there?" His voice remained at a whisper.

I pulled back to look at him. "I don't want to find out, and if you want me to go along with this whole you-being-in-charge thing, you'd better deliver, Hale."

He smiled and inched his hand a fraction farther away from its destination, making me both hotter and more frustrated. He pulled the pin holding my hair up, and I could feel my hair loosening at my neck as he ran his fingers through it. I moaned. "Please, Dylan. You have me on the brink." I buried myself in his shoulder, letting my hair cascade around my face, and I clamped my thighs shut, trying to curb his assault. He forced them open again with his strong hands and let a finger sink into me, making me gasp softly. I was so unbelievably close.

He withdrew his finger and brought it to my lips, dampening them with my own wetness. "You see how wet this makes you, Lydia? Me in charge? Let me do this for you." He kissed me softly and licked his own lips. "You taste so good." I realized in that moment just how bossy, how controlling, he'd become in our sexy encounters. He needed it—something about him craved being in charge, but what shocked me was that I needed it too. I wanted it. I was fucking *loving* it. The car came to a stop, and he held me tight for a moment, while Lloyd rounded the car to open the door. Dylan put my hand firmly in his, and helped me out of the car. I could barely walk, my legs wobbly and numb in my current state. I could feel the evening's cool air skate across my sex, and it made me shiver. He pulled me to his side, holding me, as though he were protecting me from the world, and took my keys from my hands to unlock the door.

We weren't a foot inside when he closed the door behind him and said, "Turn around, damsel," indicating I should face away from him. I complied, and he slowly came up behind me, running his hands along my bare upper back and down my arms. He unzipped the dress and pulled it off my shoulders so it pooled at my feet. I was naked except for my insanely high heels. Grabbing my hips, he pulled my naked ass into his front, and I could feel his hardness pushing against the seam of his trousers. "Can you feel how much I want you? How much I want this?" he said firmly, increasing his grip on my hips, pulling me even closer.

I tilted my head back and to the side to try to steal a glimpse of him, and he rested his chin on my shoulder. His hands wrapped around and palmed my breasts. He pushed them in and up, molding them in his palms, and he began to tug at my nipples, rolling them between his thumb and finger, teasing them to the point where pain met pleasure.

"I'm breaking all sorts of rules for you, aren't I?" He was kissing my neck, sucking my skin, nipping it gently between his teeth, devouring me in motions that mimicked what he was doing to my breasts.

"What rules have you broken for me?" I asked, practically whispering, searching for steadiness in my breath.

He spun me around and lifted me by my ass in one swift move. I locked my ankles behind his back. "For starters I rarely sleep with the same woman twice, at least not in the same week. I don't spend the night. Ever. And neither do the women I see. And I don't invite women into my office. Ever. But I couldn't resist with you. I'd been dreaming about having my mouth on that pretty pussy on that table for weeks. Picturing you just as you were."

"Did it live up to the dream?" I nuzzled into his cheek, desperate to get to a place where he was naked, where I could feel his skin on my skin.

"The dream didn't stand a chance."

"Well, I wouldn't want you breaking any of your rules, would I? I mean, maybe we better stop now, and you could sleep on my sofa. Or you can get back on your horse—"

"Not on your life, smartass." He started to carry me upstairs, and when we reached the second floor, he paused. "Bedroom?"

I pointed him in the right direction. My body was still pulsing, completely on edge from his fondling over the last hour. I was shivery, alert with anticipation.

"Are you still sore?" he asked, the pads of his fingers grasping my ass as we walked and nearly grazing the sweet spot that was already trembling for him.

"A little."

"Shall I make you sore again?" He laid me on the bed and began to undress himself with steady restraint, but the look in his eyes betrayed him. He was just as desperate to touch me as I was to touch him.

"Yes, please." Anticipation stretched my smile wide.

"Roll over. On your hands and knees, baby."

I quickly complied.

"Lean down, and perch that little ass in the air for me, Lydia. I want to see it in the moonlight." I did as I was told. He stroked my ass for a moment, and then suddenly there was a resounding smack. He'd spanked me! Hard. Holy shit. I lurched forward but quickly regained my standing. I turned around to look at him, shocked. It had brought all my blood to the surface.

He replied to my surprise with a sensual, stern look. "*That* was for the knickers."

I was still reeling from the palm of his hand, but I found myself wanting to push myself into him, onto him.

"Holy shit," I uttered, under my breath.

"You want more." He wasn't asking. He could tell I did. "Soon. Right now, I'm going to take you from behind, and hard."

"God, yes." I heard him fumbling with his pants and tearing at the condom wrapper. I felt his cock brushing my entrance, and I willed him to enter me. I didn't think I could wait another moment. This whole evening of sensual torture had been leading me here, and I didn't think he could take me hard enough.

His hands glided from my shoulders down my back. He took in my whole ass with his hands, massaging it, and his thumbs ran down my crack, softly parting me as he went. It was as though he were examining me, appreciating every inch of me as his fingers tenderly grazed my skin. I leaned back into him, desperate for him to be inside me. He paused between my cheeks, skimming his thumb over the tender opening. "Have you ever enjoyed your ass, Lydia? Has anyone ever played with you here?"

"No." My heart rate picked up, and I turned to look at him nervously. What was he going to do? God, I needed him in me. Now. I was dripping for him, and much to my surprise his touch there ignited me further.

"Good. I'll be the first." He ran a finger through my slit and slid the wetness up to where his thumb still pressed gently. He inserted the tip of his finger, just past the rosy opening. I gasped at the sudden intrusion. Was he going to do this now? He obviously sensed my surprise, because he leaned over and whispered in my ear, "Don't worry. I'm only going to give you a taste." And pushed his finger in a little farther. "Your ass is so beautiful."

The slight intrusion was so new, intense, and somehow set my clit on fire. I clenched my pussy in response. "That's right, my sweet girl. I can feel you," he said, his voice seductive and appreciative, like he was luxuriating in me.

"Dylan. I'm throbbing for you. Please." I'd sunk to my forearms, feeling weak with neediness, and I didn't think I'd make it another minute without him inside me.

"Happily." He withdrew his finger and entered me in one quick move, pushing me forward with the force of his thrust.

He was so deep this way, deeper than before. I could feel his balls brushing up against the lips of my entrance. "That's right, baby, take all of me." At this angle, he hit that fiery bundle of nerves inside me with every perfect thrust, and I could feel myself tightening, the coil stretching and shrinking, winding me tighter, bringing me closer with his every move. I hadn't thought women could come from sex, but I had with him, and there was no doubt that that was where I was headed now. "You're so sweet and wet. So tight." He was breathing hard and slamming into me, ravishing me.

"Keep going," I cried in breathy bursts. I couldn't get enough. His hands were gripping into my hips, and I could hear him slap against my ass. He pushed himself into me and pulled me back with every thrust in a perfect rhythm, intensifying each time. He was possessing me completely, as deeply as he could.

"I couldn't stop if I wanted to. I can't get enough of you." He mirrored my thoughts, and he grunted through his teeth, "You're close, I can feel it. Come now, baby. Now!" And I did. I felt my body combust at his command, a chaotic shiver took hold of me, and everything went cloudy. I was lost in a haze of sweat, his smell, and my own body quaking beneath him. I fell to the duvet, and he fell with me, remaining deep inside me. He propped his weight up with one of his arms, and used the other to caress my back and ass, gliding his hand down my body in one long stroke. There was so much tenderness in his touch, so much care, as though he was checking me over after ravishing me so completely. He slid out of me and stepped back to quickly dispose of the condom. He came back to the bed and pulled me into his arms, cradling me as he leaned up against the headboard, stroking my hair. "You ok?" he asked as he kissed me softly on the top of my head.

"Can't you tell?" I murmured. "I'm so content right now, Dylan. So...sated. I never knew it would be like this." I nuzzled into his chest.

"And we're just getting started. There's so much more I'm going to do to you. I'm making it my mission to ruin you for anyone else."

"If sex is like this for everyone, I don't really understand how anyone gets anything done." I was here in my bed, in his arms, and marveling at his sexual expertise. I couldn't imagine a life where this was a regular occurrence, but I was also beginning to not be able to imagine a life without it.

"Then unless you stay stop, I'm going to keep going. I'm not done with you yet." I could feel his smile in my hair. His arm tightened around me, and his other hand cupped between my legs, one finger slowly massaging my clit. "Or with this."

"Do your worst," I said and smiled, completely relaxing in his arms.

"What? No comments about voting and walking?"

"Don't be so surprised. I can play nice. I'm all yours." I suddenly had never been so willing in my life, and my blood sang with excitement.

"Yes, you are." He lay down and pulled me with him, keeping our bodies locked together, me on my back and him sidled up against me on his side. His ministrations increased in intensity, and I bucked my hips, pushing myself into his palm. My breathing started to quicken and he sank two and then three fingers into me, stretching me, taunting me. "That's right, my sweet girl," he whispered into my ear. I could feel his breath on my neck. I lifted my arms above my head and grabbed the pillow behind me, folding my elbows over my face, hiding my eyes as my insides began to quake. With his free hand he grabbed my wrists firmly and pulled them higher above my head, exposing my face to his. He locked them in place against the headboard, and I couldn't budge. "Look at me. Look at me while you come," he instructed firmly. I opened my eyes and my gaze met his. In that moment I came wildly into his hand, writhing beneath him, stuck in his hold.

He slowly withdrew his fingers and rolled over on top of me, supporting himself on his forearms, continuing to lock my hands in his own, our faces nearly touching. "You're all mine," he said. And then his voice dropped, and more seriously he continued: "And you'll do as I say." Holy hell, it did something to me when he went all dominant, like my body was destined to do his bidding. He leaned in and kissed my forehead, his arms framing my face.

Suddenly, he released me and shifted us around onto our sides, pulling me to his back, spooning me. "And right now, I want you to sleep."

"What?! You can't hold out now!" My orgasm had left me needy for more. I was still tightly wound, and he could feel my resistance.

"Can't I?" he said, as he stroked my arm and side, bringing me down from my heightened arousal. "We have all of tomorrow, and I promise I'll take care of you." He wrapped me tightly against him, securing me in his arms, and I didn't even remember drifting off.

Chapter 18

I blinked awake to the sun streaming in through my windows and to Dylan standing in the doorway, in boxer briefs, with two mugs of coffee. My god he was gorgeous. It was the first time I'd seen his near-naked body in the daylight, and he was as perfectly cut as he felt in the darkness. His briefs slung from hip to hip, bordering his six-pack abs. He was simply exquisite.

"Like what you see?" He smirked, having caught me ogling.

"You know you're gorgeous." I scoffed.

He shrugged. "The benefits of having a personal trainer. Now, you—you're actually beautiful." He sauntered over, put one coffee down next to me, and pulled the covers away from me. I instinctively went to curl my knees up, covering myself in the daylight, but he scolded and pushed my knees firmly down. "I want to look at you. Don't be embarrassed around me."

I growled. "You're so pervy. You're like the Earl of Perv."

He laughed. "The Marquess of Perv. Please. Be precise."

I giggled, trying to relax. I figured, *Hey, if this is really what he wants*—I embraced it and sat cross-legged, warming my hands with my cup of coffee. He sat next to me, facing me, taking me in and stroking my thigh, but he seemed thoughtful all of a sudden. "What? Did I say something?" I asked.

"No. I just…I was just reminded of something my family needs me to do. I hate that shit."

"What shit?"

"Forget it. My parents can be…relentless. That's all."

"You strike me as someone who only does do what *he* wants."

He bristled. "It's one thing to buck a parent's request to have dinner, Lydia, but another to buck six centuries of tradition. You wouldn't understand." He was looking at me with determination, like he was going to will himself to ignore whatever had just come into his head.

"Hey. Look." I sat up and shifted away from him. "I'm sorry for touching a nerve, but—"

He grabbed me and pulled me back. "I'm sorry. I'm sorry. Sore subject. You didn't deserve that." He sighed, brushing his hand through his hair. "What is your family like?"

I hated answering this question. It was bad enough when it was just a no-show mom, but now that my dad had died, it incited a level of pity, and even worse, discomfort in whoever had asked, which I couldn't stand. But what was I going to do? Lie?

"I don't have any," I replied and took a sip of my coffee. I still hadn't figured out the best words to use when announcing this, but these clearly weren't right, because he was too silent for too long.

"What do you mean? What about your parents?" he asked, while cupping my shoulder, a touch that somehow communicated sympathy but also tension. This obviously wasn't what he'd expected.

"My mother hasn't been in the picture since before I remember, and my dad died in April."

"That's terrible," he said, his hand pulling me closer.

I was so relieved he hadn't said he was sorry—I never knew how to reply to that one except to say it was ok, which of course it wasn't.

"He'd been sick for a long time," I replied. I took another long sip of my coffee. He was silent again, looking reflective in a way that I didn't understand.

"That must have been awful," he said sweetly. "Cancer?"

I nodded. When I looked back to Dylan, he looked blank, staring out the window. I knew about the whole British reserve thing, and I'd probably just broken some unwritten English rule about never talking about such things. Well, at least it was out there.

I left the bed and headed to the bathroom to brush my teeth. A moment later, Dylan was behind me, his arms wrapped around me. He leaned down and kissed my shoulder. "Do you want to talk about it?" I knew he would let me if I wanted to, but the truth was I didn't want to. Not yet. I wasn't sure I wanted to let him in that deep, or any deeper than he was already.

"No." I forced a smile. I put my toothbrush down and rested my hands over his, our naked bodies pressed together.

"What do you want to do today?" he asked, kissing my neck.

"You're actually letting me decide something?"

"I'm letting you make suggestions," he replied, now holding my hair up as he trailed his kisses along the back of my neck.

"Hmm, well, I want to see Primrose Hill," I started, pausing to think. "Or the Portobello Road Market. I've been in London almost a week, and I feel like I haven't seen anything apart from my office and the tube. And you." He frowned, obviously surprised. Did he think it was lame? And suddenly I realized that I was supposed to have said something along the lines of *Fuck me every which way until sundown.* I had just slipped, fallen into an idea of us that was so obviously against his "just sex" rules.

Eventually, he smiled. "Lydia...I know a lot of people in Primrose Hill—not a good idea. And the Market will be tricky. It's a very public place." His smile widened, and he continued, "I think we could make it work, though. Could be kind of fun, actually." His chin rested on the top of my head, and he smiled at me in the mirror. He seemed settled on it all of a sudden, and I felt the tension in my gut release.

"But first, shower," he said, firmly grabbing my hips. He didn't exactly mince words once he was decided.

He turned on the shower and then faced me, standing at attention, condom in hand. As he tore through the package with his teeth, I brought myself flush against him and grabbed it. I stood on my tiptoes and planted a firm kiss on his lips. He looked at me, eyes wide. Without taking my eyes off of his, I slid my hands down between us and felt for him. And with only a little fumbling, I slid the condom onto his thickness.

He tilted his head back. "Christ, Lydia." I finished, and he looked at me with a fire in his eyes. "As much as I enjoyed that, do you have anything against going on birth control?"

"Um, I don't have anything against it. I just hadn't thought about it." But I was thinking about it now. And I couldn't help but feel like it meant he thought we might be doing this for a while.

Our bodies were flush, and his arm was firmly wrapped around my waist. His erection was pressed against my leg, and my brain was starting to go fuzzy the way it seemed to when we were this close. "I don't want anything between us." He reached down and gently tugged at my pubic hair. "Same goes for this. Let's rid you of this today, shall we? I want skin on skin."

I gave him an "oh really?" look.

"I warned you I was bossy," he said. Of course I could protest, but the truth was I didn't want to. He grabbed my ass and pulled me up and close to him, letting me feel his erection digging into me. "Plus, you'll love it. Trust me."

"I do," I said as I returned his smile, and as I said it I realized just how true it was.

The look on his face was heating me from the inside out. He lifted me by my ribcage, and I instinctively wrapped my legs around him. We stepped into the shower, and he practically slammed me against the tile wall, shifting so he could position himself at my entrance. He slid right into place, my slick folds hugging him. Safely seated inside me, he moved us so the shower door was at my back, and the steaming stream of water poured at his back, sliding in rivulets around him and into the space between us.

"Hands up," he said. "Grab the top of the shower door." I complied immediately and was half supported by him holding me and half by the shower stall itself. "That's right, baby. Hold on tight. Don't let go."

He began driving his hips ruthlessly up into me, lifting me, sliding himself in and out, deeper with each thrust. He buried his head between my breasts and took one nipple between his teeth, relentlessly assaulting the tender peak and then shifting to the other one. No one before him had ever dared treat my breasts with anything but gentle reverence, and this was an awakening. When he twisted one particularly hard the sensation flew straight to my clit, like a jolt of electricity, fast-tracking my orgasm. I threw my head back against the glass door, unable to contain the riot building inside me. What had been a slow build was quickly becoming a tidal wave. I moved one of my hands, hoping to grab his shoulder and gain some control over his onslaught, but he briskly grabbed my wrist, firmly replacing it above my head. "Not unless I say so." His voice was breathy, authoritative, and sexy as hell.

He continued his punishing assault, thrusting into me with increasing fierceness. He had me on the brink, my body about to unravel around him. "I'm about to come, Lydia. Are you close?"

"God yes, Dylan." I breathed out, gasping as he propelled me up and down his perfect dick.

"Come now, baby. Now," he commanded, and within seconds, I detonated, completely coming apart around him. He came with me, his balls firmly pressed against my swollen, sensitive flesh. He let loose a guttural moan, his breathing thick and warm against my chest. We stayed that way for a long moment, catching ourselves, coming down from our orgasms. He pulled out of me and let me down to standing. He rid himself of the condom and gently turned me into him, holding me, my cheek against his chest.

He proceeded to soap me gently, cradling my hypersensitive breasts in his sudsy palms, planting kisses at my collarbone. He raised my hands and washed under my arms. He knelt before me, and glided soapy hands up my legs, around my butt, and between my thighs with care. He washed my hair and massaged me as he went. He was exquisitely gentle. I'd gone from being assaulted with rough aggressive sex to receiving his tender caresses in a matter of minutes, and each was perfect and sensual in its own way. I'd never felt so taken care of, so cherished.

"Your turn," I said, looking at him, and he handed me the body wash. I created a lather between my palms and decided to have fun with this. I stepped towards him so our bodies crushed against each other and began massaging his back, sliding my soapy hands from his shoulders down around his perfect ass, cupping it, making long smooth strokes with my hands and sliding them back up his sides. I made the same loop, creating a rhythm and kissing his chest while doing so. Finally I let my hands move to his front and continued my attack. I purposely and lovingly washed every part of his body except the one he was waiting for, the one *I* was waiting for, and in the meantime I saw him grow with anticipation.

"Lydia?" he scolded. "I know what you're doing."

"I know," I teased, looking up at him.

I finally gripped him firmly in both hands and stroked him at a steady beat. I let one hand slide down and cup his balls, massaging them gently. He reached out each arm and braced himself against the stall walls, and I increased my pace as I felt him stiffen even further. "Good god, baby, I'm going to come. You're killing me. Christ, Lydia!" He tilted his hips, rocking his cock into my hands, fucking them. It was clear he was close, his sense of urgency palpable. I stepped in close, using one hand to grab his ass firmly, and I tightened my grip just as his cum spilled over my hand. His head fell forward, our foreheads meeting, and he draped his arms over my shoulders. "If we don't get out of this shower, we'll never leave the house." I smiled, hearing his implicit compliment.

"That's ok. I think I changed my mind about wanting to go anywhere. Can't we just stay here in this shower all day?"

"No. I love that you want to, but no." He kissed the top of my head, and turned off the water.

Chapter 19

He told me to head down to the Market on my own and that he'd find me. Presumably it wouldn't do for us to be walking hand in hand, not that I even knew if he would be into that if we *weren't* in stealth mode. Lloyd had brought him clean clothes, and we'd eyed each other appreciatively while we dressed. He had caught me grabbing panties from my drawer, and it earned me another slap on my naked ass, one which he'd had the indecency to ask me to bend over the bed to receive. The disciplinarian side of him was enticing, seductive, but I also felt him taking my temperature, gauging how much I liked it. The answer: way more than I probably should.

But so soon after such an intimate morning, I was outside in the world and would have to pretend not to know him. Didn't I deserve more than this? This wasn't what I wanted, but staying away was beginning to feel impossible—I was straight-up addicted.

After a few blocks, I stopped looking over my shoulder to see if Dylan was following. I wrapped my light jacket around me to protect me from the cool morning air—fall was definitely on its way—and I began to get absorbed in the Market. Many of the stalls and shops appeared to sell junk—cheap tourist trinkets or knock-off handbags and paintings. But there were several that perfectly represented what I'd imagined and hoped to find at a London street market.

One stall sold Scottish cashmere, and I fingered the scarves and blankets carefully, admiring the brilliantly colored plaids. I asked the vendor about the price of one particularly beautiful cream-and-blue scarf I was touching and he replied that it was four hundred pounds. I dropped it immediately. That was more than my new dress had cost, and certainly more than I'd ever be able to spend on a scarf.

Another stand sold stylish umbrellas with handcrafted wooden handles in the shapes of animals—a fox, a rabbit, a duck. A narrow storefront sold finely crafted letterpress stationary and cards—thick white cardstock with hints of antique-y fonts and historical inks. The market was quickly beginning to crowd with tourists and locals alike, everyone carrying their morning coffee, and no one in a rush.

I decided to duck into one of the larger indoor antique malls bordering the street market, when someone behind me held the door for me. I turned half=way and smiled as Dylan planted his palm at my lower back, urging me in. He walked past me, gripping my hand as he passed, and he quickly dragged me into a quiet shop selling large old paintings. I stood in front of him, barely an inch between my back and his front, admiring an English country landscape in a thick ornate gold frame. Suddenly I felt soft fabric being draped over my shoulders and around my neck. Looking down I saw the edges of the Scottish scarf I'd been admiring moments before.

"What? Dylan, I—" I whispered, not believing the extravagant gift being wrapped around me. "Were you watching me?" His arms settled behind me, not touching me, but so close. "That's kind of trench coat creepy, you know."

I could feel him rolling his eyes. "Whatever happened to attentiveness being a good thing? The other guys you dated must have been right idiots."

"You're not wrong, but it's still a little creepy."

"Stop. You were looking at this so dreamily. Let me," he whispered in my ear, but he was sure to keep some distance between us. Anyone who saw us might think we were standing awfully close, but nothing more.

"Thank you," I said quietly, and he slipped his hand underneath the side of my jacket and brushed my midriff with his fingers. His touch ignited me.

"Follow me," he ordered, withdrawing his hand.

I turned around and saw his back navigating through the indoor market, and I followed him from a short distance through the web of tiny shops. We dodged tourists and slow-moving window shoppers, and I finally followed him into a tiny elegant estate jeweler's. The shop was completely empty and dark, lit only by a simple chandelier hanging in the center of the room and the light coming in from the shop's front window. Only a short old man with a wool vest and low bifocals manned the counter, and he was currently hunched over some trinket with an eyeglass and a bright desk lamp. He barely raised his head when we first entered, but begrudgingly began to shadow Dylan as he eyed the contents of the long cases bordering the shop. I somehow doubted that this guy read *Hello!* magazine or had a clue that anyone was interested in Dylan's love life.

I stepped over to the window, pretending to examine the

items on display, dragging my fingertips along the edge of the shelf. Pretending quickly turned to genuine interest when I realized how beautiful the pieces were. Delicate filigreed necklaces and long chandelier earrings harkened back to a bygone era of velvet gowns and top hats. There were tiaras and more unusual pieces like brooches, hair combs, and hatpins, all of which summoned the intrigue and elegance of horse-drawn carriages and filled-up dance cards. While I was lost in my reverie, Dylan had started a conversation with the shopkeeper. He was pretending to be in the market for a gift. I began to pay attention, conscious that I was supposed to be a stranger. There was a charge between us that it made it nearly impossible for me to keep my distance. I wanted nothing more than to be in his grasp, tucked into his side.

"For someone special, sir?" the shopkeeper asked, looking over the edge of his spectacles, assessing Dylan and trying to ascertain exactly what type of customer he was dealing with.

He nodded. "I'd like something unusual, one of a kind," Dylan replied with confidence. He'd know what he wanted when he saw it.

"Yes, sir. And did you have a price in mind, a limit?" the shopkeeper asked.

"No," said Dylan matter-of-factly.

"Ahh, well. I have a few items that might work. One moment." The shopkeeper began retrieving jewelry and placing the items in a velvet-lined box, creating a collection. When he caught my gaze, he asked, "Can I help you, miss?"

"No, no. I'm just looking. Thank you," I replied, moving over to the case. I stood just a couple of feet down from Dylan, splitting my attention between his magnetic pull and the gorgeous antiques in front of me.

I heard Dylan nix several things, and then point to something in the case in front of him. "I'd like to see those."

"Of course, sir," said the shopkeeper, sounding pleased. I tried to see what they were looking at, and they seemed to be a pair of dangly earrings. I could see them catching the light as the shopkeeper held them up. "Do you know if she wears long earrings, sir? They can overwhelm some, and sapphires don't complement everyone, I'm afraid."

"I see." Dylan held the earrings in his hand. He glanced at me. "Perhaps she could help." He turned, giving me his full attention, and I could feel my face heat up.

He was roping me into his scene, and I wasn't at all sure I'd be able to keep up the act, playing this game for the shopkeeper's benefit. Actually, the way I was beginning to feel that familiar pulsing tingle on my skin, I suppose it was for my benefit too.

Dylan looked right at me expectantly and asked, "Would you mind?"

Another couple calmly walked into the shop and began to browse. I coughed out of nervousness, clearing my throat. "Not at all. How can I help?" I approached Dylan, placing one hand on the counter to steady what were becoming shaky legs. The other couple was paying attention now too, and I heard the man make an admiring comment about the jewelry in a haughty tone. I couldn't take my eyes off of Dylan's and still hadn't even looked at what he was holding. I was transfixed, paralyzed by Dylan's gaze.

"I'm thinking about buying these as a gift, you see, but they're a surprise," Dylan continued, and I nodded. "She's about your size—you look similar. I was wondering if you'd try them on for me. If it wouldn't be a bother."

The way the sun was coming in through the windows behind

me and lighting him, I would have stripped naked right there and then and done whatever he asked. "Happily," I replied, summoning my inner actress. I approached him and unwrapped the scarf from my neck, placing it on the case. I tucked my hair behind my ears and removed my tiny silver studs, placing them on the counter. I expected him to hand me the earrings, but in a gesture I'm sure revealed us, he reached up and slipped the earrings into my ears. His touch ignited me, striking me like a match. His fingers grazing my cheek and neck, his face so close to my own. How did he expect me to refrain from kissing him? But he knew exactly what he was doing—this whole incognito thing was intensifying everything, bringing the chemistry between us to a boil. Fighting kissing him was like fighting an oncoming tsunami.

When he was done, he stepped back, leaned on the counter, and took me in. But in a moment his "I know exactly what I'm doing to you" smirk fell away. He was captivated, almost stunned. Was something wrong? I held my hair back and turned to look in the mirror the shopkeeper had brought out. The earrings were astonishingly beautiful. They were far more intricate than I had first appreciated. Each one was an elegant web of diamonds surrounding a cluster of large sapphires, creating an Art Nouveau floral feeling. They were teardrop shaped, outlined with a thin line of tiny diamonds, and had a sophisticated whimsy about them. I'd never pined for jewelry, but seeing these, I completely got the appeal.

It took me a moment to realize that everyone in the shop was staring at me. The woman who had walked in looked closer. "Those are absolutely exquisite! Darling, did you see these?" Then she looked at me. "They look incredible on you, dear."

I blushed intensely, suddenly feeling like everyone in that

room knew exactly what and who was flashing in my mind. "Do you think she would like them?" I asked. I looked right into Dylan's eyes, both afraid of getting us caught and also not being able to pull away.

He remained lost, mesmerized. "Undoubtedly." He was almost whispering, the word catching in his throat.

I was the center of attention and suddenly it scared the crap out of me. I felt overwhelmed and exposed. I needed to get out of there. I felt like we'd just had some kind of moment neither of us was ready for—the way he was looking at me felt all encompassing, and it was as though I could feel myself bleeding into him and disappearing. I carefully slid the earrings out of my ears and laid them in the velvet-lined box. I quickly wrapped my new beautiful scarf around my neck, grateful for its protection, and grabbed my own earrings from the counter.

"Excuse me." I smiled at everyone, and ducked out of the shop.

Chapter 20

I was halfway home and had left the bustle of the market behind me when I saw the Jaguar pull up alongside. I hesitated, and then reached for the door. Before I was even fully in the car, Dylan had hauled me onto his lap. He reached behind me, grabbed the door closed, and brought his arms right back to my body. He looked at me, pleading and commanding.

"Don't run off like that, Lydia. Please." The words were desperate and authoritative.

"Sorry. It just got, I don't know, intense all of a sudden." I pulled my face back, so I could see him.

"I know. You just looked so unbelievably beautiful. I...I wasn't prepared for it. I can imagine you spread across my bed in a thousand different ways, and it excites the fuck out of me, but that? Seeing you there, looking so guileless, so gorgeous, so, I don't know, just goddamn angelic—it fucking undid me." He gulped. He looked almost panicked. "And then you were gone. Don't do it again."

"Ok. Ok. I won't." Had he been worried? "Hey, what's wrong?"

"Nothing. Look, Lydia. I can't give you more, ok?"

"Dylan, I'm not asking you to. What are you saying?"

"It's not that I don't want... This is just who I am, what my life is. But don't run off. Not yet."

"I'm not. I won't." I put my head back onto his chest, and the car was idling in front of my house as he held me to him fiercely. I didn't really know what he was saying or what was eating him, but I did get the sense that he was sharing about as much as he could. What he'd said simultaneously made me feel safer in this thing with him and also aware that its ending was inevitable. If I wanted a relationship I was going to have to look elsewhere. Slowly he loosened his grip, and his hands settled around my waist. The moment had passed.

"I'm hungry," I said, sighing into his chest.

He laughed. Finally, tension broken. "Let's feed you, then." Rain was starting to drum the windshield. "But first—" He held out a square flat velvet box, and opened it to reveal the earrings I'd just been wearing. They looked even more brilliant in the light outside the dark shop.

"Are you fucking kidding me?" I exclaimed, sounding slightly horrified. I didn't even want to know how much those cost.

"'Thank you' will suffice, Lydia." His exasperated tone was muted by the sound of the rain pounding harder now on the roof of the car.

"These are an outrageous gift. I mean, they're unbelievable, and it was fun to pretend, but you shouldn't be giving these to me."

"Fuck should and shouldn't. If you had seen how incredible these looked on you... There was no way I could leave them behind. They're yours. I want you to have them." He wasn't to be argued with.

"Thank you, Dylan. And for the scarf, which felt like an

extravagant gift on its own. These—" I fingered the earrings lovingly. "I don't think I'll ever have the occasion to wear them, but I love them." I kissed him softly and leaned into him.

"Good. Ok, food." He stroked my back and then tugged me out of the car.

It had started raining so hard that by the time we made it to the door we were nearly soaked through. Once inside, I went to my room to shed my wet clothes, and reemerged in a clean, dry V-neck t-shirt and jeans. By the time I got to the kitchen, Dylan was on the phone ordering us takeaway Thai food. He held his cell phone away from his ear as he spoke to me, "I'm assuming you're not allergic to peanuts?" I shook my head in confirmation, but that was the only input I was asked for food-wise.

"The food will be here soon, but I have to go. I have some things I have to do this afternoon."

"You're not going to stay and eat with me?" I was more disappointed than I realized I'd be.

"No, but you'll eat with me tonight. And bring an overnight bag. You're sleeping over," he said, smiling. His rakish smile was his way of asking permission to be as bossy as he was being, and it was fine by me. "Lloyd will pick you up at five forty-five."

"Sleeping, huh?"

"Is that a challenge?" He looked both incredibly pleased at my playfulness and also completely firm. "You have no idea how I already plan to put that delectable little body of yours to work. I've been incredibly gentle with you so far, so you might want to think twice before asking for more." His voice was low and husky.

"I thought we weren't going to go to your house," I said.

"We'll be careful," he replied, coming towards me. "You really are making me break my own rules." He sighed, sounding almost confused.

He put his finger under my chin and tipped my head up, his lips meeting mine. "Now. Be good. Eat your lunch. Stay warm and dry, and be ready when Lloyd comes to get you." He kissed me again, squeezed me in his arms, and walked away. He turned once more before shutting the door behind him, "And, Lydia? Wear a dress."

* * *

At 5:45, I was at my door, ready to go. I wore a printed, capped-sleeved wrap dress with nude heels and my denim jacket. I debated for a moment about the panties. Was I really not going to wear underwear just because Dylan said so? But this crazy desire he had? I had it, too, and the truth was that it was *fun* letting him push my limits, letting him pry open the door to my naughtier side. Although it was definitely going to take some getting used to, especially when it came to dresses. I threw my hair in a messy ponytail and threw everything I really needed for an overnight into my tote. I wasn't exactly a high-maintenance girl.

I was in the car with Lloyd for five minutes, the Jaguar again, when he received a call. All I could here was "Yes, sir" and "Yes, Mr. Hale." Not a lot required of Lloyd in the talking department, I guess. Then he caught my eye in the rearview mirror, "Miss Bell, Mr. Hale has asked me to have you make a stop before we go to his home."

"Ah—" I was about to press him when my phone vibrated with a text. It was from Dylan.

SATURDAY, 5:56 pm
Trust me.

What did he mean? Just then we pulled up in front of a town house with a large glossy blue door and a discreet sign indicating it was a day spa. Oh god. He'd mentioned parting me from my pubic hair, and I had a feeling that's what this was about. I'd gotten my bikini line waxed before for swimsuit season, but I had a feeling he was thinking of something a little more drastic.

Out of instinct or some long-held habit of being an agreeable person, I opened the car door and walked the few steps to the spa door. I even opened the door and went inside. I even enjoyed the blast of warm air and the smell of cucumbers and mint. But very quickly, on the heels of taking in the soothing spa music, I had a moment of *What the fuck am I doing letting some guy tell me how or when to groom my nether regions?*

He'd asked me to trust him, and every other thing he'd pushed me to do I'd liked. Not just liked, loved. But still, there was the principle of the thing. The more I thought about it, the more I realized Dylan deserved to have *his* limits pushed too.

My conflicting mess of thoughts was disrupted by the pleasant woman at the front desk, who smiled and asked, "Miss Bell?" I must have been the only client, because it looked as though they weren't officially open—the hallways were so dim and abandoned.

"Yes," I nodded

"Right this way," she said as she stood, ready to guide me somewhere.

"Excuse me," I halted her. "Could you remind me what services I'm signed up for?"

"Of course," she began, looking down at the paper in front of her. "Our calendar says you've requested our full Brazilian bikini wax."

That fucker. He'd phoned in his directives, and he wanted me completely bare.

My well-engrained script for what happens in a salon prompted me to follow this elegant woman down the hall, but most of my brain was still standing slack-jawed back in the reception area, trying to figure out what exactly I was going to do. It's not that I was opposed to waxing—if I skirted around my outrage for just a minute, I could admit that I was slightly aroused by the idea that Dylan was this focused on my pussy. But there was also the who-the-hell-does-he-think-he-is factor that needed to be considered.

By the time my brain caught up with my body, I was standing in a warm, dark room with a massage table. It was set up like any other waxing room, only more nicely. "Yvette, your aesthetician, will be right with you. Please undress from the waist down, or um, you can just put on one of these robes, and lay on the table faceup. There is a blanket over here if you're cold while you wait."

I pulled together my resolve and lay on the table. Dylan may have gotten me in the door, but he wasn't going to dictate the events that unfolded now that I was here. The door opened, and a tiny, fierce-looking woman with a severe ponytail walked in.

"Yvette?" I asked, before she could even shut the door behind her. She nodded, and we began our negotiations.

When she was done doing her business—and she was *all* business—I felt as though I might need physical therapy to recover. I had been forced to arrange myself in ways I'd never been arranged outside the bedroom, or actually even in the bedroom, although I had a feeling that would soon change. Thankfully, Yvette was fast. Before I had time to fully adjust to the pain, she had finished waxing and trimming and was done. Looking down revealed my version of a compromise—the only

hair remaining south of my neck was a narrow, inch-long rect-
angle above my slit.

When I attempted to pay, I was informed it was all taken care
of. *What a gentleman*, I huffed to myself.

But the bastard knew what he was doing. Since I wasn't wearing underwear, and I was wearing a dress, I could feel every
breeze, every shift in the air, skate over my bareness. I felt insanely wanton. He knew it would feel good. He knew I'd like it,
and there was part of me that hated that he was right. There was
also part of me that loved it.

Chapter 21

Lloyd drove me around the back of the house—the reminders of our non-public status seemed to be constant—and Dylan was leaning in the open doorway, waiting. He was barefoot, wearing sexy-as-hell jeans and a faded grey t-shirt. I could see the outlines of his muscles beneath the soft, worn-in fabric, and I wanted nothing more than to nuzzle into it.

"How very tricky of you, having your henchman kidnap me and take me to get denuded," I said, and smirked at him as I approached.

"How does it feel?" he asked and pulled me closer. "The flush in your cheeks is giving you away. You've never waxed before?" He ran his fingers up and down my back, and then let his hand rest on my upper ass. I wouldn't have been surprised if he was just double-checking to make sure I wasn't wearing underwear.

"I've waxed before."

He laughed with a raised his eyebrow and then leaned down, bringing our faces within a hair's distance. "I'm willing to bet you're wet under that dress, just from having that pretty pussy of yours so exposed."

Holy fuck. How did he know that?

He reached into my dress, placing his whole hand over my sex, and stopped when he ran into the tiny patch of hair. "Lydia?" he looked at me, waiting for me to respond.

"I heard your offer, and I countered." I was speaking into this cheek, and I punctuated my words with a kiss.

"You naughty, naughty girl. Putting me in my place, are you?" His words were barely above a whisper, and he allowed a finger to slide in between the lips and stroke where there'd been hair just twenty minutes prior. I gasped, suddenly desperate for air.

"It needed to be done," I replied and began laying kisses down his neck, getting desperate to move this to the bedroom.

"This is mine, you cheeky girl," he said, still stroking me. "No one else sees this, understand?" I nodded, feeling the flush rise to my face. "Now, I want to see what you've done."

He retrieved his hand and grabbed mine, bringing me inside. I followed him upstairs to the sitting room adjoining his bedroom. The room was dark and warmly lit, bookcases filled the walls, and there was a couch and a couple of leather-and-steel urban-design-y looking chairs. It was a neat, tidy masculine room.

He took my jacket and my bag from my shoulder and deposited them beside the couch. We were standing in the middle of the room, and he reached an arm over his shoulder, dragged the back of his shirt up and over his head, and dropped it on the couch. The back of his hand started at my shoulder and slowly drifted down the side of my body, nudging my breast as it passed and reached the tie on my dress.

"This dress is perfect." He pulled, and the front fell open. He pushed it off my arms, leaving me standing in nothing but my bra and heels. I was warm and cold all at once, the reliable goose bumps rising to the surface. His gaze said nothing but hunger and appreciation. He reached behind me and unclasped my bra, letting it pool with my dress at my feet. My nipples were already rock hard, taut and tiny, perched on my breasts.

He came behind me, and holding my hands, turned me towards a mirror on the wall. He ran his large hands down my sides and rested them on my hips. I'd never looked at myself this way, and I felt so exposed, but also, surprisingly, beautiful. I actually loved the way I looked, wrapped in him. He was making me see my body in a new light. Reaching down in front of me, he gently slid a finger over my bare entrance, and a shiver flew up my spine, making me shift in his arms.

"Sensitive, isn't it?" he whispered.

"Yes. God, your touch is so much, so much more *there*."

"You're too sensitive for us to fuck." I spun around to meet his gaze. *What?*

"Lydia, you're not supposed to have sex for at least twelve hours after you've been waxed."

I pushed him away. "What?" I said harshly. "Wait a minute. A) Why do you know that? That's just weird. But B) why the *fuck* did you have me get waxed tonight?" I was outraged! He'd been on my mind all afternoon, he had me horny as hell, and now he was going to *deny* me?

"Lydia. I know what I'm doing. I wanted to see this." He turned me back to face the mirror, pushed my arms aside and gently outlined the tiny patch of hair with his finger and thumbed it, teasing and sending me flying. I loved the look on his face, how turned on he was. I loved his hands on me—I never wanted them off of me again. "And we'll still play. I promise. I'm just not going to be able to fuck you the way I want to so badly right now." He frowned. "It's never been so hard to keep my hands off anyone before." He said it like he didn't understand it himself.

"Don't," I said. He looked quizzically at me, and I put my own hand over his, locking it in place over my sex. "Don't take them off of me again." I tilted my head back into his shoulder, and his palms moved up to my waist, crossing my belly. I tried to urge his hands back between my legs, but he held firm.

"Ah ah," he scolded sweetly. "Patience, baby." I grumbled, but acquiesced. He rested his chin on my shoulder. "Have you ever been tied up before, Lydia?" His voice was low, but I could hear the excitement. I gulped and shook my head slowly.

"Are you ok with it?" he asked in a whisper. I gulped and nodded.

"You'll have to trust me. And just tell me if you want me to stop." I nodded in understanding, because I *did* trust him, instinctively. He grabbed my hand and brought me into the bedroom. "On the bed, hands and knees, and show me that gorgeous ass." He gestured so that I understood I was to be kneeling parallel to the bottom of his bed. All of a sudden, every cell in my body was on fire. I'd fantasized about being restrained before, but I'd never been sure if it was something I'd actually want in real life. My whole body was screaming at me that it definitely was.

I positioned myself as requested, and I could feel the dampness spreading between my legs, could feel myself swelling in anticipation. Of course, he'd just said he wouldn't be fucking me. What the hell did he have in mind?

"Put your forearms down," he ordered. He left for a minute, fetching something from the closet. "That's it."

He leaned over me and grabbed my upper arms from behind

and dragged them back until they made contact with my knees, effectively spreading my cheeks and perching my butt even higher in the air. I felt so insanely exposed. He dragged a finger through my wet folds, and sighed, "Goddamn, I was a fool to let you get waxed tonight. I so badly want to sink into you." He stood at my side, and I angled my face so I could see him. He was dangling two pieces of soft thick rope in front of me. "This shouldn't hurt, but it will be intense." I nodded. I was practically panting. He proceeded to deftly tie my left knee to my left elbow, checking the knot to be sure it was snug. He repeated the process on the other side. I couldn't stretch out if I tried. I couldn't budge an inch.

"Your ass is so beautiful, Lydia, and I can't wait to claim it." I tensed. He was stroking up and down my bottom, grazing over my anal opening, He leaned over and shocked me when he kissed it, sending a shiver up my back. "Shh, baby. Relax. We're just going to start playing. I won't fuck you there till you're ready." I felt warm liquid being spread between my cheeks. "We have to work up to that. Tonight, I'm going to put this in you." I felt a cool object being slid over my opening. "You'll wear this plug, and I'm going to fuck your mouth. And then I'm going to make you come. You're not going to come until I want you to, understand?" How was he going to stop me? I was so riotously turned on. I was quaking with anticipation, with nerves, with a feeling of *holy shit is this really happening?*

I began to feel him gently work my opening with his thumb and then a finger, massaging it and spreading the warm liquid. Then I felt the head of the plug pressing against me. "I need you to relax, baby. I don't want to hurt you. Breathe and lean into it when you're ready," he instructed, his free hand gently resting on my back. I closed my eyes and exhaled, willing myself to relax into the intrusion. I pushed back against it, and he pushed it into me in equal measure, working it deeper. We repeated this move a few more times; each time he worked it farther into me. "That's right, my sweet girl, take it all." He stroked my back as he pushed the plug in completely.

The fullness was overwhelming. It felt so foreign, so wrong, but also shockingly *good*. All of my instincts said to tense and to push it away, but I settled into it, accepting the intrusion. My heart was racing. He steadied me and smoothed his hand over my ass, caressing my cheeks.

"Good girl, Lydia. You look so beautiful."

He reached around and thumbed my clit. "See how much you like it already? Can you imagine what it will be like when I can come in your pretty ass?" When he talked dirty I could feel the heat in his words, his near desperation. He slipped his thumb inside me, and I could feel how tight it was, could feel the added pressure. It made every touch feel exponentially more intense. I was so close to coming, and I could feel my body tightening, quickening around his thumb, but he withdrew. "Not yet, baby. This time, I go first." He came around to where my face was, and held my cheeks in his palms. He kneeled down and kissed me, and looked into my eyes searchingly, making sure I was ok, still with him. My eager smile satisfied him, and he stood. He slid his jeans and briefs down and I was face-to-face with his impossibly perfect cock.

I tilted my face up and forward, straining for him, but I wouldn't be able to reach him at this angle. All of a sudden I'd never wanted anything more than to get my lips around him. I wanted to give him the blow job to end all blow jobs. I wanted to rock his fucking world with my mouth. I'd never given head without my hands before, but I was completely game. I licked my lips in anticipation and looked up through my lashes into his eyes.

He came around and sat on the bed next to me, my head directly over his lap. He gently placed his hand on the back of my head, guiding me, and used the other to brush my lips with the head of his penis. He got no resistance from me. I opened and swallowed him in. His large hand exerted gentle pressure, and he began slowly and gently entering me, tilting into me, finding his rhythm.

With each entry, I lowered my head farther, took him deeper, guiding him with my tongue to the roof of my mouth, then to the back of my throat. As he exited I flicked my tongue onto his tip and heard him groan in response. I could feel my own body responding, clenching, as I found my own rhythm. I could taste him on my tongue, and I knew he was close. His pace was increasing. He was reaching his fever pitch. As he tried to withdraw on a thrust, I tightened my lips around him and forced him to slow. "Christ, Lydia!" I sank back onto him, and he came fast and hard into my mouth. I swallowed fiercely, desperately trying to keep up as he tilted into me once more. He slowed, and I licked him clean as he withdrew. I knew without a doubt that I had never given a blow job that good before. "And here I was thinking I was the one fucking you," he said. "You blow my mind."

I smiled. "Only your mind?" I let out breathless chuckle. I was giddy with success.

"Thank god you're laughing. You should probably be running from me, but I don't think I'd let you." He came and leaned over me as he untied me, stroking my ass. "You ok?" he whispered. I nodded. "Just accept it, baby. I love seeing that plug in you." The fullness was still so present, and the pressure shifted as he moved me gently onto my back. He took a moment to rub my elbows and knees, massaging the tightness away.

He got on the bed, leaned against the headboard, and pulled me between his legs, my back flush against his warm chest. He grabbed my knees and pulled them towards my shoulders, aligning our legs, knee to knee.

"What are you doing?" I asked.

"Trust me." He took one of the ropes in his hand, and quickly and expertly tied my left knee to his own left knee. He repeated the process on the right and firmly spread his legs apart, bringing mine with them. I was so riotously turned on, the sweet spot between my legs was ringing, begging to be touched, and I was desperate to quell that need. I tried to pull my legs together, to get some control over my desire, but he grabbed my knees and pried. "Relax, baby," he urged. "Don't fight me. I've got you."

I leaned back into his rock-solid chest and took a deep breath, trying my best to relax. The warmth of his body made his earthy sweet smell all the more potent, and it was its own special brand of aphrodisiac, as if I needed any more. I was open and available to him, and there was nothing I could do about it. He elbowed my arms out of his way—there was no way he was going to let me interfere—and he cupped my breasts with his hands. He toyed with each nipple, pinching, kneading, and the sensations shot straight to the apex of my thighs. He pulled at my breasts with my nipples, creating a pinching pain that brought all my blood to the surface. My legs tried to get some purchase on the sheets, and my hips lifted, but he pulled his own legs taut, reminding me of my restraints. I was trying to will him to touch me or gain some control over the mutinous sensations between my legs. When that failed, I attempted to reach my own hand around to touch myself, but he left one of my breasts in time to snatch my wrists. "When I say, baby. You're so impatient."

"Ugh! You're driving me crazy!" I growled at him, and he laughed. My eyes closed, and I turned my cheek into his chest and did my best to writhe beneath his touch. Was he actually going to make me come just by toying with my breasts? He kissed my neck, and finally, as I was sure I was going to combust, he reached both hands down to my pussy. With one hand he gently parted me, and stroked my landing strip with his thumb. With the other he sank two fingers deep into me, stroking my g-spot and pressing against the plug from the inside. Pleasure radiated, pulsing through me. I was right on the edge, and my chest was heaving in anticipation.

"Come for me, baby. You can come now," he whispered, as he finally exerted the perfect pressure to my clit. I unhinged and came apart around him in an instant, my back arching, my legs desperately trying to close to contain the pleasure. He kept them at bay, forcing me to take it all. And the orgasm just kept going, spiraling through me. I was sure it was dying down as I could feel the intense sensitivity rising, but he paused for a moment, allowing it to settle, and then resumed his assault. I couldn't believe it when the orgasm resumed, more intense than before.

I moaned and turned to bite his arm to muffle my own cries. Just when I was peaking—I was sure I was being ripped apart by this pleasure—he reached further back and gently tugged at the plug, and I let it go. As the fullness left me, my continuing orgasm took its place, reverberating through my ass and down my legs. The feeling was otherworldly. I was actually writhing from the pleasure radiating through my limbs. Slowly, I began to come down, completely wasted. Dylan untied my legs from his, and I instinctively curled them up and folded myself into him. He let me, wrapping his legs around me, and he held me tightly to his chest, kissing the top of my head.

"Hush, baby." He stroked my hair.

"How did you?...I never..." Finally, I settled on "God, that was good."

He let go a light laugh. "Good."

"But *fuck*. I think I should be in charge next time."

He chuckled again into my hair as he kissed my shoulder. "What would you do with me?"

"What *will* I do, you mean? I'm not sure yet. Maybe I'll just put you on that horse of yours and send you galloping so I can recover." I sighed into him, my eyes closed in total exhaustion.

"Hungry?"

"Famished. Although I don't think I can move."

He righted us, and hopped out of bed, reaching for his jeans. He threw me a t-shirt from his bureau, and it hit me in the face. I gave him a horrified expression and threw the shirt right back at him, which he dodged expertly. Damn, the man had reflexes. Dylan picked the shirt up off the floor, marched towards me with a grin on his face, and slipped the shirt over my head before landing a kiss to my lips. "Dinner, baby. Come."

"I just did!" I shouted at him as I fit my arms into the shirt and he went into the bathroom. I heard another laugh, and even if I wouldn't admit it then, even if I was patting myself on the back for keeping my cool and embracing our casual fling, I felt a deeper part of me let go and let him in. I was about to fall hard, and somewhere deep inside I knew it.

Chapter 22

After a delicious meal of creamy ravioli and fresh roasted vegetables, eaten on the floor of his upstairs living room, we exchanged stories about teen years and joked about tricking the shopkeeper in the jewelry store. Dylan had nailed the perfect imitation of the snooty couple who'd come in. It was amazing to me that this half-dressed man sitting on the floor with me, telling me about a prank he'd pulled at boarding school, was a highly respected, aristocratic, and intimidating architect by day who scared the shit out of his assistants. It was also hard to believe that he couldn't give me more than just sex because it felt like he was so close to giving me everything.

Without even realizing it, we fell into a deep sleep in his bed. I was so warm and so at home. I woke once in the night and found myself completely enveloped by Dylan, his leg resting over mine, and my whole back pressed firmly against his front. His arm tightened around me, and I drifted back into sleep.

The next time I woke, the light was peeking through the drapes. I was on my back, and I found myself looking up into his very awake, very sexy face. His nose was inches from mine, and his legs were parting my own, spreading my thighs. His two-day-old stubble was better than any cup of coffee—between it and his cock pressing between my legs, I was instantly awake.

"Don't worry—I'm wearing a condom," was the only thing he actually managed to say to me before he thrust into me. Hard. My knees flew up to help accommodate him. Apparently I woke up wet for him, because there was no doubting my readiness. He met no resistance. His elbows at my shoulders, his forearms framing my face, he kissed me hard and deep as he found his rhythm. His possessiveness and his neediness were written all over his body. This was not slow and gentle—he wasn't working me up, he was going to come soon, and hard. He tilted back, changing his angle, and all of a sudden I felt him, right there, hitting me inside in the perfect place, and my body quickly caught up with his. I felt the now-familiar feeling pulse through me, as though a fist inside me began to pull all the strings taut, the rise of desire right at the base of my belly. And we came together, crying out each other's names breathlessly. He stilled inside me, and I threw my head back, arching my chest into his, trying to capture and contain the remains of my orgasm. He returned down to me, kissing me softly on my lips and cheeks. He was still in me when he kissed my nose and said, smiling, "Good morning."

"Good morning, yourself," I said, returning the smile. He withdrew and rolled onto his back, taking me with him. I perched above him as he quickly removed the condom. I curled my knees up his sides, righting myself so I was sitting atop his still-hard cock, nestled between the folds of my still-wet pussy. I put my hands down, fingers spread, onto his chest. "I guess it's been twelve hours."

He reached up and tucked my hair behind my ears. "Indeed."

"That was quite the wake-up call. Do all your sex slaves get that kind of service?"

"Very funny. Although if that's the title you'd prefer, I'm sure it can be arranged."

"As opposed to what? Fuck buddy?" I asked, and his look cooled instantly.

"Lydia, I'm sorry. You know you're more than that, right?" Not this again. How was I supposed to keep my head on straight about us being not being anything more than "just sex" casual fling partners when he said stuff like that? Now, I was getting pissed.

"Am I? I mean, I don't mean to be cold about it, but we should probably be clear on this, right? Call a spade a spade and all that. You said we can't be more, so aren't I? Technically? A fuck buddy, I mean."

He winced again. "Please stop. Just, don't call yourself that, ok? I don't want to talk about this now."

I sat up and looked at him sternly. Even if I *had* just had in- credible mind-bending sex, I needed to get this straight. "Well, I do. Dylan, if you really don't want this to go anywhere, I have to see other people." God, I didn't want to do that, but I needed to see him react. And I also needed to keep him at bay. "I know you like to call me yours and in the heat of the moment say 'you're mine' and all that, but the reality is, I'm not, and you don't actu- ally want that. I can't just be your secret stash of kink forever. I need to, well, I need to protect myself."

Dylan was sitting up now too and looked pissed beyond all hell.

"Bloody hell, Lydia. Come out and say what you're thinking, why don't you. You think I don't *want* that? That I don't want you to be mine? Lydia, *you* don't want it. Trust me. If you need to go out and fuck someone else to keep your head on straight, fine. Fuck!" He was sitting up now, running his hands through his hair, and I slid off of him. "You should, in fact. Do that. Because you don't want my world. I won't see you destroyed by it. And if you feel yourself slipping into it, you should leave."

I could feel the tears welling in my eyes, and I did not want him to see how destroyed I was by his reaction. Maybe I could have been gentler in my approach, but fuck him. I slid off the bed and went into the bathroom, closed the door, and started the shower.

I was standing under the stream, letting the hot water dilute my tears, when the bathroom door opened. Dylan walked into the shower and pulled me to him, so our bodies were flush against each other. He used his fingers to tilt my chin, but I couldn't bear to open my eyes. The tears were still falling steadily, but he brushed them aside, kissed my cheeks, and pulled my face to his chest. He just held me while the water pummeled my back.

"I'm sorry," he started. "I'm so sorry. I never should have kissed you, never should have roped you into this. Especially given everything you've been through."

"How can you say that to me?" I tried to push against him, remove my body from his, but he wouldn't let me. He just held me tighter. "You wish this hadn't even started?" I asked in disbelief.

In that moment, I could feel just how much of myself I'd already let go, so much more than I realized, because every ounce of me was feeling crushed, lost inside his rejection.

"Will you shut it? Let me finish. Of course I don't wish that, but it's probably what I should have done. Christ!" he said furiously, running his hand through his now-wet hair.

"What is it, Dylan?"

He sighed heavily. "Lydia, when I was younger, before Caroline, I had this friend, Grace."

Seriously? Another girl? "A girlfriend?"

"No, never. A childhood friend. Her mother had died. Her prick of a boyfriend dumped her at the funeral, and she was a mess." He paused, closing his eyes and rubbing hands over his face. "She wasn't getting along with her father, and she had nobody. She was one of my closest friends, so I invited her to stay with me at my flat in London while she got some space and figured things out. We'd go out with friends, get drinks—I did my best to cheer her up. I took her on a mini-break, anything to take her mind off it all. And it was working until the press caught wind and went mad." He paused, almost as though he was bracing himself, and when he spoke again his voice was tinged with anger and regret.

"They were horrible. My grandfather had just been on an international tour with the Queen—our family was in the spotlight, and people had noticed that I wasn't a kid anymore. They were speculating about whom I'd marry and what I'd do and all that shite. When I'd asked her to stay with me, it was because I cared, because I wanted to *help* her. What I hadn't realized was that I was no longer free to do that. The paps started trailing us endlessly, saying we had eloped, that she was pregnant, that we'd already had a baby, anything. Everything. She couldn't go to the bloody chemist's without the papers writing about the cold medicine she'd purchased. She couldn't go to work without someone from fucking *Hello!* magazine popping out of a bush. I couldn't make it stop no matter what I did—those heartless vultures must have been able to tell what it was doing to her, but they just wouldn't. Fucking. Stop." He sounded heartbroken, like whatever had happened had broken a part of him too.

I wrapped my arms around his waist, tightening them, wanting to comfort him, even though I didn't fully understand. I hadn't seen any references to this on Google, when I'd searched for him. I wanted to ask him, but I'd have to do it later. I didn't want to interrupt when he was finally opening up to me, finally shedding some light on how he'd become the way he was.

"It finally broke her. She couldn't handle it, no one could have. The scrutiny was oppressive. Finally...Finally, I came home one day and she was in my bathroom, on the floor...God, Lydia, she was gone. No note. She just hadn't been able to take it anymore."

"Oh god. I can't imagine, Dylan." I looked up and his eyes were glistening. This was obviously an incredibly painful memory for him. I gripped him tighter and looked up into his eyes. "Dylan, you know that wasn't your fault, right?"

"Of course it wasn't my fault, but it does mean she shouldn't have come to me for help. I made it *worse*. She had been such a vibrant girl. She was going through some terrible things of course, but it was being with me, around me, that brought her over the edge. My life is toxic, Lydia. Do you understand that? I can't be a haven for anyone—I'm a goddamn war zone."

I looked into his eyes and saw nothing but pure determination—a conviction bred over nearly a decade of him rehearsing this explanation for the tragedy he'd witnessed. It was coated in a thick sadness, an airtight regret. I wanted nothing more than to cut through it, to bring warmth into those eyes in that moment. He gripped my shoulder with one hand and tilted my chin towards his face with the other, ensuring I was focused on him. As if I could be focused anywhere else.

"Lydia, selfishly, I will take you for as long as you let me, but we can't be more, and it has to be private. I won't do that to you. Do you understand? I won't have happen to you what happened to her."

"Dylan, you're older now, smarter about the press. And most importantly, I'm not—"

"No. I won't do it. I won't do that to you." He was shaking, almost imperceptibly, but I could feel it, just below the surface. "That's why Caroline and I got engaged. She's in the same boat I'm in, only far worse. We figured if we were together then at least no one would get hurt. We were both already embedded in this insanity."

The determination remained in his voice, laced with emotion, and I could see now how it had guided him through his adult life. It had probably served him well, keeping the guilt beneath the surface at bay. He'd nearly *married* someone because of it.

"Why didn't you go through with it?"

"It turns out marrying someone you're not in love with is harder than it looks. But, Lydia," he started and then paused, exhaling deeply into my hair as he held me against him. "If you need to date, to see other people, I understand." His fists were clenched and his arms stiff around me. I hoped that meant that it was killing him to say those words, because it was killing me to hear them.

"It can't possibly be as bad as you say. Can't you see that she was depressed, that it wasn't you?"

"Please, stop, Lydia. Trust me. I've been privy to this bullshit longer than you have. And it's just gotten worse. I'm sure you heard about the phone-tapping scandal?" I nodded in confirmation—the British paparazzi tapping the phones of high-profile celebrities and politicians had been international news. "My phone was tapped, and thank god, there was no one in my life that could have gotten hurt. In some cases even the police were helping those crooks—there is no one to trust. It's just gotten *harder* to have privacy, not easier. Less possible to escape it."

"So why not leave it behind? It wouldn't be like this for you in the States, you know. No one would care who you dated."

He paused, dipping his face into the stream of water.

"No one?" He half smiled.

"Well, I live here. Remember?"

"I do. Thank god. But I can't, Lydia. My family... Well, I can't just leave." I sighed into him. It was clear he was not budging on this. "Just stay, Lydia. Stay with me, my way, just a little longer."

And of course I would, even if I shouldn't, because being with him felt less and less like a choice every time we saw each other. I couldn't imagine turning away from him, even if I wanted to. And even if I was hurt by the walls he was erecting between us, I now knew, without a doubt, that he regretted their existence as much as I did.

* * *

That afternoon Dylan had to go to Athens to oversee the construction of a hotel for nearly a week. Trying to remain playful, I gave him an exaggerated pout, but I really was disappointed. Now more than ever, when it felt so clear that our non-relationship had a definite expiration date, I wanted to hold on to him, not let him go. I wanted him to stay.

He'd be back Friday, and in the meantime I was supposed to take full advantage of Lloyd, and have him take me wherever I needed to go, albeit in the incognito Jaguar. This, I protested. "Dylan, thank you, but—"

He interrupted, "I'm not being nice. I won't have you taking the tube, especially late at night. There's no need for you to use the tube at all, actually. This way I know you're safe." I rolled my eyes, but he stopped me with an "I dare you do that again" look. "Lydia, do you know how many stories there are of people getting attacked or groped on the tube?"

"Not nearly as many stories as there are of normal people happily making their way to and from work and life on it every day." He was about to protest, but this time I stopped him. "Public transportation is the great equalizer! It unifies cities, promotes democracy, brings urban access to the masses, safely transporting millions of people every day!" I smiled as I gave him my snarky impassioned speech, and he looked back at me with a smirk and a raised eyebrow.

"Running for office, are we?"

I sighed, abandoning the joking approach. "Dylan, this is important to me. Don't be a jerk." He looked dubious. "I mean it. I love taking the tube. I like walking there with all the other people in my neighborhood headed to work. I like descending the steps in a crowd, feeling a part of the hustle and bustle of this place. I love finding a seat and reading the newspaper over people's shoulders. It makes me feel a part of London. I *like* it. A lot. You're veering over the line, Captain Creepy." He looked surprised, but he also looked like he understood.

"Come on, damsel," he fake whined, "let me at least pretend you need me and my riches." I laughed—he just looked so sweetly pleading. "What about at night? Will you let him take you at night?" he challenged. He wasn't going to give up that easily apparently.

"You mean when Notting Hill is full of cloaked thieves and muggers?" He just looked at me expectantly. "Ugh! Fine! God, you're such a control freak, you know that?"

He was visibly calmer and looking at me so sweetly, just gazing at me, with this Mona Lisa smile on his face. "What?" I asked, dying to know what he was thinking.

"Nothing. Come here." He pulled me into hug, and held me there for a minute. "I really don't want to leave you."

Chapter 23

I took the tube home, on principle, and Dylan grumpily stayed behind to pack and head off for his trip. I spent the afternoon taking care of business. I paid some bills, sent overdue emails, and made lists of things needing to be done. By evening I was feeling like I truly had things in order. A week seemed to be all a girl needed to move to a new city, become someone's kinky fuck buddy, and put her life in order. *Not bad*, I laughed to myself.

I put on my iPod and plugged it into a set of speakers in the kitchen, selecting a playlist of Brooklyn indie bands Daphne's boyfriend, er, now ex-boyfriend, had put together for me. I turned the volume way up, and with a glass of wine in hand, I got to work on dinner. I truly enjoyed moving around the kitchen by myself, barefoot in my panties, which I'd recently come to treasure, and a tank top. For the first time, possibly ever but certainly since losing my dad, I felt completely free. I can't say I was perfectly happy—I knew that everything Dylan had disclosed to me presented a real barrier, but I also knew he cared about me. Even though nothing was settled upon or firmed up, really in any area of my life, I still felt like I was right where I was supposed to be. I was doing it, putting myself out there. Living life to the fullest.

Maybe it was knowing that this overbearing gorgeous fiend had completely awakened me sexually. Maybe it was the fact that I was finally living in a town I'd always dreamed of. Maybe it was simply being far away from my old self. I put on my fancy new earrings and had my dinner at the kitchen island, my feet dangling off the high stool, and not really caring why.

* * *

In spite of Tubegate, I allowed Lloyd to pick me up early Monday morning, because I'd made a doctor's appointment to get myself on some birth control. I was as happy as Dylan was at the prospect of abandoning condoms—I now understood his compulsion for removing the barriers between us.

When I was back in the car clutching a prescription for the pill, a clean bill of health, and the latte Lloyd had brought me, I felt my phone ring.

"Hi," I said shyly when I saw it was Dylan. I couldn't believe myself. Couldn't I at least try to sound as though him calling me didn't make me completely melt?

"Morning, damsel," he said in an impossibly sexy way.

"Morning. Where are you?"

"I'm about to walk into a meeting here. Did you go to the doctor?"

"Yes, although I'm sure you knew that already," I said, catching Lloyd's eye in the rear view mirror.

I think I could actually hear him smiling. "Well, Lloyd is my driver. Is it a crime that I know what he's up to?" I guffawed au-dibly into the phone. "Doesn't it count that I asked as though I didn't?" He was definitely smiling. "Are you ok? You sound a lit-tle off."

"Fine. I, um, have my period."

"Oh. Sorry?"

I rolled my eyes. "It's ok. I just have cramps. Anyway, we're good to go in a week."

"Good timing. Are you sure you have to go to work? I'd pre-fer you just go home." Oh good god.

"Dylan, don't be ridiculous. You know you sound insane, right?"

"I do," he replied in a way that clearly conveyed he didn't give two shits if he sounded crazy.

"Well at least there's that." I wished he were here with me, al-though if he were he might want to get up to some adventures that my body just wasn't up for at the moment. "Don't you have a building to go supervise or a kingdom to rule or something?"

"In a minute." Lloyd was pulling up in front of my office. "What are you wearing?"

"Seriously?" I said through my laughter. "You really want to know? Or do you want me to make something up? Tell you I'm going to work in nothing but a negligee?"

"No. Don't lie. I'll call Lloyd and find out if you do. I want to be able to picture you." God—he wasn't *acting* like someone just using me for sex.

"Well, I'm wearing a navy pleated skirt, which ends around the middle of my thighs. A blousy ivory-colored silk camisole, and a cropped brown leather jacket. Nude flats. A necklace. Anything else you need to know?"

"Is your hair in that sexy ponytail?"

I laughed again—did he miss nothing? "Well, I don't know about sexy, but yes, it's in a ponytail. Dylan, I should go. It's almost nine fifteen, and I have a feeling it's going to be an insanely busy week. The fashion show is only two weeks away, and—"

"I know. I've gotta go too, baby. Be good."

"You too."

When I stepped out of the car, I saw Josh leaning against the building smoking. His jaw dropped when he saw me exit. "Well, I can't *wait* to hear about this." Shit, how was I going to explain being dropped off and picked up in a chauffeured Jaguar?

"Oh, it's an Uber. I'm super crampy today." I clutched my abdomen. I knew the mention of menstrual business would end the conversation quickly.

"Say no more, lovey. Although, damn. That was the nicest Uber I've ever seen." I was going to have to ask Lloyd to pick me up around the corner. This could get tricky. All the more reason he shouldn't be driving me to and from work in the first place.

Monday morning flew by without a hitch. Hannah was incredibly pleased with how the museum party had gone. She'd gotten several calls about the gown, her Fashion Week show was sold out, and she'd heard the *Times*, the *Guardian*, and several foreign papers planned on covering it. It was all hands on deck. It was clear that we'd all be working late nights to see us through.

Fiona and I were working feverishly on fielding client calls and scheduling fittings with the models. I was just about to ask her about breaking for lunch when Josh came through the door carrying a white paper shopping bag, "Delivery for *Miss* Lydia Bell." He eyed me suspiciously. "Did you order lunch from Quaglino's?" Josh was clearly trying to assess how he had missed the fact that I was the type to order in extravagant lunches to work, and Fiona looked at me for an explanation.

"Huh. Um, let me see that." I took the bag and looked in. There was a container of some kind of chowder, some bread, and what looked to be some kind of chocolate concoction.

Dylan! Gah!

"Um, yeah I've heard my friend talk about this restaurant, and I wanted to try it. Thanks, Josh."

I was going to have to get better at lying on the fly. How did he expect me to keep us a secret if he kept inserting his own upscale life into my own? Not that I didn't appreciate it. Josh darted back to his desk, and I grabbed my phone and texted him:

MONDAY, 12:45 pm
Any ideas for how to explain a fancy surprise lunch delivery to my coworkers?

MONDAY, 12:46 pm
Make something up. I don't want you going out.

MONDAY, 12:47 pm
That creepy line we talked about? You crossed it. Back away from the line, Hale.

MONDAY, 12:47 pm
You're maddening. Fine.

MONDAY, 12:48 pm
You're forgiven, but no more work surprises that I have to explain. When you get back, you can treat me to lunch. In person.

As soon as I hit SEND I realized that we couldn't have lunch out in public together.

Fuck. Foot. Mouth.

MONDAY, 12:48 pm
I mean . . . you know what I mean. Sry.

MONDAY, 12:48 pm
It's ok. Talk to you later. Enjoy your last lunch delivery, damsel.

God, this was a messed-up situation. I mean, sure I loved that he wanted to send me lunch, but it wasn't fair. He couldn't demand that we keep emotional distance, be this massive secret, but then bend the rules on his terms.

If I wasn't allowed to act like his girlfriend, it didn't feel fair that he could act like my boyfriend, sending me presents at the office whenever he wanted. If he wanted us to stay this casual just-sex thing, the least he could do was help me out and refrain from acting so damn sweet. I wanted to scream at him to make up his mind—were we nothing or were we something?

But every time I tried to think straight about it, or even try to hold on to my anger, images of us tied together in his bed invaded and I sank into a sexy daydream. Fiona interrupted my reverie. "Um, what is *that* smile about?" *Shit.*

"Oh, nothing," I replied, trying to sound as blasé and back-to-business as possible. "Let's get these fittings scheduled."

"Not so fast. Did you hook up with someone? You look different. You definitely look like you've been shagged, and recently." I blushed instantaneously. Dammit, why did I have to be the most transparent person on the planet? Fiona clearly interpreted my hesitation as confirmation, because she enthusiastically continued, "Ohmygod. You have! Who?! Is that who lunch is from? You have to tell me everything!" She dropped the papers in her hands and looked at me, riveted. What was I going to do?

I cleared my throat. "I *may* have had some action this weekend, but it wasn't anything really. I don't think I'll see him again. The lunch is from him, but I'm not that into it." Nothing could be further from the truth.

"Um, the way you just smiled while looking at your phone would suggest otherwise."

"No, no. I just went out and had some fun. I'll tell you if it turns into anything. I promise." Ugh, I hated lying. "Plus, I am drowning in period cramps today. I don't think I ever want to get intimate with anyone ever again. I feel hideous." Diversion.

"Aw, bless. Poor thing." She said while giving me a distinct no-sympathy look. "We have a ton to do, so get your face out of that chocolate and let's get to work."

At six p.m. we took a break to order some supper. I texted Dylan, missing him more at the realization that there was still an entire week to get through before I'd see him again.

> MONDAY, 6:03 pm
> Working late. Probably won't head home for a couple of hours. How are you?

> MONDAY, 6:05 pm
> Do you feel up to it? I'll have Lloyd come get you at 8? Things fine here—work work work.

> MONDAY, 6:06 pm
> Yes, please (thank you!) And feeling fine. Hope it's all going smoothly. Talk later.

While everyone finished up their Thai food in the conference room, I went to the bathroom—I was exhausted and counting down the minutes until it seemed appropriate to head home. As I passed through the reception area, I caught a glimpse of Josh's computer and saw that his browser was open to a gossip page, the website for *Hello!* magazine.

It took a moment to register what I was seeing. I'd been drawn to the picture of Dylan—even though I hadn't known him long, I'd know that suit, that body anywhere. But the thing I didn't expect was to see him walking next to another woman. It was clear from the Greek writing on the side of a passing cab that they were in Athens, and they were walking down a posh-looking street together. Him and Amelia. Smiling. With his hand firmly placed on her back.

Chapter 24

The headline of the article read, "*Has Top Bachelor Dylan Hale Finally Found his Lady?*" It looked like the picture was from the previous evening. Was this why he didn't want me to leave the office today? He thought I'd see this picture spread across every news agent?

I was furious. I couldn't help it. Couldn't he at least have given me a heads-up? Were they actually dating? Was I his sweet little thing he was keeping around on the side for kinky kicks while he started to a build a public life with Amelia Fucking Reynolds? Was everything he'd told me the day before total bullshit? I didn't think so, but then what the hell? This was so humiliating. I suddenly felt like the pathetic mistress in a made-for-TV movie.

* * *

Lloyd drove me home in silence. He asked me how I was, but I couldn't pull off much more than a brief polite response. When

I walked up to my door I saw another huge bouquet of flowers—even more gorgeous than the last—and I brought them inside, practically slamming them on the table. The card read,

Here's to skin on skin. Feel better. —DLWH

Did I even have a right to be mad at him? I did. I know I did. I felt like I did. Maybe it wasn't what it looked like, but it felt like that's what it was. Why even bother telling me there'd be no other women, when he was just going to do this?

All I wanted to do was sink into a steaming bath with a glass of wine. I was crampy, tired, and now annoyed. I missed Dylan, in spite of my fury, but in this moment, I missed Daphne more.

I heard my phone vibrate with a text, but I didn't want to deal with anyone, especially not Dylan if that's who it was. I'd get to it when I'd get to it.

A while later, as I let the hot water strip away the day, I heard the phone, perched on a wooden stool in the corner of the bathroom, buzz again. And again I ignored it.

I was postbath but still in my towel, sprawled across my bed, when it buzzed a third time. Then it started ringing. I willed myself to ignore it. I flung my arm over my eyes, just hiding. Within a minute, I could hear the sound of a voicemail registering. What would I achieve by ignoring him? I'd never been good at hiding my feelings, and he'd know I was angry the minute he heard my voice. I grunted in frustration at my inability to resist.

I grabbed my phone and sank right back into the bed. There were three texts and a voicemail, all from Dylan.

MONDAY, 8:00 pm
Home? Get some rest, baby. Athens is boring without you.

MONDAY, 8:41 pm
Lydia? Are you ok?

MONDAY, 9:23 pm
Goddammit, Lydia.

I listened to the voicemail, which contained no actual message, but I could hear a trail of expletives before the message ended. Just then the phone starting ringing again. I answered this time.

"Lydia?"

I didn't say anything.

"Are you there?"

"Yes."

"What's wrong?" Oh please.

"So, Athens is boring, huh? You needed to spice it up with some female company?"

"Amelia. This is about Amelia," he said, sounding instantly irritated. My silence was a clear confirmation. "Lydia, Amelia is a family friend, and I have no interest in her. I told you this."

"A family friend who desperately wants in your pants, whom your mother desperately wants you to marry, and whom you allowed yourself to be photographed with, when you're never photographed with anyone. I feel like you're asking me to trust you, but you tell me you don't date, and then I feel like an asshole for believing you when I'm faced with evidence to the contrary in the freaking newspaper!"

"Ok" He sighed in resignation. "I'm sorry. Let me explain. Christ, I'm not used to this." I heard another longer sigh. "I had to go to a dinner last night with the investors in this library project, one of whom is Piers Reynolds, Amelia's father. He must have told her he was meeting with me, and she came along. Or hell, I wouldn't be surprised if my mother told her. I didn't know she was going to be here. She made a fool of herself all evening—it was completely inappropriate for Piers to have his daughter there, but I'm a gentleman, Lydia. I wasn't going to make her feel bad, and we've known each other a long time. We had a pleasant conversation. We left the restaurant together, and I gave her a ride to her hotel. That was it."

"Dylan. I'm not saying you should be mean to her, but can you imagine how this feels? What this seems like? You've given me six versions of the 'no dating, no public' speech, and you've made it perfectly clear that we'll never be together, that the buck stops with our agreement that we'll fuck like teenagers and then move on. Then I see your photo, her photo, the two of you so *together*, so *public*. I felt like a fool."

I heard him sigh yet again on the other end, and it seemed like a full minute passed. "I'm sorry." He said the words quietly, and they sounded almost foreign coming from his mouth.

"I could just…Well, if you know a photograph like that has been taken, or if you see it in the paper, I'd prefer it if you were the one that told me about it. Finding it on my own and you not telling me made me feel like you were keeping it from me."

"Lydia, the truth is I let them photograph us."

"What? Why?" His apology had tipped the scales in his favor, and now I was instantly hurt all over again.

"To throw them off your scent." Was he serious? What, were we in some kind of caper movie now? "You've been at my house a couple of nights. You and I left that party together—who knows who saw, and then there was the Market. I want to protect you from those vultures, Lydia. If they want to think I'm dating Amelia Reynolds, they can goddamn well think that. She'll be thrilled about the media attention, and she's used to it. As long as it's not you they're harassing, I don't give a crap what they think." I was taking this all in. "Lydia?"

I understood what he was saying and why he was saying it, but I didn't like it. What one was supposed to say in this moment is that it was ok, but it wasn't. Not really.

"Lydia?" he asked again.

"I hear you," I said. "Can you understand that the world thinking you're dating Amelia isn't exactly my ideal solution to this problem? Can you imagine how else this might unfold? If you feel compelled to feel me up in public again only this time someone photographs *us*? Now I actually am an American harlot."

"I would never let that happen."

"Right. Well…" I could fight about this all night, but it wasn't making me feel any better. I felt completely torn between wanting to hang up on him and wishing he were right there in my bed with me.

"You're still mad."

"I'm hurt, Dylan. And mad."

"You need to trust me on this. I just want to protect you." He sighed again as he said it. I wished I could see his face, could try to decipher what he was actually feeling.

I didn't want to fight anymore, but I didn't want to be the first one to give in either. I contemplated what to say as I rolled under the sheets.

"What are you doing?" he asked after another long beat.

"I just had a bath, now I'm lying in bed."

"The bath? That has real possibilities. I can think of a hundred different ways I could make this whole thing up to you." I smiled in spite of myself.

"Actually, I still feel kind of lousy, and I'm cold."

"Baby. Turn the heat up. Stay home tomorrow."

"Dylan, I'm fine. It's not the 1950s. I'm not staying home because I have my period. Oh, and that reminds me, Lloyd is going to have to drop me off a block away from work if he takes me again. Josh saw me get out of your car this morning, and he was obviously suspicious as to how I had upgraded from the tube to a Jaguar overnight. I'm just telling you so that when you call Lloyd and ask him all about where I've been, you already know the answer to that one."

"You know me well." I wasn't so sure, but maybe I was starting to.

"Where are *you*?" I asked. "Shouldn't you be off schmoozing?"

"I was supposed to be, but then my trying damsel in distress decided to get her knickers in a twist. Knickers she shouldn't even be wearing."

"Personally, I think it was your knickers that were in a twist, and they still need some straightening out," I replied, and he let go a resigned chuckle. I could practically hear him cracking his neck, trying to release the stress. "You're there to work. Go. And I do trust you, Dylan." I was eighty-five percent sure that last sentence was true. Maybe ninety.

"Thanks, baby. I...I'm sorry about the photo, Lydia, but honestly, I'd do it again to keep those assholes at bay. Get some rest, baby. I'll be back soon."

* * *

Tuesday and Wednesday flew by in a flurry of activity. Most of the days were spent at Hannah's studio readying the models and working on fittings. We were all there late every night, ordering in takeout and blasting music as we worked to get everything in order for fashion week. It felt like theatre, like summer camp, like we were on some crazy ride together. I was loving every minute.

Dylan provided continuous evidence that he was thinking about me. He texted religiously. There were fresh flowers on my doorstep daily. He'd found me a yoga studio, and booked me a class on Tuesday morning. Of course Lloyd had driven me, and there had been a yoga mat and all the accessories waiting for me in the car. He was thinking about me, making gestures, his version of an apology about Amelia ringing in loud and clear.

The yoga studio was in the Primrose Hill neighborhood, and we passed the park on the way. It was the closest I'd gotten, but I still wanted to sit on that hill in the sun and try to imagine my parents there, be in the place they were happy. I had imagined it would be the first place I'd go when I got here, but I was in my second week, and it hadn't happened yet. Maybe I'd get there this weekend, but I was beginning to think I'd rather go alone, and I had a feeling Dylan would keep me occupied once he got back from Athens.

Thursday night Josh, Fiona, and I were still working with Lucy, one of the assistant designers, at 6:45, and we decided to order dinner in. I quietly texted Dylan to check in, and he replied immediately,

THURSDAY, 6:47 pm
Let me know when you get home safely? At stuffy benefit.
Wish you were with me.

THURSDAY, 6:48 pm
You wouldn't be bored if I were there. But I'm here, wearing my panties. And there's nothing you can do about it.

THURSDAY, 6:50 pm
You miss my palm on your ass, do you? We can take care of that soon. But on second thought, I want you wearing panties when I'm not there. No one but me needs easy access.

THURSDAY, 6:51 pm
And I thought you were a gentleman

THURSDAY, 6:51 pm
You thought wrong. Gotta go.

Getting to Friday night was torture. Dylan said he'd be back that night, and in the meantime minutes passed as hours. Ever since Dylan Hale had come into my life there was a permanent knot of desire in my belly, an ache between my thighs that made me edgy and alert. It never seemed to dissipate. If I was lucky I could hold it at bay, but if I so much as thought of him, I felt myself dampen. As much as I loved the idea of going out with my new friends, and I knew I needed to, I didn't know how I'd make it until the end of the night, and I still wasn't sure exactly how and when I'd see him.

"Do you have a good clubbing dress, Lydia?" Josh asked, as we were leaving the office. I'd agreed to go clubbing with him, Fiona, and one of the designers that night. He was looking at me like this dress business was a very serious matter.

"Um, I'm sure I have something. Tight? Short?"

"Definitely." Josh confirmed. "And, Miss Bell, you have the perfect little bod to pull it all off. Seriously, how do you stay so fit? I saw you inhale that fancy lunch. Where does it all go?"

I shrugged. "I told you—cocaine! Plus—" I pointed at my chest "—no boobs to speak of!"

"Oh shut it. Fine, keep your diet secrets to yourself. Also, so many guys dig little boobs."

"He's right," interrupted Fiona. "These enormous things are a blessing and a curse." Fiona was well-endowed to say the least, and she completely pulled them off.

"Ok, Lydia," Josh said, clearly impatient to get to the fun part of the evening. "Go home and find a frock. We meet at Fiona's in two hours. Takeaway, cocktails, I'm going to go crazy on your makeup." Well, at least this would be a good distraction until Dylan got home. I sent him a quick text letting him know my plans and hoping that somehow he'd become a part of them. Fighting while he'd been away had made me even more eager for or reunion.

I waved goodbye and turned to walk towards the tube, but as I rounded the corner I saw Lloyd smiling at me. What was he doing here? He gestured down the street, and I could just see the bumper of the Mercedes peeking out from a driveway. I all but ran towards the car, and as I approached I could see those long lean legs through the slightly open car door. My heart jumped from my chest right into that car. I was deliciously aroused in a heartbeat—his mere presence catapulting me from on edge to totally fucking ready.

Chapter 25

I leapt into the car and crawled eagerly into Dylan's lap, straddling him as he shut the door behind me. He laughed. "Miss me?" His hands immediately went to my shirt, untucking it, and finding the bare skin above the waistband of my skirt.

"Desperately." I rested my elbows on his shoulders and put my hands in his hair, gripping. I wanted so much to be kissed, but not being able to wait, I knelt down and sank my mouth onto his. He immediately returned the favor, prying me open with his tongue, giving soft licks to my palate and rimming my lips. He grabbed my lower lip between his teeth, bit gently, and pulled.

"I should go away more often," he said, smiling seductively.

"Please don't."

"Or I should just bring you with me. This would have been fun." His hands were pushing my skirt up my legs. He reached my ass and paused when he had a run-in with my thong. "Tsk tsk." He grabbed the elastic and it snapped against my hip. "Naughty girl. Let's rid you of these, shall we?" Thankfully

Lloyd was standing back on the sidewalk, and the tinted windows and alley walls meant we were mostly protected from the wandering eyes of passing pedestrians. He grabbed the lace on each side and slid the thong off one leg, as I hitched it up, and then the other. He fisted them and put them in my purse. "I'm going to have to hide your knickers, Lydia. I don't intend to leave you long enough for you to ever need them again."

Fucking hell, I was saturated with desire. I could feel my blood humming through my veins—all sounds and sights beyond Dylan faded into the background.

"Kneel up, baby." I looked nervously outside the rear car window.

"Don't worry, I told Lloyd to wait outside, and no one can see us." Reassured, I complied and rose, allowing him to access his zipper and free his thick hardness from his briefs. He reached into his pocket and retrieved a condom. "Three more days of this bullshit." His impatience was evident as he tore through the wrapper with his teeth and handed it to me. I slid it on as fast as I could, trying to speed every second that was between now and when he would be firmly inside me. "Impatient, are we?" He was smiling. "Ok, baby, I'll take care of you. We can do this fast, because the truth is I can't wait either. But later we do this my way, understand? I need to get you back under me. And soon."

"Whatever, boss man," I replied, and without waiting for him, I grabbed his cock and sheathed him with my waiting sex, sinking him deep, taking more of him than seemed possible.

I was instantly relieved and let out a low moan. I wanted to stay just like this, being possessed by him and possessing him, forever. He took over quickly. "Hands on my shoulders, baby." I obeyed without hesitation. "That's right, now lift yourself a little." He let out his own moan as I shifted over him. "That's my girl."

I suspended myself on my knees a fraction, steadying myself with his shoulders, and then sank onto him. He used his hips and raised and lowered me to create a punishing ferocious rhythm. This was so physical, so intense, and I could hear my own moans escaping. I wanted nothing more than him, harder and faster. He was relentless, and as much as I wanted him, it was clear this time was not about slowly cultivating pleasure. He needed to get off and soon. And so did I. In confirmation, he hissed through his panting uneven breaths, "Touch yourself, baby. Find your way. I'm going to come soon—keep up."

I reached down and found my clit between my fingers, but I didn't need much to catch up—I was so ripe and ready for him. His muscles strained through his sleeves as he lifted and shifted me back to perfect the angle, power and control emanating from every inch of him. Finally, he rammed into me, pulling me down deep, and he stilled inside me as he came. The desire was radiating through me. I had come, but I still felt that needy ache in my belly.

"God, Lydia, in my fucking car? What's wrong with me?" I started to move off of him, but he held me down. "Where the hell do you think you're going?" He pulled me into his chest. I paused and took him in.

He withdrew and swiftly removed the condom, tying it off and shoving it back into its wrapper and into his pocket. Holding me by the waist, he looked into me and tucked my stray strands of hair behind my ear.

"You're so fucking sweet." He reached between us and slid his hand down to cup me. "And I know you need more." I gasped as he quickly filled my still throbbing pussy with three of his fingers, pulling me taut and drumming against that sensitive spot inside me. "Your hungry, sweet pussy is perfect."

I tilted my head back, taking him in. He felt so good. Then he slid his other hand behind me and pressed his thumb against my rear opening. "And so is this."

Holy shit.

He gently pressed against the opening, working it slowly with his thumb and the dampness from my pussy. The dull ache became ferocious again. He was working me back up, and it was happening fast.

"Oh god, Dylan, I—" I felt so wanton, so sexy, so desirable under his touch. I'd never loved my body more than when he was touching it, commanding it. As soon as I felt like I was close, on the brink, he pulled back. "What? No, Dylan, please, don't stop. I need your hands on me."

He grinned seductively. "Should I let you come? You're leaving me for the evening. Do you think that's fair?" Ugh, he was so cruel. I needed him now. I was in a state of total desperation.

"Yes. No. I don't know. Oh god, please, Dylan. Please. Please let me come." My hair fell over my face, and I put my forehead against his. "Please. Pretty please." I gave him the sweetest plea I could muster in my current state.

He laughed. "Well, how could I deny that?" He reached back and resumed his assault and unraveled me again. His expertise was astounding. He knew exactly how to work me over. There was no doubt he knew my body better than I did. He brought me to the surface within seconds, had me clawing at the window, gasping for breath, and feeling myself convulse. I lost control of my body completely, flying headfirst into my orgasm.

As I came down, I leaned my head into his chest, and cleared the hair from my face, tucking it behind my ears again. He was smiling and planting light kisses on my cheek. "It's so fun to make you come," he said, stroking my cheek with the back of his hand.

"The pleasure was all mine—I guarantee it."

"No, baby. Your pleasure is all *mine*, and don't you forget it."

I looked up at him, curious at his sudden possessiveness, and gave him a lifted eyebrow. "Don't get too crazy there, mister," I said, giving him a permissive smile.

He smiled back, but then said, with a plea, "I know I said you should date people, but can I ask you not to? I know it's not fair of me, but Christ, Lydia, the idea of you with someone else makes me livid. Can I have you to myself? At least for a while?"

"Dylan. Don't be an idiot. I'm yours, and you know it." I was being honest, and it made him smile and hug me fiercely in return. But my admission was also said with a sigh, because I knew deep down that I should be dating other people. I was handing myself over without hesitation, offering my heart to him on a silver platter. And while it certainly wasn't freaking him out, he also wasn't making any moves to return the favor. This could only end with my heart breaking.

He put himself away and pulled my legs in front of him, covering me with my skirt and cradling me in his lap as he knocked on the window, clearly his signal for Lloyd to return to the car. Lloyd smoothly navigated the streets of London back to my house. I could barely walk to the door, but I let us in, dropping my bag as I entered. I yawned and leaned into him again.

He laughed. "Sleepy? How are you going to go clubbing in this state?"

"I'll be fine." I yawned again.

"Come, take a disco nap."

"No, I'll never wake up again."

"Trust me—I'll make sure you wake up."

He carried me to my bedroom, and stood me up. I had begun to lazily unbutton my blouse when Dylan put his hands over my own. "Let me," he said softly. I dropped my hands, closed my eyes, and stood still as he undressed me. He freed my hair from its ponytail and ran his fingers through it. He tucked me into bed, and then surprised me as he sat down next to me with his laptop. "I'm going to work for a bit. Sleep now. I'll wake you." He stroked my arm with his fingers, and before I knew it I had drifted off.

Chapter 26

I woke a half hour later to Dylan's erection at my back, still fully clothed. "Time to wake up, baby," he whispered.

He rolled me onto my stomach, and I tried to shake my grogginess. My arms were stretched out behind me at my sides, my fingers grazing my thighs, and suddenly, Dylan lifted me by my hips and pushed my knees beneath me. In a matter of seconds, he had positioned me to his liking. I wasn't even awake yet when I felt his palms stroking my bare ass. "Lydia, I think you need a reminder of who you belong to before you go out tonight. I want to mark this ass, and I want you to enjoy it, understand?" Well, he was definitely getting my attention. "Have you ever been spanked?"

Now I was definitely awake. As promised. "Not by anyone but you."

"Those weren't spankings, baby. Those were hints of what you're about to get from me. This is all about pleasure, I promise. You want this?" *Holy shit.* This was really going to happen. I was wide awake now.

"Yes." I sucked in my breath and licked my lips in anticipation.

One hand held me firmly at my hip, and all of a sudden the other hand was gone. It landed firmly and squarely across my ass cheek. My back clenched and my head flew up as I tried to adjust to the feeling. He placed his palm in the center of my back and held it for a moment, stilling me. "Shh, baby. We'll do fifteen." He was in full-on dominant mode, and it was hotter than hell.

He resumed, shifting his strikes from left to right, soothing my ass between the blows by running the cool back of his hand over me. Each one seemed to resonate deep in my belly. They hurt, but not as much as they were turning me on, and the pain was welcome. It spoke right to my desire, like a scratch to my itch, fueling it and soothing it at the same time. I'd never imagined that this was what this would feel like. My clit was begging, pleading for his attention. The slaps felt like teases, each one readying me more for him. I was wishing and hoping that his fingers would at least graze me, as each sting brought me closer and closer to an orgasm that was promising to blow me apart.

How did he know? How did he know this was going to do this to me? Did he see right through me from the beginning? Did every woman like this?

I could hear his ragged breath behind me, and could feel that he was in his own sensual rhythm. Finally his hand stilled, and he began peppering my ass with gentle kisses. "Look at you, Lydia. You look glorious." He took his fingers and tested my entrance. I was practically dripping, and I could feel him withdraw, soaked in my dampness. "And you loved it, baby. Look at you, so ready for me."

He flipped me over onto my front and looked straight into my eyes.

"Holy fuck, that was incredible," I said, barely being able to catch my breath.

He smiled knowingly. "God, I can't wait to be inside you." He dropped his pants, quickly sheathed himself, and entered me hard and fast, slamming into me deeply.

"Knees up." I obeyed, and he pressed my knees into my shoulders, exposing my entire bottom to him and allowing him deeper entry. He entered slowly and became more deliberate in his assault. He leaned back, angling his thrusts so his hardness connected directly with the sensitive bundle of nerves inside me. With each entry, the dull ache vibrated and pulsed, pushing me towards my climax.

"You're close, baby, I can feel you." I clenched around him, trying to gain control over the onslaught of pleasure. "Let go, Lydia. I want to feel you come all around me."

I stopped trying to control it and released, letting my body fly away into the intense earth-shattering orgasm. He was undoing me, more and more each time he was inside me, making me more and more his, making the idea of ever doing this with anyone else seem more and more remote.

He leaned over me, twisting me into him, so we were lying tangled in my bed. He looked into my eyes, stroking my cheek tenderly. "Are you ok?"

I smiled up at him. "Yes." But I was also shocked. I had just never expected to have a reaction like that to being spanked. It was so crazy good, and I had *needed* to be fucked by him afterwards. My pussy had been aching for him. I opened my mouth to tell him more, but I stopped. I didn't want to interrupt this moment—he looked so insanely pleased. He was radiant.

"What?"

"I just didn't know."

"Didn't know what?"

"That I'd like this so much. That I'd *want* you to spank me, to be so bossy in bed with me, that it would turn me on so much…and—"

"You're wondering what it says about you?" I nodded. He did get it. "All it says is that you are open. That's it. You're strong, you're receptive, you're delightful, funny, accomplished, and open. And you're all mine." He was emphatic in his possession.

"Could you see that I'd like this from the beginning?"

"I hoped." He thought for a minute. "And when I kissed you in Canada, I could feel how turned on you were, even though I was being my domineering asshole self. But Christ, Lydia, when I saw you in that bikini, I've never wanted anything more in my life." I grinned at his admission and he continued to gently stroke my ass, his hand a cooling balm for where he'd spanked me. "Now, let's get you into the shower."

I gave him a frustrated pout. I still had an ache for him. He shot me a disapproving glance. "Don't give me that look. I know you want more, but you'll have to wait, baby. It's getting late, and you're the one with other plans. Not me."

He luxuriated over every inch of me in the shower, paying careful affectionate attention to my ass. When we got out he filled his hands with lotion and ordered me to face the mirror. "Hands on the sink. Bend over, let me take care of you." I complied, and he gently rubbed the cream into my ass. It felt heavenly. "Sore?"

I shook my head. "I'm actually more sore here." I looked down and pressed my thighs together.

"I'm breaking you in." He smiled.

"In so many ways." I stood, and let him place his hands on

my hips as he stood behind me, both of us naked, looking in the mirror. He stroked his hand down my arm, and I leaned back into him. We stayed that way for a moment, just long enough for me close my eyes and think about how I didn't want to be anywhere else.

* * *

Josh, Fiona, and I stepped from the cab and into the glowing lights brightening the entrance to the club. Dylan had gone off, promising to see me later. I was feeling somewhat self-conscious in a dress that Daphne had insisted I bring with me, but which I had never actually worn—a mini brightly patterned dress that hit above mid-thigh, but was otherwise rather demure with three-quarter-length sleeves and a modest neckline. This dress was all about the legs. I left my hair down, and accessorized only with a pair of gold heels and a black clutch.

Josh looked the perfect hot companion in a very fitted suit, and Fiona sported a tight dress that fit her like a glove. Lucy had apparently arrived early and was already on the dance floor. "Let's do this!" Josh gave a battle cry. Then he clutched my arm as we entered the club, "We are going to find a perfect proper chap for you to take home tonight, Lydia."

Oh lordy.

We managed to get ourselves drinks and were hanging on the sidelines taking in the scene. Before long we made our way to the dance floor, and I lost myself completely in the music, the four of us dancing together. Perhaps it was the third drink, the much-needed disco nap or having been spanked and actually enjoying it, but I felt refreshed and quickly submitted to the music.

I hadn't been dancing in forever, and it was the perfect balm after a long week.

Every ten minutes, Fiona or Josh would lean over and point out some good-looking suited guy, but I managed to distract them or find some flaw, make some excuse. I figured they'd eventually give up. I looked at my phone and it was well after midnight. I'd slowed down on the drinks, but I really needed a rest from the dance floor. My feet were positively throbbing. I looked at the large banquettes and tables longingly. They were apparently reserved for those purchasing extremely expensive bottles of alcohol, which were a few notches above our pay grade, so I'd have to settle for leaning against a pillar. I was there for a moment, and Josh had gone to get a refill when I saw Michael, my next-door neighbor, approaching with a smile.

"Well, hello there, Lydia. I see you found the hottest spot in town."

"Hi!" I shouted over the music. "Yes! How are you? This place is wild!"

"It's a favorite among my friends, but it gets to be a little much as the night wears on." He looked around, and we took in the increasingly drunk crowd.

"I can see that."

"Can I get you a drink?"

"No, no, I'm fine. Thank you. I'm just taking a break."

"What about a date?"

Had I heard him correctly? "What?"

"A date. You know. I'd pick you up. We'd get dressed in our smartest. I'd take you out for dinner. Chatting, laughing, eating more than we should. A date." He was smiling.

My mind was reeling. It was so strange to hear someone asking me out on a date when in my mind I was dating someone else, someone who would never take me out for dinner. I mean dating is what I *should* be doing. I must have waited too long to respond, because eventually he just said, "How about just a dance, eh?"

I shrugged my shoulders, "Ok. Just one, though—my feet are killing me." He gave me a big smile, and all of a sudden I felt guilty. I didn't want to lead him on. *It's just a dance*, I told myself. Josh was approaching, and I signaled him, making my intentions clear. He gave me a huge thumbs-up and skipped off to find Fiona and Lucy.

I followed Michael onto the dance floor, and we took to the music. It was a fast song, thankfully, and I attempted to keep some distance. He grabbed my hip, and I let him for a moment, but then I raised my hands and tried to pull some moves that made touching me more difficult. I was so uncomfortable. The whole thing felt so wrong.

Finally the music shifted into the next song, and I leaned over and half screamed, "Thanks for the dance!" with a smile. I signaled that I had to use the bathroom and walked away. I headed towards a set of stairs that promised toilets at the top, but as I got close I saw a familiar imposing figure leaning against the railing, just out of the light.

Dylan did not look happy—a combination of frustration and something else marred his features. He grabbed my hand firmly and practically dragged me beneath the staircase, so we were hidden, our faces lit only by the pulsing lights of the dance floor. I was leaning against a wall, and Dylan was leaning over me, tension radiating from every muscle.

His face was stern, and his jaw was locked shut. His eyes didn't contain a hint of threat; instead, they were searching, scanning me with an infuriating combination concern and frustration. "Who the fuck was that?"

Chapter 27

W hat are you doing here? Couldn't you just text and let me know you were coming?"

"I did. You didn't respond." Shit. I hadn't felt or heard my phone in my bag. "But I'm talking about that dance. Who was that?"

"I'm sorry about missing your texts, Dylan. I am, really. But that *dance* was nothing. It was a distraction. Do you know how many dances I avoided tonight? Josh and Fiona were trying to throw me in the path of every guy in here. They were starting to think I was crazy or celibate! That *dance* was the exact same thing as a photograph with Amelia Reynolds. How dare you come in here and act all affronted when we're this giant secret? When we're *just sex*. What else do you expect me to do?" My arms were crossed, and I was deploying my best angry eyes and pursed lips at him.

He sighed and ran his hand through his hair. "Are you done?"

"No. Dylan, you can't stop me from dancing—"

"You told me there wouldn't be anyone else," he said, all of a sudden looking more wounded than angry.

"Dylan, you have to trust me! I wasn't going to do anything but dance, and if you were watching surely you could tell that I wasn't enjoying myself. You must have been able to tell that there was no threat." I looked at him with my best "come on!" look. "Do you really think you have two legs to stand on after the Amelia photo?"

He sighed in resignation and ran his hand through his hair again, his frustration showing. "I wanted to go over there and tell that arse that you were with me…I…" His voice was trailing off. I could barely hear what he had said. He seemed so torn all of a sudden. "Plus, Lydia, that guy wants in your pants."

"Don't be ridiculous. He's my next-door neighbor—he was just being nice." I didn't totally believe it, but Dylan had nothing to worry about.

His eyes widened. "He lives next door to you?" *Crap.* "Lydia, it's obvious that he likes you. Admit that, or I won't ever let you go home alone again. Ever. I dare you to see if I'm joking about this." *Christ.*

"Ok," I retreated as I spoke. He clearly needed to be reassured, and there was no getting around him. "Yes, he flirts. But you have nothing to worry about. Remember, baby? I'm yours." It was the first time I'd used the term of endearment with him, and I could tell instantly that he liked it.

He sighed heavily, as though he forcing the uncomfortable feelings out with his breathe. "Thank god for that. Shit. I'm sorry, baby. I…" He held me tightly to his chest.

He didn't get a chance to finish his thought before my phone beeped audibly, and we both glanced into my purse. How convenient that now I could hear my phone. Dylan's hand left my ass and grabbed my phone, showing me the several texts that had come in from him, and I rolled my eyes at him. But the latest one was from Josh.

SATURDAY, 12:59 am
Where are you? We're at the downstairs bar.

Dylan sighed, and I could feel some of his tension falling away. "Are you ready to go?" he said as he released me. I nodded, grateful.

"I'll just text." I wrote Josh and Fiona.

SATURDAY, 1:01 am
Was in bathroom. Exhausted. I'm gonna grab a cab and head home.

Dylan had been looking over my shoulder, "They're not going to let you just go get a cab by yourself are they?"

"I'm not getting a cab by myself. I'm going home with you, you idiot."

"They don't know that," he said in frustration. His fierce mood had been replaced by concern. Just then a text came in from Fiona.

SATURDAY, 1:03 am
We're all ready to go. Meet at entrance.

I looked up to Dylan showing him the text. "What should we do?" I wanted so badly for him to just decide that this secrecy wasn't worth it, that I was important enough to him to be with publicly, and we could just go home in his car together.

"Have the taxi drop them off first and then bring you to mine." I frowned. I didn't want to leave his side.

"Isn't that a little excessive?"

"Better safe than sorry, baby. It won't take long." He pulled me close, and his hands were now resting on my ass. He reached down and pulled up the hem of my dress, and cupped my bare ass. "This dress is too short, but I love it. You're right here for me."

I looked at him for a moment, giving him a "seriously?" look and raised eyebrow. I felt my phone vibrating again—Josh and Fiona were clearly waiting for me, and I was too tipsy to form a coherent argument.

"Go," he said. "I'll see you soon." I sighed and kissed him before I turned and left.

* * *

When the car finally pulled away from dropping off Fiona, it was after two in the morning. The alcohol had fully caught up with me. I texted Dylan to let him know I was on my way. When the car pulled along the side of his house, he was there to open the car door, and I practically fell into him. He paid the driver, and lifted me into his arms.

"'Snot necessary," I slurred and halfheartedly tried to fight my way out of his arms.

"You're completely legless. Let me get you inside." I surrendered into his arms. He carried me inside and upstairs and stood me up in front of the couch in the sitting room adjoining his bedroom. There was a warm fire going, and I saw a glass of water on the table. He unzipped my dress, and it fell to the floor. My eyes were closed from exhaustion the whole time. He carefully removed my bra and shoes, and pulled me down onto his lap on the couch. He handed me the water. "Drink up." I complied, and he pulled me into him.

"Are you still all worked up about Michael?" I asked, my eyes closed.

"Michael? Is that his name? No, Michael is not the one I'm worked up about," he replied while laying gentle kisses in my hair. I started to doze off, my skin warmed by the fire, and he leaned in close. It was barely above a whisper, and I wasn't sure if it was a dream or reality, but I heard "I missed you" right before I drifted off.

* * *

I woke in the middle of the night in Dylan's bed, my back flush against his front, under the thick duvet. I needed the bathroom badly, and I tried to extricate myself without waking him. I lifted his arm, but he wrapped it back around me firmly. "Dylan, I need to use the bathroom." He grumbled but let me go.

I stood in front of the mirror and marveled that I didn't feel worse. It was four thirty in the morning, so maybe I was still drunk. I drank down another glass of water, and used Dylan's toothbrush to brush my teeth. I found some painkillers in a drawer and swallowed them—anything to ease the inevitable crap I'd feel like tomorrow. My face was a wreck, so I took a moment to wash it, gently massaging my eyelids to rid them of the smoky eye makeup Josh had painted on. When I opened them, Dylan was in the doorway, naked.

He pulled me into him, and I could feel his erection growing. "Back to bed." He was oozing sex, and suddenly I felt very awake. I jumped up and wrapped my legs around him, taking him by surprise. He let out a laugh, and said, "You're feeling bold, aren't you? I might have to rein that in, little one." He slapped my ass and took me back to the bedroom.

He laid me on my bed and slid in next to me, pulling the warm duvet around us. "I know you're tired, Lydia, but I can't wait. You feel ok?" I looked up at him and smiled sweetly, giving him my consent. I heard him get a condom, then he rolled me away from him, so we were spooning, and he lifted my top leg with his hand. He positioned himself at my entrance, and slowly, gently fed himself into me. He was slow and patient, holding me to him as he took me from behind, on our sides. He held my breasts, and caressed my belly, curling around me and touching me gently everywhere. This time it was his tenderness that turned me on more than anything. The orgasm brewing in me was slow and steady, but no less powerful. Finally, he reached around and began massaging my clit, as he continued to thrust deeply into me.

"Come with me, baby," he whispered sweetly. He worked us both up and over the edge, and I reached above and behind me, putting my hands into his hair and pulling his face over my shoulder to bring him closer. It was the first time that it almost felt more like making love than fucking. There was no doubt in my mind that there was no other place he'd rather be.

He stayed in me for a long moment and then slowly withdrew to dispose of the condom. When he returned, he held me just as close. Even though the sun was beginning to creep through the windows, he whispered, "Sleep, baby. Sleep," and we drifted back off together.

* * *

When I woke again, Dylan was sitting in bed next to me, working on his laptop. There was a coffee and a croissant on the bedside table. I pushed myself up, and started to take the covers with me. Dylan closed his laptop firmly, placing it next to him on the bed, and swiftly yanked the covers down from my chest. "No covering up." And he pulled the covers away from my bottom half as well, staring appreciatively. "Especially now that you're waxed." He was grinning.

I hit him with a pillow. "Dylan!"

He tried to duck and block me with his forearm, but I got him square in the forehead, and Dylan Hale actually giggled. "I like you here in my room. Completely starkers," he said, smiling, observing. "How do you feel?" He reached over and handed me my coffee.

"Fine, actually." Which I didn't deserve after last night. "What time is it?" I asked.

"Twenty past eleven." He replied, looking at his large gold watch, which by the looks of it had probably cost more than my college education. "Why? Have any plans I don't know about?"

"No." I wrapped my hands around the warm mug, and looked over to the Adonis next to me. "So now that you have me here, with no clean clothes, what are you going to do with me?"

"Oh, I'm sure I'll think of something." Just then his home phone started ringing, and he reached to pick it up, giving me the universal shush sign, a finger to his lips. Obviously I was not supposed to be here.

"Yes…Good morning, Thomas." He sounded irritated to have been pulled away. "It's not a good time…He wants to meet today? Did you ask if it could wait until Monday?…I see." He rolled his eyes, at poor Thomas presumably, and not at me. "Wait, what?…Goddammit. Fine. Tell him I'll be there…The

Goring, twelve thirty. Thank you, Thom—…What?" Clearly poor Thomas had more than one message to deliver. "Tristan Bailey called again? Fuck that weasel…No, no, I'll deal with it." He looked at his watch and sighed.

He put down the phone and looked at me. "Well, we don't have as much time as I thought, baby. I'm sorry. I have a command performance work lunch in just over an hour." I could feel my frown settle in. He returned to the bed, leaned over to me, and brushed my lips with his thumb. "Don't worry, I'm going to make good use of this hour. Lean back against the headboard." Who needed coffee when I had Dylan barking orders that set every cell in my body on fire? I immediately complied as I readied myself for whatever kinky sexual foray he had planned for me.

Dylan fluffed the pillows behind me. He slid up next to me and pulled the duvet over our laps—what happened to being *starkers*? He put my own coffee back in my hands, and then he reached over to his bedside table and grabbed the Saturday papers and began rifling through them.

I was looking at him, confused, my coffee cup frozen in my hand, when he looked back to me and asked, "What?"

"Um…Nothing, I guess. I just assumed 'making good use of this hour' was going to involve some orgasms."

He smiled broadly. "Later. I can't remember the last time I lazed in bed with the papers, and I've never done that with a gorgeous naked woman next to me."

I smiled at him, loving this new side of Dylan Hale. "Hand me the *Guardian*."

After indulging in our domesticity for as long as we could, we showered and I began getting ready to go home. I was standing by the bed, untangling my rumpled dress, when I felt his damp warm body right behind me.

"Now, before you get dressed, come here." He urged me closer to the bed and leaned into my back with his chest. "Forearms on the bed, and present that pretty ass to me, Lydia. I've got something for you." I knew that tone of voice, and the *something* he had for me probably, hopefully, involved moaning, begging, and a handful of *oh god*s.

"Don't you have to be somewhere?"

"Lydia," he said in a warning tone. I sighed and did as I was told. A moment later, I felt the spread of warm lube beginning to run between my cheeks. I gasped, and Dylan began to run his fingers down the crack until he found my anal opening. "I'm going to put this plug back in you, baby, and you're going to wear it all day, and think of me. Understand?"

Holy shit. Was he serious? "Dylan…I—" Was I even going to be able to walk with it in?

He must have been able to hear my concern, because he reassured me. "It's going to feel good, baby." He was working the opening with his finger, and then the tip of the plug. "Breathe, Lydia, just relax. Trust me." I breathed deeply, closed my eyes, and opened myself up to it, and he worked the plug in, in small thrusts. It felt so full, so intense. "Good girl. Now it stays there until I take it out."

"You are one kinky bossy sex fiend, you know that?"

"I do, but I also know you're totally into it," he whispered in my ear from behind me.

* * *

Dylan dropped me at home before going to his lunch, and I spent the afternoon trying to distract myself from the foreign object up my ass, which was, much to my surprise, seriously turning me on. I'd been here two weeks, and I still hadn't properly stocked the shelves or gotten fully settled. I put on a bra, finally, and headed to Sainsbury's market, which thankfully was only a short walk away. I texted Dylan to let him know, in case he arrived while I was gone.

SATURDAY, 1:05 pm
Grocery store run.

SATURDAY, 1:07 pm
I doubt you're running anywhere.

SATURDAY, 1:10 pm
Very funny.

SATURDAY, 1:11 pm
Making you wet though, isn't it?

SATURDAY, 1:13 pm
I don't need a butt plug for that.

SATURDAY, 1:15 pm
Don't come without me, Lydia. That's an order.

SATURDAY, 1:15 pm
I can't believe I ever compared you to a knight in shining armor. Perv.

SATURDAY, 1:16 pm
I am actually knighted.

SATURDAY, 1:16 pm
Of course you are. Get your ass back on that horse and back to me asap, knighty.

SATURDAY, 1:16 pm
KNIGHTY? KNIGHTY?!

SATURDAY, 1:17 pm
You heard me.

SATURDAY, 1:17 pm
As soon as I can, damsel. Hold tight;-)

SATURDAY, 1:17 pm
Not funny

Chapter 28

An hour later, I had chopped the fruits and veggies and taken the first bite of my salad when I heard the front door open. I entered the front room to see Dylan, closing the door behind him.

"You need to lock the door, baby. I'd expect a Brooklyn girl to know that."

"Maybe I was distracted." A plug in the ass could do that to a girl.

"I'm not kidding, Lydia." He really wasn't. The look on his face said this wasn't a joke to him.

"Ok. I'll remember next time."

"Good." He exhaled and visibly relaxed, as though he could check that item off his list. "Now—" he was suddenly back in the moment "—come here." Without hesitating, I walked directly into his arms. He reached behind me and, pulling up my skirt, brushed the end of the plug, pushing on it lightly, and I gasped in response. "How do you feel?"

"Full."

"You're about to feel fuller." *Oh my god.* Was he really going to fuck me with the plug up my ass? He shed his jacket, placing it on a kitchen chair. "I've been thinking about this for the past three hours, nothing else."

He pulled my shirt over my head and unhooked my bra, leaving me only in my skirt. He grasped me under my arms and lifted me, spreading his large hands across my bare back. I wrapped my legs around his waist—it was habit now. He held me by my ass, his hands under my skirt, and carried me over to the couch.

He placed me down and quickly removed the rest of his clothing. He sat down, placed me on his lap, and pulled me in close, burying his face in my hair. "I missed you." He said it as though he were surprised by it and wasn't quite sure what to do with the information. Then he urged me up. "On your hands and knees, baby." I did as I was told.

"I missed you too." I said it to the sofa, almost embarrassed to look at him, feeling like I wasn't supposed to have those feelings for him yet. Ever. He reached forward, grabbing my hair that had fallen in front of my face and tucking it behind my ear, and he placed a kiss on my cheek.

He climbed behind me on the sofa, and I heard him open a condom. He stroked my back once again, gliding his fingers over the end of the plug and then into the folds of my sex.

He lightly rubbed my entrance with the head of his cock, stroking, teasing. "This is going to be intense, baby. You're tight without the plug, but with it, you're going to be fucking majestic." I was raw with desire—an afternoon of being teased and distracted by anticipation, and I was going to break the moment he entered me. He began to push into me, and I was completely overwhelmed. I hadn't understood what he meant by tight, but I did now. I felt like I could barely accommodate him.

He slowly and deliberately sank into me. I had to get accus-

tomed to the invasion, to his total possession. Slowly he began moving in deep leisurely thrusts. The feeling was exquisite,
and my blood pumped at an almost musical beat. We found
a rhythm, and I lost myself completely; the world, my house,
everything but Dylan dropped away, and our bodies were completely in sync. A sweat broke out on my forehead and across
my chest as I rocked into him, taking him fully and deeply. Each
thrust came with a slight pain accompanying the increased pressure, but it was welcome—it accented the razor-sharp pleasure
perfectly, marking my admission of him. I could feel every slight
movement, as though we were making love in slow motion, and
it felt shockingly intimate. That we were so in sync, so perfectly
matched in our movements heightened everything that much
more. The whole thing, this crazy heated dance, was more than
the sum of us. His hands were stroking my sides and then gently palming my breasts. He was being so gentle, so slow. I felt
his warm cheek against my back and a kiss before he rose again.
I felt more vulnerable in this moment than I ever had before.
My body began to quiver, quaking with the inevitable onslaught.
His hips were meeting my ass with gentle pressure, and we could
both hear my wetness with every tilt of his body. He picked up
his pace, and my body rose with his.

"I can feel you perfectly. Come with me, baby. Come." He
was so quiet, as though anything greater than a whisper would
have been more than either of us could handle, would have
risked disrupting this moment. As we both collapsed into our
orgasms, I arched my back, throwing my head up, trying to take
him as far in as I could, trying to register every sensation. I was
literally vibrating with pleasure. And he withdrew the plug at
the peak of the riot, sending the waves of pleasure reverberating even further into my body. Being freed from that intrusion

so suddenly, after hours, was a sensation unto itself. I fell back into him, the orgasm still sending ripples through me. He pulled back and entered me again, slowly but with determination, and he stilled, deeper than he had ever been.

My heart was still pounding in my chest, and I was reeling from what had just happened between us. He lightly kissed my back, and I was so comforted by his huge hands spread over my hips. He slowly withdrew, and taking both of us by surprise, I turned, pushing him against the arm of the sofa, and crawled frantically into his arms. I wanted nothing more than for all of us to be to touching in the wake of that intimacy. I needed my mouth on his. I kissed him aggressively, fanatically.

"Baby, are you ok?" He pulled me away and he saw the tears in my eyes.

"That was so intense, so…It was so unexpected, Dylan. I didn't know I could feel this way."

"Hush, baby. I know." He stroked my hair. "I'm pushing you too hard."

"No, no. I can't get enough," I cried as I buried my face in his neck.

Dylan removed his condom and then returned to me, reaching for a throw blanket and covering us, laying us down into an entangled mess. He stroked my back, and I felt myself calming down, but I still felt like somehow the sex we'd just had had stripped me bare and pushed my feelings for him to the surface. We were drifting off, just curled up into one another, and I wanted to tell him. I wanted him to know that I was falling for him, but I was too scared of those feelings to be honest about them with myself. I was too scared and too aware that it wouldn't matter. I could feel my chest opening, my heart opening. I could feel myself wanting him in a way that scared the shit out of me. He was pulling me into a place where there was no hope, or all hope, I wasn't even sure. Before I had the chance to overanalyze, we were in a deep nap.

* * *

I woke to his palm under my chin raising my sleepy face to his own, looking me in the eye. "Enough sleeping."

I grabbed his wrist and looked at his watch; it was nearly six p.m. "Do you have to go anywhere?" I asked, hopeful that the answer was no.

"Nowhere but back in you." I feigned shock, and he chuckled in response. "Not yet. Now, I'm hungry."

I was struck by an idea. "Can I cook for you?" He raised an eyebrow. "I've just been grocery shopping."

"Should I be worried?"

"No!" I slapped his chest playfully. "I'm a good cook. Just keep me company."

I grabbed his blue button-down shirt from the floor and put it on, and I threw my hair into a ponytail with the tie around my wrist. I put some music on the radio and I went to work. He came into the kitchen, donning his briefs and nothing more, and leaned into one of the counters to watch me cook.

"Do you have any wine?" he asked, as he tapped his fingers against the lip of the counter.

"No, I'm sorry. I'm not well prepared for company I guess." I shrugged apologetically. "Wanna go out and get some?"

"I'm enjoying watching you dance around this kitchen in my shirt way too much. I'll have Lloyd go pick some up."

I frowned. "Is that in his job description?"

"Baby, trust me, Lloyd is very well compensated. It's all part of his job description." He picked up his cell phone but then looked at me. "What are we eating?"

"Tagliatelle with prosciutto, parmesan, gruyere, and fresh peas."

He raised his eyebrow at me, impressed, and turned into his phone and gave Lloyd a list of several bottles of wine to pick up.

I looked at him skeptically, my hand on my hip. "Are you going to get me drunk?"

He leaned across the counter and grabbed an apple out of a nearby bowl, chomping into it as though he was settling in for the show of watching me cook. "I might as well get you stocked."

I came up to him at the counter, and he opened his chest, spread his arms, invited me in. The water was coming to a boil for the pasta, and my fingers were dusted with cheese. I leaned into him, soaking him up. He ran his fingers through my hair, and I buried my forehead into his chest. He was kissing me on the top of my head when the doorbell rang.

"That was fast," I said, looking up at Dylan.

"That's not Lloyd." He looked down at me, almost as if to ask me to explain.

I shrugged my shoulders and moved to go answer the door.

"Uh, Lydia. You can't answer the door like that."

I looked down and was reminded that I wore nothing but Dylan's dress shirt and laughed at the idea that I nearly answered the door that way. I ran upstairs and came back down, buttoning my jeans as I took the steps two at a time. The doorbell rang a third time. I peeked into the kitchen but didn't see Dylan. He must have been hiding. I swung open the door and found myself face to face with Michael. *Shit.*

"Hello there, Lydia." His smile was large. I felt naked, braless in Dylan's oversized shirt and my just-fucked ponytail. "You obviously got home ok last night."

I smiled and wrapped my arms around myself. "Yeah, no worries." He made a move to come into the house, but I half closed the door. "I'd invite you in, but it's actually not a great time."

"Oh." He stepped back. "Sorry, I just—"

"No, no." I hated lying and felt bad kicking him out. "It's just, I'm hungover, you know?" I tried to wipe the post-coital glow from my face and willed the dark circles under my eyes to get darker.

He looked relieved by my excuse, clearly buying it. "Totally understand. Shall we get dinner this week?" *Double crap.* This guy wasn't going to give up, was he?

"I'd love to. We'll make it happen." I saw Michael opening his mouth, getting ready to try to firm up plans. "So I should go. I'm sorry. I'm meant to call a friend in the States in a few, and I really do feel under the weather."

"Of course." He stepped off my stoop. I feared I hadn't been discouraging enough, but at least I was getting rid of him for the moment. "I'll see you soon, Lydia."

"Absolutely. Have a good night, Michael." I closed the door behind him and leaned up against it, sighing from relief.

Dylan stepped out from the hallway. "Persistent lout, isn't he?"

"He is." I was relieved he was gone, happy to be getting back into my playful evening with Dylan.

But he was no longer playful. I was met with solemnity. "Let's eat. We're going to my place after dinner."

"What? Why?"

"I don't trust that guy, and you forget to lock your door."

I rolled my eyes and was about to argue, when he interrupted me. "I'm serious. I'm not leaving you near him."

"You're ridiculous. Plus, even if there *were* a threat, you're here to protect me." But as soon as I said it I realized he wasn't. He wouldn't protect me—not that I even needed protecting—because no one was supposed to know he was here, that he was with me. He was powerless as long as we were a secret. This was the first time it bugged me, really bugged me. If he was so jealous, so possessive, why not just tell people we were together? It was beginning to feel like he cared more about us being a secret than he did about me. The secret felt like he was just keeping the wheels greased, so he could slide out of this non-relationship as easily as he'd slid in. Secrecy meant he always had an easy escape route, and a small part of me sank at another reminder that we were a temporary casual thing.

He ignored my comment and headed back to the kitchen. I quickly finished putting together dinner, while Dylan laid out plates. He brought the wine in from Lloyd, but we didn't open a bottle. We ate quickly, and I packed an overnight bag. It felt like we were on the run from a harmless goofy neighbor.

Chapter 29

It was eight thirty when we got back to his house. When we walked in the door, he kissed me, but there was nothing to it. He kissed me the way someone does automatically, while they're making lists in their head or, I don't know, designining buildings. Like I didn't even have to be there for it

"I have to work. Make yourself at home—there's a television in the lounge by the bedroom. I might be late, so go to sleep without me." His tone was distant and cold, dismissive.

"You're being an asshole."

"What?"

"You heard me."

"Lydia—" He looked at me like he was pleading for me to just let him be that way.

"You are. I'm going to go upstairs and watch something funny on TV. I'm only staying because I *want* to be with you, and I *hope* that at some point over the evening you realize how ridiculous you're being about Michael."

"Lydia, I have to work." He said it as though I'd misunderstood why he was being distant and weird. But I hadn't.

"If that were true, then there'd be no reason for me to be here with you."

* * *

I had no idea what time it was when I rolled over sleepily, looking for a clock, but I ran straight into the firm wall of Dylan's naked chest. It was the middle of the night, and I'd woken with a deep need for the restroom. I must have fallen asleep on the couch, but somehow I'd ended up in the bed. I was wearing one of Dylan's t-shirts, which had ridden up, and I pulled it down as I shimmied out of bed, trying not to wake him. When I came back, he was leaning up on his elbow and patting the spot I'd just occupied next to him.

"Come back to bed."

I just stood by the side of the bed, waiting. When I'd gone to sleep I was still annoyed with him. Now I didn't know what I felt.

"I woke because you left. Come back."

"What was going on with you tonight?" I started, staying in place by the side of the bed. "This afternoon we had the best sex we've ever had—you were incredible—and then this evening you acted as though I was an annoying kid sister you were forced to look after. You were so...cold."

Dylan sat up and sighed, running his fingers through his hair. "Can we leave it at me feeling out of my depth and not handling it well? You absolutely deserve more of an explanation than that, but...Christ." He groaned and fully rubbed his hands over his face, like some kind of tug-of-war was unfolding inside him. "I hated not being able to…Lydia, I've never felt that way before."

"What way?"

"Helpless," he said, and he swallowed hard as he spoke. He was looking at me like he still felt that way. Helpless. Like by simply telling me how he felt he'd been stripped bare before me. I probably should have pressed him, but I didn't need to. I may not have fully understood what had made him feel that way, but I knew with total certainty that, if anything, we were closer than either of us had expected to be. The question was whether it would matter in the end.

* * *

We showered together in the morning, and Dylan was fully back to being his attentive self. We didn't have sex, almost as if we were giving ourselves a reprieve after our intense encounter the day before. I brushed and dried my hair, pulling it into a messy side braid, which I could just pull off with my shoulder-length hair. When I emerged from the bathroom, he handed me my jeans. "It's cool outside today. Do you have a sweater?"

"Are we going out?" I asked as I rummaged through my bag for my old NYU sweatshirt.

"Yes. I'm taking you out of here for the day. And we'll be outside." He looked out the window as he said it, eyeing the grey skies. "I think the weather will hold."

"Where are we going?" I slipped on my jeans and oxfords. I was reaching for my long-sleeved t-shirt, but I stopped when I saw Dylan emerge from his closet in those perfect jeans and a t-shirt that draped over him perfectly.

He came up behind me, wrapping his arms around me. "I'm

not telling," he whispered and unbuttoned the jeans I'd just put on. He slipped his hands down the front, cupping me in his hands. "No panties. Good girl." He slipped first one and then two fingers into me, massaging me.

I surrendered to his touch, leaning back into him. I reached my hands up into his hair, gripping and pulling it between my fingers. "Two fingers. Good boy." I grinned, and felt him grinning into my hair. I was instantly damp, and he spread the wetness, allowing him easier, more fluid strokes. His fingers found the delicious sweet spot inside me, and I felt myself tremble under his touch, the sensation spreading down my thighs, weakening me.

"That's right, baby, come into my hand, Lydia. I want to feel you," he whispered. I clenched around him as he thumbed my clit, propelling me completely into the intense white space of my orgasm. I couldn't believe how quickly he could bring me so deeply into pleasure. My eyes were closed, and as I came down from my orgasm, he dragged his hands up my body, pulling me into him. "I love making you come, baby. I could do it all day."

"Sounds ok to me." I was still half groaning, luxuriating in the wake of my orgasm.

I could feel him smiling into my back. "No." He buttoned up my jeans and gave me a playful slap on my ass. Next thing I knew he was across the room, throwing my t-shirt at me. "Get dressed, baby. Let's go."

* * *

I found him in the kitchen, pouring coffee into two to-go mugs, and handing me a piece of toast. He looked almost excited. He grabbed his keys from a hook on the wall, and we walked out the back door. It was unseasonably cool, an early hint of fall in the air.

"Where's Lloyd?" He was nowhere to be seen, and where the Mercedes had dropped us off the night before there was now a tall black Land Rover.

"Day off. Just you and me." He opened the passenger door for me before rounding the car to slide into the driver's seat. He pressed a button and all the mirrors and the driver's seat automatically shifted and calibrated to him. He fiddled with the controls on the steering wheel and the Rolling Stones started humming through the speakers. "Ready?"

"For what exactly? Are you taking me to like a seventeentht-century English theme park where all the women obediently follow around their knighted menfolk?"

He punched me playfully in the leg, and I shrieked and laughed. "Very funny." He then reached to my side and tickled my belly, throwing me into a total fit.

"Stop! Dylan! Stop!" I was going to pee my pants if he didn't relent. "Please! Seriously! Dylan!" He finally stopped, but he was glowing with victory. Bastard.

He expertly navigated the city streets, and we were quickly on a highway headed out of town.

"So tell me more about what happened with Caroline. " He winced at my question, but I wasn't going to back down. I wanted to know more.

"Didn't Google give you all the details?"

"All I saw was that you were engaged. The palace didn't seem enthused and the press billed it as some kind of rebellion on her part, which strikes me as odd, given how accomplished you are."

"I wasn't then." He half winced, clearly not wanting to remember something. "I don't like talking about that part of my life." His eyes were on the road as he spoke.

"Can you just give me some highlights? I want to know you."

"You do."

"I want to, like, know the shit out of you. Like if knowing Dylan Hale were an Olympic event, I'd compete for the USA and win against all the other Knights of the Templar or whatever." He looked at me skeptically. "Please?"

He touched my thigh and sighed. "Fine. It's not easy to explain to someone outside my antiquated world, but I grew up with a lot of…duty. Obligation. Titles don't mean much to me, but they do to my family, and it was drilled into me to keep up appearances. There is a lot of responsibility involved in being a Hale."

"That sounds heavy, and kind of boring if you're a kid."

"Boring was the least of it. One of my earliest memories was my mother and father putting me on a horse, decked out in the perfect little riding kit, and I was terrified. Absolutely terrified and crying. But they told me it was my duty to know how to ride. Duty is a weird concept for a four-year-old."

"God." I suddenly thought of all of the warmth in my own childhood, the total lack of fear. But I also thought, for the first time in a while, about my mother. What would it have been like to have had her too? There were moments, flashes, when I felt aware of not having had my parents, not in the way others had theirs, and this was one of them.

"Yes. I mean, they're not heartless people. They're not, really. But their priorities are just different. All of their life choices haven't really been choices, they've been about what's proper and expected. Well, for the most part. Anyway, none of the snobbery that my parents have has ever come naturally to me."

"You say that like it's a bad thing."

"It is to them. They can't stand that I haven't secured the title. It kills them that I haven't guaranteed that there'll be an eighteenth Duke. Anyway, so when I became friends with Grace and others who weren't from our world, my family didn't look on it kindly. And when she got hurt by association, I realized they'd been right in their own way. I shouldn't have let her in."

"Dylan, that's—"

"Lydia, stop. It's true. I realized that all of their snobbery had a purpose, that there were certain realities about my life, whether I liked them or not. I stopped caring, I got into fights. There were drugs, a lot of drinking. Mostly stupid rich-kid antics, nothing I'm proud of. And I wasn't alone. We all knew the rules. We were the offspring of titled aristocracy and London's big players. And as our antics moved from school to coming-out balls and then to benefits and Ascot and the rest of that bullshit, it became front-page tabloid news. Caroline was the culmination of all that."

"This doesn't sound like you at all. And I still don't understand what happened with Caroline."

"Getting into mischief with some asshole son of a notable family is uncomfortable gossip, but Caroline is royalty. She understood, better than me, what lay in store for us. It was her idea. She figured if we weren't going to have any choices in our lives we might as well plod through it with a friend. And when she and I started to date, the media took notice. They were everywhere. We were photographed on vacation." I recalled the references to nude photos in a tropical locale. "Eating breakfast, in uncomfortable positions at clubs. In the States it may be movie stars, but here and on the continent the tabloids are fueled by aristocracy, royalty, socialites. It's its own tawdry brand of celebrity."

"Weren't your parents pleased?"

"They would have been if we hadn't been doing everything in our power to act out. We weren't exactly following standard royal engagement protocol. The palace did as much damage control as possible, but it became clear we were making life hard for everyone. I think we both knew we'd never be happy that way. We did try to make it work, but I just didn't love her like that." I was silent, but I reached out for his hand. He wouldn't look at me, but he let me hold him in this small way. He stopped, reflecting. "I just don't like who I was then. I don't want you to know that man.

"Anyhow," he continued, "she and I finally decided it was a bad idea. But it's still my reality. Hers too, of course."

"What do you mean?"

"I don't have a choice, Lydia. I've figured out how to have as free a life as I can without hurting anyone, and it's worked so far. I'm an architect, which is mine. I earned it, and I can do it my way. My grandfather was key in that, by the way. You once asked me if he and I were close? Well, he was my only real ally. The only person who understood that I *wanted* to work hard and build something." He glanced over at me thoughtfully for a moment. "He would have adored you." He paused for a moment before continuing, staring at the road ahead of him. "My parents think architecture is an indulgence. But the rest of it, well…"

"So what? You'll marry someone of their choosing eventually?" There was bite in my words, no matter how I tried to hide it.

"No. I won't marry at all."

"Or date."

"That's right."

"Or have children."

"If it can be helped."

It was so sad. He really believed that love was closed to him, that a life with people in it was something he wasn't allowed.

"I don't understand how you became so successful if you were so busy being this bad boy. How'd you pull it off?"

"I'm lucky. Talent helps—I just get architecture, and I love it—and hard work gets you far."

"Can I ask you something about Grace?" I was going to take total advantage of this openness. I felt like I had somehow caught him in a confessional state.

He sighed, but gave in. "Sure."

"I Googled you and the name 'Grace' and nothing came up. Why aren't there any pictures of you guys on the Internet anymore?"

"I hired a lawyer and we managed to get them all removed. It was the least I could do. For her family. I wanted to sue for damages, but her family didn't want a big trial, anything to continue to fuel the madness. But we were able to get all mentions of her removed from the Internet. My legal team still has to pursue media outlets about it from time to time."

He was starting to make sense to me, why he felt like he needed so much control. Taking control had brought him so much. He'd built his life, repaired relationships, kept public troubles at bay, all by being in total control and leaving no room for others' errors. The wall he'd built around himself was tall and firm, and it was also breaking my heart.

Chapter 30

After about an hour's drive from the city, we pulled up to set of unobtrusive dark metal gates that opened when Dylan entered a code into his phone. We proceeded down a seemingly endless wooded driveway, passing a field on the right, with a large curved steel sculpture in the center of it that I couldn't take my eyes off of and recognized immediately.

"Is that a Richard Serra sculpture?" I asked, my mouth hanging open and following it with my eyes as we passed. I'd only ever seen his sculptures in museums and public spaces.

"It is," Dylan replied, clearly surprised and maybe even impressed that I'd recognized it. I was still looking at it when I saw deer meandering at its edges.

We rounded a corner, and I saw a large arc of glass panels forming the front of an elegant modern house. A circular gravel drive with perfect modern stone and wood accents marked the entrance. Despite the grand nature of the front of the house, it somehow seemed like it naturally emerged from the ground, like it was part of the earth. I saw glimpses of a couple of small outbuildings set back from the home—a garage, and what looked like large sheds. There was a small garden near the house, but mostly it seemed to be bounded by beautiful hilly wilderness.

Dylan helped me from the car and retrieved a large shopping bag from the backseat. "What is this place?" I asked, spinning, taking it all in, my eyes wide with appreciation.

"It's my hideout."

"You designed it?"

He nodded and guided me to the front door, opening the lock by waving his phone in front of a panel. This place was clearly state-of-the-art.

We entered the large front space, one large room divided into living and dining areas. Despite the impressive height of the windows lining this space, the house didn't actually appear to be that big. It was clear there were some private rooms behind the main space, but it was one level. It was furnished with a mixture of midcentury modern pieces and more traditional antiques. It seemed to perfectly represent Dylan. He grabbed my hand and pulled me back into a warm open kitchen, and I saw that the back of the house was lined in glass as well. I could see a large stone patio and fire pit beyond a slim kitchen door.

I noticed that there were sandwiches on the counter and a bottle of white wine, sweating at having just been taken from the refrigerator. I looked at him questioningly. "Are we not alone?"

"There's a caretaker, Mrs. Upton. I told her we were coming. She'll be back at her cottage by now," he said as he deposited the bag by the rear door and opened the wine. We leaned against the island in the middle of the room and ate our lunch.

"So what are you going to do with me, now that you have me here?" I sidled up next to him, tucking myself into his side, holding my wine in my free hand.

He wrapped his arm around me and looked down into my face. "I'm going to fill those lungs with proper country air. So eat up—we're going for a walk."

Dylan took out some wool socks and Wellington boots from the shopping bag, just my size, and retrieved his own from a closet. We stood by the back door, and he grabbed a waxed dark coat with a high collar and fitted it onto me—it was far too big, but he rolled up the sleeves. "You'll do."

"I feel like a giant gnome."

He wrapped my new scarf snugly around my neck and pulled its ends down my chest, "You look beautiful." But he was smirking when he said it. He untucked my hair from the scarf and brushed my bangs from my eyes. "I don't want you getting cold. I'll get you a proper jacket for the next time we come here."

He wore a thick chunky cream sweater and his own scarf, and once again looked like he was stepping off the pages of a fashion spread. So unfair. He opened the door and ushered me out.

We walked for at least three hours. He pointed out spots he loved—a brook and a cropping of rocks—and gestured for me to be quiet when we saw a stag. He loved this place. I could see him come alive before my eyes. A cool breeze swept over the field, and I shivered. He stopped and turned me into him, kissing me on the top of my head and rubbing his hands up and down my arms.

"You're getting cold. Let's head back. Let's get you warm in front of the fire. And naked."

* * *

Dylan was quick to build a fire in the master bedroom. The

space was large but cozy, sparse but with all the essentials, and it had an old roughed-up leather sofa in front of a beautiful fireplace. I nursed a cup of tea while he worked. I could watch him leaning into the fireplace all day. In his t-shirt, his features lit by the flames he was coaxing to life, he was truly beautiful, and I was so fiercely attracted to him, but it was becoming more than that. It *was* more than that. My intense sexual attraction to him was still present and completely unavoidable, but now, looking at him, my chest and cheeks warmed in addition to the usual places. I cared for him deeply, but I wouldn't let myself think beyond that—I couldn't. I'd only known him a short time, and after everything he'd told me in the car, it was clear he wasn't going to bring me fully into his life. But I was going to go down with this ship, even if its sinking seemed inevitable.

When he was satisfied with his handiwork he returned to me and took the mug from my hand. "Undress, Lydia." He went and sat down on the low long couch and gestured for me to stand in front of the fire. I would have made a joke about calling him "sire" or something similarly knight-in-shining-armor related, but I thought that might actually be insensitive given what he'd said about his family.

I moved in front of him and immediately felt the warmth of the fire at my back. Dylan was relaxed on the couch, one of his feet resting on his other knee, his arms spread across the back of the sofa. He looked completely irresistible. I was already barefoot, but I unbuttoned my jeans and slowly dropped the zipper. Gripping the sides with my thumbs, I shimmied out of them, letting them rest at my feet. As I kicked them to the side, I became aware of my bare ass warming from the fire behind me. I crossed my arms in front of me and grabbed the hem of my shirt, pulling it up in a deliberately slow move, exposing my bra as I lifted the shirt over my head. Finally, I reached behind and unclasped my bra, letting it fall from my front to my feet. My cheeks were warm from being outside, and now my skin was tingling as its temperature rose from the roaring fire. I reached up to tuck the hair that had come loose from my braid behind my ears and sweep my too-long bangs from my eyes.

"Take your hair down," he said firmly as he leaned forward and uncrossed his legs, never once taking his eyes from my own. I complied and dragged my fingers through my hair, loosening the braid and letting it fall to my shoulders. "Fucking stunning," he whispered, eyeing me with total appreciation. I smiled, bit my lip, and looked up in both pleasure and embarrassment.

As he rose to meet me, he removed his own t-shirt. I didn't think I'd ever get enough of that sight—him, barechested, the light from the fire against his skin. He ran the backs of his hands down my goose bump–covered arms, which was when I noticed the length of soft rope in one of this hands.

"You've got a fire in you, damsel. You know that, don't you?"

I guess I did. He saw right through me. I'd never felt shy before because I'd never felt seen before. He was exposing parts of myself that I didn't know existed, and it made me feel so acutely vulnerable. I'd always been able to manage what others saw when they looked at me. But Dylan saw through it all, and the kicker? He liked what he saw, or he certainly made me feel like he did.

"Give me your hands." I held out my palms for him, and he made quick work of binding them at my wrists. Holding me by my bound wrists, he guided me behind the couch to the large modern four-poster, like a canopy bed with no canopy. He leaned me up against one of the bedposts and pulled my hands above my head.

"Tiptoes. Stretch those arms up, Lydia." I obeyed without hesitation. "Good girl." He used the loose ends of the rope to affix my hands to top of the bedpost, and I could barely touch the ground, my arms hugging the sides of my face.

Dylan took a step back to appreciate his handiwork, and smirked with a combination of eagerness and what looked like devotion, maybe even more. He took a condom from his jeans pocket before letting them and his briefs fall to the floor. Watching him stalk me like a panther coming for me made me clench, and I could feel some of the dampness release onto my thighs. I was so wet for him, aching for him.

"Dylan." I felt alive with anticipation, but it was no longer the slightly nervous kind. I was excited, eager, already loving whatever he was going to do next.

"What do you want, baby?"

"You, Dylan, please. I just want you. Inside me."

He tickled my side, and I shrieked, totally unable to protect myself, but he still maintained his bossy glare when he said, "When I say, baby." Only now, I caught the adoration hiding in plain sight behind those dominant eyes. His bossiness wasn't just a turn-your-brain-to-mush level of sexy, it was *fun*. It had become something we both sought. And I caught myself wondering how that had happened.

He kneeled down in front of me and lifted one of my feet, taking my toe in his mouth and biting. The sensation went right up my leg to my sex, igniting me. He proceeded to place featherlight kisses slowly up my inseam, and I convulsed on the inside, waiting for him to reach the top of my thighs. Because I was stretched so taut I couldn't gain any purchase to actually move—I simply had to take it all in. His nose brushed my entrance, and a shiver radiated through me. But he retreated.

"No, Dylan." I groaned. "Please."

"Patience, my greedy girl." He released my foot and began his assault anew with my other leg.

I was practically writhing with need. This man owned me completely, body and soul, and I needed him more than I had ever needed anything in that moment. My pussy craved him, frantic for his touch. No, not just my pussy—all of me craved him. This time when he reached his goal, he inhaled deeply and blew a long cool breath over me. I twisted my hips, attempting to manage the sensation.

"Still, Lydia." He grabbed my hips to still me, and licked me, kissed me, not enough to bring me to the surface, all enough to drive me completely insane. I wanted nothing more than to wrap my arms around his neck and pull him into me. I could feel his lips, dampened by me, trailing wet kisses around the small patch of pubic hair above my entrance.

He stood and pressed me into the bedpost. "Wrap your legs around me." I immediately did as I was told, and he lifted me, providing relief to my arms and allowing them to bend. He reached under me and put on the condom. "I can't wait for tomorrow and to be rid of these. To come in you and on you. God, baby. To have nothing keeping us apart." Were we still talking about birth control? I groaned, and he kissed and tweaked at my nipple between each syllable, and the bites of pain fueled the swirling liquid desire in my belly. I was so close to coming, and he wasn't even in me yet. He grinned, knowing exactly what he was doing.

"Dylan!" I groaned his name impatiently, and he impaled me fiercely and swiftly. It hit the ache inside me square on. He thrusted, lifting me on and off of him, and I pulled myself by my arms, dropping myself onto him, yearning for his impossibly deep penetration. He found his rhythm and my body began to deliver on its promise, quaking, convulsing in his grasp.

"That's right baby. I can feel you. Kiss me when you come." I molded my mouth to his hard and fast and unraveled in his arms. The pleasure took over my limbs, making them drift away from me, replete with the intense gratification. There wasn't just hunger there. There wasn't just fun. And there was no fucking way this was casual. I let him take me completely.

"I don't think I'll ever get used to this," he said, more to himself than to me. He deftly unworked the knot at my wrists and brought me down to the floor with him. My legs were in a tangle with his, and he was rubbing my wrists, massaging the indentations from the rope away.

"I wish we could spend the night, but I think it's best we head back." The sun had gone down, and it had to be at least seven in the evening.

"Ok." I was in my own dreamy fog and was so sated and pliant, happy to have him make the decisions.

"We'll eat here and then be off. Spend the night with me? We can pick up an overnight bag on the way." I probably should have said no, taken some space, but I didn't want to. How could I imagine spending the night anywhere else? God, I was in too deep, and it was definitely too quick.

I gave him an *mmm* in assent and nuzzled into his chest.

"Have I actually fucked you into submission?" I could hear the smile in his words.

"Mission accomplished." I burrowed just a little deeper into him. "Can I ask you something?"

"Of course," he said.

"In Canada, when you kissed me…" I paused.

"Mmm hmm," he replied while lightly kissing the top of my head.

"Why did you walk away that night? Why not just sleep with me and have a one-night stand?"

He stopped the kissing, and I looked up at him. A flash of regret registered in his brow. He ran his hand through his hair.

"I wanted to—god, I wanted to. But I didn't want to hurt you, Lydia. You're different."

"So what made you change your mind and leave me that note?" I said, remembering the hope I felt when Charles had delivered that notecard with Dylan's number.

"I just couldn't stay away. I still can't."

Chapter 31

W hen I woke I was in Dylan's bed, and the sun was pouring through his windows. I looked at the clock on his side of the bed, and it was 5:45 in the morning. How had that even happened? The last thing I remembered had been falling asleep in his car the night before. I looked next to me at Dylan, sleeping soundly, his lips slightly parted, his leg over my own. He looked so peaceful. I laid back down as I had been and put my head on his chest.

Within a moment I felt his hand in my hair. "Morning, baby."

I lifted my head to look at him. "Did I wake you?" I asked.

"Not at all."

"How did I even get here?"

"Oh, well, I drugged you, naturally." The corners of his mouth were tilted up into a lazy morning smile, even though his eyes were still firmly closed in sleepiness.

I grabbed a pillow and hit him in the face. His arms flew up in surprise and he laughed. "I'm serious!" I protested. "The last thing I remember is falling asleep in the car." I looked and saw my overnight bag by the bathroom door. "And how did that get here?"

"You were dead asleep," he began to explain, as he inched himself up into a sitting position, rubbed the sleep from his eyes and pulled me with him. "I didn't have the heart to wake you. I went to your house, and left you in the car—I locked it, obviously. I packed you an overnight bag, brought you back here, and brought you up to bed."

"You carried me?" I asked, and he nodded and yawned in confirmation. "And I never woke up?"

"It was rather remarkable. You were dead to the world." He smiled and was thoughtful for a moment.

I snuggled into him. What a surprise this guy was. The idea of him—the same guy who apparently told Sheiks to go F themselves—rummaging through my clothes, packing me a bag. It was just so damn *domestic*.

"Thank you." I reached up and kissed him on the lips.

"Well you'd better be well rested." He smirked, and I hit him with the pillow again, sending him rolling over me to protect himself. He landed atop me, pinning me down, his eyes suddenly wide. "It's Monday morning," he added, obviously referring to our deadline for no more condoms. "Time for your wake-up call."

He reached between my legs and stroked me, and I was instantly aroused. I placed my hands on his chest and took in all his strength. Within moments he was in me, skin on skin. It was my first time without a condom, and I was startled by the difference. I felt so outrageously close to him, so sensitive to his movements. The way we'd both been anticipating it, I would have thought it would have been loud and rough, but instead we made love quietly, and apart from my riotous orgasm, without kink or fanfare. It was lovely, intimate, and felt like we were the only two people awake in London.

Two hours later we were finally out of bed, in the shower, and Dylan's strong hands were in my soapy hair, but it was as though some part of us were still making love, like we couldn't fully leave each other. He dragged his fingernails against my scalp and kissed my nose through the water running across my cheeks, taking an extra second just to look at me. I found myself gently squeezing where my hands were resting on his hips.

"You have a busy couple of weeks ahead of you." he said, looking as though he were making calculations in his head, planning. "The fashion show is next Wednesday?"

I nodded while tilting my hair back into the stream of water. " And I can only imagine how frantic things will be before then. Hannah said that she may need me or Fiona to go with her to some of the other shows this week, but who knows."

"Just tell me what your plans are. I want to know when I can see you."

"Of course." The water was pouring over us, and as excited as I was for this busy week, I never wanted to get out—something about this weekend felt like a major wall had been chipped apart. He was letting me in, and I wanted to let him in too. "I could just share my work calendar with you."

"Do it," he said, nodding.

"Will you share yours with me?" I asked, looking up into his blue eyes.

"You want to know where I am?"

"I like imagining you in your tower, designing, commanding, instructing."

"I'll do it as soon as I get to the office."

I leaned up and kissed him, smiling. "Thank you."

"And it's your birthday next Thursday." I snapped my head up to look at him. "You think I wouldn't know that?"

"It is," I confirmed. "Twenty-five. Getting long in the tooth over here."

He jauntily slapped me on the ass. "Hardly." He kissed me on the lips, holding my face in his hands. "Ok, you're clean. Out. We both have to get to work."

After drying my hair, I examined what he'd chosen for me to wear to work. I giggled while swatting Dylan's hand away from my breast and removed a grey sleeveless tailored dress with red panels running down the sides from the bag. He'd also picked my one pair of black heels, a reliable workhorse pair I'd had resoled three times already. Looking at them now and imagining Dylan picking them up made me slightly embarrassed—they were scuffed badly and seriously in need of repair. Or replacement.

Dylan turned to me from the closet and looked like the perfectly turned-out sexy millionaire architect he was. A bespoke suit and straight narrow tie. Not a hair out of place. He reached for my hand and pulled me towards the door. "Let's go get coffee. I'll walk you to work."

I raised my eyebrow up at him. He was going to let me walk? And he was going to walk *with* me? "We'll be discreet," he said quietly, as though he were throwing caution to the wind. He stopped us on the stairs headed towards the foyer and pulled me close against him. "Lydia, where did you come from and what are you doing to me?" He was searching, questioning, looking into me trying to figure us out.

I was basking in this warmth as he shut the door behind us, with his hand at my back. But reality set in the moment we turned onto the sidewalk and that hand dropped away. If someone he knew passed us, it would be easy to make it appear as though we were strangers. I suddenly felt isolated, alone even, walking with him that way. More than I ever had before. The closer we were in private, the harsher this public distance felt.

I shook the lonely feelings aside as we ducked into the coffee shop, determined to revel in the closeness we'd had all weekend. Everything about being out, in public, together called to me—I wanted to smell him out here, feel him. While the barista was turned away, I leaned in next to him, feeling his wool jacket against my cheek. The narrow shop was otherwise empty, and we both took our time eyeing the artisanal coffees and pastries. Dylan ordered our drinks, and we stood waiting, our hands surreptitiously grazing each other. I giggled slightly when he pressed his thumb into my palm, and I could see his smile out of the corner of my eye. It was the closest I'd been to feeling like his girlfriend, to feeling like I was a part of his life.

He was opening his wallet, preparing to pay, when the shop door swung open, the bell above it rang, and a gorgeous well-turned-out couple swept in. Dylan's head turned towards them, and his face went blank. His hand instantly fell away from my own. By the time I'd blinked, he'd stepped a foot away from me and the air had turned frigid between us. The tall woman walked excitedly towards Dylan, gripped his shoulders, and exclaimed, "Dylan Hale! We haven't seen you in ages!"

In a flash he was gone. I was gone. Invisible.

Everything we'd built over the weekend shattered like glass, like the illusion it probably was.

Dylan fully abandoned me at the counter and moved in to greet his friends. I could actually see as his posture shifted, could feel the moment when his public jovial in-control mask fell into place. I stood there, cold, bewildered, and looked up at the threesome. The camaraderie between the three of them was unmistakable. They were instantly laughing, recalling having all recently run into someone else they knew, an inside joke tossed between them. The Dylan I'd entered the shop with was gone, and this Dylan, the one for whom a secret was more important than anything, was back.

For a moment, I hoped. I *believed* he would turn back around and bring me into their fold. Hadn't we achieved something this weekend that would make the secrecy impossible?

I gave him this expectant hopeful moment, keeping my eyes locked on him, but his friend caught my stare and gave me an odd look. He was wary, clearly wondering about me and my prying gaze, and gave Dylan a concerned whisper. Dylan glanced back at me and then offered his friend a shrug, as if to say he had no idea who I was.

Gone. It was gone.

Every ounce of delicious intimacy, each gram of joy fell to the floor and puddled around me. I'd never felt so small in my life as I did in that moment. Then I looked to the counter and saw that he'd left a five pound note for my coffee, and in *that* moment, I'd never felt so cheap. I was a complete and utter fool.

I hastily paid for my coffee with cash from my own wallet and took the hot cup in my hands. I carefully skirted the boisterous threesome and left, letting that bell clang above me. As the door was shutting behind me, I heard the woman he was talking with say, in her posh exaggerated accent, "So, Amelia Reynolds…" and I was grateful to be gone before I could hear Dylan's reply.

Chapter 32

I stepped into the first taxicab I saw and directed the driver to my office. Before he was around the corner the hot tears were collecting in my eyes. I knew I had signed up for this. I knew that secrecy was part of the deal, that we were a just-sex fling, only meant to last so long, but what I hadn't known is how it would hurt. The secrecy meant something different now than it had a week ago. I had been kidding myself if I thought I could throw myself in Dylan's path, allow myself to be so vulnerable with him, and then also allow myself to be compartmentalized into this sliver of his life.

But the thing was *he'd* thrown these signs my way that we were more. My fists clenched as I thought about all the moments he'd looked at me, told me, even if it wasn't with words, that this was *more*. He'd just spent the entire weekend with me and had been so loving. He'd told Caroline about me. But, then again, *what* he'd told her about me I didn't know. I'd probably never know. He could have just been pointing out his latest conquest.

I was so confused. I was hurt. I was *furious*. I was furious with him for looking at me the way he did. For kissing me the way he did. For brushing my goddamn hair out of my eyes. What right did he have if he was just going to shove me away like I was nothing? And I was furious with myself. How could I have been so stupid?

I was pulling up to the curb when Dylan's first text came in.

MONDAY, 8:39 am
Where are you?

> MONDAY, 8:41 am
> Work.

I don't know why I replied at all. He didn't deserve it. The phone immediately started ringing, but I sent it to voicemail. I wouldn't talk to him right now. I'd been too absorbed in him for three days straight. I needed myself back.

MONDAY, 8:46 am
Goddammit, Lydia. Answer.

> MONDAY, 8:47 am
> Can't talk. Walking into meeting with Hannah.

I was suddenly incredibly grateful I hadn't yet shared my work calendar with him. I needed space, but I didn't want to text him that. I silenced my phone, put it in my bag, and tackled work email for a bit to try to put the morning behind me. He had disappeared on me, and now I needed to disappear. If for no other reason than for self-preservation. It wasn't long before there was an actual meeting, and I was able to fully distract myself from the growing pit in my stomach.

* * *

The pace at work was frenetic, and all hands were busy accomplishing our own work plus that of three other people. Fiona leaned over and assured me that the parties following these hellish weeks would be well worth it. But at that moment I couldn't imagine enjoying anything. The way he had so easily switched from attending to me to pretending I meant nothing felt like a knife to the chest. It hurt because it was cruel. But more than that it hurt because it was a *lie*.

At one thirty lunch was brought in for everyone from a local restaurant, and we took a miniscule break to feed ourselves, although I could barely touch the food. I just wasn't up for it. I took the time to check my phone. There were three missed calls from Dylan and one text.

MONDAY, 1:08 pm
You're mad. I get it. But will you please talk to me? I'm worried.

I had no idea what to do. Part of me wanted to give him the silent treatment all day, shut him out the way he'd shut me out. But really, I didn't *want* to punish him. I didn't even know *what* I wanted. I just needed to be by myself.

MONDAY, 1:10 pm
Can I just have some space?

I'm sure he wanted an explanation, but I didn't know how to explain. I didn't even know if I'd be able to stay away, but right then I couldn't breathe. The tension between what I knew I was starting to feel for him, maybe already felt for him, and his own limited feelings for me was possibly more than I could bear. I felt like I was being shoved through the door of something that would forever make me regret having let someone in.

I looked at my phone and saw the indicator that he was replying. It appeared and disappeared several times, but finally a reply arrived.

MONDAY, 1:14 pm
OK

I suspected he wasn't quite sure what to make of my own sudden change in mood. Well, I wasn't either. He'd just have to wait for me to figure it out.

* * *

When I arrived home, I found myself sending Dylan an *I'm home* text out of habit. I immediately cursed myself.

The text was marked as "read" but I didn't receive a reply right away. The signal that he was typing appeared and disappeared as it had before, but then it disappeared and didn't come back. I had asked for space, and I suppose he was actually going to give it to me. I didn't know what I was expecting, but maybe there was something he would be able to say that would make this sick feeling go away.

I sighed audibly and headed upstairs to get out of my work clothes. I changed into leggings, a t-shirt, and my favorite worn-in NYU hoodie and came down to the kitchen to put together some dinner. This was one of those nights when not having a mom to call stung and missing my father made my chest hurt. As part of my vow to get back to myself I vowed to get to Primrose

Hill that week—maybe it would be the balm I needed. I made my dad's famous macaroni and cheese, poured myself a glass of wine, and settled onto the couch to call Daphne. Thankfully she picked up on the second ring.

"Lydia! I'm so glad you caught me. I am getting ready to go to class in a bit. How was your weekend with Dylan?"

Oh god. Hearing Daphne's voice brought all of my feelings to the surface, and I started to cry. "I…I—" I couldn't even get the words out.

"Oh no, Lydia! What's going on? What did that bastard do to you?"

I breathed through the tears and tried to organize my thoughts. "Nothing, I mean he didn't do anything. Or everything. God, I don't even know."

"You sound terrible."

"I know. I just…you were right to be concerned about the secrecy thing." I heard her voice agreement. "It was fine, really it was going fine. And he actually explained his fear of the press more to me this weekend. This weekend we were closer than ever…Or I thought we were." I told her about the house, the walk, and how I'd fallen asleep in his car. "And, Daphne, I mean, I'm sure you saw this coming, but I think I'm falling in love with him—"

"Lydia, I think that ship has sailed."

"You're probably right, but I can't say it to myself yet." I told her about what happened at the coffee shop in the morning, "And it just hurt in a way I didn't expect it to. He has been completely upfront with me, he's given me no reason to have different expectations. He told me we weren't going to be public. It's not fair of me to feel this way."

"That's complete and utter horseshit, Lydia. Maybe you both thought that'd be fine, but no one has any business setting the parameters of a relationship like this in advance. There's no way to know how anyone will feel. It was naïve of him to think he could put up this barrier and assume it wouldn't change things or that you guys wouldn't change and run up against it. It was naïve of him to think he wouldn't fall in love with *you*!" She sounded so reasonable, but she also didn't know Dylan. If there was someone who was impervious to normal human behavior, it was probably him.

I couldn't help but laugh. "You have to say that because you *already* love me."

"Not true! I mean, yes, of course I love you. You're lovable." I loved Daphne's emphatic support. "But Lydia, he doesn't *sound* like someone who is keeping his emotional distance. Everything that he's done, everything you've talked about? He can say it's meaningless all he wants, but his actions say something else. I mean, of *course* you were falling in love—I think you both were, even if the dipshit doesn't want to admit it. "

"I know, but Daphne, this guy is like the king of seduction." She laughed out loud, and I began to see through my tears. "I wouldn't put it past him to use romance as a way into my pants—not that that makes him different than any other guy, I guess—but, I mean, he'd be able to do it without feeling it. He is like master of his universe. " And mine apparently. "He's never out of control for a second. You don't get that successful that fast by getting emotionally involved."

"Who is this cynical person I'm talking to? And where is Lydia? You're kind of making him sound like a psychopath. Do you really believe that about him?"

Did I? I thought for a moment. "No, I don't. I just want to understand this. I know in my gut that he cares about me. So how could he do this?"

"Lydia, I can't answer that. Maybe he's freaked out? Maybe he's just a lame-ass guy who doesn't know how to express himself. Who knows?! But Lydia, there's only one way to find out. You have to talk to him." Ugh, I knew she was going to say that. "I think he cares about you. I know he does. Don't you think he deserves to know if this secrecy thing isn't working for you? Don't you think he deserves to know how *you* feel about *him*?" She was making it sound like a healthy adult conversation would solve this problem, but she didn't know Dylan and his extenuating circumstances.

"But what if that means it's over?" In my gut I knew that it would be. He'd been pretty clear that it was his way or the highway.

"I can't answer that one for you, L. You'll be ok though, no matter what."

"Thanks, Daph. I miss you."

"I miss you too. I wish I were there, so we could drink a bottle of wine and watch *Mean Girls* and paint our toes."

"Me too." And as I said it, I realized just how much I missed my best friend.

"Let's do it from afar!" She said, suddenly bubbly.

"What? Now? Don't you have to go to class?"

"Eh, whatever. If there was ever a reason to miss class, it'd be this. Do you have the movie on your computer?"

"Yes! Let's switch to video chat, so we don't go broke."

"Perfect."

Daphne and I spent the rest of my evening watching the movie together and chatting. Thank god for her. Eventually I fell asleep on the couch, a little less despondent, a little bit drunk, and so grateful for my best friend.

Chapter 33

I woke to soft strokes against my forehead, and I opened my eyes to see a haggard-looking Dylan leaning over me.

"Baby, I'm sorry. I know you asked for space, but I couldn't stay away."

I fluttered my eyes fully open, and started to try to sit myself up on the couch. But Dylan reached under me and lifted me into his arms. "I'm sorry I woke you—I just didn't want to scare you. I'm taking you to bed."

"What time is it?"

"Nearly one."

"How did you get in?"

He rounded the corner and began climbing the stairs. "You left the door unlocked again." He held me tightly as he made his way to my room. He put me down in bed, and tucked me under the covers. He stood at the side of the bed and ran his hand through his hair. "Can I stay?"

I nodded and rolled to my side, facing away from him. Was I ever going to be able to stay away? I did want him there, but

I also wanted him away. I was fighting with myself as much as I wanted to fight with him. He stripped out of his clothing and slid in next to me, pulling me into him so my head was lying on his firm chest. I started to outline his muscles with my fingers, stroking him gently. I wanted so badly to be where we were twenty-four hours earlier. He smelled so good, and just being this close to him was awakening all of my senses, awakening all of my wants, all of the closeness. The feel of him next to me, holding me, was turning me on, and it felt like there was nothing I could do to stop it. He rolled to face me and brought his hand between us to unzip my sweatshirt. He looked into my face, asking permission to continue, but suddenly the whole day and all of its pain flooded back to my senses. The anger. The hurt. It was there again. Fresh.

I grabbed his hand and stopped him. He looked alarmed for a moment, but his look changed to curiosity when I resumed the unzipping myself.

I shed my hoodie and began to sit up, pulling the straps of my tank top from my shoulders. He reached out and tried to touch, but I pulled away and removed my top completely. I could see the slight panic in his eyes.

"I'm sorry," he said. "I hurt you."

"Yes." I felt a tear escape, but I pulled them back before they had a chance to let loose. I wasn't ready to talk about this. I could feel the end of us coming, like we'd been swimming in high seas, and the tide was about to go out.

"Baby," he said, as he wiped the stray tear from my cheek. "I wanted to introduce you, Lydia. I did. You know I can't—"

I cut him off. "I just want to forget about it right now." I could hear Daphne's voice flash through my head—we *should* talk. But I didn't want to. I wanted to fuck. I wanted to fuck *him*.

He leaned over me and started to curl his hands into the waistband of my leggings, trying to bring me to him. But I swatted his hand away and made quick work of getting rid of them myself.

I flipped over him, rose to straddle him, and pushed his shoulders into the mattress. I leaned over to kiss him. My lips hovered over his mouth, but I couldn't bring myself to kiss him there, as though if I did he might be able to swallow me whole, drain me of any strength I had left. Instead I put my lips against his neck and sucked. Hard. Determined to leave my own mark on Dylan Hale. His eyes were wide, but willing. For the first time I was calling the shots.

I reached between us to position him at my entrance and sank onto him, taking him in completely in one swift movement.

"Lydia." He groaned. He angled his pelvis and, putting his hands at my hips, tried to lift and lower me, but I grabbed his wrists and moved them to the side of his head, pinning them there. I'd do the lifting and lowering. I'd do the kissing and not kissing. I'd summon his body the way I'd let him summon mine.

I closed my eyes and lost myself in him completely. I couldn't bear to look at him, afraid of the emotions I'd feel if I did. And he must have sensed it, because he didn't ask me to open my eyes or to look into his. He was quiet and let me lead. He was so deep this way, and angled so perfectly, we reached a fever pitch, and I could feel his groans vibrating in his chest. I threw my head back as I felt myself tighten, clenching through the oncoming orgasm. I'd never felt so alone with him, nor had I ever needed him so badly. I didn't know where we were headed, but right now, I needed this. I cried out as the raw pleasure released through me. Dylan came at the same time, and let his hips fall to the mattress. I collapsed on top of him, inhaling his scent and letting my cheek and chest be warmed by him.

Finally, he withdrew, and I rolled off of him onto my side, my back facing his front. He took a tissue from the bedside table and dried between my legs, carefully cleaning me. He pulled me close and caught his breath in my hair. We didn't speak, but I could feel the tension, the concern, the distance. Eventually, well after I heard his breathing even into a relaxed rhythm, I drifted back into a restless sleep.

* * *

The light was just creeping into the room, and he continued to sleep as I tiptoed around my bedroom and readied myself for work. It wasn't even six in the morning, but the truth was that I couldn't bear to have another morning with him, knowing that I was in love with him, and he was never going to love me back, never going to give me more. If last night was any indication, I simply couldn't handle it. I wasn't built for this level of hurt, this kind of helpless anger. I had let myself fall too far down the rabbit hole. I wasn't sure I'd ever fully recover, but the sooner I got out, the better chance I'd have.

I could feel a cloud settling over me. Before I left the room, I kissed him while he was sleeping and left a note on my pillow:

I can't do this anymore. I'm sorry. —L

I was grateful for the early-morning quiet walk to the tube. There were far fewer of us making the trek at this hour, but I certainly wasn't alone. I replayed the last night in my mind. He said that he had wanted to introduce us, but then why didn't he? Dylan Hale did as he pleased. If he'd really wanted to introduce me to his friends, he would have. This was going to be torture, and I'd have to find some way to stay away. But fuck, I just couldn't resist him. He came into my house in the middle of the night like some kind of stalker, and instead of confronting him, or letting him have it, I threw myself at him. I shook my head in frustration at myself—surely making every early-morning commuter think I was crazy.

I emerged from the tube and headed to my office, which I prayed would be unlocked at this hour, and felt my phone vibrate. He'd already called three times, and the first text had come in.

TUESDAY, 6:49 am
You're ending this? Lydia, talk to me.

Why couldn't he just let me figure this out on my own? He was apologizing. Maybe that should count for something, but what did it matter? We wanted different things.

TUESDAY, 6:52 am
I'm sorry.

TUESDAY, 6:53 am
Lydia, we need to talk about this. Tonight.

Why did this have to be so hard? Why couldn't he let me just leave, escape before he destroyed me completely? I knew Daphne thought that somehow he and I could talk this through, but she hadn't heard the determination in his voice when he talked about how he would never date, would never marry, would never have a life with someone. No. I had to be strong if I was going save any piece of myself.

TUESDAY, 6:52 am
No. I'm sorry, Dylan.

* * *

Dylan texted me throughout the day and called several times, but I doggedly deleted the texts without reading them and the voicemails without listening. I needed a clean break. Eventually he'd leave me alone. I took crying breaks in the bathroom and somehow managed to convince Fiona I was just in a fight with a friend back home.

By Thursday night I was able to stop crying while at work. By Saturday I was able to eat at least one meal a day other than a latte. And by Monday, Dylan had stopped calling and texting, allowing me to limit my morning crying to the period between waking and finishing my shower. I was slowly coming back into the driver's seat, slowly finding my façade again.

That night I was home picking at the pizza I'd ordered when Daphne called. She only let me ask her questions about her for so long. She could tell I wasn't ok, and was only going to let me pretend otherwise for so long.

"Lydia, are you sure you shouldn't call him back?" she asked.

"Daphne, you should have heard him, back when this all started. He was so absolute about not dating. If I had stuck around he just would have talked me into stretching out our sex fest for another few months, allowing for another handful of emotionally-intense awesome weekends that ultimately meant nothing. What if was he never going to be able to get past that?

No matter how close we got? Wasn't it smarter of me to walk away?" *Please say yes. Please say yes.*

"No."

"What?! You're my friend. You're supposed to be on my side!" I said indignantly.

"I *am* on your side, and I think you should talk to him. Listen, I've been thinking about this, and I just don't buy it. I don't buy his bullshit about this being casual no matter what. Sure, he said that in the beginning, but you have no idea what he was going to say now. I mean, look at the dude. He was spending basically every second of his free time with you, when he said he hardly ever slept with the same person twice. He's a busy guy, Lydia, and not once did he pass you over. He was thinking about you when you weren't around, texting you, buying you gifts, the works. I mean, I want to know what he was going to say if he had convinced you to talk to him! I think he might have surprised you."

I sighed. "Maybe."

"Look," she continued. "I know he's a formal stuffy Earl doing his Earl thing, but he also sounds like he really cares about you. Honestly, I think he loves you too, Lydia." She sounded pleading as she spoke. She really wanted me to give him a chance.

I groaned in frustration. "Daphne. I mean. I don't think I can go back—I just started to feel like one percent normal again. And by tomorrow, if I'm lucky, I'll feel two percent normal. I don't know if I can risk backtracking."

"Just think about it, Lydia. You never told him how you felt. He never knew that the status quo wasn't enough for you. He didn't know that you love him."

We chatted for a few more minutes, but my heart wasn't in it.

I needed to go to sleep, and I couldn't muster much energy for anything these days.

* * *

The next morning on the way to work I replayed my conversation with Daphne in my mind. She really believed I should talk to him, that I hadn't given him a fair shot. I'd never been honest about my feelings. I left that note for him because I didn't actually believe that he'd be able to hear me, but if there was any chance at all, no matter how small, that this could work, I needed to be open, to let him in again. Wouldn't I be mad at myself forever if I didn't at least hear him out?

When I got off the tube, I gulped and sent him a text.

> TUESDAY, 7:04 am
> Hey, can we talk?

My phone immediately started ringing and his face showed up on my screen—a picture from his hideaway house, a selfie of us in one of the fields, smiling broadly at the camera. I sent the call to voicemail. I couldn't do this over the phone.

> TUESDAY, 7:05 am
> In person.

TUESDAY, 7:06 am
Of course. Tonight? 7pm? Dinner?

> TUESDAY, 7:06 am
> Sure.

TUESDAY, 7:06 am
I'll pick you up at work.

I sighed. That was over, and now I had the whole day to figure out what I needed to say. I was grateful to meet the security guard at the entrance to the office, unlocking the doors just as I arrived. I'd been getting there so early these days that he and I had become buds.

I immediately picked up with work where I left off the night before, grateful to be able to throw myself into something. Later in the morning, Lucy and I were organizing the clothes for the show, and stacking the Polaroids of the models, makeup, and accessories. We were in a fever, getting ready, and I happily immersed myself in the work.

I was quiet, lost in my rumination, as I picked at my pad thai over lunch.

"What will you wear to the party tomorrow?" Fiona said, trying once again to pull me into conversation.

"What party?" Had I been told about this already? I had been so distracted I wasn't positive I hadn't missed half of what my coworkers had told me lately.

"The Designers Gala? At the Savoy? Did Hannah really not tell you?" Fiona was looking at me as though I'd missed the biggest news since the Internet.

"Maybe? I don't think so though." I honestly wasn't sure.

"It's a huge deal, Lydia, and we'll have to look stunning. Seriously—everyone who is anyone will be there. It's the culmination of all of the Fashion Week parties. You should peruse the closet today, because there won't be much time tomorrow. The show is at four, and the party is at seven. We'll be in a mad rush."

It was hard to imagine a party at that moment, but maybe I

could get in the right headspace, given enough alcohol. I looked at Fiona, who was clearly eager to talk details about the party, and did my best to indulge her and to let her good mood bring me out of my own bad one.

It wasn't until after four p.m. that I had a chance to even look at my phone again, but when I did I saw a missed call and two texts from Daphne.

TUESDAY, 12:07 pm
What an asshole! Is it true!?!

TUESDAY, 12:07 pm
Forget any nice thing I said about him last night! What a lying douchebag!

What was going on? I quickly logged into my email and there was one from Daphne at the top with the subject, *Saw this. OMG. Call me. Are you OK?* There was single link in the email and I clicked on it. A page from *Hello!* magazine popped up, and there, looking right at me, were two photographs of Dylan walking out of a London hotel next to Amelia Reynolds. In one his hand was on her elbow, and he was kissing her on the cheek. She had a huge smile on her face. His parents and another older couple were emerging with them, all looking jovial. In the other it was just the two of them, emerging side by side. She was wearing sunglasses, but didn't exactly look unhappy. He looked weirdly satisfied. The headline, posted only a few hours before, was displayed in bold lettering, *"Wedding Bells for London's Most Eligible Bachelor."* The brief article read,

Renowned architectural genius, Marquess of Abingdon, and eligible bachelor, Dylan Hale, famously known for having once been engaged to Princess Caroline in his wilder days, is finally settling down for good. Dylan is the son of shipping tycoon Geoffrey Hale, 16th Duke of Abingdon. He was seen emerging from the Goring Hotel last Saturday afternoon with Lady Amelia Reynolds, daughter of Baron and Baroness Piers and Louise Reynolds. And again yesterday, just the two of them emerging from San Lorenzo. Dylan, owner and chief architect at Hale Architecture & Design, was the youngest person to ever be awarded the prestigious Stirling Prize for the Cathedral Hospital in Canterbury and has been considered one of the city's most eligible bachelors for 6 years running. A source confirms that the two have a "significant relationship" and did not deny an engagement. Lunch with the parents certainly looks "significant" to us!

Chapter 34

I nearly hyperventilated. I crumpled on the inside, deflating. I could feel the tears coming fast, and I had to get out of there. The past week of regaining myself was lost, obliterated. I had thought I had hit rock bottom, but I was wrong—*this* was rock bottom. And I thought I'd felt like a fool before at the coffee shop? Hah! That was nothing. *Now* I felt like a fool. Not only had I believed all of his caring gestures were real, but I'd gullibly fallen for the story he'd told me about Amelia, complacently let him guide me into the little secret place he'd carved for me. I wanted to vomit. The panic was rising. I quickly ducked into Hannah's office where Fiona was sorting through the Polaroids of the models on the floor, and it was immediately clear to both of them that I wasn't well.

"You look terrible, Lydia. Are you ok?" Hannah asked, concerned.

"You know, I think it's something I ate. Would it be ok if I headed home? I'll be in first thing again tomorrow to prep for the show. I'm so sorry."

"Of course, of course," Hannah said kindly. "Get home safely, and thank you for getting in so early this morning. Your hard work is paying off. I don't know how we'd be getting this done without you."

I nodded in gratitude, but I needed to get out of there before I lost it completely. I grabbed my jacket and bag and quickly replied to Dylan's earlier text.

TUESDAY, 4:16 pm
Don't bother.

Then I purposely left my phone on the desk. I needed to be alone. I left the office and began walking north. I just walked and walked, letting the city zoom past me. I passed the media executives pouring out of their offices in Soho and crossed the traffic mayhem of Oxford Street and Centre Point. I meandered around Bloomsbury and passed signs for the University College of London, twisting and turning down mews and streets just to avoid stopping. For the first time since I arrived I wasn't blissful walking through these streets, but I was grateful for the anonymity they provided, for reminding me that there was a whole city here beyond Dylan.

After about an hour I realized where I needed to go, where I had been going all along. I consulted my A-Z guide to make sure I wasn't too far off track. I entered Regent's Park and headed straight up its long straight narrow path. My feet were starting to hurt, but I didn't care. My eyes were wet, and I kept bringing my fingers up to brush away the tears. More than one reserved Londoner eyed me oddly, presumably wondering about the strange crying girl marching purposefully through the elegant park.

The thoughts were reeling through my mind, a million per

second, all contradictory, all searching for answers. How had I been so stupid? Had he been using me? But then why bother? Wasn't I too much trouble to deal with if he really didn't care? Why even try to talk to me or apologize the week before? What would he even have said to me? Why hadn't he told me that his lunch had been with Amelia and her family unless he wanted to hide it? And how on earth had I let my guard down so profoundly?

Eventually, I passed the London Zoo, crossed the street, and entered Primrose Hill Park. I looked up and began climbing the famed hill. The park was far from crowded on a late Tuesday afternoon. I saw a group of high school students loitering at the base of the hill. An older couple was walking down from the viewing point at the top. An artist had perched an easel and was carefully taking in the scene. There were a few parents or nannies with strollers and children frolicking around them. I thought how recently I had been looking after Maddy and Cole, and I was suddenly reminded about how much I'd changed in these few weeks. How alive I had been feeling but also how innocent I had been before, how simple and doe-eyed my life pre-Dylan now seemed. And I could never go back.

I nearly reached the top and picked an empty grassy spot to park myself, as far from the path as I could manage. I took out the long blanket-like Scottish cashmere scarf and wrapped it around my neck, burying my face in its fabric, and I cried. I gave in to the tears, to the slight heaves in my breath, and let go. I replayed every moment with Dylan in my mind, every touch, every sweet gesture and sexy instance between us. It was clear how I'd fallen in love with him—he'd made me feel so safe, safer than I'd ever felt before. He made me vulnerable, but my vulnerability had been ok, a signal that I was opening up and taking risks. I'd allowed him to be the first person I'd ever truly let take care of me. He made me love myself just a little more than I had, and not just my body. Every time I'd made him laugh, I'd found more of my own humor. Every time he'd listened so intently, I saw more of myself through his eyes. He saw me so clearly, and it had made me see myself more clearly. I'd been confidently un-earthing myself. But now, now I felt more foolish than ever. Was I ever going to find that with someone else? Ever?

I took the photo of my parents out of my bag and examined them closely, searching their faces. I was seeing what they'd seen that day, taking in the same view. Was my current feeling what came next for them? Had they ever felt about each other the way I was feeling about Dylan? It seemed impossible.

I hugged my knees and closed my eyes and tried to just breathe in the view and relax. The sun had set, and the park had mostly emptied, but I hadn't moved an inch. I dreaded the idea of having to go back to my house, for the reality, the finality of this to set in. I'd never felt more alone in the world than I did in that moment.

I wasn't sure how much time had passed, but I looked up when I heard someone shouting my name. Dylan was jogging up the steep hill towards me. *Shit.* How the hell had he found me *here*? Why couldn't he just leave me alone? Could this be any more humiliating? I stood and started walking away from him.

"Lydia!" He shouted from downhill. He still hadn't caught up to me. "Goddammit, Lydia. Turn around. Look at me. It's not true. I swear it's not true." His shout turned to a determined tone as he got closer.

I turned and was about to shout, but was caught off guard. He looked terrible, shattered. His eyes were bloodshot. His nor-mally trim hair was mussed. His collar askew. His sleeves rolled around his elbows. But then all of my anger flooded back, making my lungs burn.

"You are such a psycho!" I breathed fire into the words. "How did you even find me here? Why can't you just leave me alone? Are you getting off on roping me in, making me feel things for you and then blindly, cowardly standing by and watching as I crumble? Did you enjoy it each time I fell for your lies, believed in what was happening between us? You're a sick fuck, you know that?"

"Lydia." He sighed, and I heard a slight catch in his breath. He ran his hand through his hair, which was already standing on end, as thought that hand had been in that hair all day. "For fuck's sake, I'm *not* engaged to Amelia."

"Why should I believe you? It makes perfect sense. She is perfect for you, the perfect answer to all of your concerns." I spoke harshly, angry as much at the world and myself as I was at him. "I mean, why wouldn't you have just told me about that lunch unless you were trying to hide it from me? That was your 'work lunch,' right? And why else hide me from your friends? They're not the press—if they're your friends surely they wouldn't run to the nearest tabloid and reveal the shocking news that you're casually fucking a nobody. I've never felt so humilated." I stopped for a moment, running my hands through my own mussed hair. "You know, I don't even know why the fuck I'm even talking to you about this—"

"Enough!" He shouted and interrupted me. "Christ, Lydia."

I turned and continued to walk away from him, but he caught up to me and grabbed my arm. I looked up at him, tears streaming down my cheeks, and pulled my arm away. He reached back more gently, and held me by both arms, looking right into my face, right past my skin and into my core.

"Lydia, listen to me." His eyes were so wide, so raw. I should have turned and kept walking, but that ever-present pull was there. I stayed. I stared blankly into those eyes, trying to keep my tears at bay. "I'm sorry. I'm so sorry, baby." He brushed an errant tear off my cheek with his thumb. "God, I'm so glad I found you." He looked into my eyes, and his relief was evident. "Let me explain. Please." His words were soft, pleading, and his chest rising and falling, barely containing the energy radiating off of him. I stood there, still debating whether to hear him out. Wouldn't it be better to leave rather than risk being sucked back in? But I was hopeless in his presence. I gave him a quick look of assent, and then fixed my stare past him, focusing on the horizon.

He covered his eyes with his hands in what looked like despair as he caught his breath. "I'm sorry. Look, I was holed up all day working on the building in Jordan. I've been burying myself in work since you left me. I was zoned in, and I gave strict instructions about not being interrupted. I didn't know. I had no idea about those photos—none. If I had I would have preempted this whole thing or at least warned you. I noticed I was getting a lot of calls, but I wasn't going to answer my phone for anyone but you. I haven't been able to face anyone. God, Lydia, I haven't slept in a week." That, at least, was believable. He looked like shit.

"As soon as I saw your text," he continued, "I stopped to figure out what was going on. I had a zillion voicemails and emails, and it didn't take me long to figure out what had happened." He was talking fast, trying to get it all out. He wouldn't let go of me, but I could feel him wanting to throw his arms up to his face in exasperation.

"Lydia. The work lunch that Saturday. What happened was

Amelia's mum learned that Piers needed to meet with me and, apparently, she urged him to make it a Saturday meeting. She let Amelia know, called my mum and got her on board, decided that it should be a big old happy family lunch. No one told me of course, knowing I'd have shut the whole ridiculous thing down. Not ten minutes into the meal I was surrounded. That's my mum, Lydia. She and Louise are school mates, and they've been hell-bent on setting their children up, forcing us into the same kind of shite marriages that were foisted upon them. My mother thinks I'm single, and as far she knows I haven't dated anyone since Caroline. She thought that if she gave me a nudge I might just fall into it. I didn't tell you before, because I didn't know she was going to be there. And then when she was, well, I thought I could shut it down. I wanted to protect you from it. I thought I *should* protect you from it, but now I realize I should have told you."

I opened my mouth to speak, to tell him, *Hell yes, you should have told me,* but he kissed me quickly on the lips to hush me and pulled back. "Let me finish. The second time I met Amelia to tell her to back off, that there was never going to be anything between us, to put an end to all of it. I should have told you about that, about all of this, and I tried. But you stopped answering my texts or taking my calls a week ago. Maybe I could have tried harder, but I didn't think you'd listen. And fuck, I didn't want to push you away any more than I already had. I thought you'd take one look at this absolute insanity—the newspapers, the lies, the god-awful family crap—and run. I was worried you wouldn't believe me. I've made quite a cock-up of the whole thing now, haven't I?"

"You have," I said sternly.

"This all probably sounds ludicrous to you. But I'm quite certain Amelia is to blame for the photographer being there both times, for grabbing me as we exited, and for leaking some bullshit about us having a relationship. The rest is what the press does best—make something out of nothing. I'm so sorry about that, Lydia. I promise there is nothing to any of it. I'm not talking to either of my parents right now because of this. And I obviously won't be speaking with Amelia anytime soon."

What was I supposed to say? I did believe his explanation. And he was right—I didn't answer a single call over the past week. How was he supposed to tell me? If he'd come to my door I would have shut it in his face. I relaxed a little in his arms, but the truth was that this was only part of our issue—a big part obviously, but still only a part. I brought my own hands to my eyes to shield them, to throw my head into them in confusion.

"Dylan, I—"

"I know. As long as we're not public, things like this will keep happening. The thing that makes me the furious is that if we *had* been public—if my mother, Amelia, all of that lot knew about us—this never would have happened. I knew it the night Michael showed up, and I know it even more now. The world needs to know you're mine." I shot a look up at him, and I could feel the hope written all over my face. "*I* need the world to know you're mine. That I'm yours. Because I am. Even if you won't take me back, I'm yours. I didn't mean to hurt you, Lydia. I felt horrible ignoring you at the coffee shop. It felt so wrong. I felt like a fraud. I'm so sorry, baby. It was automatic—I've been used to shielding anything I care about from the world, but I never meant to hurt you. This is completely new to me—I've trained myself carefully over years to keep this part of my life shut down, simple, private and you come in…Lydia you have upended me completely. Everything's different with you. I don't know how to do any of this." Possibly for the first time since I'd met him, he looked his age—young, unsure, wanting.

"Me either." I sniffled and smiled slightly. He returned my smile with relief.

"I love you, Lydia." Three little words and my heart boomeranged back to me. He loved me. "And I want the world to know." I looked up at him, stunned. My smile was growing. I couldn't have wiped it from my face if I'd tried. He pulled me in, not being able to keep his distance any longer. "And if you ever call yourself a nobody again, especially in comparison to a twat like Amelia Reynolds, I'll give you a spanking you'll remember." He whispered this last bit in my ear, his relieved playfulness returning.

I sank into his embrace, letting relief settle over me. There had been an explanation, but more importantly he'd known, he hadn't needed to be wrangled or told. He'd found me, found us, on his own. Suddenly something occurred to me. "How'd you find me here?"

"Creepy?"

"Just a little."

"Can't we put this in the knight-on-a-white-horse column?" he asked with a pleading smile, and I smirked at him in return, pulling into him, holding him to me. "I called Daphne."

I pulled back in surprise. "You did? How'd you get her number? What did she say?" Daphne must have been shocked. Not to mention worried. I'd have to call her as soon as this conversation was over.

"While Lloyd was driving me around town looking for you, I had Thomas look up Daphnes who'd graduated from NYU last year. I woke up three different Daphnes before I found yours."

"Really?" I let out a laugh. "Poor Thomas. What did you say to them?"

"I said, 'Are you the Daphne who might know where Lydia Bell is?' When I got yours, well—"

"Oh." I laughed. "I can only imagine that call. She must have given you a hard time." Daphne was fiercely loyal.

"She gave me quite an earful. She doesn't like me much."

"Can you blame her? She's the one who sent me that horrible picture today. You must have said something right though if she was willing to help you."

"I told her I loved you. And she knew you'd be here. She said, 'If she's not with you, and she's not home or at work, then she's at Primrose Hill.'" He paused, curious all of a sudden. "What *are* you doing here?"

I reached into my bag and handed him the photo.

"Your parents?" he asked, and I nodded. "Is that why you're in London?" I nodded again, wiping the last of my tears from my cheeks and feeling myself calm down. "And this is you." He pointed at my mother's pregnant belly. I nodded again.

"They were happy here. They were in love here," I explained.

He reached down and picked me up, bringing me into a swinging hug. "And now you're in love here." I raised my eyebrow—I hadn't told *him* that I loved him. He immediately stopped swinging me, realizing his faux pas. He looked nervous for a moment. "I mean—"

"I love you too, Dylan." I rescued him. "I mean, obviously. I love you too." I jumped into his arms and wrapped my legs around him, kissing him deeply.

He kissed me back long and hard and moved the kisses across my cheeks to my ear and neck, holding me tightly the whole time. Finally, he put me down and straightened me up, tucking my hair behind my ears, wiping away the mascara that had run under my eyes, and fixing my scarf. "Come. I'm taking you to dinner. *Out* to dinner. You'll tell me all about your parents while we eat. I'm going to take you somewhere where I know everyone. I'm going to kiss you at the table and embarrass you."

I laughed, and took his hand. "Can we go home and shower first? I feel like I'm a mess."

"No. It's nearly eight, and I want to feed you. We're not going anywhere fancy, and you look beautiful." He planted a steady and firm kiss on my lips, like he was holding on to me for dear life, and led me down the hill to his car.

While Dylan spoke to Lloyd, I used Dylan's phone and shot Daphne a quick text.

TUESDAY, 7:52 pm
It's me, Lydia. Thank you for knowing me so well. All's good. Really good. I'll call you tomorrow.

She wrote back immediately.

TUESDAY, 7:53 pm
Dying to hear. That guy can be very persuasive.

Chapter 35

Dylan never let go of my hand. He took me to a tiny restaurant, tucked away between some shops in Soho. There was a chalkboard with the menu on the wall, and the place had an unfinished and unpretentious atmosphere, not the place you'd go looking for a young ex-bad-boy famous aristocratic architect. But as soon as we walked in, the host greeted Dylan with a hug. Dylan immediately guided me forward. "Jamie, this is my girlfriend, Lydia." Jamie's eyes widened in surprise, and he offered his hand warmly.

Girlfriend!

"Pleased to meet you," he said, eyeing me curiously. I reached out for his hand in return.

He was right that he seemed to know everyone. The chef, Will, came out to greet us, and the waitstaff continued to bring out tidbits that we hadn't ordered, and addressed Dylan by name. He knew everyone's story, and by the end of the night they all knew who I was.

"You come here often, I take it?" I looked at him, confused. It was like these people were his family.

"All the time. Will is an old friend. I helped him start this place—we're partners."

"You own this place?" I asked surprised.

He nodded in confirmation. "With Will. I invested when he was ready to open. We've known each other since we were kids. He's one of the good ones, one of the few people from my past who understands what it's like to actually want to do something with your life other than ride horses and drink tea and listen to your grandparents talk about life before the war."

"I have trouble imagining you here with your family or clients—you seem so relaxed, so yourself."

"Oh, I've never taken anyone here." I looked up to Jamie, who was bringing another bottle of wine, and he nodded at me in confirmation.

Over dinner I told him more about my family than I'd ever told anyone. He was sweetly riveted, and he shared more over that dinner than he had in three weeks of being together.

Had it really only been three weeks?

"Are we insane? Isn't it too fast to fall in love?" I asked him.

"What makes you think I have any idea what's normal?"

"Good point. I mean, you're kind of a perv." I smiled at him.

"Your perv. And who cares? All I know is that I'm not letting you out of my sight. For a second."

"Does this mean you're going to be even more overprotective?"

"You think I'm overprotective?" I gave him an "oh please" look. "Lydia, I like control. That's never going away." He gave me a look that left no room for error in this department. "And can't you see why? Look at the havoc that one stint with the press wreaked on my life, on your life." He had a point. But of course his control reached far beyond protecting me from the press.

"Plus, the world is more dangerous than you think," he said, moving his eyes to his plate. I got the sense he was talking about something specific, but I didn't want to interrupt our evening to probe.

* * *

When we got back to his house, it was nearly midnight, and I was completely spent. He helped me shed my jacket, and lifted me into his arms. I rested my head against his chest and closed my eyes, inhaling him. He put me down in his bedroom, and began removing his clothes. He pointed to a drawer in his dresser, and I went over and opened it. It was nearly full of clothing in my size. There were a couple of beautiful lacey bras, t-shirts, a pair of jeans, a skirt, and some other items. All new. No underwear, I noticed. Some things wouldn't change, and I didn't want them to.

"What's all this?" I asked.

"I had Thomas pick some things up for you while we were at dinner. I want you here more. Fill that drawer up. And there's one for you in the bathroom as well."

"You want me clothed?" I smirked at him.

"Almost never," he said, smiling back at me. "But if we're going to be seen in public together, clothing will be an unfortunate necessity."

"Fair enough."

"And never in here." He sauntered up to me and lifted my shirt over my head. He threw the shirt into the corner, and smiling that mischievous smile, traced where it had been with his fingers. His light touch had my skin singing, and my nipples stiffened immediately. Yearning settled low in my belly, and I pushed my hips into him, and putting my hands on his ass, pulled him into me. "I'm still in charge, you know," he said. I had zero doubts.

He ran his hands up my arms and settled them in my hair, and, gripping my head, he pulled my face to his, devouring me with a purposeful, steady, intensely deep kiss. I rested my hands on his biceps and felt them firm as he lifted me onto the bed. He hovered over me and unbuttoned my jeans. "Ass up, baby." I complied immediately, and he dragged my pants down and off my legs.

He buried his face in my belly, breathing me in, and I fingered his hair, massaging his scalp, wanting my hands on him as much as was humanly possible. He dragged his tongue across my lower stomach, skirting where my pubic hair once was and leaving a cool path behind him, sending a shiver rippling up my body. "You are intoxicating, Lydia. I'm going to make you come. And come. And come." God, how could he say that? His words spoke directly to the desire congregating between my thighs. "I love you." The words, just three little words, filled the space between us.

His kisses moved south, carefully abstaining from my sweet spot, circling me in some kind of torturous assault. I could feel my wetness spreading between my legs. I arched my back to bring my sex to his mouth, but he instantly retreated. "Ah ah, Lydia. Patience." He zeroed in on my clit, and flicked it with his tongue, sending an outrageous bolt of covetous desire down my legs. "I missed you so much. Please, please, never leave me again."

I groaned and luxuriated in having him with me again. "Never," I said.

"First, I am going to fuck you here," he used his fingers to part my pussy lips and thrust his tongue into my entrance. "Mine, baby." Then he gripped the backs of my thighs and pushed them into my belly, exposing me fully to him. He trailed kisses back to my rear and softly licked me there. "And soon, here," he said, and I sighed in response. "This is mine too."

"Oh god, Dylan. I'm yours. All yours, and you're mine. I want you. So. Badly."

"I want you too, baby. And you have me." He rose to my face and kissed me fiercely, taking no prisoners. He rose to kneel, sitting on his feet, and he pulled me up with him. "Wrap your legs around me, Lydia. That's right." He lifted me onto him, filling me with his hardness. He groaned deeply as I took him in. He supported my back with his steely arms as I threw my head back, spreading myself for him. He was so deep in me, in every way.

I used my knees to rise and fall on him, and we quickly found our pace, syncing with each other. I gripped his hips with my thighs, pulling us more tightly together, molding us to each other.

"Oh god, Lydia!" He reached in between us with one of his hands, and strummed my clit. "I want you to come with me baby, are you close?"

"Yes! Touch me, Dylan." I heaved out the words, and he relentlessly and expertly worked my clit with his fingers. We rose into our orgasms together, crying out each other's names, and he finally settled deeply inside me. The sweat on our bodies made us sticky as we embraced, and I could feel his come in me, pouring out of me. He held my body to him as though for dear life, crushing my breasts to his chest.

"I feel like a fool. How did I not see you coming?"

My chin rested on his shoulder, another way of hugging him

closer. "You think I saw *you* coming, Dylan? You've opened my world."

He withdrew, cleaned us up, and laid me down gently on the bed. He propped himself on his arm, so he could look down at me, and stroked his fingers down my body, from my chin down to my sex and back.

"I want to give you everything, Lydia. Never leave."

"I'm not going anywhere. Not until you've done that to me at least ten more times." I closed my eyes again and just indulged in the feeling of his trailing fingers on my skin.

"No. I mean ever." I flashed my eyes open again and looked at him, confused. "I want you here, living with me."

"Don't you think that's a little fast?"

He shifted inched closer, so our bodies were touching, and he laid his palm against my cheek, threading his fingers through the hair at my nape. "Lydia, I want you here, safe, where I can look after you. I don't like thinking of you alone in that house. And I don't want to spend any more nights apart than we have to. Move in."

"Dylan, that's nuts. It's too soon. One thing at at time, ok?"

He exhaled in defeat. "Well then prepare yourself."

"For what?"

"For me asking you. Every day. Until you say yes."

I didn't give him an answer, but I rolled my eyes, which earned me a raised eyebrow swiftly followed by a kiss to my lips.

"You don't make me sore anymore." I smiled. "You've officially broken me in."

"Good. Now I can really get crazy with you." I gaped and stared at him playfully, but also in true shock. He really was going to show me things I didn't know existed. "As you're ready, and if you're willing, of course."

I turned into him, hiding my face, embarrassed by my thoughts of all he was going to do to my body. He pushed my hair from my face and found my eyes. He rose and brought me into his arms. "Time to sleep, baby. You have a busy day tomorrow." He kissed me on top of my head and squeezed me tighter.

He was right. The fashion show was the next afternoon and there was the grand designers' gala that night. We slipped beneath the heavy duvet, and I sidled up next to him, finding the perfect nook in his shoulder to use as a pillow.

The last thing I heard before drifting into sleep was Dylan. "I'm so glad I found you, Lydia. I love you."

Chapter 36

The next day, the day of the fashion show, I spent zipping between the office and Hannah's studio for spare zippers or forgotten sketches. I was in a taxi, having just picked up lattes for everyone, when I felt my phone buzz with a text from Dylan.

WEDNESDAY, 9:17 am
Check your email. XX

I quickly brought up my email on my phone and saw one from Dylan at the top. There was no subject heading, but just a link to *Hello!* magazine. The page linked to the same story from the day before about him and Amelia. Only now there was a big red X blinking across the photo. Underneath, the word *update* flashed in bold and was followed by a brief description.

Official word from Dylan Hale's publicist at Hale Architecture & Design denies any romantic involvement with Amelia Reynolds. "Dylan and Amelia's families have long been friends, but there is no romantic involvement between the two, and they are absolutely not engaged to be married. Dylan Hale is romantically involved with someone else." So, ladies and gentlemen, place your bets. WHO could the lucky lady be?

There were already nearly three hundred comments on the article containing the names of various socialites and celebrities. This was Dylan's form of an apology, and it was also a huge step forward for us, out of the shadows. In every corner of my body, where doubt, shame, and fear had crept in the day before, lightness, joy, and pure excitement now resided. I couldn't believe this was happening.

I quickly forwarded the email to Daphne with a short note,

He's doing his best to make up for it. Today is crazy—fashion week! I promise to call as soon as I can, but it might not be till tomorrow. Thanks again for all the support lately. XO —L

And before delving back into work, I sent of a quick reply text to Dylan.

> TUESDAY, 9:25 am
> Thank you, knighty. Into the fray—it's crazy here. XX

TUESDAY, 9:28 am
Have fun. I'll be at the show.

TUESDAY, 9:28 am
Oh, and stop calling me knighty.

TUESDAY, 9:28 am
Oh, and I love you.

TUESDAY, 9:29 am
I love you too.

TUESDAY, 9:29 am
Knighty.

TUESDAY, 9:29 am
Maddening. You're absolutely maddening.

* * *

The show would begin at four, and at three thirty we were still in the throes of preparations. I felt like we were running a collective marathon. Running between models, throwing each other clipboards, and making last-minute edits. It was frantic, engrossing, and crazy fun.

When the pre-music for Hannah's show began, I was at the entrance to the runway with her, lining the models up. I peeked through the curtain from the side and scanned the room. It took a few moments, but I found him, front row with an empty seat next to him. He was chatting with someone behind him whom he clearly knew when I noticed an elegantly dressed woman approach and take the seat next to him. When she turned I saw it was Caroline. He stood, and they exchanged quick kisses on the cheeks. She said something, and he nodded and smiled. She looked happy for him, pleased. And now I knew she knew.

The music changed, the show began, and there was no more time to dwell—we were instantly performing, everyone on the runway and backstage working their butts off, making the culmination of the hard work come to life. The show was over in what felt like a heartbeat, and I noticed Hannah visibly relax. It had happened. No one had tripped. No one had lost their skirt on the runway. And the applause had spoken for itself. As the models danced in relief and the backstage area began to flood with well-wishers, it became immediately clear that the show was an enormous success.

The frenetic energy continued as we began to break the show down, and Hannah disappeared into the postshow mayhem. While unzipping a model, I felt my phone vibrate.

WEDNESDAY, 4:35 pm
Well done, you! I'm off. Tell me where to pick you up for party, 7pm.

WEDNESDAY, 4:36 pm
You're coming with me?

WEDNESDAY, 4:36 pm
Baby, I'm your date. You think I'd let you go alone?

WEDNESDAY, 4:36 pm
:) The office

All of a sudden I realized that this would be it. We'd be in public, really in public, together. Every time he'd tried to warn me about the press or talked about protecting me from the paparazzi, it had seemed so far away from me. I'd thought it was just an excuse to keep us secret. But since then I'd seen how invasive they could be, and I was throwing myself into that world. I shuddered, suddenly feeling frantic and shy about having my own photo in the papers. The pit in my stomach grew as I eyed the perfect-looking models around me—what was *I* going to look like on camera? Ugh.

At that moment, I heard Fiona calling my name, pulling me

out of my ruminations. Hannah was still mingling with the press and the celebrities who'd attended her show, while Fiona and I began returning the clothing to garment bags, accounting for every piece. It was 5:30 by the time we were piling into a car to go back to Hannah's studio.

"Well, girls, we did it. You were a fabulous help. And, Lydia, I'm so glad you're feeling better—you looked positively ill yesterday afternoon, but my god you were on fire today. Thank god! Tomorrow we all need a rest. Take the day off." I smiled. It was my birthday the next day, and the break was going to be appreciated.

"It was such a rush, Hannah." I said, feeling the excitement spill off of me. "I can't imagine how you must feel. Everyone seemed so pleased." I really had been overwhelmed by the whole experience.

"Well, we'll see what the press says tomorrow and the bloggers say tonight. I'll be afraid to look," she replied. "At least we'll have the party to distract ourselves. Why don't you girls come with me in my car?" Fiona happily accepted on the spot. I got the sense that Hannah, while kind, was not always this chummy. Her good mood was making her generous.

"Um," I said softly, "well, I actually already have a ride to the party, but thank you so much for the invitation." I tried to be as gracious as possible without prompting further questions. Maybe I should have just accepted. Dylan would have understood, but then again, it felt important for us to go together.

Fiona saw right through me. "Spill the beans, Bell." *Oh god.* I didn't necessarily want to talk about this in front of my boss. Although, if the zillion comments on that Internet post were any indication of London's interest in Dylan's love life, she would find out anyway.

I could feel my cheeks heating up. "I have a date." I cleared my throat and looked nervously at Hannah. Fiona's expression was horrified at having been kept out of the loop. She was clearly waiting for me to continue. "I'm, um, dating someone. Dylan Hale. I'm dating Dylan Hale."

Chapter 37

I immediately covered my face with my hands in anticipation of their reactions. I was blushing—I could feel my hot cheeks, and there was a self-conscious pit in my belly. I peeked through my fingers and Hannah's eyes were wide. It was possibly the only time I'd ever seen real emotion on her face.

"Shut. Up!" Fiona was nearly speechless for a moment, but she quickly found her words. "I can't *believe* you've been holding out on me."

I looked back to Hannah, whose wheels were turning. She looked like a light bulb had gone off. She reached into her bag and grabbed her cell phone and made a call. "Hello, Stephen? It's Hannah…Thank you…Yes, yes…Listen, I need your help for another hour. Meet me at my studio." Stephen was the hair and makeup guru who had overseen the looks for her show.

Turning back to me, Hannah continued with a businesslike determination, "Your job's not over tonight, Lydia. If you let me, I'm going to make you the last model of the show. The press has been going nuts trying to figure out who Dylan Hale's girlfriend

is, and you two are going public tonight?" I nodded. *Oh god.*
Where was this going? "You're going to be photographed to the
hilt, and I want you wearing one of my gowns."

What girl hadn't fantasized about being dressed by a designer
for a night out? This was beginning to feel like a dream. Only it
was a dream we had about an hour to make come true.

Fiona saw me looking at my watch. "Can you tell him to get
you at seven fifteen? I'm sure we can pull this off in an hour and
a half." She looked at Hannah, who nodded.

"Um, sure. But are you sure about this?" I looked to Hannah.
"I mean, wouldn't it be better to stick with the actual models
and the royals?"

Hannah shook her head ferociously. "We don't have time to
boost your self-esteem. This will be perfect." By this point we
were all hustling from the car into the studio.

I texted Dylan about the time and location change, and
Hannah instructed Fiona to prep a press release about the
gown in case people asked. As soon as we got inside, Hannah
started rifling through the racks and holding pieces up to
me—I clearly wasn't going to have a say in any of this. She
quickly settled on an A-line silk gown with V-neck halter. The
dress hung elegantly and was fitted, hugging the few slight
curves I had, but it was also unstructured, with the draped fabric meeting in an elegant ruched knot at my waist. It also had
a subtle but high slit running up the front below the knot. The
back was dangerously low, as low as it could go without being tasteless. The silk was a warm cream color but was accented
with subtle pale pink beading, running in vertical lines down
the dress, which gave me added length. It was old Hollywood
glamour but also somehow undeniably contemporary. It also,
thankfully, fit me like a glove and just needed to be hemmed,

which would have to be done quickly.

While Hannah went to work on the gown herself, Stephen attacked my hair and face. He worked ferociously, creating soft waves in my hair, and finally just trimmed my bangs when he couldn't figure out what else to do with them. His makeup job was thankfully subtle and natural-looking. It was 7:05 by the time they were done zipping me up. Fiona was frantically running out the door to get ready herself, and Hannah had left to get ready once she was sure the gown would hold up. I was suddenly alone and grateful to have a few minutes to settle my nerves. I snagged the only pair of heels that fit—thankfully one of the models had had little feet—and I looked in the full-length mirror.

I couldn't believe what I saw starring back at me. I felt like a movie star, and apart from when I'd been in Dylan's arms, I'd never felt more beautiful. I felt like myself, only far far more glamorous. Just then I heard my phone ding, and it was Dylan.

WEDNESDAY, 7:14 pm
I'm here.

WEDNESDAY, 7:15 pm
Almost ready. I'll be right down.

I took one more look in the mirror, commanding myself to have the courage to act the way I felt, and bracing myself for the inevitable attention. I was collecting my clothes and putting them in my tote when I felt the room heat up. I stood, faced the doorway, and saw Dylan, in his killer suit and a dark purple narrow tie. His mouth was hanging open, and he braced himself in the doorway.

"Good god, Lydia." He sauntered towards me. My body blossomed under his gaze, and I could feel the color rising to my cheeks. "You look like a complete dream." He took my arms and spread them, stepping back to take me in. His smile was enormous. "I can't believe I get to be the one to walk into this party with you." He stepped in and cupped my chin with his hand, lifting my face to his. "Are you ready for this? You're sure?"

"Definitely."

He smiled back at my reply. "Me too. Let's go, shall we?"

"One minute." I reached into my bag and dug around for my final accessory. I pulled out the black velvet box and held it up for him to hold. "I finally get to wear these." I pulled the beautiful earrings he'd bought for me out of their box and fixed them into my ears. "What do you think?"

"Fucking gorgeous." He leaned in and pulled me into him, kissing me hard. "I'm not going to be able to keep my hands off you tonight. We'd better go—the sooner we get there, the sooner we can leave and I can get you into my bed."

* * *

Dylan held my hand in the car, drumming my palm with his thumb the whole time. Was he nervous too?

"You ok?" I asked.

"Of course." He smiled at me. The car slowed and we were waiting in the circular driveway of the Savoy hotel, a line of cars ahead of us. "Just stay close. No running off."

I nodded. Finally, he exited his side of the car and flashbulbs instantly starting popping. He came around to my side of the car, and opened the door. He reached in and gave me a wink before I slid out. He held me tightly around the waist, and I put one arm around his back and used the other to hold up my skirt as I stepped up onto the curb. The din of the clicking cameras became furious. The flashbulbs were blinding, and the blur of voices coming from the pool of journalists made me feel like I was lost. I didn't know where to look. Dylan used all of his carefully deployed strength to guide me through and keep me steady, surely knowing I'd find this overwhelming.

He paused before the door, and we faced a row of photographers and journalists, all shouting his name and asking me mine. I held onto his back for dear life. Suddenly, he leaned down, and placing two fingers under my chin, raised my face to his, and planted a long and deliberate kiss onto my lips. The press rallied in response. He pulled back and gave me a quick reassuring smile before spelling my name for a waiting journalist. I smiled and waved. After answering a few questions about his work and the building in Jordan, he quickly ushered me up the steps and in the front door.

That had been completely bizarre and far more intense than I'd anticipated. As soon as we were in the door, he pulled me aside. "You ok?"

I reassured him by squeezing his arm. "Is it always that insane?"

"No. That was bloody bonkers. The last time I experienced that was after Caroline and I got engaged." I winced. She was a princess, for crying out loud, and it still hurt to think of him engaged to someone. He gave me a look of warning. "I'm not justifying that wince." He leaned in close. "I love *you*. My publicist chiming in this morning must have gotten everyone going.

It will die down." He reached around and firmly grabbed my ass. "Now let's go have some fun, and then I'm going to get you home and give you a birthday spanking—one for each year." My jaw dropped, and he smiled at my shock. "And you'll love every one."

Chapter 38

He kept his hand at my back as we navigated around the room, but we were never able to get very far. Dylan seemed to know everyone, and everyone seemed to be curious about his date. I hadn't processed that Dylan hadn't brought a girl anywhere with him in public in seven years. There was no small amount of interest in this sudden change.

In spite of the onslaught of attention and the sheer amount of chitchat and introductions that were happening, he never lost sight of me, noticing when my drink needed refreshing, stopping waiters so we could grab appetizers, and, best of all, giving my hip the occasional squeeze or planting the occasional kiss on my lips to let me, and the entire room, know that we were together.

He introduced me to business partners, celebrities, politicians, and famous fashion designers. At one point a tall older sophisticated woman wearing a formal suit approached Dylan and kissed him on each cheek. "My Lord," she began, but Dylan waved her off, rejecting the formal address.

"Deirdre, I'd like you to meet my girlfriend, Lydia Bell." I loved hearing the word come out of his mouth.

The woman politely reached out for my hand, which I shook firmly. Dylan continued, "Lydia is currently working for Hannah Rogan."

The woman's eyes widened. "Of course. Hannah's show today was simply breathtaking." I smiled proudly.

Dylan turned to me. "Lydia, Deirdre Rocker is the president of the BFC."

Holy shit. Of course. The BFC was the British Fashion Council, the premier fashion organization in the UK, and the host of London Fashion Week. I had tried to get an informational interview with Deirdre Rocker when I was looking for jobs, but I had been told there was little hope of that happening. She knew everything and everyone there was to know when it came to the fashion world, both in the UK and abroad.

I managed to summon my professional self, and replied, "Of course. It's such an honor to meet you." I continued to chat with her about the BFC and was in the middle of discussing my experience with New York Fashion Week when I felt Dylan's grip tighten at my hip, prompting me to look up. For the first time since the party in Canada, I saw his family approaching us. Dylan politely excused us from our conversation with Deirdre, and braced me against him as his parents and sister reached us.

"Dylan." His mother came in for a hug. She clearly wanted to brush everything under the carpet. But Dylan firmly held his grip on me and made no move to hug her back, making for an extremely awkward moment.

I reached out my hand, determined to be graceful and welcoming. "Duchess, I'm Lydia Bell. We met in Canada this past summer." I figured using the title, now that I knew she had one, wouldn't hurt insofar as making amends went.

She took my hand, relieved by my cheerful politeness, and possibly embarrassed. I'm sure she guessed that I had been filled in on her antics. "Of course, dear. Charlotte, please," she said. "It's so lovely to see you again. You look absolutely beautiful." Her words were polite, but I couldn't help but feel she wasn't completely satisfied with this situation. "I didn't realize that you and Dylan had stayed in touch." I wouldn't have exactly described her words as sincere.

I reached out for Geoffrey's hand. "Duke, it's nice to see you again." He had been silent, clearly used to letting his wife handle these awkward emotional family matters. He issued a polite reply. This wasn't going to get anywhere with me here. I saw Dylan's sister hanging back, looking shy amidst the tension between her brother and parents. She looked beautiful in an ivory long-sleeved gown, which was startling against her long dark brown hair.

Dylan continued to ignore his parents and reached his free hand towards his sister, smiling at her with an expression I hadn't seen before. It was almost parental, filled with intense love and caring. He summoned her forward and said, "Emily, I'd like you to meet Lydia." I could feel him presenting me to her, smiling above my head with pride.

Emily stepped forward towards her brother, and Dylan put his hand on her arm. I noticed the gesture and it occurred to me that perhaps I wasn't the only one to know his overprotective side. I reached out and clasped her hand. Her face had lit up with her brother's attention, and it was clear she worshiped him.

"It's lovely to meet you," she said. "I know we saw each other in Canada, but I was horribly rude, I'm afraid—"

"Oh no, you weren't! You were on vacation with your family, and we barely met!" She brightened a little—relieved to be rescued and forgiven. I felt like an intruder with his parents there, and I saw my opportunity to help Dylan smooth things over with his parents, if that was even possible. "I'm dying for another drink. Do you want to come find the bar with me?"

Dylan's hand resumed its fierce grip on my hip, but I looked up and pried his hand free. I planted a swift kiss on his lips, and could immediately feel the surprise register from his parents. Their eyes wide and glued to us. I whispered, "I'll be back," remembering the first time he'd said those words to me, at a different party, and how far we'd come since then. He smiled slightly and let me go.

Emily and I left the awkward threesome behind us. "We haven't seen Dylan with a girl in a long time. I think my parents are kind of in shock."

We made the rounds, and Emily pointed out the who's who of the party, even chiming in with mnemonic devices should I need them. With drinks in hand I turned from the bar, and we began to head back into the party.

As we moved back into the boisterous throng, Dylan emerged, walking towards us with a look of determination until his eyes settled on me. As they did, I felt that familiar warmth spread through my veins. He practically collapsed into me and immediately pulled me into his protective grasp again, replacing his hand on my hip. I could feel his body relax as we settled into each other again.

He looked at Emily. "Are you doing alright?"

Emily nodded and rolled her eyes slightly. Yup, she was definitely used to his overprotective side. Dylan smiled, reassured, and continued, "Mum and Dad are off talking to the Spencers." He pointed towards a far corner of the room, dismissing her. Lovingly, but dismissing her all the same. Perhaps he'd missed the fact that she had grown up—she and I were practically the same age, after all.

Emily looked less than thrilled to be off in search of her parents again, but she lit up when she saw someone she knew. "There's Peter Fisher." And she waltzed off towards a young man with a bored expression on his face. His eyes brightened up when he saw Emily coming.

I glanced up at Dylan, and who eyed poor Peter Fisher suspiciously. I wouldn't have been surprised if he was making a mental note to check up on the poor guy later. In a moment, his eyes were back on me. I turned in to give him a full-on hug, folding myself into his grasp. "Everything ok?" I asked him.

"Yes. And don't think I don't know what you were doing." I looked up at him and gave his own mischievous smile back at him. "They were bloody shocked when you kissed me."

"And that was just a kiss." I was smiling into his chest. He clasped his hands around me and rested them on my lower back, skin on skin. The familiar pleasurable tug was there, always present, but it was also bathed in something bigger and warmer now.

He rested his chin on the top of my head and then kissed it—it started out sweet and innocent. But then his hands slid up my sides, landing at my ribcage, and his thumbs surreptitiously skirted the edge of my dress and grazed the sides of my breasts.

"Come." He took my hand and led me down a long hallway away from the party. When we came to a hidden corner past a bank of elevators, he backed me against the wall, leaned into me, and spoke softly. "It's time to get you home. Out of this unbelievable dress. And for you to feel my palm on your ass." All of my muscles, right down *there*, tightened, heeding him. "But I can't wait that long. I need to touch you now."

His intense desire for me was evident in every fiber of his body—the way he stood, ready to pounce, hovering over me. And his posture registered in my own. I reached my hands into his jacket and gently untucked the back of his shirt, so I could feel his skin beneath it. I lifted my leg through the high slit of the dress and pushed my thigh into his growing erection.

I couldn't help but look over his shoulder to make sure no one was coming, but he cupped my chin in his hand and turned my face to his. "Look only at me, baby. Don't worry about being caught—you don't have to worry. I'll never let anyone see anything they shouldn't." And I surrendered to him.

He looked down and saw my exposed leg. "Fucking hell, I love this dress."

He reached down to my knee, and slowly dragged his hand up my thigh. Every centimeter closer he got to my bare slit, the wetter I became, the hungrier, the more intense the craving. My heart was racing at the thought of being caught, but I gladly relinquished any fear to him. If anyone passed, we'd just look like a young couple in love. His whole body was protecting the scene unfolding between us.

His fingers finally reached their destination, and he dragged one through my folds. I could feel my slickness, how easily his fingers glided through me. He sank two fingers deep inside me, and I allowed a moan to escape. "Shh, baby. Those moans are only for me. You need to be quiet. And don't come." How was I going to stop? And why was he torturing me if he wasn't going to let me come?

After another riotous moment, he withdrew his fingers and

brought them to my lips. "Taste yourself." Holy fuck this was dirty. I pulled his fingers into my mouth and tasted my saltiness. "Good girl." He stepped back, and left me panting, leaning against the wall. I would have been happy to collapse right there, but he grabbed my hand and led me towards the hotel entrance.

As we walked it became immediately clear why he hadn't let me come. The throbbing ache between my legs was begging for him, and I could already feel how being spanked was going to catapult me into another universe. I was already craving the sweet stings that would come and how they would both satisfy and fuel this needy ache in my groin. There was a sheen of sweat forming on my skin in anticipation. I couldn't *wait* to get home.

"Ready?" We began to descend the stairs of the hotel, and I realized that the throng of photographers was still there, awaiting our exit.

I stopped in my tracks. "Dylan! I can't be photographed like this."

"Like what?" He was whispering softly, so no passersby would be able to hear, "Randy? Ready to come for me?"

I blushed fiercely. "Yes!"

"You look stunning, Lydia. Don't worry. I've told you already—I would never expose or embarrass you. Trust me."

And of course I did. We walked out, and he held my hand firmly in his. This time we didn't speak to any of the press, but we both smiled, and his hand never left mine. We ducked into his car, with Lloyd at the wheel, and were instantly protected from the crowd of cameras.

As soon as the door had closed, I tried to haul myself into Dylan's lap, but he stopped me, and buckled my seatbelt for me instead.

"Since when do you care about automobile safety?" I asked,

feeling bereft of his touch and wanting nothing more than to be ensconced in his arms. The dull throb between my thighs was intensifying with every passing minute.

"I care deeply about your safety. I also know that you want to touch me and want me to touch you, but you'll have to wait. Thankfully the car comes with a handy restraint system."

"You're driving me crazy!" I practically panted the words. My breathing was shallow, and my skin was hypersensitive, anticipating and craving his touch.

"I know." He reached out and ran a finger from my ear, down my jaw and neck. Somehow, the light touch registered as bolts of lightning headed straight for the growing ache in my belly. The car meandered through the London streets, and I wished I could push Lloyd's foot onto the gas pedal, make him red run lights and get me to Dylan's bedroom faster.

As soon as we arrived at his house—at the front entrance—I eagerly unclasped my seatbelt and reached for the door handle. I had it mostly open by the time Dylan had come around to help me out of the car. "Patience, baby," he admonished gently, and he took his sweet time sauntering to the door, unlocking, and ushering me inside.

But once inside, even his patience had been exhausted. "Aw, fuck it," he said as he kissed me with all the fervor he'd been holding back and hauled me into his arms, and in record time we were where he'd been leading me all evening. In his bed. And he delivered on every promise.

* * *

I blinked awake to the sun pouring through the curtains and

onto the bed. As I rolled over, I saw Dylan propped on his arm looking at me, smiling, and I immediately groaned and shut my eyes again. He seemed way too chipper.

"Look at me, baby." I turned my head to face him. "Open those pretty eyes." I reluctantly looked through my lashes up into his face.

"Happy birthday," he said, with a Cheshire cat grin. I couldn't help but smile back, but I still buried my head back under the pillow.

"No hiding." He unearthed me from the pillows and pushed my hair out of my face. "Hey, it's your birthday."

"Uh-huh." I was lying on my side, facing him, and he was facing me, running his fingers up and down my side and looking at me with a sweet reverence that was almost unnerving.

"And we're celebrating. I'm taking the morning off. I've got plans for you."

Dylan hopped out of bed with an unnatural energy for eight in the morning. He threw me one of his t-shirts, and before I knew it I was being dragged down the stairs towards the smell of coffee and freshly baked croissants.

I looked up at him questioningly—when did he make coffee? "Molly made the coffee," he said, answering my unasked question as though this explained everything. I looked up at him, even more confused. "My housekeeper? She lives in a flat on the third floor."

Dylan had a housekeeper? Who lived there? Before I had a chance to ask for clarification, the doorbell rang. We were only twenty minutes into this day, and already I felt like I had no idea what was going on.

"That will be your first birthday present." Dylan's grin was that of a teenage kid with a surprise up his sleeve. *Oh god.* What had he done? If it was one of those singing telegrams or something equally embarrassing I might have had to kill him in his sleep.

I heard Dylan greet someone at the door, and they were making their way back to the kitchen. Then I heard a very familiar female voice say, "Now where *is* the birthday girl?"

Chapter 39

Daphne!" I shrieked and jumped over to her, gripping her fiercely. "What are you doing here?" My face was huge with delight and the world was spinning as I oriented to my best friend being here in Dylan's kitchen.

"Dylan flew me over. I just got in. Surprise!" She leaned into our hug and whispered, "Did you know he had a private plane?" I spun my gaze to meet Dylan's, and he just shrugged.

I broke my hug with Daphne and went to Dylan, burying myself in him and prompting him to hug me back. I looked up, my chin to his chest. "Thank you." I reached up and kissed him hard. "Thank you so much."

His eyes looked glassy, and his grip on me deepened. "You're welcome," he said. "You two have fun. I'm going to get showered and changed." I released him and moved to a breakfast stool, encouraging Daphne to take a seat.

"Whoa," said Daphne, with her eyes like saucers. "You guys are serious, huh?"

"I guess we are." I smiled.

"Well the press certainly thinks so. Look what I picked up at the airport." Daphne put the newspaper on the counter in front of me, and there was a large photograph of Dylan and me kissing from the night before. The headline read, "*Dylan Hale's Mystery Woman Revealed.*" There was no real story, apart from describing my name and age, mentioning that I was a British-born American, was working in fashion, and was wearing a Hannah Rogan gown, which Hannah would be pleased with.

"Wow," I said, not fully believing it was anything more than a joke. The idea that there were more copies of this paper besides the one sitting in front of me was kind of mind-blowing. "This was from last night."

"I'm going to want every. Single. Detail. I mean, that dress! You look incredible." I nodded with excitement. "But for the love of god, go get dressed. I'm only here for three days, and we have some serious catching up to do."

"Oh, Daphne, I'm so glad you're here. So, so glad." I directed her to coffee, and then hustled upstairs.

The shower was still running, and I quickly stripped and slipped in, roping my arms around Dylan from behind. He held my hands to his front, and I laid my cheek against his back. "Thank you, Dylan. Thank you so much."

He turned and pulled me into a hug, resting his hands on my bare ass. "You're welcome. I don't think I've ever seen you so happy."

"She's my best friend," I said by way of an explanation. "How did you do it?"

"I worked it out with her when I called to find you. I figured either way—if you never wanted to talk to me again or if you forgave me—you'd want her here. Plus, I couldn't think of a better birthday present."

"Thank you," I said, reaching up to kiss him softly on the lips.

"The real present is me having to share you for three days." He wrapped his arms tightly around me. "Don't misunderstand me—I want to meet Daphne, but a whole weekend when I can't have you exactly when I want you? When we have to be quiet? It's going to fucking kill me."

I smiled as I laid my forehead against his firm chest, breathing in the heat of his body in the steamy shower. His hands began slowly stroking up my back.

"She's probably tired from her flight," I said, and I laid a kiss on his shoulder.

"Undoubtedly. I wouldn't be surprised if she'd prefer a few moments to rest before starting her day," he said, running his fingers through my dampening hair.

"I'm sure." I sighed, and giggled into his skin. I had every intention of seducing him, of making him moan, but before I had a chance, he leaned down to give me a surprisingly slow, unexpectedly reverent kiss. Not the kind that would lead to my legs wrapped around his waist, but the kind that was a kiss in its own right. He wrapped his hands around my face and made every peck, every gentle laying of his lips count. When I looked up into his eyes, with the water cascading around his shoulders and down his chest, I found myself marveling at what had happened. The dream of it all dawning on me. This man loved me, and I loved him.

We stood in that shower, kissing until the water ran cold. And all the seemingly innocuous moments that had led to that love flashed before my eyes. How he'd brushed my hair from my eyes so he could see me. How he'd look at me when I was unsure. How he made me laugh. How I made *him* laugh. How he'd cracked me open and made me feel alive. How every doubt and moment of fear was worth it. How he felt like home.

When we finally rejoined Daphne in the parlor, Dylan urged us out the door for brunch. The three of us sat in the lush dining room at the Connaught hotel, during which Daphne grilled him, sized him up as though he were on some kind of job interview. He withstood the inquisition well, keeping his arm around me the entire meal. It was his way of telling her that he'd be damn hard to get rid of, and I could tell she respected it. He wasn't going to back down, and I was pretty sure that was all she wanted for me: loyalty and adoration, both of which Dylan demonstrated in spades. Before leaving us he handed Daphne his credit card and told her, "Daphne, if she finds anything she loves, use this."

"Will do, sir," replied Daphne, with a hint of mocking in her tone.

"And sorry I can't join you ladies," he continued, looking back to Daphne smiling mischievously. "You know, I'm just a formal stuffy Earl doing his Earl thing."

Daphne's jaw dropped and she blushed and looked at me like she was about to kill me. I was laughing so hard I nearly fell off my seat.

The day—a day that should have been filled with grief from missing my father—was somehow perfect. We perused Liberty of London, tried on half of Selfridges, and ducked into a dozen boutiques in between. I convinced Daphne that I really didn't want Dylan spending loads of money on me, but she confessed he'd made her promise to buy me things. Apparently they'd bonded over my stubbornness. So we came to a compromise, and I let Dylan get me a new pair of black heels to replace my old worn-in pair: a pair of Manolos that I knew would please us both.

As I walked her down one of my favorite hidden mews in Mayfair, shopping bags dangling from my arm, I felt calmer, more content, more seamlessly happy than I had in a long time. And I reveled in the fact that I'd have both my boyfriend and my best friend in the same place for three whole days.

* * *

By the end of the day Monday, my first day back at work after what had been a perfect weekend, I sat at my work computer enjoying the quiet. My day had been spent wading through Josh's insane reaction to the news that I was Dylan's girlfriend and having a postmortem with Hannah and Fiona about how the gown had been received. Finally, by six in the evening, the office was quiet enough to scroll through the emails that had accumulated over the previous four days.

One email was from Deirdre Rocker, inviting me for a meeting, a meeting I'd been unable to secure months earlier. Another email was from a fashion photographer asking if I had any interest in that side of the business, and there were half a dozen more like that one. Being introduced by Dylan Hale had clearly brought my name up to the top of some people's lists, and I wasn't sure yet how I felt about it. He'd warned me that things would change, that I was entering a different world, and he'd been right, but he'd been wrong about which part of being in his world would throw me for a loop. Being hounded by paparazzi didn't scare me—Dylan made me feel safe, and I couldn't imagine feeling any more than annoyed by that nuisance. But this, the way things looked to be falling into my lap, the way his name carried weight, the free rides being offered, this was the new world that I was afraid might change me. I wanted to build my life, not just glide through on unsolicited emails. If I was going to stick around, if I was going to *move in* with him—and I still hadn't wrapped my head around that one—we were going to have to jump these hurdles.

I sighed audibly into the empty office—I needed to get home to Dylan, to the night we had planned, but I needed just a moment. I leaned back in my chair, closed my eyes, and thought about how right it had felt to wake up in his bed, his arms wrapped tightly around me. I could imagine the feel of those arms perfectly and suddenly wanted desperately to get back to them. I gathered my things into my bag, and I was just about to close my email when I heard the ping of a new message in my personal account.

The email had the subject line *A Warning*, and the sender was a series of numbers and letters in no discernable pattern. I would have deleted the email, assuming it was spam, if I hadn't glimpsed the preview of the text within it: *He's not who you think he is.* I opened the email and below the foreboding message was a grainy up-close photograph of Dylan and me in a dark room. I recognized the moment immediately from his house in the country, and my breathing hitched. My arms tied tightly above my head. Dylan's face, in clear profile, kissing the side of my breast.

My heart was beating furiously. Whoever this was had caught an intimate moment—one of the *most* intimate moments—weeks ago and hadn't shared it with the press. Yet. I scrolled farther down the image and in large bold font, three words were typed across Dylan's naked back: *LIAR, CRIMINAL, TRAITOR.*

About the Author

Parker Swift grew up in Providence, Rhode Island, and then grew up again in New York, London, and Minneapolis and currently lives in Connecticut. She has spent most of her adult life examining romantic relationships in an academic lab as a professor of social psychology. Now, she's exploring the romantic lives of her fictional characters in the pages of her books. When she's not writing, she spends her time with her bearded nautical husband and being told not to sing along to pop music in the car by her two sons.

Learn more at:
Twitter @the_ParkerSwift
Facebook.com/ParkerSwiftAuthor
Instagram @Parker.Swift

Don't miss the thrilling next installments of Dylan and Lydia's story!

Parker Swift's Royal Scandal series continues!

Royal Disaster

and

Royal Treatment

Available for pre-order now

www.ingramcontent.com/pod-product-compliance
Ingram Content Group UK Ltd.
Pitfield, Milton Keynes, MK11 3LW, UK
UKHW022259280225
455674UK00001B/106